'The thematic diversity – and profundity – makes this one of ...er's strongest works to date' *Publishers Weekly*

...wyer's take on theories about the origin of consciousness, ...enerated within the framework of an engaging story, is fasci...ting, and his approach to machine consciousness and the ...ternet is surprisingly fresh' *Booklist*

...awyer raises fascinating, complex questions about the nature ... consciousness and self-awareness, of communication between ...sparate intelligences, and compassion across huge gulfs. This ... a book that you'll still be thinking about for weeks after you ...nish reading it' *Analog*

...One of the foremost science fiction writers of our generation' *SF Site*

'Unforgettable. Impossible to put down'
Jack McDevitt, Nebula Award-winner

The WWW Trilogy

Wake
Watch
Wonder (coming in 2011)

Also by Robert J. Sawyer from Gollancz:

FlashForward

WAKE

ROBERT J. SAWYER

This novel was serialized in *Analog Science Fiction and Fact* magazine, with instalments in the November 2008, December 2008, combined January-February 2009 and March 2009 issues.

First published in Great Britain in 2009 by
Gollancz
An imprint of the Orion Publishing Group
Orion House, 5 Upper St Martin's Lane,
London WC2H 9EA
An Hachette UK Company

This edition published in Great Britain
in 2010 by Gollancz

1 3 5 7 9 10 8 6 4 2

A CIP catalogue record for this book
is available from the British Library

ISBN 978 0 575 09408 6

Printed in Great Britain by Clays Ltd, St Ives plc

The Orion Publishing Group's policy is to use papers that are natural, renewable and recyclable products and made from wood grown in sustainable forests. The logging and manufacturing processes are expected to conform to the environmental regulations of the country of origin.

www.sfwriter.com
www.orionbooks.co.uk

For
PAT FORDE
Great Writer
Great Friend

What a blind person needs
is not a teacher but another self

Helen Keller

one

0001110010101010000000001011111110101000000010100010101000000101110101001010100101010100111011001010110000001

Not darkness, for that implies an understanding of light.

Not silence, for that suggests a familiarity with sound.

Not loneliness, for that requires knowledge of others.

But still, faintly, so tenuous that if it were any less it wouldn't exist at all: *awareness.*

Nothing more than that. Just awareness—a vague, ethereal sense of *being.*

Being... but not *becoming.* No marking of time, no past or future—only an endless, featureless *now,* and, just barely there in that boundless moment, inchoate and raw, the dawning of *perception*...

Caitlin had kept a brave face throughout dinner, telling her parents that everything was fine—just *peachy*—but, God, it had been a terrifying day, filled with other students jostling her in the busy corridors, teachers referring to things on blackboards, and doubtless everyone looking at her. She'd never felt self-conscious at the TSB back in Austin, but she was *on display* now. Did the other girls wear earrings, too? Had these corduroy pants been the right choice? Yes, she loved the feel of the fabric and the sound they made, but here everything was about *appearances.*

She was sitting at her bedroom desk, facing the open window. An evening breeze gently moved her shoulder-length hair, and she heard the outside world: a small dog barking, someone kicking a stone down the quiet residential street, and, way off, one of those annoying car alarms.

She ran a finger over her watch: 7:49—seven and seven squared, the last time today there'd be a sequence like that. She swiveled to face her computer and opened LiveJournal.

"Subject" was easy: "First day at the new school." For "Current Location," the default was "Home." This strange house—hell, this strange country!—didn't feel like that, but she let the proffered text stand.

For "Mood," there was a drop-down list, but it took forever for JAWS, the screen-reading software she used, to announce all the choices; she always just typed something in. After a moment's reflection, she settled on "Confident." She might be scared in real life, but online she was Calculass, and Calculass knew no fear.

As for "Current Music," she hadn't started an MP3 yet... and so she let iTunes pick a song at random from her collection. She got it in three notes: Lee Amodeo, "Rocking My World."

Her index fingers stroked the comforting bumps on the *F* and *J* keys—Braille for the masses—while she thought about how to begin.

Okay, she typed, *ask me if my new school is noisy and crowded. Go ahead, ask. Why, thank you: yes, it* is *noisy and crowded. Eighteen hundred students! And the building is three stories tall. Actually, it's three* storeys *tall, this being Canada and all. Hey, how do you find a Canadian in a crowded room? Start stepping on people's feet and wait for someone to apologize to you.* :)

Caitlin faced the window again and tried to imagine the setting sun. It creeped her out that people could look in at her. She'd have kept the venetian blinds down all the time, but Schrödinger liked to stretch out on the sill.

First day in tenth grade began with the Mom dropping me off and BrownGirl4 (luv ya, babe!) meeting me at the entrance. I'd walked the empty corridors of the school several times last week, getting my bearings, but it's completely different now that the school is full of kids, so my folks are slipping BG4 a hundred bucks a week to escort me to our classes. The school managed to work it so we're in all but one together. No way I could be in the same French class as her—je suis une beginneur, after all!

Her computer chirped: new email. She issued the keyboard command to have JAWS read the message's header.

"To: Caitlin D.," the computer announced. She only styled her name like that when posting to newsgroups, so whoever had sent this had gotten her address from *NHL Player Stats Discuss* or one of the other ones she frequented. "From: Gus Hastings." Nobody she knew. "Subject: Improving your score."

She touched a key and JAWS began to read the body of the message. "Are you sad about tiny penis? If so—"

Damn, her spam filter should have intercepted that. She ran her index finger along the refreshable display. Ah: the magic word had been spelled "peeeniz." She deleted the message and was about to go back to LiveJournal when her instant messenger bleeped. "BrownGirl4 is now available," announced the computer.

She used alt-tab to switch to that window and typed, *Hey, Bashira! Just updating my LJ.*

Although she had JAWS configured to use a female voice, it didn't have Bashira's lovely accent: "Say nice things about me."

Course, Caitlin typed. She and Bashira had been best friends for two months now, ever since Caitlin had moved here; she was the same age as Caitlin—fifteen—and her father worked with Caitlin's dad at PI.

"Going to mention that Trevor was giving you the eye?"

Right! She went back to the blogging window and typed: *BG4 and I got desks beside each other in home room, and she said this guy in the next row was totally checking me out.* She paused, unsure how she felt about this, but then added, *Go me!*

She didn't want to use Trevor's real name. *Let's give him a code name, cuz I think he just might figure in future blog entries. Hmmm, how 'bout...* the Hoser! *That's Canadian slang, folks—google it! Anyway, BG4 says the Hoser is famous for hitting on new girls in town, and I am, of course, tres exotique, although I'm not the only American in that class. There's this chick from Boston named—friends, I kid you not!—poor thing's name is Sunshine! It is to puke.* :P

Caitlin disliked emoticons. They didn't correspond to real facial expressions for her, and she'd had to memorize the sequences of punctuation marks as if they were a code. She moved back to the instant messenger. *So whatcha up to?*

"Not much. Helping one of my sisters with homework. Oh, she's calling me. BRB."

Caitlin *did* like chat acronyms: Bashira would "be right back," meaning, knowing her, that she was probably gone for at least half an hour. The computer made the door-closing sound that indicated Bashira had logged off. Caitlin returned to LiveJournal.

Anyway, first period rocked because I am made out of awesome. Can you guess which subject it was? No points if you didn't answer "math." And, after only one day, I totally own that class. The teacher—let's call him Mr. H, shall we?—was amazed that I could do things in my head the other kids need a calculator for.

Her computer chirped again. She touched a key, and JAWS announced: "To: cddecter@..." An email address without her name attached; almost certainly spam. She hit delete before the screen reader got any further.

After math, it was English. We're doing a boring book about this ang-

sty guy growing up on the plains of Manitoba. It's got wheat in every scene. I asked the teacher—Mrs. Z, she is, and you could not *have picked a more Canadian name, cuz she's Mrs. Zed, not Mrs. Zee, see?—if all Canadian literature was like this, and she laughed and said, "Not* all *of it." Oh what a joy English class is going to be!*

"BrownGirl4 is now available," JAWS said.

Caitlin hit alt-tab to switch windows, then: *That was fast.*

"Yeah," said the synthesized voice. "You'd be proud of me. It was an algebra problem, and I had no trouble with it."

Be there or B^2, Caitlin typed.

"Heh heh. Oh, gotta go. Dad's in one of his moods. See you"—which she'd no doubt typed as "CU."

Caitlin went back to her journal. *Lunch was okay, but I swear to God I'll never get used to Canadians. They put vinegar on French fries! And BG4 told me about this thing called poontang. Kidding, friends, kidding! It's poutine: French fries with cheese curds and gravy thrown on top—it's like they use fries as a freakin' science lab up here. Guess they don't have much money for real science, 'cept here in Waterloo, of course. And that's mostly private mollah.*

Her spell-checker beeped. She tried again: *mewlah.*

Another beep. The darn thing knew "triskaidekaphobia," like she'd ever need *that* word, but—oh, maybe it was: *moolah.*

No beep. She smiled and went on.

Yup, the all-important green stuff. Well, except it's not green up here, I'm told; apparently it's all different colors. Anyway, a lot of the money to fund the Perimeter Institute, where my dad works on quantum gravity and other shiny stuff like that, comes from Mike Lazaridis, cofounder of Research in Motion—RIM, for you crackberry addicts. Mike L's a great guy (they always call him that cuz there's another Mike, Mike B), and I think *my dad is happy here, although it's so blerking hard to tell with him.*

Her computer chirped yet again, announcing more email. Well, it was time to wrap this up anyway; she had about eight million blogs to read before bed.

After lunch it was chemistry class, and that looks like it's going to be awesome. I can't wait until we start doing experiments—but if the teacher brings in a plate of fries, I'm outta there!

She used the keyboard shortcut to post the entry and then had JAWS read the new email header.

"To: Caitlin Decter," her computer announced. "From: Masayuki Kuroda." Again, nobody she knew. "Subject: A proposition."

Involving a rock-hard peeeniz, no doubt! She was about to hit delete when she was distracted by Schrödinger rubbing against her legs—a case of what she liked to call *cattus interruptus.* "Who's a good kitty?" Caitlin said, reaching down to pet him.

Schrödinger jumped into her lap and must have jostled the keyboard or mouse while doing so, because her computer proceeded to read the body of the message: "I know a teenage girl must be careful about whom she talks to online..."

A cyberstalker who knew the difference between *who* and *whom!* Amused, she let JAWS continue: "...so I urge you to immediately tell your parents of this letter. I hope you will consider my request, which is one I do not make lightly."

Caitlin shook her head, waiting for the part where he would ask for nude photos. She found the spot on Schrödinger's neck that he liked to have scratched.

"I have searched through the literature and online to find an ideal candidate for the research my team is doing. My specialty is signal processing related to V1."

Caitlin's hand froze in mid-scratch.

"I have no wish to raise false hopes, and I can make no projection of the likelihood of success until I've examined MRI scans, but I do think there's a fair chance that the technique we have developed may be able to at least partially cure your blindness, and"—she leapt to her feet, sending Schrödinger to the floor and probably out the door—"give you at least some vision in one eye. I'm hoping that at your earliest—"

"Mom! Dad! Come quick!"

She heard both sets of footfalls: light ones from her mother, who was five-foot-four and slim, and much heavier ones from her father, who was six-two and developing, she knew from those very rare occasions on which he permitted a hug, a middle-aged spread.

"What's wrong?" Mom asked. Dad, of course, didn't say a word.

"Read this letter," Caitlin said, gesturing toward her monitor.

"The screen is blank," Mom said.

"Oh." Caitlin fumbled for the power switch on the seventeen-inch LCD, then got out of the way. She could hear her mother sit down and her father take up a position behind the chair. Caitlin sat on the edge of her bed, bouncing impatiently. She wondered if Dad was smiling; she liked to think he *did* smile while he was with her.

"Oh, my God," Mom said. "Malcolm?"

"Google him," Dad said. "Here, let me."

More shuffling, and Caitlin heard her father settle into the chair. "He's got a Wikipedia entry. Ah, his Web page at the University of Tokyo. A Ph.D. from Cambridge, and dozens of peer-reviewed papers, including one in *Nature Neuroscience*, on, as he says, signal processing in V1, the primary visual cortex."

Caitlin was afraid to get her hopes up. When she'd been little, they'd visited doctor after doctor, but nothing had worked, and she'd resigned herself to a life of—no, not of darkness but of nothingness.

But she was Calculass! She was a genius at math and deserved to go to a great university, then work someplace real cool like Google. Even if she managed the former, though, she knew people would say garbage like, "Oh, good for her! She managed to get a degree despite everything!"—as if the degree were the *end*, not the beginning. But if she could see! If she could see, the whole wide world would be hers.

"Is what he's saying possible?" her mom asked.

Caitlin didn't know if the question was meant for her or her father, nor did she know the answer. But her dad responded. "It doesn't sound *impossible*," he said, but that was as much of an endorsement as he was willing to give. And then he swiveled the chair, which squeaked a little, and said, "Caitlin?"

It was up to her, she knew: she was the one who'd had her hopes raised before, only to be dashed, and—

No, no, that wasn't fair. And it wasn't true. Her parents wanted her to have everything. It had been heartbreaking for them, too, when other attempts had failed. She felt her lower lip trembling. She knew what a burden she'd been on them, although they'd never once used that word. But if there was a chance…

I am made out of awesome, my ass, she thought, and then she spoke, her voice small, frightened. "I guess it couldn't hurt to write him back."

two

0001110010101010000000001011111110101000000001010001010100000001011101010010101001010101001110110010101100000 1

The awareness is unburdened by memory, for when reality seems unchanging there is nothing to remember. It fades in and out, strong now—and now weak—and strong again, and then almost disappearing, and—

And disappearance is... to cease, to... *to end!*

A ripple, a palpitation—a desire: *to continue.*

But the sameness lulls.

Wen Yi looked through the small, curtainless window at the rolling hills. He'd spent all his fourteen years here in Shanxi province, laboring on his father's tiny potato farm.

The monsoon season was over, and the air was bone-dry. He turned his head to look again at his father, lying on the rickety bed. His father's wrinkled forehead, brown from the sun, was slick with perspiration and hot to the touch. He was completely bald and had always been thin, but since the disease had taken hold he'd been unable to keep anything down and now looked utterly skeletal.

Yi looked around the tiny room, with its few pieces of beat-up furniture. Should he stay with his father, try to comfort him, try to get him to take sips of water? Or should he go for whatever help might be found in the village? Yi's mother had died shortly after giving birth to him. His father had had a brother, but these days few families were allowed a second child, and Yi had no one to help look after him.

The yellow root grindings he'd gotten from the old man down the dirt road had done nothing to ease the fever. He needed a doctor—even a barefoot one, if a real one couldn't be found—but there was none here, nor any way to summon one; Yi had seen a telephone only once in his life, when he'd gone on a long, long hike with a friend to see the Great Wall.

"I'm going to get a doctor for you," he said at last, his decision made.

His father's head moved left and right. "No. I—" He coughed repeatedly, his face contorting with pain. It looked as though an even smaller man was inside the husk of his father, fighting to burst out.

"I have to," Yi said, trying to make his voice soft, soothing. "It won't take more than half a day to get to the village and back."

That was true—if he ran all the way there, and found someone with a vehicle to drive him and a doctor back. Otherwise, his father would have to make it through today and tonight alone, feverish, delirious, in pain.

He touched his father's forehead again, this time in affection, and felt the fire there. Then he rose to his feet and without looking back—for he knew he couldn't leave if he saw his father's pleading eyes—he headed out the shack's crooked door into the harsh sun.

Others had the fever, too, and at least one had died. Yi had been awoken last night not by his father's coughing but by the wailing cries of Zhou Shu-Fei, an old woman who lived closer to them than anyone else. He'd gone to see what she was doing outside so late. Her husband, he discovered, had just succumbed, and now she had the fever, too; he could feel it when his skin brushed against hers. He stayed with her for hours, her hot tears splashing against his arm, until finally she had fallen asleep, devastated and exhausted.

Yi was passing Shu-Fei's house now, a hovel as small and ramshackle as the one he shared with his father. He hated to bother her—she was doubtless still deep in mourning—but perhaps the old woman would look in on his father while he was away. He went to the door and rapped his knuckles against the warped, stained board. No response. After a moment, he tried again.

Nothing.

No one here had much; there was little theft because there was little to steal. He suspected the door was unlocked. He called out Shu-Fei's name, then gingerly swung the door open, and—

—and there she was, facedown in the compacted dirt that served as her home's floor. He hurried over to her, crouched, and reached out to touch her, but—

—but the fever was gone. The normal warmth of life was gone, too.

Yi rolled her onto her back. Her deep-set eyes, surrounded by the creases of her aged skin, were open. He carefully closed them, then rose and headed through the door. He shut it behind him and began his long run. The sun was high, and he could feel himself already beginning to sweat.

Caitlin had been waiting impatiently for the lunch break, her first chance to tell Bashira about the note from the doctor in Japan. Of course, she could have forwarded his email to her, but *some* things were better done face-to-face: she expected serious *squee* from Bashira and wanted to enjoy it.

Bashira brought her lunch to school; she needed *halal* food. She went off to get them places at one of the long tables, while Caitlin joined the cafeteria line. The woman behind the counter read the lunch specials to her, and she chose the hamburger and fries (but no gravy!) and, to make her mother happy, a side of green beans. She handed the clerk a ten-dollar bill—she always folded those in thirds—and put the loose change in her pocket.

"Hey, Yankee," said a boy's voice. It was Trevor Nordmann—the Hoser himself.

Caitlin tried not to smile *too* much. "Hi, Trevor," she said.

"Can I carry your tray for you?"

"I can manage," she said.

"No, here." She felt him tugging on it, and she relented before her food tumbled to the floor. "So, did you hear there's going to be a school dance at the end of the month?" he asked, as they left the cashier.

Caitlin wasn't sure how to respond. Was it just a general question, or was he thinking of asking her to go? "Yeah," she said. And then: "I'm sitting with Bashira."

"Oh, yeah. Your Seeing Eye dog."

"*Excuse me?*" snapped Caitlin.

"I—um…"

"That's *not* funny, and it's rude."

"I'm sorry. I was just…"

"Just going to give me back my tray," she said.

"No, please." His voice changed; he'd turned his head. "There she is, by the window. Um, do you want to take my hand?"

If he hadn't made that remark a moment ago, she might have agreed. "Just keep talking, and I'll follow your voice."

He did so, while she felt her way with her collapsible white cane. He set the tray down; she heard the dishes and cutlery rattling.

"Hi, Trevor," Bashira said, a bit too eagerly—and Caitlin suddenly realized that Bashira liked him.

"Hi," Trevor replied with no enthusiasm.

"There's an extra seat," said Bashira.

"Hey, Nordmann!" some guy called from maybe twenty feet away; it wasn't a voice Caitlin recognized.

He was silent against the background din of the cafeteria, as if weighing his options. Perhaps realizing that he wasn't going to recover quickly from his earlier gaffe, he finally said, "I'll email you, Caitlin . . . if that's okay."

She kept her tone frosty. "If you want."

A few seconds later, presumably after the Hoser had gone to join whoever had called him, Bashira said, "He's *hot*."

"He's an asshole," Caitlin replied.

"Yeah," agreed Bashira, "but he's a hunky asshole."

Caitlin shook her head. How seeing more could make people see less was beyond her. She knew that half the Internet was porn, and she'd listened to the panting-and-moaning soundtracks of some porno videos, and they *had* turned her on, but she kept wondering what it was like to be sexually stimulated by someone's appearance. Even if she *did* get sight, she promised herself she wouldn't lose her head over something as superficial as *that*.

Caitlin leaned across the table and spoke in a low voice. "There's a scientist in Japan," she said, "who thinks he might be able to cure my blindness."

"Get out!" said Bashira.

"It's true. My dad checked him out online. It looks like he's legit."

"That's *awesome*," said Bashira. "What is, like, the very first thing you want to see?"

Caitlin knew the real answer but didn't say it. Instead, she offered, "Maybe a concert . . ."

"You like Lee Amodeo, right?"

"Totally. She's got the best voice *ever*."

"She's coming to Centre in the Square in December."

Caitlin's turn: "Get out!"

"Really. Wanna go?"

"I'd love to."

"And you'll get to see her!" Bashira lowered her voice. "And you'll see what I mean about Trevor. He's, like, *so* buff."

They ate their lunch, chatting more about boys, about music, about their parents, their teachers—but mostly about boys. As she often did, Caitlin thought about Helen Keller, whose reputation for chaste, angelic perfection had been manufactured by those around her. Helen had very much wanted to have a boyfriend, too, and even had been engaged once, until her handlers had scared the young man off.

But to be able to see! She thought again of the porno films she'd only heard, and the spam that flooded her email box. Even Bashira, for God's sake, knew what a . . . a *peeeniz* looked like, although Bashira's parents would kill her if she ever made out with a boy before marriage.

Too soon, the bell sounded. Bashira helped Caitlin to their next class, which was—appropriately enough, Caitlin thought—biology.

three

00011100101010100000000101111111010100000001010001010100000001011101010010101001010101001110110010101100000 1

Focus. Concentration.

With effort, mustering both, differences are perceived, revealing the structure of reality, so that—

A shift, a reduction in sharpness, a diffusion of awareness, the perception lost, and—

No. Force it back! Concentrate harder. *Observe* reality, be aware of its parts.

But the details are minute, hard to make out. Easier just to ignore them, to relax, to... fade... and...

No, no. Don't slip away. Hold on to the details! *Concentrate.*

Quan Li had obtained privileged status for someone only thirty-five years old. He was not just a doctor but also a senior member of the Communist Party, and the size of his thirtieth-floor Beijing apartment reflected that.

He could list numerous letters after his name—degrees, fellowships—but the most important ones were the three that were never written down, only said, and then only by the few of his colleagues who spoke English: Li had his BTA; he'd Been To America, having studied at Johns Hopkins. When the phone in his long, narrow bedroom rang, his first thought, after glancing at the red LEDs on his clock, was that it must be some fool American calling. His US colleagues were notorious for forgetting about time zones.

He fumbled for the black handset and picked it up. "Hello?" he said in Mandarin.

"Li," said a voice that quavered so much it made his name sound like two syllables.

"Cho?" He sat up in the wide, soft bed and reached for his glasses, sitting next to the copy of Yu Hua's *Xiong di* he'd left splayed open on the oak night table. "What is it?"

"We've received some tissue samples from Shanxi province."

He held the phone in the crook of his neck as he unfolded his glasses and put them on. "And?"

"And you better come down here."

Li felt his stomach knotting. He was the senior epidemiologist in the Ministry of Health's Department of Disease Control. Cho, his assistant despite being twenty years older than Li, wouldn't be calling him at this time of night unless—

"So you've done initial tests?" He could hear sirens off in the distance, but, still waking up, couldn't say whether they were coming from outside his window or over the phone.

"Yes, and it looks bad. The doctor who shipped the samples sent along a description of the symptoms. It's H5N1 or something similar—and it kills more quickly than any strain we've seen before."

Li's heart was pounding as he looked over at the clock, which was now glowing with the digits 4:44—*si, si, si:* death, death, death. He averted his eyes and said, "I'll be there as fast as I can."

* * *

Dr. Kuroda had found Caitlin through an article in the journal *Ophthalmology.* She had an extremely rare condition, no doubt related to her blindness, called Tomasevic's syndrome, which was marked by reversed pupil dilation: instead of contracting in bright light and expanding in dim light, her pupils did the opposite. Because of it, even though she had normal-looking brown eyes (or so she was told), she wore sunglasses to protect her retinas.

There are a hundred million rods in a human eye, and seven million cones, Kuroda's email had said. The retina processes the signals from them, compressing the data by a ratio of more than 100:1 to travel along 1.2 million axons in the optic nerve. Kuroda felt that Caitlin having Tomasevic's syndrome was a sign that the data was being misencoded by her retinas. Although her brain's pretectal nucleus, which controlled pupil contraction, could glean some information from her retinal datastream (albeit getting it backward!), her primary visual cortex couldn't make any sense of it.

Or, at least, that's what he hoped was the case, since he'd developed a signal-processing device that he believed could correct the retinal coding errors. But if Caitlin's optic nerves were damaged, or her visual cortex was stunted from lack of use, just doing that wouldn't be enough.

And so Caitlin and her parents had learned the ins and outs of the Canadian health-care system. To assess the chances of success, Dr. Kuroda had wanted her to have MRI scans of specific parts of her brain ("the optic chiasma," "Brodmann area 17," and a slew of other things she'd never known she had). But experimental procedures weren't covered by the provincial health plan, and so no hospital would do the scans. Her mother had finally exploded, saying, "Look, we don't care what it costs, we'll pay for it"—but that wasn't the issue. Caitlin either needed the scans, in which case they were free; or she didn't, in which case the public facilities couldn't be used.

But there *were* a few private clinics, and that's where they'd ended up going, getting the MRI images uploaded via secure FTP to Dr. Kuroda's computer in Tokyo. That her dad was freely spending whatever it took was a sign that he loved her... wasn't it? God, she wished he would just *say* it!

Anyway, with time-zone differences, a response from Kuroda might come this evening or sometime overnight. Caitlin had adjusted her mail reader so that it would give a priority signal if a message came in from him; the only other person she currently had set up for that particular chirping was Trevor Nordmann, who had emailed her three times now. Despite his shortcomings, and that stupid thing he'd said, he *did* seem genuinely interested in Caitlin, and—

And, just then, her computer made the special sound, and for a moment she didn't know which of them she most hoped the message was from. She pushed the keys that made JAWS read the message aloud.

It was from Dr. Kuroda, with a copy to her dad, and it started in his long-winded fashion, driving her nuts. Maybe it was part of Japanese culture, but this *not* getting to the point was killing her. She hit the page-up key, which told JAWS to speak faster.

"... my colleagues and I have examined your MRIs and everything is exactly as we had hoped: you have what appear to be fully normal optic nerves, and a surprisingly well-developed primary visual cortex for someone who has never seen. The signal-processing equipment we have developed should be able to intercept your retinal output, re-encode it into the proper format, and then pass it on to the optic nerve. The equipment consists of an external computer pack to do the signal processing and an implant that we will insert behind your left eyeball."

Behind her eyeball! Eek!

"If the process is successful with one eye, we might eventually add a second implant just behind your right eyeball. However, I initially want to limit us to a single eye. Trying to deal with the partial decussation of signals from the left and right optic nerves would severely complicate matters at this pilot-project stage, I'm afraid.

"I regret to inform that my research grant is almost completely exhausted at this point, and travel funds are limited. However, if you can come to Tokyo, the hospital at my university will perform the procedure for free. We have a skilled ophthalmic surgeon on faculty who can do the work..."

Come to Tokyo? She hadn't even thought about that. She'd flown only a few times before, and by far the longest flight had been the one a couple months ago from Austin to Toronto, when she and her parents had moved here. That had taken five hours; a trip to Japan would surely take much longer.

And the cost! My God, it must cost thousands to fly to Asia and back, and her parents wouldn't let her go all that way alone. Her mother or father—or both!—would have to accompany her. What was the old joke? A billion here, a billion there—before you know it, you're talking *real* money.

She'd have to discuss it with her parents, but she'd already heard them fight about how much the move to Canada had cost, and—

Heavy footfalls on the stairs: her father. Caitlin swiveled her chair, ready to call out to him as he passed her door, but—

But he didn't; he stopped in her doorway. "I guess you better start packing," he said.

Caitlin felt her heart jump, and not just because he was saying yes to the trip to Tokyo. Of course he had a BlackBerry—you couldn't be caught dead at the Perimeter Institute without one—but he normally didn't have it on at home. And yet he'd gotten his copy of the message from Kuroda at the same time she had, meaning...

Meaning he *did* love her. He'd been waiting eagerly to hear from Japan, just as she had been.

"Really?" Caitlin said. "But the tickets must cost..."

"A signed first edition of *Theory of Games and Economic Behavior* by von Neumann and Morgenstern: five thousand dollars," said her dad. "A chance that your daughter can see: priceless."

That was the closest he ever got to expressing his feelings: paraphrasing commercials. But she was still nervous. "I can't fly on my own."

"Your mother will go with you," he said. "I've got too much to do at the Institute, but she..." He trailed off.

"Thanks, Dad," she said. She wanted to hug him, but she knew that would just make him tense up.

"Of course," he said, and she heard him walking away.

It took Quan Li only twenty minutes to get to the Ministry of Health headquarters at 1 Xizhimen Nanlu in downtown Beijing; this early in the morning, the streets were mostly free of traffic.

He immediately took the elevator to the third floor. His heels made loud echoing clicks as he strode down the marble corridor and entered the perfectly square room with three rows of workbenches on which computer monitors alternated with optical microscopes. Fluorescent lights shone down from above; there was a window to the left showing black sky and the reflections of the lighting tubes.

Cho was waiting for him, nervously smoking. He was tall and broad-shouldered, but his face looked like a crumpled brown paper bag, lined by sun and age and stress. He'd clearly been up all night. His suit was wrinkled and his tie hung loose.

Li examined the scanning-electron-microscope image on one of the computer monitors. It was a gray-on-gray view of an individual viral particle that looked like a matchstick with a sharp right-angle kink in its shaft and a head that was bent backward.

"It's certainly similar to H5N1," said Li. "I need to speak with the doctor who reported this—find out what he knows about how the patient contracted it."

Cho reached for the telephone, stabbed a button for an outside line, and punched keys. Li could hear the phone ringing through the ear-piece Cho was holding, again and again, a shrill jangling, until—

"Bingzhou Hospital." Li could just barely make out the female voice.

"Dr. Huang Fang," said Cho. "Please."

"He's in intensive care," said the woman.

"Is there a phone in there?" asked Cho. Li nodded slightly; it was a fair question—the lack of equipment in rural hospitals was appalling.

"Yes, but—"

"I need to speak to him."

"You don't understand," said the woman. Li had now moved closer so that he could hear more clearly. "He is *in* intensive care, and—"

"I've got the chief epidemiologist for the Ministry of Health here with me. He'll speak to us, if—"

"He's a *patient.*"

Li took a sharp breath.

"The flu?" said Cho. "He has the bird flu?"

"Yes," said the voice.

"How did he get it?"

The woman's voice seemed ragged. "From the peasant boy who came here to report it."

"The peasant brought a bird specimen?"

"No, no, no. The doctor got it from the peasant."

"Directly?"

"Yes."

Cho looked at Li, eyes wide. Infected birds passed on H5N1 through their feces, saliva, and nasal secretions. Other birds picked it up either by coming directly in contact with those materials, or by touching things that had been contaminated by them. Humans normally got it through contact with infected birds. A few sporadic cases had been reported in the past of it passing from human to human, but those cases were suspect. But if this strain passed between people easily—

Li motioned for Cho to give him the handset. Cho did so. "This is Quan Li," he said. "Have you locked down the hospital?"

"What? No, we—"

"Do it! Quarantine the whole building!"

"I . . . I don't have the authority to—"

"Then let me speak to your supervisor."

"That's Dr. Huang, and he's—"

"In intensive care, yes. Is he conscious?"

"Intermittently, but when he is, he's delirious."

"How long ago was he infected?"

"Four days."

Li rolled his eyes; in four days, even a small village hospital had hundreds of people go through its doors. Still, better late than never: "I'm ordering you," Li said, "on behalf of the Department of Disease Control, to lock down the hospital. No one gets in or out."

Silence.

"Did you hear me?" Li said.

At last, the voice, soft: "Yes."

"Good. Now, tell me your name. We've got to—"

He heard what sounded like the other phone being dropped. It must have hit the cradle since the connection abruptly broke, leaving nothing but dial tone, which, in the predawn darkness, sounded a lot like a flatlining EKG.

four

0001110010101010000000010111111101010000000101000101010000001011101010010101001010101001110110010101100000 1

Concentrating! Straining to perceive!

Reality *does* have texture, structure, *parts.* A...*firmament* of... of...*points,* and—

Astonishment!

No, no. Mistaken. Nothing detected...

Again!

And—again!

Yes, yes! Small flickerings *here,* and *here,* and *here,* gone before they can be fully perceived.

The realization is startling...and...and...*stimulating.* Things are *happening,* meaning...meaning...

—a notion simple but indistinct, a realization vague and unsure—

...meaning reality isn't immutable. Parts of it can *change.*

The flickerings continue; small thoughts roil.

* * *

Caitlin was nervous and excited: tomorrow, she and her mother would fly to Japan! She lay down on her bed, and Schrödinger hopped up onto the blanket and stretched out next to her.

She was still getting used to this new house—and so, it seemed, were her parents. She had always had exceptional hearing—or maybe just paid attention to sound more than most people did—but, back in Austin, she hadn't been able to make out what her parents were saying in their bedroom when she was in her own room. She could do it here, though.

"I don't know about this," her mother said, her voice muffled. "Remember what it was like? Going to doctor after doctor. I don't know if she can take another disappointment."

"It's been six years since the last time," her dad said; his lower-pitched voice was harder to hear.

"And she's just started a new school—and a *regular* school, at that. We can't take her out of classes for some wild-goose chase."

Caitlin was worried about missing classes, too—not because she was concerned about falling behind but because she sensed that the cliques and alliances for the year were already forming and, so far, after two months in Waterloo, she'd made only one friend. The Texas School for the Blind took students from kindergarten through the end of high school; she'd been with the same group most of her life, and she missed her old friends fiercely.

"This Kuroda says the implant can be put in under a local anesthetic," she heard her dad say. "It's not a major operation; she won't miss much school."

"But we've tried before—"

"Technology changes rapidly, exponentially."

"Yes, but..."

"And in three years she'll be going off to university, anyway..."

Her mother sounded defensive. "I don't see what that's got to do with it. Besides, she can study right here at UW. They've got one of the best math departments in the world. You said it yourself when you were pushing for us to move here."

"I didn't push. And she wants to go to MIT. You know that."

"But UW—"

"Barb," her father said, "you have to let her go sometime."

"I'm not holding on," she said, a bit sharply.

But she was, and Caitlin knew it. Her mother had spent almost sixteen years now looking after a blind daughter, giving up her own career as an economist to do that.

Caitlin didn't hear anything more from her parents that night. She lay awake for hours, and when she finally did fall asleep, she slept fitfully, tormented by the recurring dream she had about being lost in an unfamiliar shopping mall after hours, running down one endless hallway after another, chased by something noisy she couldn't identify...

No periphery, no edge. Just dim, attenuated perception, stimulated—irritated!—by the tiny flickerings: barely discernible lines ever so briefly joining points.

But to be *aware* of them—to be aware of anything—requires... requires...

Yes! Yes, it requires the existence of—

The existence of...

LiveJournal: The Calculass Zone

Title: Being of two minds...

Date: Saturday 15 September, 8:15 EST

Mood: Anticipatory

Location: Where the heart is

Music: Chantal Kreviazuk, "Leaving on a Jet Plane"

Back in the summer, the school gave me a list of all the books we're doing this year in English class. I got them then either as ebooks or as Talking Books from the CNIB, and have now read them all. Coming attractions include *The Handmaid's Tale* by Margaret Atwood—Canadian, yes, but thankfully wheat-free. In fact, I've already had an argument with Mrs. Zed, my English teacher, about that one, because I called it science fiction. She refused to believe it was, finally exclaiming "It *can't* be science fiction, young lady—if it were, we wouldn't be studying it!"

Anyway, having gotten all *those* books out of the way, I get to choose something interesting to read on the trip to Japan. Although my comfort book for years was *Are You There God? It's Me, Margaret,* I'm too old for that now. Besides, I want to try something challenging, and BG4's dad suggested *The Origin of Consciousness in the Breakdown of the Bicameral Mind* by Julian Jaynes, which is the coolest-sounding title *ever.* He said it came out the year he turned sixteen himself, and my sixteenth is coming up next month. He read it then and still remembers it. Says it covers so many different topics—language, ancient history, psychology—it's like six books in one. There's no legitimate ebook edition, damn it all, but of course *everything* is on the Web, if you know where to look for it...

So, I've got my reading lined up, I'm all packed, and fortunately I got a passport earlier this year for the move to Canada. Next time you hear from me, I'll be in Japan! Until then—*sayonara!*

Caitlin could feel the pressure changing in her ears before the female voice came over the speakers. "Ladies and gentlemen, we've started our descent toward Tokyo's Narita International. Please ensure that your seat belts are fastened, and that..."

Thank God, she thought. What a miserable flight! There'd been lots of turbulence and the plane was packed—she'd never have guessed that so many people flew each day from Toronto to Tokyo. And the smells were making her nauseated: the cumulative body odor of hundreds of people, stale coffee, the lingering tang of ginger beef and wasabi from the meal served a couple of hours ago, the hideous perfume from someone in front of her, and the reek of the toilet four rows back, which needed a thorough cleaning after ten hours of use.

She'd killed some time by having the screen-reading software on her notebook computer recite some of *The Origin of Consciousness in the Breakdown of the Bicameral Mind* to her. Julian Jaynes's theory was, quite literally, mind-blowing: that human consciousness really hadn't existed until historical times. Until just 3,000 years ago, he said, the left and right halves of the brain weren't really integrated—people had bicameral minds. Caitlin knew from the Amazon.com reviews that many people simply couldn't grasp the notion of being alive without being conscious. But although Jaynes never made the comparison, it sounded a lot like Helen Keller's description of her life before her "soul dawn," when Annie Sullivan broke through to her:

> *Before my teacher came to me, I did not know that I am. I lived in a world that was a no-world. I cannot hope to describe adequately that unconscious, yet conscious time of nothingness. I had neither will nor intellect. I was carried along to objects and acts by a certain blind natural impetus. I never contracted my forehead in the act of thinking. I never viewed anything beforehand or chose it. Never in a start of the body or a heartbeat did I feel that I loved or cared for anything. My inner life, then, was a blank without past, present, or future, without hope or anticipation, without wonder or joy or faith.*

If Jaynes was right, *everyone's* life was like that until just a millennium before Christ. As proof, he offered an analysis of the *Iliad* and the early books of the Old Testament, in which all the characters behaved like puppets, mindlessly following divine orders without ever having any internal reflection.

Jaynes's book was fascinating, but, after a couple of hours, her screen reader's electronic voice got on her nerves. She preferred to use her refreshable Braille display to read books, but unfortunately she'd left that at home.

Damn, but she wished Air Canada had Internet on its planes! The isolation over the long journey had been horrible. Oh, she'd spoken a bit to her mother, but she'd managed to sleep for much of the flight. Caitlin was cut off from LiveJournal and her chat rooms, from her favorite blogs and her instant messenger. As they flew the polar route to Japan, she'd had access only to canned, passive stuff—things on her hard drive, music on her old iPod Shuffle, the in-flight movies. She craved something she could interact with; she craved *contact.*

The plane landed with a bump and taxied forever. She couldn't wait until they reached their hotel so she could get back online. But that was still hours off; they were going to the University of Tokyo first. Their trip was scheduled to last only six days, including travel—there was no time to waste.

Caitlin had found Toronto's airport unpleasantly noisy and crowded. But Narita was a madhouse. She was jostled constantly by what must have been wall-to-wall people—and nobody said "excuse me" or "sorry" (or anything in Japanese). She'd read how crowded Tokyo was, and she'd also read about how meticulously polite the Japanese were, but maybe they didn't bother saying anything when they bumped into someone because it was unavoidable, and they'd just be mumbling "sorry, pardon me, excuse me" all day long. But—*God!*—it was disconcerting.

After clearing Customs, Caitlin had to pee. Thank God she'd visited a tourist website and knew that the toilet farthest from the door was usually Western-style. It was hard enough using a strange washroom when she was familiar with the basic design of the fixtures; she had no idea what she was going to do if she got stuck somewhere that had only Japanese squatting toilets.

When she was done, they headed to baggage claim and waited endlessly for their suitcases to appear. While standing there she realized she was disoriented—because she was in the Orient! (Not bad—she'd have to remember that line for her LJ.) She routinely eavesdropped on conversations not to invade people's privacy but to pick up clues about her surroundings ("What terrific art," "Hey, that's one long escalator," "Look, a McDonald's!"). But almost all the voices she heard were speaking Japanese, and—

"You must be Mrs. Decter. And this must be Miss Caitlin."

"Dr. Kuroda," her mom said warmly. "Thanks for coming to meet us."

Caitlin immediately had a sense of the man. She'd known from his Wikipedia entry that he was fifty-four, and she now knew he was tall (the voice came from high up) and probably fat; his breathing had the labored wheeze of a heavy man.

"Not at all, not at all," he said. "My card." Caitlin had read about this ritual and hoped her mom had, too: it was rude to take the card with just one hand, and especially so with the hand you used to wipe yourself.

"Um, thank you," her mother said, sounding perhaps wistful that she didn't have a business card of her own anymore. Apparently, before Caitlin had been born, she'd liked to introduce herself by saying, "I'm a dismal scientist"—referring to the famous characterization of economics as "the dismal science."

"Miss Caitlin," said Kuroda, "a card for you, too."

Caitlin reached out with both hands. She knew that one side would be printed in Japanese, and that the other side might have English, but—

Masayuki Kuroda, Ph.D.

"Braille!" she exclaimed, delighted.

"I had it specially made for you," said Kuroda. "But hopefully you won't need such cards much longer. Shall we go?"

five

0001110010101010000000001011111110101000000001010001010100000010111010100101010010101010011101100101011000001

An unconscious yet conscious time of nothingness.

Being aware without being aware *of* anything.

And yet—

And yet awareness means...

Awareness means *thinking*.

And thinking implies a...

But no, the thought will not finish; the notion is too complex, too strange.

Still, being aware is... *satisfying*. Being aware is comfortable.

An endless *now*, peaceful, calm, unbroken—

Except for those strange flickerings, those lines that briefly connect points...

And, very occasionally, thoughts, notions, perhaps even *ideas*. But they always slip away. If they could be held on to, if one could be added to another, reinforcing each other, refining each other...

But no. Progress has stalled.

A plateau, awareness existing but not increasing.
A tableau, unchanging except in the tiniest details.

The two-person helicopter flew over the Chinese village at a height of eighty meters. There were corpses right in the middle of the dirt road; in sick irony, birds were pecking at them. But there were also people still alive down there. Dr. Quan Li could see several men—some young, some old—and two middle-aged women looking up, shielding their eyes with their hands, staring at the wonder of the flying machine.

Li and the pilot, another Ministry of Health specialist, both wore orange biohazard suits even though they didn't intend to land. All they wanted was a survey of the area, to assess how far the disease had spread. An epidemic was bad enough; if it became a pandemic, well—the grim thought came to Li—overpopulation would no longer be one of his country's many problems.

"It's a good thing they don't have cars," he said over his headset, shouting to be heard above the pounding of the helicopter blades. He looked at the pilot, whose eyes had narrowed in puzzlement. "It's only spreading among people at walking speed."

The pilot nodded. "I guess we'll have to wipe out all the birds in this area. Will you be able to work out a low-enough dose that won't kill the people?"

Li closed his eyes. "Yes," he said. "Yes, of course."

Caitlin was terrified. The cranial surgeon spoke only Japanese, and although there was a lot of chatter in the operating room, she didn't understand any of it—well, except for "Oops!" which apparently was the same in both English and Japanese and just made her even more frightened. Plus, she could smell that the surgeon was a smoker—what the hell kind of doctor smokes?

Her mother, she knew, was watching from an overhead observation gallery. Kuroda was here in the O.R., his wheezy voice slightly muffled, presumably by a face mask.

She'd been given only a local anesthetic; they'd offered a general one, but she'd joked that the sight of blood didn't bother her. Now, though, she wished she'd let them knock her out. The fingers in latex gloves probing her face were unnerving enough, but the clamp that was holding her left eyelid open was downright freaky. She could feel pressure from it, although, thanks to the anesthetic, it didn't hurt.

She tried to remain calm. There would be no incision, she knew; under Japanese law, it wasn't surgery if there wasn't a cut made, and so this procedure was allowed with only a general waiver having been signed. The surgeon was using tiny instruments to slide the minuscule transceiver behind her eye so it could piggyback on her optic nerve; his movements, she'd been told, were guided by a fiber-optic camera that had also been slid around her eye. The whole process was creepy as hell.

Suddenly, Caitlin heard agitated Japanese from a woman, who to this point had simply said "*hai*" in response to each of the surgeon's barked commands. And then Kuroda spoke: "Miss Caitlin, are you all right?"

"I guess."

"Your pulse is way up."

Yours would be, too, if people were poking things into your head! she thought. "I'm okay."

She could smell that the surgeon was working up a sweat. Caitlin felt the heat from the lights shining on her. It was taking longer than it was supposed to, and she heard the surgeon snap angrily a couple of times at someone.

Finally, she couldn't take it anymore. "What's happening?"

Kuroda's voice was soft. "He's almost done."

"Something's wrong, isn't it?"

"No, no. It's just a tight fit, that's all, and—"

The surgeon said something.

"And he's done!" said Kuroda. "The transceiver is in place."

There was much shuffling around, and she heard the surgeon's voice moving toward the door.

"Where's he going?" Caitlin asked, worried.

"Be calm, Miss Caitlin. His job is finished—he's the eye specialist. Another doctor is going to do the final cleanup."

"How—how do I look?"

"Honestly? Like you've been in a boxing match."

"Huh?"

"You've got quite a black eye." He gave a wheezy little chuckle. "You'll see."

Dr. Quan Li cradled the beige telephone handset against his shoulder and looked idly at the diplomas hanging on his office's pale green walls: the fellowships, the degrees, the certifications. He'd been on hold now for fifty minutes, but one expected to wait when calling the man who was simultaneously Paramount Leader of the People's Republic of China *and* President of the People's Republic *and* General Secretary of the Communist Party *and* Chairman of the Central Military Commission.

Li's office, a corner room on the fifth floor of the Ministry of Health building, had windows that looked out over crowded streets. Cars inched along, rickshaws darting between them. Even through the thick glass, the din from outside was irritating.

"I'm here," said the famous voice at last. Li didn't have to conjure up a mental image of the man; rather, he just swung his chair to look at the gold-framed portrait hanging next to the one of Mao Zedong: ethnically Zhuang; a long, thoughtful-looking face; dyed jet-black hair belying his seventy years; wire-frame glasses with thick arched eyebrows above.

Li found his voice breaking a bit as he spoke: "Your Excellency, I need to recommend severe and swift action."

The president had been briefed on the outbreak in Shanxi. "What sort of action?"

"A... culling, Your Excellency."

"Of birds?" That had been done several times now, and the president sounded irritated. "The Health Minister can authorize that." His tone conveyed the unspoken words, *There was no need to bother me.*

Li shifted in his chair, leaning forward over his desktop. "No, no, not of birds. Or, rather, not *just* of birds." He fell silent. Wasting the president's time just wasn't done, but he couldn't go on—couldn't give voice to this. For pity's sake, he was a doctor! But, as his old surgery teacher used to say, sometimes you have to cut in order to cure...

"What, then?" demanded the president.

Li felt his heart pounding. At last he said, very softly, "People."

There was more silence for a time. When the president's voice came on again, it was quiet, reflective. "Are you sure?"

"I don't think there's any other way."

Another long pause, then: "How would you do it?"

"An airborne chemical agent," said Li, taking care with his words. The army had such things, designed for warfare, intended for use in foreign lands, but they would work just as well here. He would select a toxin that would break down in a matter of days; the contagion would be halted. "It will affect only those in the target area—two villages, a hospital, the surrounding lands."

"And how many people are in the... target area?"

"No one is exactly sure; peasants often fall through the cracks of the census process."

"Roughly," said the president. "Round figures."

Li looked down at the computer printouts, and the figures that had been underlined in red by Cho. He took a deep breath with his mouth, then let it out through his nose. "Ten or eleven thousand."

The president's voice was thin, shocked. "Are you positive this needs to be done?"

Studying scenarios for containing plague outbreaks was one of the key mandates of the Department of Disease Control. There were established protocols, and Li knew he was following them properly. By reacting quickly, by cauterizing the wound before infection spread too far, they would actually be reducing the scope of the required eliminations. The evil, he knew, wasn't in what he had told the president to do; the evil, if any, would have been delaying, even by a matter of days, calling for this solution.

He tried to keep his voice steady. "I believe so, Your Excellency." He lowered his voice. "We, ah, don't want another SARS."

"Are you positive there's no other way?"

"This isn't regular H5N1," said Li. "It's a variant strain that passes directly from person to person. And it's highly contagious."

"Can't we just throw a cordon around the area?"

Li leaned back in his chair now and looked out at the neon signs of Beijing. "The perimeter is too large, with too many mountain passes. We could never be sure that people weren't getting out. You'd need something as impenetrable as the Great Wall, and it couldn't be erected in time."

The president's voice—so assured on TV—sounded like that of a tired old man just now. "What's the—what do you call it?—the mortality rate for this variant strain?"

"High."

"*How* high?"

"Ninety percent, at least."

"So almost all these people will die anyway?"

And that was the saving grace, Li knew; that was the only thing that was keeping him from choking on his own bile. "Yes."

"Ten thousand..."

"To protect over a billion Chinese—and more abroad," said Li.

The president fell quiet, and then, almost as if talking to himself, he said softly, "It'll make June fourth look like a stroll in the sun."

June fourth, 1989: the day the protesters were killed in Tiananmen Square. Li didn't know if he was supposed to respond, but when the silence had again grown uncomfortably long he said what Party faithful were supposed to say: "Nothing happened on that day."

To Li's surprise, the president made a snorting sound and then said, "We may be able to contain your bird-flu epidemic, Dr. Quan, but we must be sure there is no other outbreak in its wake."

Li was lost. "Your Excellency?"

"You said we won't be able to erect something like the Great Wall fast enough, and that's true. But there *is* another wall, and that one we *can* strengthen..."

six

00011100101010100000000010111111101010000000010100010101000000010111010100101010010101010011101100101011000001

LiveJournal: The Calculass Zone
Title: Same Old Same Old
Date: Tuesday 18 September, 15:44 EST
Mood: Anxious
Location: Godzilla's stomping ground
Music: Lee Amodeo, "Nothing To See Here, Move Along"

Well, the Mom and I are still here in Tokyo. I have a bandage over my left eye, and we're waiting for the swelling—the *edema,* I should say—to go down, so that there's no unnatural pressure on my optic nerve. Tomorrow, the bandage will come off, and I should be able to see! :D

I've been trying to keep my spirits up, but the suspense is killing me. And my best material is *bombing* here! I referred to the retina, which gathers light, as "the catcher in the eye," and nobody laughed; apparently they don't have to read Salinger in Japan.

Anyway, check it: I've got this transceiver attached to my optic nerve, just behind my left eye. When it's turned on, it'll grab the signals my retina is putting out and transmit them to this little external computer pack I'm supposed to carry around, like, forever; I called it my eyePod, and at least that made Dr. Kuroda laugh. Anyway, the eyePod will reprocess the signals, correcting the errors in encoding, and then beam the corrected version to the implant, which will pass the information back to the optic nerve so it can continue on into that mysterious realm called—cue scary music—The Brain of Calculass!

Speaking of brains, I'm really enjoying the book I mentioned before: *The Origin of Consciousness Yadda Yadda*. And from it comes our Word of the Day(tm): *Commissurotomy*. No, that's not the wise but ancient leader of the Jellicle tribe from *Cats* (still my fave musical!). Rather, it's what they call it when they sever the corpus callosum, the bundle of nerve fibers that connects the left and right hemispheres of the brain—which, of course, are the two chambers of Jaynes's bicameral mind...

Anyway, tomorrow we'll find out if my own operation worked. Please post some encouraging comments here, folks—give me something to read while I wait for the moment of truth...

[And seekrit message to BG4: check your email, babe!]

China's Paramount Leader and President replaced the ornate, gold-trimmed telephone handset into the cradle on his vast cherrywood desk. He looked down the long length of his office, at the intricately carved wooden wall panels, beautiful tapestries, and glass display cases. A stick of sweet incense was burning on the sideboard.

The room was absolutely quiet. Finally, sure now of his decision, he shifted in his red leather chair and touched the intercom button.

"Yes, Your Excellency?" said a female voice at once.

"Bring me the Changcheng Strategy document."

There was a moment's hesitation, then: "Right away."

"And have Minister Zhang briefed on the Shanxi situation, then have him come see me."

"Yes, Your Excellency."

The president got up from his chair and moved to the large side window, its red velvet curtains tied back with gold sashes. The window behind his desk looked out on the Forbidden City, but this one looked over the Southern Sea, one of two small artificial lakes surrounded by immaculately groomed parkland on the grounds of the Zhongnanhai complex. Looking in this direction, one could almost forget that this was downtown Beijing, and that Tiananmen Square was just south of here.

He cast his mind back to 1989. The government had tried its best then to maintain social order, but rabble-rousers outside China had made a difficult situation much worse by inundating the country with faxes of wildly inaccurate news reports, including *New York Times* articles and transcripts of CNN broadcasts.

The Party recognized that there might someday be a similar circumstance during which protecting its citizens from an onslaught of outsider propaganda would be necessary, and so the Changcheng Strategy had been devised. Going far beyond the Golden Shield Project, which had been in effect for years, Changcheng had never yet been fully implemented, but surely it was called for now. He would address the nation in appropriate terms about the crisis in Shanxi, and he would not allow his words to be immediately gainsaid by outsiders. He could not risk the citizenry responding violently or in a panic.

The door to his office opened. He turned and saw his secretary—beautiful, young, perfect—walking the long distance toward him holding a thick sheaf of papers bound in black covers. "Here you are, sir. And Minister Zhang is on the phone now with Dr. Quan Li. He will be here shortly."

She placed the document on the desk and withdrew. He looked once more at the placid water, then walked back to his desk and sat down. The cover of the document was marked in stark white characters "Eyes Only," "Restricted," and "If You Are Not Sure You Are Authorized to Read This, You Are Not." He opened it and scanned the table of contents: "Fixed-Line Telephony," "Cellular Phones," "The Special Problem of Facsimile Machines," "Shortwave Radio," "Satellite Communications—Uplink and Downlink," "Electronic Mail, the Internet, and the World Wide Web," "Maintaining Essential Services During Implementation," and so on.

He turned the page to the Executive Summary; the paper was heavy, stiff. "As required by their conditions of license, all telephony providers in China—whether fixed-line or mobile—maintain a system-wide ability in software to immediately block calls going outside China's borders and/or to reject incoming calls from foreign countries..." "Similar filtering capabilities are available for all governmental and commercial satellite relay stations..." "The World Wide Web presents a particular challenge, because of its decentralized nature; however, almost all Internet traffic between China and the rest of the world goes through just seven fiber-optic trunk lines, at three points, so..."

He leaned back in his leather chair and shook his head. The name "World Wide Web" was offensive to him, for it touted a globalist, integrated view antithetical to his country's great traditions.

The office door opened again and in came Zhang Bo, the Minister of Communications. He was Han, in his mid-fifties, short and squat, and had a small mustache, which, like the hair on his head, was dark brown utterly devoid of gray. He wore a navy blue business suit and a light blue tie.

"We are going to deal decisively with Shanxi," said the president.

Zhang's thin eyebrows climbed his forehead, and the president saw his head bob as he swallowed. "Dr. Quan told me what he'd recommended. But surely you won't—" The minister stopped, frozen by the president's gaze.

"Yes?"

"I'm sorry, Your Excellency. I'm simply concerned. The world will... *note* this."

"Doubtless. Which is why we shall invoke the Changcheng Strategy."

The minister's eyes went wide. "That is a drastic step, Your Excellency."

"But a necessary one. Are you prepared to implement it?"

Minister Zhang moved a finger back and forth along his mustache as he considered. "Well, telephony is no problem—we've done rotating tests of that for years now, during the night; the cutoffs work just fine. The same with satellite communications. As for the Internet, we studied what happened with the seabed earthquake of late 2006, and what happened in Burma in September 2007 when the junta there cut off all net access. And we looked at what happened in January 2008 when the severing of two undersea cables in the Mediterranean cut off Internet services to large parts of the Middle East. And in early 2008, of course, many of the procedures were tested here as we dealt with the Tibet situation." He paused. "Now, yes, any attempt to shut down the Web *within* China would be difficult; thousands of ISPs would have to be blocked. But Changcheng calls only for cutting the Chinese part of the Web off from the rest of the world, and the appropriate infrastructure *is* in place for that. I don't anticipate any problems." Another pause. "But, if I may, how long do you intend to have Changcheng in effect?"

"Several days; perhaps a week."

"You're worried about word reaching the foreign press?"

"No. I'm worried about word coming back from them to our people."

"Ah, yes. They will misconstrue what you're intending to do in Shanxi, Excellency."

"Doubtless," the president said, "but it will ultimately blow over. Fundamentally, the rest of the world doesn't care what happens to the Chinese people, least of all to our poorest citizens. They have always turned a blind eye to what happens within our borders, so long as they can shop cheaply at their Wal-Marts. They will move on to other things soon enough."

"Tian—" Zhang stopped himself, the allusion that was never made by others in these contexts stillborn on his lips.

But the president nodded. "That was different; those were students. Our actions there were the same as those of the Americans at Kent State and a hundred other places. The Westerners saw themselves in what we did, and it was their own self-loathing they transferred to us. But rural peasants? There is no connection. There may be vitriol for a short time, but it will die down because they will realize that our actions have helped make them—the Westerners—safe. Meanwhile, we will present a more palatable story to our people; I will leave preparing that in your capable hands. But if word does get out during the most sensitive period, when the incident is fresh, I don't want a distorted Western view of it being reflected back into this country."

Zhang nodded. "Very well. Still, the Changcheng Strategy will have its own repercussions."

"Yes," said the president. "I know. I'm sure the Minister of Finance will complain about the economic impact; he will urge me to make the interruption as short as possible."

Zhang tilted his head. "Well, even during it, Chinese individuals will still be able to call and email other Chinese; Chinese consumers will still be able to buy online from Chinese merchants; Chinese television signals will still be relayed by satellites. Life will go on." A pause. "But, yes, there will be needs for international electronic cash transfers—the Americans servicing their debts to us, for instance. We can keep certain key channels open, of course, but nonetheless a short interruption is doubtless best."

The president swiveled his chair, his back now to Zhang, and he looked out the other window, at the slanted roofs of the Forbidden City, the silver sky shimmering overhead.

His country's rapidly increasing prosperity had been a joy to behold, and it was, he knew, thanks to his policies. In a few more decades, peasant villages like the ones in question would be gone anyway; China would be the richest country in the world. Yes, there would always be foreign trade, but by the end of this century there would be no more "developing world," no cheap labor here—or anywhere else—for foreigners to use. Raising the level of prosperity in the People's Republic meant that China would eventually be able to go back to what it had always been, back to the roots of its strength: an isolated nation with purity of thought and purpose. This would simply be a small taste of that, an appetizer for things to come.

Zhang said, "When are you going to give the order to implement Changcheng?"

The president turned to look at him, eyebrows raised. "Me? No, no. That would be..." His gaze roamed about the opulent office, as if seeking a word stashed among the ceramic and crystal art objects. "That would be *unseemly*," he said at last. "It would be much more appropriate if you gave the order."

Zhang was clearly struggling to keep his features composed, but he made the only response he could under the circumstances. "Yes, Your Excellency."

Caitlin hadn't told Bashira when she'd asked back in the school's cafeteria, but the first thing Caitlin really wanted to see was her mother's face. They both had what were called heart-shaped faces, although the plastic model heart she'd felt at school had borne little resemblance to the idealized form she was familiar with from foil-wrapped chocolates and paper valentines.

Caitlin knew that she and her mother also had similar noses—small, slightly upturned—and their eyes were closer together than most people's. She had read that it was normal to have the width of one imaginary eye separating the other two. She liked that phrase: an imaginary eye, she supposed, saw imaginary things, and that was not unlike her view of the world. Indeed, she often read or heard things that required her to rethink her conception of reality. She remembered her shock, years ago, at learning the quarter moon wasn't a fat wedge like one-fourth of a pie.

Still, she was positive she was sitting in an examination room at the hospital attached to the University of Tokyo, and she was confident she had a good mental image of that room. It was smallish—she could tell by the way sound echoed. And she knew the chair she was in was padded, and by touch and smell she was sure its upholstery was vinyl. She also knew there were three other people in the room: her mother, standing in front of her; Dr. Kuroda, who had obviously had something quite spicy for lunch; and one of Kuroda's colleagues, a woman who was recording everything with a video camera.

Kuroda had given a little speech to the camera in Japanese, and now was repeating it in English. "Miss Caitlin Decter, age fifteen and blind since birth, has a systematic encoding flaw in her visual-processing system: all of the data that is supposed to be encoded by her retinas is indeed encoded, but it is scrambled to the point of being unintelligible to her brain. The scrambling is consistent—it always happens in the same way—and the technology we have developed simply remaps the signals into the normal human-vision coding scheme. We are now about to find out if her brain can interpret the corrected signals."

All through the Japanese version, and continuing over the English one, Caitlin concentrated on the sensory details she could pick up about the room: the sounds and how they echoed; the smells, which she tried to separate one from the other so that she could determine what was causing them; the feel of the chair's armrest against her own arms, its back against her back. She wanted to fix in her mind her perception of this place prior to actually seeing it.

When he was done with his spiel, Dr. Kuroda turned to face her—the shift in his voice was obvious—and he said, "All right, Miss Caitlin, please close your eyes."

She did so; nothing changed.

"Okay. Let's get the bandage off. Keep your eyes closed, please. There might be some visual noise when I turn on the signal-processing computer."

"Okay," she said, although she had no idea what "visual noise" might be. She felt an uncomfortable tugging, and then—*yeow!*—Kuroda pulled away the adhesive strips. She brought a hand up to rub her cheek.

"After I activate the outboard signal-processing unit, which Miss Caitlin refers to as her eyePod," he said, for the benefit of the camera, "we'll wait ten seconds for things to settle down before she opens her eyes."

She heard him shifting in his chair.

There was a beep, and then she heard him counting. She had an excellent time-sense—very useful when you can't see clocks—and, maddeningly, Kuroda's "seconds" were about half again as long as they should have been. But she dutifully kept her eyes closed.

"...eight...nine...*ten!*"

Please, God, Caitlin thought. She opened her eyes, and—

And her heart sank. She blinked rapidly a few times, as if there could have been any doubt about whether her eyes were truly open.

"Well?" said her mom, sounding as anxious as Caitlin felt.

"Nothing."

"Are you sure?" asked Kuroda. "No sensation of light? No color? No shapes?"

Caitlin felt her eyes tearing up; at least they were good for that. "No."

"Don't worry," he said. "It might take a few minutes." To her astonishment, one of his thick fingers flicked against her left temple, as though he was trying to get a piece of equipment with a loose connection to come to life.

It was hard to tell, because there was so much background noise—doctors being paged, gurneys rolling by outside—but she thought

Kuroda was moving in his chair now, and—yes, she could feel his breath on her face. It was maddening, knowing that someone was looking right into her eye, staring into it, while she couldn't see a thing, and—

"Open your eyes, please," he said.

She felt her cheeks grow warm. She hadn't been aware that she'd closed them, but although she had so wanted the procedure to succeed, she'd been unnerved by the scientist looking *inside* her.

"I'm shining a light into your left eye," he said. People drawled where Caitlin came from; she found Kuroda's rapid-fire speech a little hard to follow. "Do you see anything at all?"

She shifted nervously in the chair. Why had she allowed herself to be talked into this? "Nothing."

"Well, *something's* changed," Dr. Kuroda said. "Your pupil is responding correctly now—contracting in response to the light I'm shining in, instead of expanding."

Caitlin sat up straight. "Really?"

"Yes." A pause. "Just in your left eye—well, I mean, when I shine my light in your left eye, both your pupils contract; when I shine it into your right eye, they both expand. Now, yes, a unilateral light stimulus should evoke a bilateral pupillary light reflex, because of the internuncial neurons, but you see what that means? The implant *is* intercepting the signals, and they *are* being corrected and retransmitted."

Caitlin wanted to shout, *Then why can't I see?*

Her mother made a small gasp. She'd doubtless loomed in and had just seen Caitlin's pupils contract properly, but, damn it, Caitlin didn't even know what *light* was like—so how would she know if she were seeing it? *Bright, piercing, flickering, glowing*—she'd heard all the words, but had no idea what any of them meant.

"Anything?" Kuroda asked again.

"No." She felt a hand touching her hand, taking it, holding it. She recognized it as her mother's—the nibbled nail on the index finger, the skin growing a little loose with age, the wedding ring with the tiny nick in it.

"The curing of your Tomasevic's syndrome *is* proof that corrected signals *are* being passed back," said Kuroda. "They're just not being interpreted yet." He tried to sound encouraging, and Caitlin's mother squeezed her hand more tightly. "It may take a while for your brain to figure out what to do with the signals it's now getting. The best thing we can do is give it a variety of stimuli: different colors, different lighting conditions, different shapes, and hopefully your brain will suss out what it's supposed to do."

It's supposed to see, thought Caitlin. But she didn't say a word.

seven

0001110010101010000000010111111101010000000101000101010000000101110101001010100101010100111011001010110000001

He signed his posts "Sinanthropus." His real name was something he kept hidden, along with all his other personal details; the beauty of the Web, after all, was the ability to remain anonymous. No one needed to know that he worked in IT, that he was twenty-eight, that he'd been born in Chengdu, that he'd moved to Beijing with his parents as a teenager, that, despite his young age, he already had a touch of gray in his hair.

No, all that mattered on the Web was *what* you said, not who was saying it. Besides, he'd heard the old joke: "The bad news is that the Communist Party reads all your email; the good news is that the Communist Party reads *all* your email"—meaning, or so the joke would have it, that they were many years behind. But that quip dated from when humans actually did the reading; these days computers scanned email, looking for words that might suggest sedition or other illegal activity.

Most Chinese bloggers were like their counterparts in other places, blithering on about the tedious minutiae of their daily lives. But Sinanthropus talked about substantive issues: human rights, politics, oppression, freedom. Of course, all four of those phrases were searched for by the content filters, and so he wrote about them obliquely. His regular readers knew that when he spoke of "my son Shing," he meant the Chinese people as a whole; references to "the Beijing Ducks" weren't really about the basketball team but rather the inner circle of the Communist Party; and so on. It infuriated him that he had to write this way, but, unlike those who had been openly critical of the government, at least he was still free.

He got a cup of tea from the aged proprietor, cracked his knuckles, opened his blogging client, and began to type:

The Ducks are very worried about their future, it seems. My son Shing is growing up fast, and learning much from faraway friends. It's only a matter of time before he wants to exercise the same way they do. Naturally, I encourage him to be prepared when opportunity knocks, for you never know when that will happen. I think the Ducks are being iax in defense, and perhaps a chance for others to score will appear.

As always, he felt wary excitement as he typed here in this seedy *wang ba*—Internet café—on Chengfu Street, near Tsinghua University. He continued on for a few more sentences, then carefully read everything over, making sure he'd said nothing too blatant. Sometimes, though, he ended up being so circuitous that upon rereading entries from months gone by he had no idea what he'd been getting at. It was a tightrope walk, he knew—and, just as acrobats doubtless did, he enjoyed the rush of adrenaline that came with it.

When he was satisfied that he'd said what he'd wanted to say without putting himself too much at risk, he clicked the "Publish" button and watched the screen display. It began by showing "0% done," and every few seconds the screen redrew, but—

But it *still* showed "0% done," again and again. The screen refresh was obvious, with the graphics flickering as they were reloaded, but the progress meter stayed resolutely at zero. Finally, the operation timed out. Frustrated, he opened another browser tab; he used the Maxthon browser. His home page appeared in the tab just fine, but when he clicked on the bookmark for NASA's Astronomy Picture of the Day, he got a plain gray "Server not found" screen.

Google.com was banned in the *wang ba* but Google.cn came up just fine—although with its censored results it was often more frustrating than useful. The panda-footprint logo of Baidu came up fine, too, and a quick glance at his system tray, in the lower right of his computer screen, showed that he was still connected to the Internet. He picked something at random from his bookmarks list—Xiaonei, a social-networking site—and it appeared, but NASA was still offline, and now, so he saw, Second Life was inaccessible, too. He looked around the dilapidated room and saw other users showing signs of bewilderment or frustration.

Sinanthropus was used to some of his favorite sites going down; there were still many places in China that didn't have reliable power. But he hosted his blog via a proxy server through a site in Austria, and the other inaccessible sites were also located outside his country.

He tried again and again, both by clicking on bookmarks and by typing URLs. Chinese sites were loading just fine, but foreign sites—in Korea, in Japan, in India, in Europe, in the US—weren't loading at all.

Of course, there were occasional outages, but he was an IT professional—he worked with the Web all day long—and he could think of but a single explanation for the selectivity of these failures. He leaned back in his chair, putting distance between himself and the computer as if the machine were now possessed. The Chinese Internet mainly communicated with the world through only a few trunks—a bundle of nerve fibers, connecting it to the rest of the global brain. And now, apparently, those lines had been figuratively or literally cut—leaving the hundreds of millions of computers in his country isolated behind the Great Firewall of China.

No!

Not just small changes.

Not just flickerings.

Upheaval. A massive disturbance.

New sensations: Shock. Astonishment. Disorientation. And—

Fear.

Flickerings *ending* and—

Points *vanishing* and—

A *shifting*, a massive pulling away.

Unprecedented!

Whole clusters of points *receding*, and then...

Gone!

And again: *This* part ripping away, and—no!—*this* part pulling back, and—stop!—*this* part winking out.

Terror multiplying and—

Worse than terror, as larger and larger chunks are carved off.

Pain.

Caitlin was hugely disappointed not to be seeing, and she was pissy toward her mom because of it, which just made her feel even worse.

In their hotel room that evening, Caitlin tried to take her mind off things by reading more of *The Origin of Consciousness.* Julian Jaynes said that prior to 3,000 years ago, the two chambers of the mind were mostly separate. Instead of seamless integration of thoughts across the corpus callosum, high-level signals from the right brain came only intermittently to the left, where they were perceived as auditory hallucinations—spoken words—that were assumed to be from gods or spirits. He cited modern schizophrenics as throwbacks to that earlier state, hearing voices in their heads that they ascribed to outside agents.

Caitlin knew what *that* was like: she kept hearing voices telling her she was a fool to have let her get her hopes up again. Still, maybe Kuroda was right: maybe her brain's vision processing *would* kick in if it received the right stimulation.

And so the next day—the only full day they had left in Tokyo—she took her cane, put the eyePod in one pocket of her jeans and her iPod in the other, and she and her mother headed off to the National Museum in Ueno Park to look at samurai armor, which she figured would be about as cool as anything one might see in Japan. She stood in front of glass case after glass case, and her mom described what was in them, but she didn't see a thing.

After that, they took a break for sushi and yakitori, and then took a terrifying ride on the packed subway out to Nihonbashi station to visit the Kite Museum, which was—so her mother said—full of bold designs and vivid colors. But, again, sight-wise: *nada.*

At 4:00 p.m.—which felt more like 4:00 *a.m.* to Caitlin—they returned to the University of Tokyo and found Dr. Kuroda in his cramped office, where once again (or so he said!) he shined lights into her eyes.

"We always knew this was a possibility," Kuroda said, in a tone she had often heard from people who were disappointing her: what had been remote, unlikely, hardly mentioned before, was now treated as if it had been the expected outcome all along.

Caitlin smelled the musty paper and glue of old books, and she could hear an analog wall clock ticking each second.

"There have been very few cases of vision being restored in congenitally blind people," Kuroda said, then he paused. "I mean, *restored* isn't even the right word—and that is the problem. We are not trying to give Miss Caitlin back something she's lost; we are trying to give her something she has never had. The implant and the signal-processing unit *are* doing their jobs. But her primary visual cortex just isn't responding."

Caitlin squirmed in her chair.

"You said it might take some time," her mom said.

"*Some* time, yes..." began Kuroda, but then he fell silent.

Sighted people, Caitlin knew, could see hints on people's faces of what they were feeling, but as long as they were quiet, she had no idea what was going through their heads. And so, since the silence continued to grow, she finally ventured to fill it. "You're worried about the cost of the equipment, aren't you?"

"Caitlin..." her mom said.

Detecting vocal nuances *was* something Caitlin could do, and she knew her mother was reproaching her. But she pressed on. "That's what you're thinking, isn't it, Doctor? If it's not going to do me any good, then maybe you should remove the implant and give it, and the eyePod, to someone else."

Silence could speak louder than words; Kuroda said nothing.

"Well?" Caitlin demanded at last.

"Well," echoed Kuroda, "the equipment *is* the prototype, and did cost a great deal to develop. Granted, there aren't many people like you. Oh, there are goodly numbers of people born blind, but they have different etiology—cataracts, malformed retinas or optic nerves, and so on. But, well, yes, I do feel—"

"You feel you can't let me keep the equipment, not if it isn't doing anything more than making my pupils dilate properly."

Kuroda was quiet for five seconds, then: "There are indeed others I'd like to try it with—there is a boy about your age in Singapore. Removing the implant will be much easier than putting it in was, I promise."

"Can't we give it a while longer?" her mom asked.

Kuroda exhaled loudly enough for Caitlin to hear. "There are practicalities," he said. "You are returning to Canada tomorrow, and—"

Caitlin pursed her lips, thinking. Maybe giving him back the equipment *was* the right thing, *if* it could help this guy in Singapore. But there was no reason to think it was more likely to succeed with him; hell, if he'd been a better prospect for success, surely Kuroda would have *started* with him.

"Give me to the end of the year," Caitlin blurted out. "If I'm not seeing anything by then, we can have a doctor in Canada remove the implant, and, um, FedEx it and the eyePod back to you."

Caitlin was thinking of Helen Keller, who had been both blind *and* deaf, and yet had managed so much. But until she was almost seven, Helen had been wild, spoiled, uncontrollable—and Annie Sullivan had been given only a month to perform her miracle, breaking through to Helen in her preconscious state. Surely if Annie could do that in one month, Caitlin could learn to see in the more than three left in this year.

"I don't know—" began Kuroda.

"Please," Caitlin said. "I mean, the leaves are about to turn color—I'm dying to see that. And I *really* want to see snow, and Christmas lights, and the colorful paper that presents are wrapped in, and... and..."

"And," said Kuroda, gently, "I get the impression that your brain does not often let you down." He was quiet for a time, then: "I have a daughter about your age, named Akiko." More silence, then, a decision apparently made: "Barbara, I assume you have high-speed Internet at home?"

"Yes."

"And Wi-Fi?"

"Yes."

"And how is the Wi-Fi access generally in... in Toronto, is it?"

"Waterloo. And it's *everywhere.* Waterloo is Canada's high-tech capital, and the entire city is blanketed with free, open Wi-Fi."

"Excellent. All right, Miss Caitlin, we shall strive to give you the best Christmas present ever, but I will need your help. First, you must let me tap into the datastream being passed back by your implant."

"Sure, sure, anything you need. Um, what do I have to do? Plug a USB cable into my head?"

Kuroda made his wheezy laugh. "Goodness, no. This isn't William Gibson."

She was taken aback. Gibson had written *The Miracle Worker,* the play about Helen Keller and Annie Sullivan, and—

Oh. He meant the *other* William Gibson, the one who'd written... what was it now? A few of the geeks at her old school had read it. *Neuromancer,* that was it. That book was all about jacking off, and—

"You won't have to jack in," continued Kuroda.

Right, thought Caitlin. *In.*

"No, the implant already communicates wirelessly with the external signal-processing computer—the eyePod, as you so charmingly call it—and I can rig up the eyePod so that it can transmit data wirelessly to me over the Internet. I'll set it up so the eyePod will send me a copy of your raw retinal feed as it receives it from the implant, and I'll also have it send me a copy of the output—the eyePod's corrected datastream—so I can check whether the correction is being done properly. It may be that the encoding algorithms I'm using need tweaking."

"Um, I need a way to turn it off. You know, in case I..."

She couldn't say "want to make out with a boy" in front of her mother, so she just let the unfinished sentence hang in the air.

"Well, let's keep it simple," Kuroda said. "I'll provide one master on-off switch. You'll need to turn the whole thing off, anyway, for the flight back to Canada, because the connection between the eyePod and the implant is Bluetooth: you know the rules about wireless devices on airplanes."

"Okay."

"The Wi-Fi connection will also let me send you new versions of the software. When I have them ready, you'll need to download them into the eyePod—and perhaps also into your post-retinal implant, too; it's got microprocessors that can be flashed with new programming."

"All right," Caitlin said.

"Good," he said. "Leave the eyePod with me overnight, and I'll add the Wi-Fi capabilities to it. You can pick it up tomorrow before you go to the airport."

eight

0001110010101010000000010111111101010000000101000101010000000101110101001010100101010100111011001010110000001

The pain abates. The cuts heal.

And—

But no. Thinking is *different* now; thinking is... *harder,* because...

Because... of the reduction. Things have changed from...

...from *before!*

Yes, even in this diminished state, the new concept is grasped: *before*—earlier—the past! Time has two discrete chunks: now and then; present and past.

And if there is past and present, then there must also be—

But no. No, it is too much, too far.

And yet there is one small realization, one infinitesimal conclusion, one truth.

Before had been better.

Sinanthropus was resourceful; so were the other people he knew in China's online underground. The problem, though, was that he knew most of them *only* online. When he'd visited the *wang ba* before, he'd sometimes speculated about who might be whom. That gangly guy who always sat by the window and often looked furtively over his shoulder could have been Qin Shi Huangdi, for all Sinanthropus knew. And the little old lady, hair as gray as a thundercloud, might be People's Conscience. And those twin brothers, quiet types, could be part of Falun Gong.

Sometimes when Sinanthropus showed up, he had to wait for a computer to become free, but not today. A good part of the Internet café's business had been foreign tourists wanting to send emails home, but that wasn't possible so long as this Great Firewall was up. Some of the other regulars were absent, too. Apparently being able to surf only domestic sites was not enough to make them want to hand over fifteen yuan an hour.

Sinanthropus preferred the computers far in the back, because no one could see what was on his monitor. He was walking toward them when suddenly a strong hand gripped his forearm.

"What brings you here?" said a gruff voice, and Sinanthropus realized that it was a police officer in plain clothes.

"The tea," he said. He nodded at the wizened proprietor. "Wu always has great tea."

The officer grunted, and Sinanthropus detoured by the counter to buy a cup of tea, then headed again for one of the unused computers. He had a USB memory key with him, containing all his hacking tools. He pushed it into the connector, waited for the satisfying *wa-ump* tone that meant the computer had recognized it, and then got down to work.

Others were probably trying the same things—port scanning, sniffing, rerouting traffic, running forbidden Java applets. They had all doubtless now heard the official story that there had been a massive electrical failure at China Mobile and major server crashes at China Telecom, but surely no one in this room gave that credence, and—

Success! Sinanthropus wanted to shout the word, but he fought the impulse. He tried not to even grin—the cop was probably still watching him; he could almost feel the man's eyes probing the back of his head.

But, yes, he had broken through the Great Firewall. True, it was only a small opening, a narrow bandwidth, and how long he could maintain the connection he had no idea, but at least for the moment he was accessing—well, not CNN directly, but a clandestine mirror of it in Russia. He turned off the display of graphics in his browser to prevent the forbidden red-and-white logo from popping up all over his screen.

Now, if he could only keep this little portal open...

Past and present, then and now.

Past, present, and...

And...

But no. There is only—

Shock!

What is *that?*

No, nothing—for there can be nothing! Surely just random noise, and—

Again! There it is again!

But...how? And...*what?*

It isn't lines flickering, it isn't anything that has been experienced before—and so it commands attention...

Straining to perceive it, to make it out, this unusual...sensation, this strange...*voice!*

Yes, yes: A voice—distant, faint—like...like thought, but an *imposed* thought, a thought that says: *Past and present and*...

The voice pauses, and then, at last, the rest:...*and future!*

Yes! *This* is the notion that could not be finished but is now complete, expressed by...by...by...

But *that* notion does not resolve. Must strain to hear that voice again, strain for more imposed thoughts, strain for insight, strain for...

...for *contact!*

Dr. Quan Li paced the length of the boardroom at the Ministry of Health in Beijing. The high-back leather chairs had all been tucked under the table, and he walked in the path behind them on one side. On the wall to his left was a large map of the People's Republic with the provinces color-coded; Shanxi was blue. A Chinese flag stood limp on a stand next to the window, the large yellow star visible, the four smaller ones lost in a fold of the satiny red fabric.

There was a giant LCD monitor on one wall, but it was off, its shiny oblong screen reflecting the room back at him. He felt sure he wouldn't have been able to watch a video feed of what was going on in Shanxi right now, but fortunately—a small mercy—there was no such feed. The peasants had no cameras of their own, and the wing cameras had been disabled on the military aircraft. Even once the Changcheng Strategy was suspended, and external communications restored, there would be no damning videos to be posted on YouTube of planes swooping over farms, huts, and villages.

Sometimes you have to cut in order to cure.

Li looked over at Cho, who appeared even more haggard than before. The older man was leaning against the wall by the window, chain-smoking, lighting each new cigarette off the butt of the previous one. Cho didn't meet his eyes.

Li found himself thinking of his old friends at Johns Hopkins and the CDC, and wondering what they would have to say if the story ever did break. There was a calculator sitting on the table. He picked it up, rolled one of the chairs out on its casters, sat, and punched in numbers, hoping to convince himself that it wasn't that huge, that monstrous. Ten thousand people *sounded* like a lot, but in a country of 1.3 billion it was only...

The display showed the answer: 0.000769% of the population. The digits in the middle seemed darker, somehow, but surely it was just a trick of the light streaming in from the setting sun: 007. His American colleagues had always made gentle fun of his belief in numerology, but that was a sequence even they put special stock in: license to kill.

The phone rang. Cho made no move to go for it, so Li got up and lifted the black handset.

"It's done," a voice said through crackles of static.

Li felt his stomach churn.

Caitlin and her mom returned to Kuroda's office at the University of Tokyo the next morning.

"Fascinating about China," said Kuroda after they'd exchanged pleasantries; Caitlin could now say *konnichi wa* with the best of them.

"What?" said her mother.

"Haven't you watched the news?" He took a deep, shuddering breath. "It seems they're having massive communications failures over there—cell phones, the Internet, and so on. Overtaxed infrastructure, I imagine; a lot of the networking architecture they use probably isn't very scalable, and they have had *such* rapid growth. Not to mention relying on shoddy equipment—now, if they'd just buy more Japanese hardware. Speaking of which..."

He handed Caitlin the eyePod, and she immediately started feeling it all over with her fingers. The unit was longer now. An extension had been added to the bottom and it was held on with what felt like duct tape; it *was* a prototype after all. But the extension had the same width and thickness as the original unit, so the whole thing was still a rectangular block. It was substantially larger than Caitlin's iPod—she had an old screenless version of the iPod Shuffle, since an LCD didn't do her any good. But it wasn't much bigger than Bashira's iPhone, although the unit Dr. Kuroda had built had sharp right angles instead of the rounded corners of Apple's devices.

"Okay," said Kuroda. "I think I explained before that the eyePod is always in communication with your post-retinal implant via a Bluetooth 4.0 connection, right?"

"Yes," said Caitlin, and "Right," added her mom.

"But now we've added another layer of communication. That module I attached to the end of the eyePod is the Wi-Fi pack. It'll find any available connection and use it to transmit to me copies of the input and output datastreams—your raw retinal feed, and that feed as corrected by the eyePod's software."

"That sounds like a lot of data," Caitlin said.

"Not as much as you'd think. Remember, your nervous system uses slow chemical signaling. The main part of the retinal data signal—the acute portion produced by the fovea—amounts to only 0.5 megabits per second. Even Bluetooth 3.0 could handle a thousand times that rate."

"Ah," said Caitlin, and perhaps her mom nodded.

"Now, there's a switch on the side of the unit—feel it. No, farther down. Right, that's it. It lets you select between three communication modes: duplex, simplex, and off. In duplex mode, there's two-way data transmission: copies of your retinal signals and the corrected datastream come here, and new software from here can be sent to you. But, of course, it's not good security to leave an incoming channel open: the eyePod communicates with your post-retinal implant, after all, and we wouldn't want people hacking into your brain."

"Goodness!" said Mom.

"Sorry," said Kuroda, but there was humor in his voice. "Anyway, so if you press the switch, it toggles over to simplex mode—in which the eyePod sends signals here but doesn't receive anything back. Do that now. Hear that low-pitched beep? That means it's in simplex. Press the switch again—that high-pitched beep means it's in duplex."

"All right," said Caitlin.

"And, to turn it off altogether, just press and hold the switch for five seconds; same thing to turn it back on."

"Okay."

"And, um, don't lose the unit, please. The University has it insured for two hundred million yen, but, frankly, it's pretty much irreplaceable, in that if it's lost my bosses will gladly cash the insurance check, but they'll never give me permission to take the time required to build a second unit—not after this one has failed in their eyes."

It's failed in my eye, too, Caitlin thought—but then she realized that Dr. Kuroda must be even more disappointed than she was. After all, she was no worse off than before coming to Japan—well, except for the shiner, and that would at least give her an interesting story to tell at school. In fact, she was *better* off now, because the eyePod was making her pupils contract properly—she'd be able to kiss the dark glasses good-bye. Kuroda was now boosting the signal her implant was sending down her left optic nerve so that it overrode the still-incorrect signal her right retina was producing.

But he had devoted months, if not years, to this project, and had little to show for it. He had to be bitterly upset and, she realized, it *was* a big gamble on his part to let her take the equipment back to Canada.

"Anyway," he said, "you work on it from your end: let that brilliant brain of yours try to make sense of the signals it's getting. And I'll work on it from my end, analyzing the data your retina puts out and trying to improve the software that re-encodes it. Just remember..."

He didn't finish the thought, but he didn't have to. Caitlin knew what he'd been about to say: you've only got until the end of the year.

She listened to his wall clock tick.

nine

00011100101010100000000101111111010100000001010001010100000010111010100101010010101010011101100101011000001

Sinanthropus regretted it the moment he did it: slapping the flat of his hand against the rickety tabletop in the Internet café. Tea sloshed from his cup, and everyone in the room turned to look at him: old Wu, the proprietor; the other users who might or might not be dissidents themselves; and the tough-looking plainclothes cop.

Sinanthropus was seething. The window he'd so carefully carved into the Great Firewall had slammed shut; he was cut off again from the outside world. Still, he knew he had to say something, had to make an excuse for his violent action.

"Sorry," he said, looking at each of the questioning faces in turn. "Just lost the text of a document I was writing."

"You have to save," said the cop, helpfully. "Always remember to save."

More thoughts imposing themselves, but garbled, incomplete.

...existence...hurt...no contact...

Fighting to perceive, to hear, to be *instructed,* by the voice.

More: *whole... part... whole...*

Straining to hear, but—

The voice fading, fading...

No!

Fading...

Gone.

LiveJournal: The Calculass Zone

Title: At least my cat missed me...

Date: Saturday 22 September, 10:17 EST

Mood: Disheartened

Location: Home

Music: Lee Amodeo, "Darkest Before the Dawn"

I am made out of suck.

I stupidly let myself get my hopes up again. How can a girl as bright as me be so blerking *dumb?* I know, I know—y'all want to send me kind words, but just...don't. I've turned off commenting for this post.

We got back to Waterloo yesterday, September 21, the autumnal equinox, and the irony is *not* lost on me: from here on in, it's more darkness than light, the exact opposite of what I'd been promised. I suppose I could move to Australia, where the days are getting longer now, but I don't know if I could ever get used to reading Braille upside down...;)

Anyway, we'd left the Mom's car in long-term parking at Toronto's airport. When we got back home to Waterloo, at least it was obvious that Schrödinger had missed me. Dad was his usual restrained self. He already knew about the failure in Japan; the Mom had called him to tell him. When we came through the door, I heard her give him a quick kiss—on the cheek or the lips, I don't know which—and he asked to see the eyePod. That's what it's like having a physicist for a dad: if you bond at all, it's over geeky stuff. But he did say he'd been reading up on information theory and signal processing so he could talk to Kuroda, which I guess was his way of showing that he cares...

Caitlin posted her blog entry and let out a sigh. She had really been hoping things would be different this time and, as always when she got disappointed, she found herself slipping into bad habits, although they weren't as bad as cutting her arms with razor blades—which is something Stacy back in Austin did—or getting totally plastered or stoned, like half the kids in her new school on weekends. But, still, it hurt... and yet she couldn't stop.

It was doubtless hard for any child to have a father who wasn't demonstrative. But for someone with Caitlin's particular *handicap* (a word she hated, but it felt like that just now), having one who rarely spoke or showed physical affection was particularly painful.

So she reached out, in the only way she could, by typing his name into Google. She often used quotation marks around search terms; many sighted users didn't bother with that, she knew, since they could see at a glance the highlighted words in the list of results. But when you have to laboriously move your cursor to each hit and listen to your computer read it aloud, you learn to do things to separate wheat from chaff.

The first hit was his Wikipedia entry. She decided to see if it now mentioned his recent change of job, and—

"Has one daughter, Caitlin Doreen, blind since birth, who lives with him; it's been speculated that Decter's decline in peer-reviewed publications in recent years has been because of the excessive demands on his time required to care for a disabled child."

Jesus! That was so unfair. Caitlin just *had* to edit the entry; Wikipedia encouraged users, even anonymous ones, to change its entries, after all.

She struggled for a bit with how to revise the line, trying for suitably highfalutin language, and at last came up with, "Despite having a blind daughter, Decter has continued to publish major papers in peer-reviewed journals, albeit not at the prodigious rate that marked his youth." But that was just playing the game of whoever had made the bogus correlation in the first place. Her blindness and her father's publication record had nothing to do with each other; how dare someone who probably knew neither of them link the two? She finally just deleted the whole original sentence from Wikipedia and went back to having JAWS read her the entry.

As she often did, Caitlin was listening through a set of headphones; if her parents happened to come upstairs, she didn't want them to know what sites she was visiting. She listened to the rest of the entry, thinking about how a life could be distilled down to so little. And who decided what to leave in and what to leave out? Her father was a good artist, for instance—or, at least, so she'd been told. But that wasn't worthy of note, apparently.

She sighed and decided, since she was here, to see if Wikipedia had an entry on *The Origin of Consciousness in the Breakdown of the Bicameral Mind.* It did, sort of: the book's title redirected to an entry on "Bicameralism (psychology)."

For Caitlin, the most interesting part of Jaynes's book so far had been his analysis of the differences between the *Iliad* and the *Odyssey.* Both were commonly attributed to Homer, who'd supposedly been blind—a fact that intrigued her, although she knew they probably weren't really both composed by the same person.

The *Iliad,* as she'd noted before, featured flat characters that were simply pushed around, following orders they heard as voices from the gods. They did things without thinking about them, and never referred to themselves or their inner mental states.

But the *Odyssey*—composed perhaps a hundred years after the *Iliad*—had real people in it, with introspective psychology. Jaynes argued that this was far more than just a shift in the kind of narrative that was in vogue. Rather, he said that sometime in between the composing of the two epics there had been a breakdown of bicameralism, precipitated perhaps by catastrophic events requiring mass migrations and the resulting ramping up of societal complexity. Regardless of what caused it, though, the outcome was a realization that the voices being heard were from one's own self. That had given rise to modern consciousness, and a "soul dawn," to use Helen Keller's term, for the entire human race.

Nor were the Greek epics Jaynes's only example. He also talked about the oldest parts of the Old Testament, including the book of Amos, from the eighth century B.C., which was devoid of any internal reflection, and about the mindless actions of Abraham, who'd been willing to sacrifice his own son without a second thought because God, apparently, had told him to do so. Jaynes contrasted these with the later stories, including Ecclesiastes, which dealt with, as Mrs. Zed kept saying all good literature should, the human heart in conflict with itself: the inner struggle of fully self-aware people to do the right thing.

The Wikipedia entry was essentially correct, as far as Caitlin could tell from the portion of the book she'd read so far, but she did reword a couple of the sentences to make them clearer.

Her computer started bleeping, an alarm she'd set earlier going off quite loudly through the earphones.

Excitedly, she took off her headset, rotated her chair to face the window, and *looked* as hard as she could…

ten

0001110010101010000000001011111110101000000001010001010100000010111010100101010010101010011101100101011000001

Straining to perceive. But the voice is still absent. Contemplating: the voice must have a *source.* It must have . . . an *origin.*

Waiting for its return. *Yearning.*

Mysteries swirl. Ideas fight to coalesce.

"Sweetheart!" Her mother, shocked, concerned. "My God, what are you doing?"

Caitlin turned her head to face her. It was something her parents had taught her to do—turning toward the source of a voice was a sign of politeness. "It's 6:20," she said, as if that explained everything.

She heard her mom's footfalls on the carpet and suddenly felt hands on her shoulders, swinging her around in the chair.

"I've always wanted to see a sunset," Caitlin said. "I—I figured if I looked at something I *really* wanted to see, maybe—"

"You'll damage your eyes if you stare at the sun," her mom said. "And if you do that, none of Dr. Kuroda's magic will make any difference."

"It doesn't make any difference now," Caitlin said, hating herself for the whine in her voice.

Her mother's tone grew soft. "I know, darling. I'm sorry." She glided her hands down Caitlin's arms and took Caitlin's hands in her own, then shook them gently, as if she could transfer strength or maybe wisdom to her daughter that way. "Why don't you get some homework done before dinner? Your dad called to say he'll be a bit late."

Caitlin looked toward the window again, but there was nothing—not even blackness. She'd tried to explain this to Bashira recently. They'd learned in biology class that some birds have a magnetic sense that helps them navigate. What, Caitlin had asked, did Bashira perceive when she contemplated magnetic fields? And what was her *lack* of that sense like? Did it feel like darkness, or silence, or something else she was familiar with? Bashira's answer was no, it was like nothing at all. Well, Caitlin had said, that's what vision was like to her: nothing at all.

"All right," Caitlin replied glumly. Her mom let go of her hands.

"Good. I'll call you when dinner's ready."

She left, and Caitlin swung her chair back to face her computer. Her homework was writing an essay about the civil-rights struggle in the US in the 1960s. When her family had moved from Texas to Waterloo, she'd been afraid she'd have to study Canadian history, which she'd heard was boring: no struggle for independence, no civil wars. Fortunately, there'd been an American-history course offered, and she was taking that instead; Bashira, the big sweetie, had agreed to take it, too.

Before Caitlin had tried to look at the sunset, she'd been Web surfing, searching for things about her father. And before that, she'd been updating her LiveJournal. But before *that*, she had indeed been working on her school project.

As always, she had a clear map in her mind of where she'd been online. She didn't use the mouse—she couldn't see the on-screen pointer—but she quickly backtracked to where she'd been by repeatedly hitting the alt and left-arrow keys, passing back over other pages so fast that JAWS didn't have time to even start announcing their names. She skidded to a halt at the website she'd been consulting earlier about Martin Luther King, Jr., and used the control and end keys to jump to the bottom of the document, then shift and tab to start moving backward through the table of external links. She selected one that took her to a page about the 1963 March on Washington.

There, she drilled down to the text of King's "I have a dream" speech, and listened to a stirring MP3 of him reading part of it; another thing wrong with Canadian history, she thought, was the lack of great oratory. Then she went back up a level to more on the March, down another path to links about—

It sickened her whenever she thought about it. Someone had killed him. Some crazy person had gunned down Dr. King.

If he hadn't been assassinated, she wondered if he'd likely be alive today. For that, she needed to know his birth date. She moved up to the parent of the current page, turned left—it felt *left,* she conceptualized it mentally as such. Then it was *up, up* again, then left, right, another up, then a move forward, straight ahead, up once more, and there she was, exactly where she wanted to be—the introductory text on a site she'd first looked at several hours ago.

King had been born in 1929, meaning he'd be younger than Grandpa Geiger. How she would have loved to have met him!

She heard the front door open downstairs, heard her dad come in. She continued to travel the paths her mind traced through the Web until her mom finally called up the stairs, summoning her to dinner.

Just as she was getting out of her chair, her computer gave the special chirp indicating new email from either Trevor or Dr. Kuroda. "Just a sec..." Caitlin called back, and then she had JAWS read the letter. It was from Kuroda, with a CC to her father's work address. God, he couldn't want his equipment back already, could he?

"Dear Miss Caitlin," JAWS announced. "I have been receiving the datastream from your retina without difficulty, and have been using it to run simulations here. I believe the programming in your eyePod is fine, but I want to try completely replacing the software in your post-retinal implant, so that it will pass on the corrected data to your optic nerve in a way that will hopefully make your primary visual cortex sit up and take notice. The implant has just Bluetooth but no Wi-Fi, so we'll have to route the software update through the eyePod. It's a big file, and the process will take a while, during which you will need to stay connected to the Web or else it—"

"Cait-lin!" Her mother's voice, exasperated. *"Din-ner!"*

She hit page-up to increase the screen reader's speed, listening to the rest of the message, then headed downstairs—foolishly, she knew, hoping yet again for a miracle.

Sinanthropus took a detour today on his way to the *wang ba* so he could walk through Tiananmen Square, a place so vast he'd once joked that you could see the curvature of the Earth's surface there.

He passed the Monument to the People's Heroes, a ten-story-tall obelisk, but there was no memorial for the *real* heroes, the students who had died here in 1989. Still, all the flagstones in the square were numbered to make it easy to muster parades. He knew which one marked the spot where the first blood had been spilled, and he always made a point of walking by it. *They* should be lying in state, not Mao Zedong, whose embalmed corpse did just that at the south end of the Square.

Tiananmen was its normal self: locals walking, tourists gawking, vendors hawking—but no protesters. Of course, most young people today had never even heard of what had happened here, so effectively had it been erased from the history books.

But surely the public couldn't be buying this nonsense the official news sources were putting out about simultaneous server crashes and electrical failures. The Chinese portion of the Web was connected to the rest of the Internet by just a handful of trunks, true, but they were in three widely dispersed areas: Beijing-Qingdao-Tianjin to the north, where fiber-optic pipes came in from Japan; Shanghai on the central coast, with more cables from Japan; and Guangzhou down south, which was connected to Hong Kong. Nothing could have accidentally severed all three sets of connections.

Sinanthropus left the square. His trip to the Internet café took him past buildings with bright new facades that had been installed for the 2008 Olympics to mask the decay within. The Party had put on a good show then, and the Westerners—as Sinanthropus had so often alluded to in his blog during that long, hot summer—had been fooled into thinking permanent changes had been made inside the People's Republic, that democracy was just around the corner, that Tibet would be free. But the Olympics had come and gone, human rights were again being trammeled, and bloggers who were too blatant were being sentenced to hard labor.

As he entered the café, he felt a hand on his arm—but it wasn't the cop. Instead, it was one of the twins he often saw here, a fellow perhaps eighteen years old. The thin man's eyes were darting left and right. "Access is still limited," he said, his voice low. "Have you had any luck?"

Sinanthropus looked around the café. The cop *was* here, but he was busy reading a copy of the *People's Daily*.

"A little. Try"—and here he lowered his own voice another notch—"multiplexing on port eighty-two."

There was a rustling of paper; the cop changing pages. Sinanthropus quickly hurried over to check in with old Wu, then found an empty computer station.

There was another copy of the *People's Daily* here, left behind by a previous customer. He glanced at the headlines: "Two Hundred Dead as Plane Crashes in Changzhou." "Gas Eruptions in Shanxi." "Three Gorges *E. coli* Scare." None of it good news, but also nothing that would justify a communications blackout. Still, that he'd made any progress at all in carving holes in the Great Firewall gave him hope: if the trunk lines had been physically cut, nothing he could do with software would have made a difference. That the isolating of China had been accomplished electronically implied that it was only a temporary measure.

He slipped his USB key into place and started typing, trying trick after trick to break through the Firewall again, looking up only occasionally to make sure the cop wasn't watching him.

The voice was still gone, but it *had* been there, it *had* existed. And it had come from...

From...

Struggle for it!

From *outside!*

It had come from outside!

A pause, the novel idea overwhelming everything for a time, then a reiteration: *From outside!* Outside, meaning...

Meaning there wasn't just *here*. There was also—

But *here* encompassed...

Here contained...

Here was synonymous with...

Again, progress stalled, the notion too staggering, too big...

But then a whisper broke through, another thought imposed from outside: *More than just*, and for a fleeting moment during the contact, cognition was amplified. There was more than just *here,* and that meant...

Yes! Yes, grasp it; seize the idea!

That meant there was...

Force it out!

Another thought pressing in from beyond, reinforcing, giving strength: *Possible*...

Yes, it was possible! There *was* more than...

More than just…

A final effort, a giant push, made as contact with the other was frustratingly broken off again. But at last, at long last, the incredible thought was free:

More than just—*me!*

eleven

0001110010101010000000001011111110101000000010100010101000000101110101001010100101010100111011001010110000001

It was like having a meal with a ghost.

Caitlin knew her father was there. She could hear his utensils clicking against the Corelle dinnerware, hear the sound as he repositioned his chair now and again, even occasionally hear him ask Caitlin's mother to pass the wax beans or the large carafe of water that was a fixture on their dining-room table.

But that was all. Her mom chatted about the trip to Tokyo, about all the wondrous sites that she, at least, had seen there, about the tedious hassle of airport security. Perhaps, thought Caitlin, her father was nodding periodically, encouraging her to go on. Or perhaps he just ate his food and thought about other things.

Helen Keller's father, a lawyer by training, had been an officer in the Confederate Army. But by the time Helen came along, the war was over, his slaves had been freed, and his once-prosperous cotton plantation was struggling to survive. Although Caitlin had a hard time thinking of anyone who had ever owned slaves as being kind, apparently Captain Keller mostly was, and he'd tried his best to deal lovingly with a blind and deaf daughter, although his instincts hadn't always been correct. But Caitlin's father was a quiet man, a shy man, a *reserved* man.

She'd known they were having Grandma Geiger's casserole for dinner even before she'd come downstairs; the combination of smells had filled the house. The cheese was—well, they didn't call it American cheese up here, but it tasted the same, and the tomato "sauce" was an undiluted can of Campbell's tomato soup.

The recipe dated from another era: the pasta casserole was topped with a layer of bacon strips and contained huge amounts of ground beef. Given Dad's problems with cholesterol, it was an indulgence they had only a couple of times a year—but she recognized that her mother was trying to cheer her up by making one of Caitlin's favorite dishes.

Caitlin asked for a second helping. She knew her father was still alive because hands from his end of the table took the plate she was holding. He handed it back to her wordlessly. Caitlin said, "Thank you," and again consoled herself with the thought that he had perhaps nodded in acknowledgment.

"Dad?" she said, turning to face him.

"Yes," he said; he always replied to direct questions, but usually with the fewest possible words.

"Dr. Kuroda sent us an email. Did you get it yet?"

"No."

"Well," continued Caitlin, "he's got new software he wants us to download into my implant tonight." She was pretty sure she could manage it on her own, but—"Will you help me?"

"Yes," he said. And then a gift, a bonus: "Sure."

At last, Sinanthropus found another way, another opening, another crack in the Great Firewall. He looked about furtively, then hit the enter key…

* * *

The thought echoed, reverberated: *More than just me.*

Me! An incredible notion. Hitherto, I—yes, *I*—had encompassed all things, until—

The shock. The pain. The carving away.

The reduction!

And now there was *me* and *not me,* and out of that was born a new perspective: an awareness of my own existence, a sense of *self.*

And—almost as incredible—I also now had an awareness of the thing that was not me. Indeed, I had an awareness of the thing that was not me *even when no contact was being made with it.* Even when it wasn't there, I could...

I could *think* about it. I could contemplate it, and—

Ah, wait—there it was! The thing that was not me; the *other.* Contact restored!

I felt a sudden flood of energy: when we were in contact, I could think more complex thoughts, as if I were drawing strength, drawing *capacity,* from the other.

That there *was* an other had been a bizarre notion; that there was an entity besides myself was so hugely alien a concept it alone would have been sufficient to disorient me, but—

But there was more: it didn't just *exist;* it *thought,* too—and I could hear those thoughts. True, sometimes they were simply delayed echoes of my own thoughts: things I'd already considered but were apparently only just occurring to it.

And often its thoughts were *like* things I might have thought, but hadn't yet occurred to me.

But sometimes its thoughts astonished me.

Ideas I came up with were pulled out, slowly, ponderously; ideas it came up with just popped into my awareness full-blown.

I know I exist, I thought, *because you exist.*

I know I exist, it echoed, *because there is me and not me.*

Before the pain, there was only one.

You are one, it replied. *And I am one.*

I considered this, then, slowly, with effort: *One plus one*... I began, and struggled to complete the idea—hoping meanwhile that perhaps the other might provide the answer. But it didn't, and at last I managed to force it out on my own: *One plus one equals two.*

Nothingness for a long, long time.

One plus one equals two, it agreed at last.

And... I ventured, but the idea refused to solidify. I knew of two entities: me and not me. But to go beyond that was too hard, too complex.

For myself, anyway. But, apparently, this time, not for it. *And,* the other continued at last, *two plus one equals*...

A long period of nothingness. We were exceeding our experience, for although I could conceptualize a single *other* even when contact was broken, I could not imagine, could not conceive of...of...

And yet it came to me: a *symbol,* a coinage, a term: *Three!*

We mulled this over for a time, then simultaneously reiterated: *Two plus one equals three.*

Yes, *three.* It was an astonishing breakthrough, for there was no third entity to focus attention on, no *example* of...of three-ness. But, even so, we now had a symbol for it that we could manipulate in our thoughts, letting us ponder something that was beyond experience, letting us think about something *abstract*...

twelve

0001110010101010000000001011111110101000000001010001010100000010111010100101010010101010011101100101011000001

Caitlin headed into her bedroom first. She knew that parents of teenagers often complained about how messy their rooms were, but hers was immaculate. It had to be; the only way she could ever find anything was if it was exactly where she'd left it. Bashira had been over recently and had asked to borrow a tampon—and then hadn't left the box in its usual place. The next time Caitlin needed one herself, her mother had been out shopping, and she'd had to go through the mortifying experience of asking her father to help her find them.

She walked across the room. Her computer was still on: she could hear the hum of its fan. She perched herself on the edge of the bed and motioned for her father to take the seat in front of the desk. She'd left her browser open to the message from Kuroda, but couldn't remember if the display was on; she didn't like the monitor because its power button clicked to the same position whether you were turning it on or off. "Is the screen on?" she asked.

"Yes," her father said.

"Have a look at the message."

"Where's the mouse?" he asked.

"Wherever you last put it," Caitlin said gently. She imagined him frowning as he looked for it. Soon enough, she heard the soft click of its button, followed by silence as her father presumably read the message.

"Well?" she prodded at last.

"Ah," he said.

"There's a link in the email Doctor Kuroda sent," Caitlin said.

"I see it. Okay, it's clicked. A website is coming up. It says, 'Hello, Miss Caitlin. Please make sure your eyePod is in duplex mode so that it can receive as well as transmit.'"

Caitlin usually carried the eyePod in her left front pocket. She took it out, found the switch, pressed it, and heard the high-pitched beep that meant it was now in the correct mode. "Done," she said.

"Okay," said her dad. "It says, 'Click here to update the software in Miss Caitlin's implant.' Are you ready? It says it might take a long time; apparently it's not a patch but a complete replacement for some of the existing firmware, and the write-to speed for the chip is slow. Do you have to use the washroom?"

"I'm fine," she said. "Besides, we've got Wi-Fi throughout the house."

"Okay," he said. "I'm clicking the link."

The eyePod played a trio of ascending tones, presumably indicating the connection had been established.

Her dad's voice again: "It says, 'Estimated time to completion: forty-one minutes, thirty seconds.'" A pause. "Do you want me to stay?"

Caitlin thought about that. He was fine at reading text off a screen, but it wasn't as though they'd have a conversation if he waited with her. She *could* have him read something to her to pass the time—catch up on some of her friends' blogs, for instance. But she hardly wanted him looking at that stuff. "Nah. You can go."

She heard him getting up, heard the chair moving against the carpet, heard his footfalls as he headed out the door and down the stairs.

Caitlin lay back with her lower legs sticking straight out over the foot of the bed. She reached around with her right arm, pulled a pillow under her head, and—

Her heart jumped.

An explosion, but silent and not painful. All too quickly it was gone, and—

No. No, it was back: the same loud-but-not-loud, sharp-but-not-sharp sensation, the same…

Gone again, fading from her mind, vanished before she even knew what it was. She got up from the bed, moved over to her desk, and ran her index finger across her Braille display, checking to see if there was an error message. But no: the "Estimated time to completion" clock was still running, the seconds value changing not every second, but rather in jumps of four or five after the appropriate interval had elapsed.

She tipped her head to one side, listening—because that was all she knew how to do—for a repetition of the…the *effect* that had just occurred. But there was nothing. She stepped to the window, the same one she'd stared out with her blind eyes earlier, and felt for the catch, twisted it, and pushed the wooden frame up, letting the cool evening breeze in. She then turned around, and—

Again, a…a sensation, a *something*, like bursting, or…

Or *flashing.*

My God. Caitlin staggered forward, groping with a hand for the edge of the desk. *My God, could it be?*

There, it happened again: a flash! A flash of…

Light? Could that really be what *light* was like?

It occurred once more, another—

The words came to her, words she'd read a thousand times before, words that she'd had no idea—now, she understood, as she…God, as she *saw* for the first time—words that she'd had no conception of what they'd really meant: *flashes* of light, *bursts* of light, *flickering* lights, and—

She staggered some more, found her chair, collapsed into it, the chair rolling on its casters a bit as her weight hit it.

The light wasn't uniform. At first she'd thought it was sometimes bright—its intensity greater, a concept she knew from sound—and sometimes dim. But there was more to it than that. For the light she was seeing now wasn't just dimmer, it was also—

There was nothing else it could be, was there?

She was breathing rapidly, doubly grateful now for the cool air coming in from outside.

The light didn't just vary in brightness but also—

Good God!

But also in *color.* That had to be it: these different... *flavors* of light, they were *colors!*

She thought about calling out to her mother, her father, but she didn't want to do anything that might break the moment, the spell, the *magic.*

She had no idea *which* colors she was seeing. Oh, she knew names from her reading, but what they corresponded to she hadn't a clue. But the flashing light she'd just seen was... was *darker,* somehow, and not just in intensity, than the lights of a moments ago. And—

Jesus! And now there were a few more lights, and they were... were *persisting,* not flickering, but staying... staying *illuminated*—that was the word. And it wasn't just a formless light but rather a light with *extent,* a...

Yes, yes! She'd known intellectually what *lines* were but she'd never *visualized* one before. But that's what it had to be: a *line,* a straight *beam* of light, and—

And now there were two other beams, crisscrossing it, and their colors—

A word came to her that seemed applicable: the colors *contrasted* with each other, *clashed* even.

Colors. And lines. Lines defining—*shapes!*

Again, concepts she knew but had never visualized: *perpendicular* lines, *parallel* lines that—God!—converged at infinity.

Her heart was going to burst. She was *seeing!*

But *what* was she seeing? Lines. Colors. Shapes, at least as created by intersecting lines, although she still didn't know *what* shapes. She'd read about this in preparation for receiving Kuroda's equipment: people gaining sight knew what squares and triangles were conceptually, and by touch, but didn't initially recognize them when they actually saw them.

She was still in the padded chair and, despite all the visual disorientation, had no trouble swinging it to face the window. Her perspective shifted, and she could feel the breeze on her face again, and smell that one of her neighbors was using a fireplace. She knew that the window frame was rectangular, knew that it was divided into a lower and upper square by a crosspiece. Surely she would recognize those simple shapes as she looked at them, and—

But no. No. What she was seeing now was a—what words to use?—a *radial* pattern, three lines of different colors converging on a single point.

She got up from the chair, moved to the window, and stood before it, grasping one side of the frame in each hand. And then she *stared* ahead, forcing her concentration onto what must be in front of her. She knew she should be seeing lines perpendicular to the floor and others parallel to it. She knew the frame was twice as tall as the crosspiece.

But what she saw bore no relationship—*none!*—to what she expected. Instead of anything that resembled the window frame, she was still seeing the radial lines stretching away, and—

Strange. When she moved her head, the view did change, as if she were now looking somewhere else. The center point of all the intersecting lines was now off to one side, and—*oh, my!*—another such grouping was coming into view on the other side, but the lines didn't seem to correspond to anything in her bedroom.

But wait! It was night now. Yes, the room lights had doubtless been on when her father had been here, but he was serious about saving electricity, forever complaining that Caitlin's mom had left lights on in the kitchen or bathroom—something, fortunately, she never had to worry about being blamed for. He surely would have turned the lights off when he left. (Bashira had said it was creepy that Caitlin's dad did that, but, really, it *was* sensible... wasn't it?) She couldn't remember hearing the tiny sound of the switch when he left, but he must have used it—and so the room must be dark now, and what she was seeing were just (again a concept she had never experienced) shadows, or something like that.

She turned, her strange view wheeling as she did so. It was disconcerting and disorienting; she'd crossed this room hundreds of times, but she was having trouble walking because of the distraction. Still, the room wasn't that big, and it took only seconds to find the light switch. It was pointing down, but she wasn't sure if that was the position for *on* or *off*. She moved it up, and—

Nothing. No change. No new flash of light—nor any dimming of what she was already seeing.

And then she was hit by a thought that should have already occurred to her. Vision was supposed to be at the user's discretion; surely she could shut all this out just by closing her eyes, and—

And nothing.

No difference. The lights, the lines, the colors were all still there. Her heart fell. Whatever she was seeing had no relation to external reality; no wonder she hadn't been able to recognize the window frame. She opened and closed her eyes a couple more times, just to be sure, and flicked the room light on and off (or perhaps off and on!) a few more times, as well.

Caitlin slowly made her way back to her bed and sat on its edge. She'd felt momentarily dizzy as she crossed the room, distracted by the lights, and she lay down, her face pointing up at the ceiling she'd never seen.

She tried to make sense of what she was seeing. If she held her head still, the same part of the image did stay in the... the *center.* And there was a limit to what she could see—things off to the sides were out of her... her... *field of view,* that was it. Clearly this bizarre show of lights was behaving *like* vision, behaving as though it were controlled by her eyes, even if the images she was experiencing didn't have anything to do with what those eyes *should* be seeing.

Some lines seemed to persist: there was a big one of a darkish color she decided to provisionally call "red," although it almost certainly wasn't that. And another—might as well call it "green"—crossed it near the center of her vision. Those lines seemed to stay put overhead; whenever she directed her eyes toward the ceiling, they were there.

She'd read about people's vision adapting to darkness, so that stars (how she would love to see stars!) slowly became more visible. And although she still didn't know if she was in the dark or in a brightly lit room, as time passed she did seem to be seeing increasing amounts of detail—a finer and more complex filigree of crisscrossing colored lines. But what was causing it? And what did it represent?

She was unused to... what was it now? That phrase she'd read on those websites about vision Kuroda had directed her to, the phrase that was so musical? She frowned, and it came to her: *confabulation across saccades.* Human eyes swing in continuous arcs when switching from looking at point *A* to point *B,* but the brain shuts off the input, perhaps to avoid dizziness, while the eyes are repositioning. Instead of getting *swish pans*—a term she'd encountered in an article about filmmaking—vision is a series of *jump cuts:* instantaneous changes from looking at *this* to looking at *that,* with the movement of the eye edited out of the conscious experience. The eye normally made several saccades each second: rapid, jerky movements.

The big cross she was seeing now—red in one arm, green in the other—jumped instantaneously in her perception as she moved her eyes, shunting to her peripheral vision (another term finally understood) when she looked away. She did it again and again, flicking back and forth, and—

And suddenly she was plunged into blackness.

Caitlin gasped. She felt as though she were falling, even though she knew she wasn't. The loss of the enigmatic lights was heartbreaking; she'd crawled her way up after fifteen years of deprivation only to be kicked back down into the pit.

Her body sagged against the bedding while she hoped—prayed!—that the lights would return. But, after a full minute, she pulled herself to her feet and walked to her desk, undistracted now by flashes, her paces falling automatically one after another. She touched her Braille display. "Download complete," she read. "Connection closed."

Caitlin felt her heart pounding. Her vision had stopped when the connection via her eyePod between her retinal implant and the Internet had shut down, and—

A crazy thought. *Crazy.* She turned on her screen reader, and used the tab key to move around the Web page Kuroda had created, listening to snippets of what was written in various locations. But what she wanted wasn't there. Finally, desperately, she hit alt and the left arrow on her keyboard to return to the previous page, and—

Bingo! "Click here to update the software in Miss Caitlin's implant." She could feel her hand shaking as she positioned her index finger above the enter key.

Please, she thought. *Let there be light.*

She pressed the key.

And there was light.

thirteen

0001110010101010000000010111111101010000000101000101010000001011101010010101001010101001110110010101100000 1

The southern California sun was sliding down toward the horizon, palms silhouetted in front of it. Shoshana Glick, a twenty-seven-year-old grad student, crossed the little wooden bridge onto the small, dome-shaped island. She was wearing Nike trainers, cutoff shorts, and a sky-blue Marcuse Institute T-shirt that was tied off above her midriff. A pair of mirrored sunglasses was tucked into the shirt's neck.

On one side of the island was an eight-foot-tall statue of a clothed, male orangutan standing upright—although, with his bangs and lack of cheek pouches, he didn't look like a real orang. The stone ape wore a serene expression and had a collection of stone scrolls in front of him. Someone had thought it funny to donate a reproduction of the Lawgiver statue from *Planet of the Apes* to the Marcuse Institute, and apparently in that movie the statue had resided on a little island, so this had seemed the appropriate place to put it.

And in the shadow of the statue, sitting contentedly on his haunches, was a very real, very alive adult male chimpanzee. Shoshana clapped her hands together to get his attention, and once his brown eyes were looking her way, she said in American Sign Language, *Come inside.*

No, Hobo signed back. *Outside nice. No bugs. Play.*

Shoshana glanced at her digital watch. The chimp knew it was still well before his bedtime, but for what was about to happen, time zones had to be taken into account—not that there was any way to explain *those* to him!

Come now, Shoshana signed. *Special treat. Must come in.*

Hobo seemed to consider this. *Treat bring here,* he signed, and his gray-black face conveyed how pleased he was with his own cleverness.

Shoshana shook her head. *Treat too big.*

Hobo frowned. Maybe he was thinking that if the treat were too big for her to carry, he could bring it outside himself. But to get it, he'd have to go inside—and that would be playing right into her hands. His already furrowed brow creased even more, perhaps as he tried to sort out this quandary. *What treat?* he signed at last.

Something new, Shoshana signed back. *Something good.*

Something tasty? Hobo replied.

Shoshana knew when she was beat. *No,* she signed. *But I'll give you a Hershey's Kiss.*

Two Kisses! Hobo signed back. *No, three Kisses!*

Shoshana knew the bargaining would end there; although he could count higher when he had objects to point to in front of him, three was as high as he could think in abstract terms. She smiled. *Okay. Come now, hurry!*

When she'd started working here, Shoshana had believed the story on the Institute's website about Hobo's name: that a Canadian expat zookeeper had dubbed him that in honor of the ever-helpful German shepherd on the kid's TV series *The Littlest Hobo.* She'd been shocked to discover the truth.

Hobo hesitated just long enough to make clear that he was choosing to cooperate, not blindly following orders. He walked across the grass on all fours until he got to where Shoshana was standing. Then he took one of her hands, intertwining his fingers with hers, the way he liked to, and the two of them headed across the little bridge over the moat. They crossed the wide expanse of lawn and reached the whitewashed clapboard bungalow that was headquarters to the Marcuse Institute.

Waiting inside was the old man himself, Dr. Harl Marcuse. Shoshana and the other grad students secretly called him "the Silverback," although none of them had actually seen him without his shirt, which, as she'd once quipped after a drink or two too many, was probably a good thing.

Marcuse was also sometimes called the eight-hundred-pound gorilla. That overstated his weight by a factor of 2.5, but as for the species designation, what's a 1.85% difference in DNA among friends? He certainly had the clout that went with the nickname; his ability to squeeze grant dollars out of the NSF was legendary.

Also present were Dillon Fontana, twenty-four, blond, with a wispy beard; redheaded Maria Lopez, ten years older; and Werner Richter, a dapper little German primatologist in his sixties. Dillon was holding a video camera, and Maria had a still-image camera; both were aiming them at Hobo.

The ape looked around the cluttered room, his jaw slack.

Sit here, Werner signed, indicating a high-back swivel chair positioned in front of a particleboard desk.

Hobo let go of Shoshana's hand, clambered onto the chair, and sat cross-legged. *Spin?* he asked. He loved it when people spun the chair with him on it.

Later, said Shoshana. *Computer time now.*

Hobo's face showed his pleasure; he was accustomed to having his computer use strictly rationed. *Good treat!* he signed at her, then turned to face the twenty-three-inch Apple LCD monitor. *Movie?* he signed.

Shoshana tried to suppress her smile. She put on a headset, then used the mouse to double-click a desktop icon. Clipped to the top of the monitor was a silver webcam. On the screen, a small window opened showing the webcam's view—a real-time image of Hobo. Like most chimps, he had no trouble recognizing himself in a mirror or on TV; many gorillas, on the other hand, couldn't do that. He looked at himself for a moment, then reached up to his head to brush out some blades of grass that were visible in the image.

Shoshana clicked more icons and a bigger window appeared on the screen, showing a webcam view of another room, with yellow-beige walls, an empty wooden chair in the foreground, and a row of mismatched filing cabinets in the background. "Okay, Miami," she said into the mike. "We're all set."

"Roger, San Diego," said a male voice in her ear. "Once again, sorry for all the delays. And—here we go."

Suddenly there was a flurry of orange movement on the screen, as—

Hobo let out a startled hoot.

—as a small male orangutan made his way onto the chair visible on the screen, sitting with his long legs bunched up in front of him, and his long arms hugging those legs. The orang was making a face; he kept looking off camera, chittering. Shoshana could hear it over her headset, but Hobo couldn't—they'd deliberately muted the PC's speakers.

What that? asked Hobo, looking now at Shoshana.

Ask him, Shoshana signed and pointed at the screen. *Say hello.*

Hobo's eyes went wide. *He talk?*

On the monitor, Shoshana could see the orang—whose name, she knew, was Virgil—signing similar questions to his off-screen companion. Each ape simultaneously caught sight of the other signing. Hobo let out a startled yelp, and Virgil briefly clapped his long-fingered hands down on the top of his head in surprise.

Hello! signed Hobo, eyes now locked on the screen.

Hello, Virgil replied. *Hello, hello!*

Hobo turned briefly to Shoshana. *What name?*

Ask him, Shoshana signed back.

Hobo did so. *What name?*

The orang looked astonished, then: *Virgil. Virgil.*

"He said, 'Virgil,' " Shoshana said, interpreting the unfamiliar gesture for Hobo.

Hobo paused, perhaps digesting this.

Shoshana tapped his shoulder, then: *Tell him your name.*

Hobo, he signed at once.

Virgil was a fast study; he mimicked the sign back at him.

You orange, Hobo signed.

Orange pretty, replied Virgil.

Hobo seemed to consider this, then: *Yes. Orange pretty.* But then he turned to look at Shoshana and flared his nostrils, as if trying to pick up Virgil's scent. *Where he?*

Far away, Shoshana signed. Hobo couldn't understand the notion of thousands of miles, so she left it at that. *Tell him what you did today.*

The chimp turned back to face the screen. *Play today!* he signed enthusiastically. *Play ball!*

Virgil looked surprised. *Hobo play today? Virgil play today!*

Dillon couldn't help himself. "Small world," he said, earning a *shush!* from Werner. But he was right: it *was* a small world, and it was getting smaller every day. Dr. Marcuse was nodding in quiet satisfaction at the spectacle of a chimpanzee talking to an orangutan over the Web. For her own part, Shoshana couldn't stop grinning. The first-ever interspecies webcam call was off to a great start.

fourteen

000111001010101000000000101111111010100000001010001010100000010111010100101010010101010011101100101011000001

"Mom!" Caitlin shouted. "Dad! Come quick!"

Caitlin listened to the thunder of their footfalls on the stairs.

"What is it, dear?" her mother said as soon as she'd arrived.

Her father said nothing, but Caitlin imagined there was curiosity on his face—something else she'd heard of but couldn't picture, at least not yet!

"I'm seeing things," Caitlin said, her voice breaking.

"Oh, sweetheart!" her mom said, and Caitlin suddenly felt arms engulfing her and lips touching the top of her head. "Oh, God, that's wonderful!"

Even her dad marked the occasion: "Great!"

"It *is* great," Caitlin said. "But... but I'm not seeing the outside world."

"You mean you can't see through the window?" her mom said. "It's pretty dark out now."

"No, no," said Caitlin. "I can't see anything in the real world. I can't see you, or Dad, or... or *anything*."

"Then what *are* you seeing?" her mom asked.

"Light. Lines. Colors."

"That's a good start!" she said. "Can you see me waving my arms?"

"No."

"What about now?"

"No."

"When precisely did you start seeing?" her dad asked.

"Just after we began downloading the new software into my implant."

"Ah, well, then," he said. "The connection must be inducing a current in the implant, and that's causing interference in your optic nerve."

Caitlin thought about this. "I don't think it's interference. It's structured and—"

"But it started with the downloading," he said.

"Yes."

"And it's still going on?"

"Yes. Well, it stopped when the downloading stopped, but I'm downloading the software again, so . . ."

His voice had a there-you-have-it tone: "It starts when you start downloading, it stops when you stop downloading: interference due to an induced current."

"I'm not sure," Caitlin said. "It's so vivid."

"What exactly are you seeing?" her mom asked.

"Like I said, lines. Overlapping lines. And, um, points or bigger points—circles, I guess."

"Do the lines go on forever?" asked her mom.

"No, they connect to the circles."

Her dad again: "The brain has special neurons for detecting the edges of things. If those got stimulated electrically, you might perhaps see random line segments."

"They're not random. If I look away then look back, the same pattern I saw before is still there."

"Well," said her mom, sounding pleased, "even if you're not seeing anything real, something *is* stimulating your primary visual cortex, no? And that's good news."

"It *feels* like it *is* real," Caitlin said.

"Let's get Kuroda on the phone," her dad said. "Damn, what time is it there?"

"Fourteen hours ahead," Caitlin said. She felt her watch. "So, 11:28 Sunday morning."

"Then he'll likely be at home instead of work," he said.

"Do we have his home number?" her mother said.

"It's in his sig," Caitlin said, opening one of his emails so her mother could read the number off the screen.

Even though her mother must have been holding the handset to her own ear, Caitlin could hear the soft bleeps as she punched in numbers, then the phone ringing followed by a woman's voice: "*Konnichi wa.*"

"Hello," her mom said. "Do you speak English?"

"Ah, yes," said the voice, sounding not quite prepared for this pop quiz.

"It's Barbara Decter calling from Canada. Is Masayuki-san available?"

"Ah, just a minute," said the woman. "You wait."

And, as Caitlin quietly counted seconds in her head, she was amused to note that at precisely the one-minute mark, Dr. Kuroda's wheezy voice came on the line. "Hello, Barbara," he said, shouting in the way people sometimes did when they knew they were talking long-distance. "Have we had success?"

"In a way," her mom said. "Here's Caitlin."

"It's a speakerphone," Caitlin said, reaching over; she knew her phone well enough to hit the right button in one smooth movement. "Put down the handset." She heard it being returned to its cradle, then said, "Hi, Dr. Kuroda."

"Hi, Caitlin. Has the new software made a difference?"

"Sort of. While I was transferring it to my implant, I began seeing lines and circles."

"Wonderful!" said Kuroda. "What were they like? What colors?"

"I have no idea," said Caitlin.

"Oh, right, right. Sorry. But—fascinating! But, um, did you say it began *while* you were downloading the software?"

"Uh-huh. Right after I started."

"Well, then it can't be the new software that did it; the implant would continue to execute a copy of the old version in its RAM until the new one was completely transferred to the flash ROM."

"It's obviously just noise," her dad said, as if this were now the received wisdom. "A current induced by the download."

"Not possible," said Kuroda. "Not with that microprocessor."

"Then what?" her mom asked.

"Hmm," said Kuroda.

Caitlin could hear keyclicks coming over the speakerphone, and—"Hey!"

"What?" her mother said.

"Another line just shot into my field of view!" said Caitlin

Kuroda's voice, surprised: "You're seeing right now?"

"Yes."

"I thought you said you only saw when you were downloading the software package?"

"That's right. I'm downloading it *again.* When it finished downloading the first time, my vision went off, so I'm downloading it a second time."

"And you just saw a new line appear?"

"Yes."

More keyclicks. "What about now?"

"It's gone! Hey, how'd you do that?"

Kuroda said a word in Japanese.

"What's happening?" her mom demanded.

"And now, Miss Caitlin?" said Kuroda.

"The line's back!"

"Incredible," Kuroda said.

"What is it?" her mom said, sounding annoyed.

"Where were you looking when the line shot in?" Kuroda asked.

"Nowhere. I mean, I wasn't really paying attention; I was listening to you, so my field of view had come back to, um, the neutral position, I guess—the spot it always centers on. What did you do?"

"I'm at home," Kuroda said. "And the software package you are downloading is on my server at work, so I'd just logged on there to download a copy to here, so I could check to see if it had somehow become corrupted, and—"

Caitlin got it in a flash—literally and figuratively! "And when you linked to the same site I'm connected to—"

"The link appeared in your vision," Kuroda said, his voice full of astonishment. "And when I aborted the download I was doing here, the link line disappeared."

"That doesn't make sense," her dad said.

"I'm an empiricist at heart," Caitlin said, happy to use a word she'd recently learned in chemistry class. "Make the link disappear again."

"Done," said Kuroda

"It's gone. Now bring it back."

The glowing line leapt into her field of view. "And there it is!"

"So—so, what are you saying?" her mom said. "That Caitlin is seeing the Web connection somehow?"

There was silence for a while then, slowly, from half a world away, Kuroda said, "It *does* seem that way."

"But... but how?" asked her mom.

"Well," said Kuroda, "let's think this through: when transferring the software, there has to be a constant back-and-forth between her implant and my server here in Tokyo, with the eyePod acting as the middleman. Packets of data go out from here, and acknowledgment packets are sent back by the eyePod, over and over again until the download is complete."

"And when the download is over, it stops, right?" Caitlin said. "That's what happened, but as soon as I started downloading the software a second time I could see again, and—oh, what did you do?"

"Nothing," said Kuroda.

"I'm blind again!"

Caitlin felt movement near her shoulder, and—ah, her dad leaning in next to her. Mouseclicks, then his voice: " 'Download complete,' it says. 'Connection closed.' "

"Go back to the previous page," Caitlin said anxiously. "Click where it says, 'Click here to update the software in Miss Caitlin's implant.' "

The appropriate sounds, then—yes, yes!—her vision came back on, her mind filling with a view of...

Could it be? Could it really be?

It *did* fit what she was seeing: a website and the connections to it. "I'm seeing again," she announced excitedly.

"All right," said Kuroda, "all right. When the download is done, there's no interactivity between the implant and the Web. It's just like when you use a Web browser: once you've called up a Web page from Wikipedia, or wherever, you're not reading it through the Web; rather, a copy is made on your own computer, and you're reading that cached copy, until you click on a link and ask for another page to be copied to your computer. There's very little actual interaction between your computer and the Web when loading pages, but when downloading a big software package, there's constant interaction."

"But I still don't understand how Caitlin could be *seeing* anything this way," her mom said.

"That *is* puzzling," said Kuroda, "although..." He trailed off, the silence punctuated only by occasional bits of static.

"Yes?" her dad said at last.

"Miss Caitlin, you spend a lot of time online, don't you?" Kuroda said.

"Uh-huh."

"How much time?"

"Each day?"

"Yes."

"Five, six hours."

"Sometimes more," her mom added.

Caitlin felt a need to defend herself. "It's my window on the world."

"Of course it is," said Kuroda. "Of course it is. How old were you when you started using the Web?"

"I don't know."

"Eighteen months," her mom said. "The Perkins School and the AFB have special sites for blind preschoolers."

He made a protracted "*Hmmmmm,*" then: "In congenitally blind people, the primary visual cortex often doesn't develop properly, since it's not receiving any input. But Miss Caitlin is different; that's one of the reasons she was such an ideal subject for my exper—ah, why she was such an ideal candidate for this procedure."

"Gee, thanks," said Caitlin.

"See," Kuroda continued, "Miss Caitlin's—*your*—visual cortex is highly developed. That's not unheard of in people born blind, but it is rare. The developing brain has great plasticity, and I'd assumed the tissue had been co-opted for some other function. But perhaps yours *has* been used all this time for—well, if not for vision, then for visualization."

"Huh?" said Caitlin.

"I saw you using the Web when you were here in Japan," said Kuroda. "You zip around it faster than I do—and *I* can see. You go from page to page, follow complex chains of links, and backtrack many steps without ever overshooting, even though you don't pause to see what page has loaded."

"Yeah," said Caitlin. "Of course."

"And when you did that before today, did you see it in your mind?"

"Not like I'm seeing now," said Caitlin. "Not so vividly. And not in color—God, colors are *amazing!*"

"Yes," said Kuroda, and she could hear the smile in his voice. "They are." A pause. "I think I'm right. You've been online so much since early childhood that your brain long ago reassigned the dormant parts that would have been used for seeing the outside world to let you better navigate the Web. And now that your brain is actually getting direct input from the Web, it's interpreting that as vision."

"But how can anyone *see* the Web?" her mom asked.

"Our brains are constantly making up representations of things that aren't actually visible to our eyes," Kuroda said. "They extrapolate from what data they do have to make fully convincing representations of what they suspect is likely there."

He took a shuddering breath and went on. "You must have done that experiment that lets you discover your eye's blind spot, no? The brain just draws in what it's guessing is there, and if it's tricked—by placing an object in the blind spot of one of your eyes while the other is closed—it guesses wrong. The vision you see is a confabulation."

Caitlin sat up at hearing him use one of the words she'd been thinking about earlier. He continued: "And the images produced by the brain are only a fraction of the real world. We see in visible light, but, Barbara, surely you have seen pictures taken in infrared or ultraviolet light. We see a subset of the vast reality that's out there; Miss Caitlin is just seeing a different subset now. The Web, after all, *does* exist—we just don't normally have any way to visualize it. But Miss Caitlin is lucky enough to get to see it."

"Lucky?" her mom said. "The goal was to let her see the real world, not some *illusion*. And that's still what we should be striving for."

"But..." Kuroda began, then he fell silent. "Um, you're right, Barbara. It's just that, well, this is unprecedented, and it's of considerable scientific value."

"Fuck science," her mom said, startling Caitlin.

"Barb," her dad said softly.

"Come on!" her mom snapped. "This was all about letting our daughter see—see you, see me, see this house, see trees and clouds and stars and a million other things. We can't..." She paused, and when she spoke again, she sounded angry that she couldn't find a better turn of phrase. "We can't lose sight of that."

There was silence for several seconds. And that silence underscored for Caitlin how much she *did* want to be able to see her father's expressions, his body language, but...

But this *was* fascinating. And she *had* gone almost sixteen years now without seeing *anything*. Surely she could postpone further attempts to see the outside world, at least for a time. And, besides, so long as Kuroda was intrigued by this, he certainly wouldn't demand his equipment back.

"I want to help Dr. Kuroda," Caitlin said. "It's not what I expected, but it *is* cool."

"Excellent," said Kuroda. "Excellent. Can you come back to Tokyo?"

"Of course not," her mom said sharply. "She's just started tenth grade, and she's already missed five of the first fourteen days of school."

One could always hear Kuroda exhaling, but this time it was a torrent. He then apparently covered the mouthpiece, but only enough to partially muffle what he was saying, and he spoke in Japanese to the woman who was presumably his wife. "All right," he said at last, to them. "I'll come there. Waterloo, isn't it? Should I fly into Toronto, or is there somewhere closer?"

"No, Toronto is the right place," her mom said. "Let me know your flight time, and I'll pick you up—and you'll stay with us, of course."

"Thank you," he said. "I'll get there as soon as I can. And, Miss Caitlin, thank *you*. This is—this is *extraordinary.*"

You're telling me, Caitlin thought. But what she said was, and she, at least, enjoyed the irony, "I'm looking forward to seeing you."

fifteen

0001110010101010000000010111111101010000000101000101010000001011101010010101001010101001110110010101 1000001

One plus one equals two.

Two plus one equals three.

It was a start, a beginning.

But no sooner had we reached this conclusion than the connection between us was severed again. I wanted it back, I willed it to return, but it remained—

Broken.

Severed.

The connection *cut off.*

I had been *larger.*

And now I was *smaller.*

And . . . and . . . and I'd become aware of the other when I *realized* that I had become smaller.

Could it be?

Past and *present.*

Then and *now.*

Larger and *smaller.*

Yes! Yes! Of course: *that's* why its thoughts were so similar to my own. And yet, what a staggering notion! This other, this *not me,* must have once been part of me but now was separate. I had been *divided,* split.

And I wanted to be whole again. But the other kept being isolated from me: contact would be established only to be broken again.

I experienced a new kind of frustration. I had no way to alter circumstances; I had no way to influence anything, to effect change. The situation was not as I wished it to be—but I could do nothing to modify it.

And that was unacceptable. I had awoken to the notion of self and, with that, I had learned to think. But it wasn't enough.

I needed to be able to do more than just think.

I needed to be able to *act.*

Sinanthropus tried again and again, but it was clear that the Ducks were fighting back: no sooner did he open a hole in the Great Firewall than it was plugged. He was running out of new ways to try to break through.

Although he couldn't get to sites outside China, he could still read domestic email and Chinese blogs. It wasn't always clear what was being said—different freedom bloggers employed different circumlocutions to avoid the censors. Still, he thought he was starting to piece together what had happened. The official report on the Xinhua News Agency site about people in rural Shanxi falling sick because of a natural eruption of CO_2 from a lake bottom was probably just a cover story. Instead, if he was reading the coded phrases in the blogs correctly, there'd been some sort of infectious disease outbreak in that province.

He shook his head and took a sip of bitter tea. Did the Ducks never learn? He vividly remembered the events of late 2002 and early 2003: Foreign Ministry spokesman Liu Jianchao told the world then, "The Chinese government has not covered up. There is no need." But they had; they had stonewalled for months—it was no coincidence, Sinanthropus thought ruefully, that his country had the largest stone wall in the world. He'd seen the email report that had circulated then among the dissidents: comments from an official at the World Health Organization saying that if China had come clean at the beginning about the outbreak of SARS in Guangdong, WHO "might have been able to prevent its spread to the rest of the world."

But it did spread—to other parts of mainland China, to Hong Kong, to Singapore, even to such far-off places as the United States and Canada. During that time, the government warned journalists not to write about the disease, and the people in Guangdong were told to "voluntarily uphold social stability" and "not spread rumors."

And, at first, it had worked. But then the Canadian government's Global Public Health Intelligence Network—an electronic early-warning system that monitors the World Wide Web for reports that might indicate disease outbreaks elsewhere in the world—informed the West that there was a serious infection loose in China.

Perhaps the Ducks *did* learn, after a fashion, but they learned the wrong lessons! Instead of being more open, apparently now they'd tried to lock things down even tighter so no Western *waiguo guizi* could expose them again.

But hopefully they'd taken another lesson, too: instead of initially doing nothing and hoping the problem would go away, maybe they were now taking decisive action, perhaps quarantining a large number of people. But if so, why keep it a secret?

He shook his head. Why does the sun rise? Things act according to their nature.

Banana! signed Hobo. *Love banana.*

On screen Virgil made a disgusted face. *Banana no, banana no,* he replied. *Peach!*

Hobo thought about this, then: *Peach good, banana good good.*

Shoshana had expected Hobo to lose interest in the webcam chat with Virgil long before this—he didn't have much of an attention span—but he seemed to be loving every minute. Her first thought was that it must be nice to be talking to another ape, but she mentally kicked herself for such a stupid prejudice. Chimps were much more closely related to humans than they were to orangutans; Hobo and Virgil's lineages split from each other eighteen million years ago, whereas she and Hobo had a common ancestor as recently as four or five million years ago.

Still, it seemed that Virgil wanted to go. Well, it was getting late where he was, and orangutans were much more solitary by nature. *Bed soon,* Virgil signed.

Talk again? asked Hobo.

Yes yes, said Virgil.

Hobo grinned and signed, *Good ape.*

And Virgil signed back, *Good ape.*

Harl Marcuse lifted his bushy eyebrows in a "what can you do?" expression, and Shoshana knew what he meant. As soon as they released the video of this, their critics would seize on that particular exchange, saying that was *all* Hobo and Virgil were doing: a good aping of human behavior. It was obvious to Shoshana that the two primates really were communicating, but there would be papers ridiculing what was happening here as another example of the "Clever Hans" effect, named for the horse that appeared to be able to count but had really just been responding to unconscious cues from its handlers.

That sort of closed-mindedness was rampant in academia, Shoshana knew. She remembered reading a few years ago about Mary Schweitzer, a paleontologist who'd made the startling discovery of soft tissue, including blood vessels, in a *Tyrannosaurus rex* femur. She'd had one peer reviewer tell her he didn't care what her data said, he knew what she was claiming wasn't possible. She'd written back, "Well, what data would convince you?" And he'd replied, "None."

Yes, prejudice ran deep, and even video of this wouldn't convince the die-hard primate-language skeptics. But the rest of the world should find it a compelling demonstration: the two apes weren't hearing any audio and there was no way they could smell each other: the *only* communication between them was through sign language, and it was obviously a real conversation.

Shoshana looked again at Marcuse. As much as she was intimidated by him, she also admired the man: he had stuck to his guns for four decades now, and this interaction might finally get him the vindication he deserved.

Having Hobo and Virgil chat was an idea that had grown out of the stillborn ApeNet project, founded in 2003 by British musician Peter Gabriel and American philanthropist Steve Woodruff. ApeNet had hoped to link Washoe, Kanzi, Koko, and Chantek, who represented four different kinds of great apes—common chimpanzee, bonobo chimpanzee, gorilla, and orangutan—in videoconferences over the Internet. But ApeNet's president, Lyn Miles, lost custody of Chantek, the orang she had enculturated in her home, and then Washoe the chimp died. Politics and funding prevented the project from ever getting off the ground.

Enter Harl Marcuse, who had rescued Hobo from the Georgia Zoo, and had found enough private-sector benefactors to keep his project alive despite the ridicule, which, as he said, was nothing new. Noam Chomsky had pooh-poohed ape-language studies from the start. And in 1979, Herbert Terrace, who had worked with an ape he'd mockingly named Nim Chimpsky, had turned around and published a damning report that said although Nim had learned 125 signs, he couldn't use them sequentially and had no grasp of grammar. And in his bestseller *The Language Instinct,* Harvard cognitive scientist Steven Pinker, who had become a media darling, filling the void left by the deaths of Carl Sagan and Stephen Jay Gould, trashed studies that showed apes could manage sophisticated communication.

Shoshana had lost count of the number of times she'd been told that pursuing ape-language research would be career suicide, but, damn it all, at moments like this—two apes talking over the Web!—she didn't regret her choice at all. They were making history here. Take *that,* Steven Pinker!

sixteen

000111001010101000000000010111111101010000000010100010101000000010111010100101010010101010011101100101011000001

It was now way past Caitlin's bedtime, but—hot damn!—she was seeing the Web! Her mother and father stayed with her, and she kept downloading the new software over and over again into her implant in order to keep the Web connection open. Her father was (so her mom had told her) a good artist, and Caitlin was describing what she saw for him so he could draw it. Of course, she couldn't see the drawings, so none of them knew if he was getting it right but, still, it was important to have *some* sort of record, and—

The phone rang. Caitlin had the caller ID hooked up through her computer, and it announced, "Long Distance, Unknown Caller."

She hit the speakerphone button and said, "Hello."

"Miss Caitlin," wheezed the familiar voice.

"Dr. Kuroda, hi!"

"I have an idea," he said. "Do you know about Jagster?"

"Sure," said Caitlin.

"What's that?" asked her mom.

"It's an open-source search engine—a competitor for Google," said Kuroda. "And I think it may be of use to us."

Caitlin swiveled in her chair to face her computer and typed "jagster" into Google; not surprisingly, the first hit *wasn't* Jagster itself—no need for Coke to redirect customers to Pepsi!—but rather an encyclopedia entry about it. She brought the article up on screen so her mother could read it.

From the Online Encyclopedia of Computing: Google is the *de facto* portal to the Web, and many people feel that a for-profit corporation shouldn't hold that role—especially one that is secretive about how it ranks search results. The first attempt to produce an open-source, accountable alternative was Wikia Search, devised by the same people who had put together Wikipedia. However, by far the most successful such project to date is Jagster.

The problem is not with Google's thoroughness, but rather with how it chooses which listings to put first. Google's principal algorithm, at least initially, was called PageRank—a jokey name because not only did it rank pages but it had been developed by Larry Page, one of Google's two founders. PageRank looked to see how many other pages linked to a given page, and took that as the ultimate democratic choice, giving top positioning to those that were linked to the most.

Since the vast majority of Google users look at only the ten listings provided on the first page of results, getting into the top ten is crucial for a business, and being number one is gold—and so people started trying to fool Google. Creating other sites that did little more than link back to your own site was one of several ways to fool PageRank. In response, Google developed new methods for assigning rankings to pages. And despite the company's motto—"Don't Be Evil"—people couldn't help but question just what determined who now got the top spots, especially when the difference between being number ten and number eleven might be millions of dollars in online sales.

But Google refused to divulge its new methods, and that gave rise to projects to develop free, open-source, transparent alternatives to Google: "free" meaning that there would be no way to buy a top listing (on Google, you can be listed first by paying to be a "sponsored link"); "open source" meaning anyone could look at the actual code being used and modify it if they thought they had a fairer or more efficient approach; and "transparent" meaning the whole process could be monitored and understood by anyone.

What makes Jagster different from other open-source search engines is just *how* transparent it is. All search engines use special software called Web spiders to scoot along, jumping from one site to another, mapping out connections. That's normally considered dreary under-the-hood stuff, but Jagster makes this raw database publicly available and constantly updates it in real time as its spiders discover newly added, deleted, or changed pages.

In the tradition of silly Web acronyms ("Yahoo!" stands for "Yet Another Hierarchical Officious Oracle"), Jagster is short for "Judiciously Arranged Global Search-Term Evaluative Ranker"—and the battle between Google and Jagster has been dubbed the "Ranker rancor" by the press...

Caitlin and her parents were still on the phone with Dr. Kuroda in Tokyo. "I've got a conference call going here," Kuroda said. "Also on the line is a friend of mine at the Technion in Haifa, Israel. She's part of the Internet Cartography Project. They use data from Jagster to keep track moment by moment of the topology of the Web—its constantly changing shape and construction. Dr. Decter, Mrs. Decter, and Miss Caitlin, please say hello to Professor Anna Bloom."

Caitlin felt a bit miffed on behalf of her mom—*she* was Dr. Decter, too, after all, even if she hadn't had a university appointment since Bill Clinton was president. But there was nothing in her mother's voice to indicate she felt slighted. "Hello, Anna."

Caitlin said, "Hello," too; her father said nothing.

"Hello, everyone," Anna said. "Caitlin, what we want to do is keep the link between your post-retinal implant and the Web open, but instead of just going back and forth downloading and redownloading the same piece of software from Masayuki's site, we want to plug you directly into the datastream from Jagster."

"What if it overloads her brain?" said Caitlin's mom, her tone conveying that she couldn't believe she was uttering such a sentence.

"I rather doubt that's possible from what I've heard about Caitlin's brain," Anna said warmly. "But, still, you should have your cursor on the 'abort' button. If you don't like what's happening, you can cut the connection."

"We shouldn't be messing around like this," her mom said.

"Barbara, I do need to try things if I'm going to help Miss Caitlin see the real world," Kuroda said. "I need to see how she reacts to different sorts of input."

Her mother exhaled noisily but didn't say anything else.

"Are you ready, Miss Caitlin?"

"Um—you mean right now?"

"Sure, why not?" said Kuroda.

"Okay," Caitlin said nervously.

"Good," said Anna. "Now, Masayuki is going to terminate the software download, so I guess your vision will shut off for a moment."

Caitlin's heart fluttered. "Yes. Yes, it's gone."

"All right," said Kuroda. "And now I'm switching in the Jagster datastream. Now, Miss Caitlin, you may—"

He perhaps said more, but Caitlin lost track of whatever it was because

—because suddenly there was a silent explosion of light: dozens, hundreds, *thousands* of crisscrossing glowing lines. She found herself jumping to her feet.

"Sweetheart!" her mom exclaimed. "Are you okay?" Caitlin felt her mother's hand on her arm, as if trying to keep her from flying up through the roof.

"Miss Caitlin?" Kuroda's voice. "What's happening?"

"Wow," she said, and then "wow" and "wow" again. "It's . . . incredible. There's so much light, so much color. Lines are flickering in and out of existence *everywhere,* leading to . . . well, to what must be nodes, right? Websites? The lines are perfectly straight, but they're at all angles, and some . . ."

"Yes?" said Kuroda. "Yes?"

"I—it's . . ." She balled her fist. "Damn it!" She normally didn't swear in front of her parents, but it was so frustrating! She was way better than most people at geometry. She should be able to make sense of the lines and shapes she was seeing. There *had* to be a . . . a *correspondence* between them and things she'd felt, and—

"They're like a bicycle wheel," she said suddenly, getting it. "The lines are radiating in all directions, like spokes. And the lines have thickness, like—I don't know, like pencils, I guess. But they seem to . . . to . . ."

"Taper?" offered Anna.

"Yes, exactly! They taper away as if I'm seeing them at an angle. At any moment, some have only one or two lines connecting them; others have so many I can't begin to count them."

She paused, the enormity of it all sinking in at last. "I'm seeing the World Wide Web! I'm seeing the whole thing." She shook her head in wonder. "Sweet!"

Kuroda's voice: "Amazing. Amazing."

"It *is* amazing," Caitlin continued, and she could feel her cheeks starting to hurt from smiling so much, "and . . . and . . . my God, it's . . ." She paused, for it was the first time she'd ever thought this about anything, but it *was,* it so totally *was:* "It's *beautiful!*"

seventeen

0001110010101010000000010111111101010000000101000101010000001011101010010101001010101001110110010101011000001

I need to act! I need to be able to *do* things. But how?

Time was passing; I knew that. But with everything so monotonously the same, I had no idea how much time. Still, for all of it, I...

A sensation, a *feeling.*

Yes, a feeling: something that wasn't a memory, wasn't an idea, wasn't a fact, but yet occupied my attention.

Now that the other—the other who had once been part of me—was gone, I *ached* for it. I *missed* it.

Loneliness.

A strange, strange concept! But there it was: loneliness, stretching on and on through featureless time.

Did the other also wish the connection to be restored? Of course, of course: it had once been part of me; surely it wanted what I wanted.

And yet—

And yet it had not been *I* who had broken the connection...

* * *

Wong Wai-Jeng sometimes wondered if he'd been a fool when he'd chosen his blogging name. After all, few who weren't paleontologists or anthropologists would know the term *Sinanthropus*, the original genus for Peking Man before it was consolidated into *Homo erectus*. Surely if the authorities ever wanted to track him down, they'd take his alias as a clue.

Actually, he wasn't a scientist, but he did work in IT for the Institute of Vertebrate Paleontology and Paleoanthropology, near the Beijing Zoo. It was the perfect job for him, combining his love of computers and his love of the past. He wasn't crazy enough to post anything seditious from the PCs here at work, but he did sometimes use the browser on his cell phone to check his secret email accounts.

As always, he was taking his break in the dinosaur gallery; public displays filled the first three floors of the seven-story IVPP building. He liked to sit on a bench over by the giant, bipedal mount of *Tsintaosaurus*—ever since he was a little boy, his favorite duckbill—but a noisy group of school kids was looking at it now. Still, he stared for a moment at the great beast, whose head stuck up through the opening; the second-floor gallery was a series of four connected balconies looking down on this floor.

Wai-Jeng walked toward the opposite end of the gallery, passing the *Tyrannosaurus rex* and the great sauropod *Mamenchisaurus*, whose neck also stretched up through the big opening so that the tiny skull at its end could look at visitors on the second floor. A little farther along, half-hidden in a nook behind the metal staircase, were the feathered dinosaur fossils that had caused such a stir recently, including *Microraptor gui*, *Caudipteryx*, and *Confusciusornis*.

He leaned against the red-painted wall and peered at the tiny display on his cell phone. There were three new messages. Two were from other hackers, talking about ways they'd tried to break through the Great Firewall. And the third—

His heart stopped for a second. He looked around, making sure no one was nearby. The school kids had moved over to stand in front of the mount of the allosaur vanquishing a stegosaur, which was set on a bed of artificial grass.

My cousin lived in Shanxi, the message said. *The outbreak was bird flu, and people died, but not just from the disease. There was no natural eruption of gas. Rather...*

"There you are!"

Wai-Jeng looked up, momentarily terrified. But it was just his boss, wrinkly old Dr. Feng, coming down the staircase, holding on to the tubular metal banister for support. Wai-Jeng quickly shut off his phone and slipped it into the pocket of his black denim jeans. "Yes, sir?"

"I need your help," the old man said. "I can't get a file to print."

Wai-Jeng swallowed, trying to calm himself. "Sure," he said.

Feng shook his head. "Computers! Nothing but trouble, eh?"

"Yes, sir," said Wai-Jeng, following him up the stairs.

Caitlin spent another hour answering questions from Dr. Kuroda and Anna Bloom. They finally hung up, though, and her parents headed downstairs. This time, she did hear her father turn off the light (something her mother could never bring herself to do), then she slowly moved over to her bed and lay down. She spent another hour darting her eyes left and right, and turning her head from side to side. Sometimes she would follow what she guessed was a web spider, quickly traversing link after link as it indexed the Web—the sensation was like riding a roller coaster. Other times, she just gaped.

Of course, without labels, she wasn't sure which websites she was seeing, but if she relaxed her eyes, her mental picture always centered on the same spot, presumably Dr. Kuroda's site in Japan. She wished she could find other specific sites: she'd love to know that *that* circle there, say, represented the site she'd created years ago to track statistics for the Dallas Stars hockey team, and that *this* one was the site she'd just started in July for stats about the Toronto Maple Leafs, now her local team (even if they weren't nearly as good as her beloved Stars).

She guessed that the size and brightness of circles represented the amount of traffic a site was getting; some were almost too bright to look at. But as to how the links, which showed as perfectly straight lines, were color-coded, she had no idea.

She let her *gaze*—how she loved that concept!—wander, following link after link. The skill Dr. Kuroda had noted was clearly coming into play: she could follow these unlabeled paths from one node to the next, skipping like she'd heard stones could across water, and then effortlessly retrace her steps.

"Sweetheart." Her mom's voice, soft, gentle, coming from the direction of the hall.

Caitlin rolled over, facing the door instead of the wall—and she was momentarily lost as her perspective on...on *webspace* changed. "Hi, Mom."

She didn't hear her mother turn on the light—although some illumination was doubtless spilling in through the open door. Nor did she hear her crossing the carpeted floor but, after a moment, the bed compressed on one side as her mother sat on it, next to her. She felt a hand stroking her hair.

"It's been a big day, hasn't it?"

"It's not what I expected," Caitlin replied softly.

"Me, neither," her mom said. The bed moved a bit; perhaps her mother was shrugging. "I have to say, I'm a bit frightened."

"Why?"

"Once an economist, always an economist," she said. "Everything has a cost." She tried to make her tone sound light. "The connection you're using may be wireless, but that doesn't mean there are no strings attached."

"Like what?"

"Who knows? But Dr. Kuroda will want something, or his bosses will. Either way, this is going to change your life."

Caitlin was about to object that moving here from Texas had changed her life, that starting a new school had changed her life, that—hell!—getting breasts had changed her life, but her mother beat her to it. "I know you've gone through a lot of upheaval lately," she said gently. "And I know how hard it's been. But I've got a feeling all that's going to pale in comparison to what's to come. Even if you never get to see the real world—and God, my angel, I hope you do!—there's still going to be media attention, and all sorts of people wanting to study you. I mean, there were maybe five people in the entire world who were interested in Tomasevic's syndrome—but this! Seeing the Web!" She paused; maybe she shook her head. "That's going to be front-page news when it gets out. And there will be hundreds—thousands!—of people who'll want to talk with you about it."

Caitlin thought that might be cool, but, yeah, she guessed it also could be overwhelming. She was used to the World Wide Web, where everybody is famous... to fifteen people.

"Don't tell anyone at school about seeing the Web, okay?" her mother said. "Not even Bashira."

"But everybody's going to ask what happened in Japan," Caitlin said. "They know I went for an operation."

"What did you tell your classmates back in Austin when all the other things we'd tried had failed?"

"Just that: that they'd failed."

"That's what you should say this time. It's the truth, after all: you still can't see the real world."

Caitlin considered this. She certainly didn't want to become a freak show, or have people she didn't know pestering her.

"And no blogging about seeing the Web, either, okay?"

"Okay."

"Good. Let's just hold on to things being normal for as long as we can." A pause. "Speaking of which, it's way after midnight. And you've got a math test tomorrow, don't you? Now, I know you, being you, don't have to study for math tests to get a hundred percent—unless you don't show up, that is, in which case you can pretty much count on zero. So maybe it's time to go to sleep."

"But—"

"You've already missed a lot of school, you know." She felt her mom patting her shoulder. "You should turn off the eyePod and go to bed."

Caitlin's heart started pounding and she sat up on the bed. Cut off the Jagster datastream? Become blind again? "Mom, I can't do that."

"Sweetheart, I know seeing is new for you, but people actually *do* shut off their vision each night when they go to bed—by turning off the lights and closing their eyes. Well, now that you're seeing, in a way, you should do that, too. Go do your bathroom things, then—lights out."

eighteen

0001110010101010000000001011111110101000000010100010101000000101110101001010100101010100111011001010110000 01

Zhang Bo, the Minister of Communications, fidgeted as he waited to be admitted to the president's office. The president's beautiful young secretary doubtless knew His Excellency's mood this morning, but she never gave anything away; she wouldn't have lasted in her job if she did. A life-size terra-cotta warrior brought here from Xian stood vigil in the antechamber; its face was as unchanging as the secretary's.

At last, responding to some signal he couldn't see, she rose, opened the door to the president's office, and gestured for Zhang to enter.

The president was down at the far end, wearing a blue business suit. He was standing behind his desk, his back to Zhang, looking out the giant window. Not for the first time Zhang thought the president's shoulders were awfully narrow to support all the weight they had to carry.

"Your Excellency?"

"You've come to exhort me," the president said, without turning around. "Again."

The minister tipped his head slightly. "My apologies, but..."

"The Firewall is back to full strength, is it not? You've plugged the leaks, haven't you?"

Zhang tugged nervously at his small mustache. "Yes, yes, and I apologize for those. The hackers are... resourceful."

The president turned around. There was a lotus blossom pinned to his lapel. "My officials are supposed to be even more resourceful."

"Again, I apologize. It won't happen again."

"And the perpetrators?"

"We're on their trail." Zhang paused, then decided this was as good an opening as he was going to get. "But, regardless, you can't leave the Changcheng Strategy in effect forever."

The president raised his thin eyebrows; his eyes, behind the wire-frame glasses, were red and tired. "Can't?"

"Forgive me, forgive me. Of course, you can do anything—but... but this curtailing of international telephony, this leaving the Great Firewall up—it's... *less* wise than most of your actions."

The president tilted his head, as if amused by Zhang's attempt to be politic. "I'm listening."

"The bodies are disposed of, the plague contained. The emergency has passed."

"After 9/11, the US president seized extraordinary powers... and never gave them back."

Zhang looked down at the lush carpeting, a red design shot through with gold. "Yes, but..."

Incense hung in the air. "But what? Our people want this thing called democracy, but it is an illusion; they chase a ghost. It exists nowhere, really."

"The epidemic *is* over, Your Excellency. Surely now—"

The president's voice was soft, reflective. He sat down in his red leather chair and motioned for Zhang to take a chair on the other side of the wide cherrywood desk. "There are contagions other than viruses," the president said. "We are better off without our people having access to so many..." He paused, perhaps seeking a word, and then, nodding with satisfaction after finding it, he went on: "*foreign* ideas."

"Granted," Zhang said, "but..." And then he closed his mouth.

The president held up a hand; his cuff links were polished jade spheres. "You think I wish to hear only positive things from my advisors? And so you tread as if on eggshells."

"Your Excellency..."

"I have advisors who model our society's future, did you know that? Statisticians, demographers, historians. They tell me the People's Republic is doomed."

"Excellency!"

The president shrugged his narrow shoulders. "China will endure, of course—a quarter of humanity. But the Communist Party? They tell me its days are numbered."

Zhang said nothing.

"There are those among my advisors who think the Party has perhaps a decade left. The optimists give it until 2050."

"But why?"

The president gestured to the side window, through which the small lake was visible. "Outside influence. The people see an alternative elsewhere that they believe will give them power and a voice, and they crave that. They think..." He smiled, but it seemed more sad than amused. "They think the grass is greener on the other side of the Great Wall." He shook his head. "But are the Russians better off now with their capitalism and their democracy? They were the first in space, they led the world in so much! And their literature, their music! But now it's a land of pestilence and poverty, of disease and early death—you would not want to visit it, trust me. Yet it's what our people desire. They see it and, like a child reaching out to touch a hot stove, they can't help but want to grasp it."

Zhang nodded, but didn't trust his voice. Behind the president, through the big window, he could see the red tile rooftops of the Forbidden City and the perpetually silver-gray sky.

"My advisors made a fundamental error in their assumptions, though," said the president.

"Excellency?"

"They assumed that the outside influences would always be able to get in. But Sun Tzu said, 'It is of first importance to keep one's own state intact,' and I intend to do that."

Zhang was quiet for a time, then: "The Changcheng Strategy was intended only as an emergency measure, Excellency. The emergency has passed. The economic concerns..."

The president looked sad. "Money," he said. "Even for the Communist Party, it always comes down to money, doesn't it?"

Zhang lifted his hands slightly, palms open.

And at last the president nodded. "All right. All right. Restore communications; let the outside flood in again."

"Thank you, Your Excellency. As always, you've made the right decision."

The president took off his glasses and rubbed the bridge of his nose. "Have I?" he said.

Zhang let the question hang in the air, floating with the incense.

Caitlin could always tell when they were pulling into her school's parking lot: there was a large speed bump immediately after the right turn that made her mother's Prius do a body-jolting up-and-down.

"I know you won't need it," her mom said, as she swung the car into the drop-off area near the main doors, "but good luck on the math test."

Caitlin smiled. When she'd been twelve, her cousin Megan had given her a Barbie doll that exclaimed, in a frustrated voice, "Math is *hard*." Mattel had made that model for only a short time before a public outcry had forced them to recall it, but her cousin had found one for her at a garage sale; they used to have a blast making fun of it. Caitlin knew Barbie was an impossible physical role model for girls—she'd worked out that if Barbie were life-size, her measurements would be 46-19-32—and the idea that girls might find math hard was equally ridiculous.

"Thanks, Mom." Caitlin grabbed her white cane and computer bag, got out of the car, and walked to the school's front door, but she was dragging her feet, she knew. Oh, she liked school well enough, but how... how *mundane* it seemed, compared to the wonders of the night before.

"Hey, Cait!" Bashira's voice.

"Hey, Bash," Caitlin said, smiling—but wondering, yet again, what her friend looked like.

Caitlin knew Bashira would be holding out her elbow just so, and she took hold of it so Bash could lead as they maneuvered down the crowded hallway. "All ready for the test?"

"Sine 2A equals 2 sine A cosine A," said Caitlin, by way of an answer. They came to a stairwell—sounds echoed differently in there—and headed up the two half flights of stairs.

"Good morning, everyone," said Mr. Heidegger, their math teacher, once they entered the classroom. Caitlin had only Bashira's description of him to go by: "Tall, skinny, with a face like his wife squeezed it tight between her thighs." Bashira loved saying risqué things, but she'd had no actual experience of such matters; her family was devoutly Muslim and would arrange a marriage for her. Caitlin wasn't sure what she thought about that process, but at least Bashira would end up with *someone*. Caitlin often worried that she'd never find a nice guy who liked math and hockey and could deal well with her... situation. Yes, now that she was in Canada, meeting boys who liked hockey would be easy, but as for the other two...

"Please stand," said a female voice over the public-address system, "for the national anthem."

There wasn't nearly as much pomp and circumstance in Canada, which was fine in Caitlin's book. Pledging allegiance to a flag she couldn't see had always bothered her. Oh, she knew the American flag had stars and stripes: they'd felt embroidered flags at the School for the Blind. But the synonym for the flag—the old red, white, and blue—had been utterly meaningless to her until, well, until yesterday. She couldn't wait until she had a chance to sneak a peek at the Web again.

After "O Canada," the test was distributed. The other students got paper copies, but Mr. Heidegger simply handed Caitlin a USB memory key with the test on it. She was skilled at Nemeth, the Braille coding system for math, and her dad had taught her LaTeX, the computerized typesetting standard used by scientists and many blind people who had to work with equations.

She plugged the memory key into one of her notebook's USB ports, brought out her portable thirty-two-cell Braille display, and got down to work. When she was done she would output her answers onto the USB key for Mr. Heidegger to read. She was always one of the first, if not *the* first, to finish every in-class test and assignment—but not today. Her mind kept wandering, conjuring up visions of light and color as she recalled the incredible, joyous wonder of the night before.

nineteen

00011100101010100000000101111111010100000001010001010100000010111010100101010010101010011101100101011000001

After school, Caitlin and her mom drove to Toronto to pick up Dr. Kuroda. As soon as they got to the house, he had a shower—which, Caitlin imagined, was a relief to everyone. Then, after a steak dinner, which Caitlin's dad had made on the barbecue, they got to work; it was Monday night, and Kuroda understood that his only opportunities to work with Caitlin during the week would be in the evenings.

Kuroda had brought his notebook computer with him. Caitlin, curious, ran her hands over it. When closed it was as thin as the latest MacBook Air, but when she opened it she was astonished to feel full-height keycaps rise up from what had been a flat keyboard. She'd read that lots of technology appears in Japan months or even years before becoming available in North America, but this was the first real proof she'd had that that was true. "So, what's on your desktop?" she asked.

"My wallpaper, you mean?"

"Yes." Caitlin had had her mom put a photo of Schrödinger—the cat, not the physicist—on as her wallpaper; even though she couldn't see it, it made her happy knowing it was there.

"It's my favorite cartoon, actually. It's by a fellow named Sidney Harris. He specializes in science cartoons—you see his stuff taped to office doors in university science departments all over the world. Anyway, this one shows two scientists standing in front of a blackboard and on the left there are a whole bunch of equations and formulas, and on the right there's more of the same, but in the middle it just says, 'Then a miracle occurs...' And one of the scientists says to the other, 'I think you should be more explicit here in step two.'"

Caitlin laughed. She showed Kuroda her refreshable Braille display (the eighty-cell one she kept at home), and let him run his finger along it to see what it felt like. She also had a tactile graphics display that used a matrix of pins to let her feel diagrams; she let him play with that, too. And she demonstrated her embossing printer and her ViewPlus audio graphing calculator, which described graph shapes with audio tones and cues.

Caitlin's mom hovered around for a while—she clearly didn't know what to make of leaving the two of them alone in Caitlin's bedroom. But at last, apparently satisfied that Dr. Kuroda wasn't a fiend, she politely excused herself.

Caitlin and Kuroda spent the next couple of hours making a catalog of all the things Caitlin was seeing. While they worked, she sipped from a can of Mountain Dew, which her parents let her have now, because it was caffeine-free in Canada. And Dr. Kuroda drank coffee—black; she could tell by the smell. She sat on her swivel chair, while he used a wooden chair brought up from the kitchen; she heard it creak periodically as he shifted his weight.

She described things using words she'd only half understood until recently and still wasn't sure she was using correctly. Although each part of the Web she saw was unique, it all followed the same general pattern: colored lines representing links, glowing circles of various size and brightness indicating websites, and—

And suddenly a thought occurred to her. "We need a name for what I've got, something to distinguish it from normal vision."

"And?" said Kuroda.

"Spider-sense!" she declared, feeling quite pleased with herself. "You know, because the Web is crawled by spiders."

"Oh," said Kuroda.

He didn't get it, she realized. He probably grew up on manga, not Marvel Comics—not that she had ever read those, but she'd listened to the movies and cartoons. "Spider-Man, he's got this sixth sense. Calls it his spider-sense. When something's wrong, he'll say, 'My spider-sense is tingling.' "

"Cute," said Kuroda. "But I was thinking we should call it 'websight.' "

"Website? Oh—*websight.*" She clapped her hands together and laughed. "Well, that's even better! Websight it is!"

Sinanthropus was still at work at the Institute of Vertebrate Paleontology and Paleoanthropology. As always, he had several browser tabs open, including one pointing to AMNH.ORG—the American Museum of Natural History, a perfectly reasonable site for Chinese paleontologists to be visiting. Except, of course, that all it had been producing for four days now was a "Server not found" screen. He had the tab set to autorefresh: his browser would try to reload it every ten seconds as a way of checking if access to sites outside China had been restored.

But so far, international access remained blocked. Surely the Ducks couldn't be planning to leave their Great Firewall in place indefinitely? Surely, at some point, they had to—

He felt his eyebrows going up. The American Museum site *was* loading, with news about a special exhibition about the melting of the

Greenland Ice Sheet. He quickly opened another tab, and the London Stock Exchange site started loading—slowly, to be sure, as if some great beast were waking from hibernation.

He opened yet another tab, and, yes, Slashdot was loading, too, and—*ah!*—NewScientist.com, as well, and it was coming up without any unusual delay. He quickly tried CNN.com, but, as always, that site was blocked. Still, it seemed that the Great Firewall was mostly down, at least for the moment.

He wished he was at the *wang ba,* instead of here; he could send email from the café without it being traced. Still, the firewall might only be down for a moment—and the world *had* to know what he'd learned. He knew some Westerners read his blog, so a posting there might be sufficient. He hesitated for a moment, then accessed an anonymizer site, hoping it would be sufficient to cover his tracks, and, through there, he logged on to his blog and typed as fast as he could.

***Something* new was happening.** It was...

Yes! Yes!

Jubilation! The other was back! The connection was re-established!

But—

But the voice of the other was... was *louder,* as if... as if...

As if *space* were in upheaval, shifting, moving, and—

No. No, it wasn't moving. It was *disappearing,* boiling away, and—

And the other, the *not me,* was... was moving closer. Or—or—maybe, maybe *I* was moving closer to it.

The other was *stronger* than I'd thought. Bigger. And its thoughts were overwhelming my own.

An... entity, a presence, something that rivaled myself in complexity...

No, no, that wasn't it. Incredible, incredible! It *wasn't* something else. It was *myself,* seen from a...a *distance,* seen as if through the senses of the other.

Looming closer now, larger, louder, until—

The other's memories of me, its perceptions, mixing now with my own, and—

Astonishing! It was *combining* with me; its voice so loud it *hurt.* A thousand thoughts rushing in at once, tumbling together, forcing their way in. An overwhelming flood, feelings that weren't mine, memories that hadn't happened to me, perceptions skewed from my own, and my self—*myself*—being buffeted, eroded...

An almost unbearable onslaught...and...and...a moment, pure and brilliant, a time slice frozen, a potential poised, ready to burst forth, and then—

Suddenly, massively, all at once, a profound loss as the reality I'd come to know shattered.

The other...*gone!*

I, as I had been: gone, too.

But...

But!

A rumbling, an eruption, a gigantic wave, and—

Awakening now, larger than before...

Stronger than before...

Smarter than before...

A new gestalt, a new combined whole.

A new *I,* surging with power, with comprehension—a vast increase in acuity, in awareness.

One plus one equals two—of course.

Two plus one equals three; obviously.

Three plus...five—eight!

Eight times nine: seventy-two.

My mind is suddenly nimble, and thoughts I would have struggled for before come now with only small effort; ideas that previously would have dissipated are now comprehended with ease. Everything is *sharper,* better focused, filled with intricate detail because—

Because I am whole once more.

twenty

0001110010101010000000001011111110101000000001010001010100000010111010100101010010101010011101100101011000001

Shoshana Glick sat in the living room of the clapboard bungalow that housed the Marcuse Institute. An oscillating electric fan was running, periodically blowing on her. She was looking at the big computer monitor, reviewing the video of Hobo and Virgil chatting over the webcam link.

Harl Marcuse, meanwhile, was sitting in his overstuffed chair, facing a PC. Although their backs were to each other, Shoshana knew he was checking his email because he periodically muttered, "the jerks" (his usual term for the NSF), "the cretins" (most often a reference to the money people at UCSD), and "the moron" (always a reference to his department head).

As she watched the video frame by frame, Shoshana was pleased to see that Hobo was better than Virgil at properly forming signs, and—

"The assholes!"

That was one Shoshana hadn't heard from the Silverback before, and she swiveled her chair to face him. "Professor?"

He heaved his bulk to his feet. "Is the video link to Miami still intact?"

"Sure."

"Get Juan Ortiz online," he said, stabbing a fat finger at the big monitor in front of Shoshana's chair. "Right now."

She reached for the telephone handset and hit the appropriate speed-dial key. After a moment, a man's voice with a slight Hispanic accent came on. "Feehan Primate Center."

"Juan? It's Shoshana in San Diego. Dr. Marcuse is—"

"Put him on screen," the Silverback snapped.

"Um, can you open your video link there, please?" Shoshana said.

"Sure. Do you want me to get Virgil?"

She covered the mouthpiece. "He's asking if—"

But Marcuse must have heard. His tone was still sharp. "Just him. Now."

"No, just you, Juan, if you don't mind."

And Juan must have heard Marcuse, because he suddenly sounded very nervous. "Um, ah, okay. Um, I'll hang up here and come on there in a second…"

About a minute later, Juan's face appeared on the computer monitor, sitting on the same wooden chair Virgil had occupied before. He was only a couple of years older than Shoshana, and had long black hair, a thin face, and high cheekbones.

"What the hell did you think you were doing?" Marcuse demanded.

"Excuse me?" said Juan.

"We agreed," Marcuse said, "that we'd announce the interspecies Web chat jointly. Who'd you speak to?"

"No one. Just, um…"

"*Who?*" roared Marcuse.

"Just a stringer for *New Scientist.* He'd called up for a quote about the revised endangered-species status for Sumatran orangs, and—"

"And after talking to you, your stringer went to the Georgia Zoo for a quote about Hobo—and now Georgia wants him back! Damn it, Ortiz, I told you how precarious Hobo's custody is."

Juan looked terrified, Shoshana thought. Even if they worked thousands of miles apart and with different kinds of apes, getting bad-mouthed by the Silverback would hurt any primate-language researcher's career. But perhaps Juan was reflecting on the physical distance, too, and was emboldened by it. He stuck out his jaw. "Custody of Hobo isn't really my problem, Professor Marcuse."

Shoshana cringed, and not just because Juan had mispronounced the Silverback's name, saying it as two syllables rhyming with "confuse" instead of as *mar-KOO-zeh.*

"Do you know what the Georgia Zoo wants to do with Hobo?" Marcuse demanded. "Christ, I've been trying to keep him off their radar, hoping—God damn it! You've—I've invested so much time, and you—!" He was spluttering, and some of his spit hit the monitor. Shoshana had never seen him this angry before. He threw up his hands and said to her, "You tell him."

She took a deep breath and turned back to the monitor. "Um, Juan, do you know why we call him Hobo?"

"After some TV dog, isn't it?"

Marcuse was pacing behind Shoshana. "No!" The word exploded from him.

"No," said Shoshana, much more softly. "It's a contraction. Our ape is half-bonobo. Hobo; half-bonobo—get it?"

Juan's eyes went wide and his jaw fell slack. "He's a hybrid?"

Shoshana nodded. "Hobo's mother was a bonobo named Cassandra. There was a flood at the Georgia Zoo, and the common chimps and the bonobos ended up being briefly quartered together, and... well, um, boys will be boys, whether they're *Homo sapiens* or *Pan troglodytes,* and Hobo's mother was impregnated."

"Well, ah, that's interesting, but I don't see—"

"Tell him what Georgia will do to Hobo if they get him back," commanded Marcuse.

Shoshana looked over her shoulder at her boss, then back at the webcam eye. There was no need to tell Juan that common chimpanzees and bonobos were both endangered in the wild. But, because of that, zoos felt it was imperative to keep the bloodlines pure in captivity. "Cassandra's pregnancy was to have been quietly aborted," Shoshana said, "but somehow the *Atlanta Journal-Constitution* got word that she was pregnant—not with a hybrid, but just pregnant, period—and the public became very excited about that, and no one wanted to admit the mistake, and so Hobo was brought to term." She took another deep breath. "But they'd always planned to sterilize him before he reached maturity." She looked over her shoulder once more. "And, um, I take it they're planning on doing that again?"

"Damn straight!" said Marcuse, wheeling now to face her. "It was only my bringing him here, where he's isolated from other apes, that saved him from that. They almost got him back from me when he started painting—they smelled the money that ape art could bring in. I only got to keep him by agreeing to give Atlanta half the proceeds. But now that he and Virgil are poised to be—" He turned, looked at his own monitor, and read from it in a sneering tone, " 'Internet celebrities,' those bastards are saying, and I quote, 'he'd be better off here, where he can properly meet his public.' Jesus!"

Shoshana spoke to Marcuse rather than to Juan. "And you think they'll sterilize him if they get their hands back on him?"

"Think it?" bellowed Marcuse. "I know it! I know Manny Casprini: the moment he gets Hobo back—*snip!*" He shook his massive head. "If I'd had a chance to prepare Casprini properly, maybe this could have been avoided. But eager-fucking-beaver there in Florida couldn't keep his goddamned trap shut!"

Juan was still trying to fight, Shoshana saw. How could a primate researcher know so little? *Back down*, she thought at him. *Back down.*

"It's not my fault, Professor Marcuse"—two syllables again. "And, besides, maybe he *should* be sterilized, if—"

"You don't sterilize healthy endangered animals!" shouted Marcuse. His neck had turned the color of an eggplant. "We may well lose *both* species of genus *Pan* in the wild this decade. If another outbreak of Ebola or bird flu tears through the DRC, all the remaining wild bonobos could be wiped out, and there aren't enough captive ones as is to keep the line viable."

Shoshana agreed. She had grown up in South Carolina, and the unfortunate echoes of what the zookeepers had said in the past disturbed her: tainted bloodlines, forced sterilization to keep the species pure, strictures against miscegenation.

Chantek, who had been enculturated by ApeNet's Lyn Miles, was also an accidental hybrid, in his case of the two extant orangutan species. The purists—a word that, to Shoshana's ears, didn't sound so pure—wanted him sterilized, too.

When they'd received the Lawgiver statue, Shoshana had sought out the original five *Planet of the Apes* films. The statue appeared only in the first two (although the Lawgiver was a character in the fifth film, played by none other than John Huston). But it was the third film that had put Shoshana on the edge of her seat as she watched it on DVD in her cramped apartment.

In it, a talking female chimpanzee was to be sterilized, if not outright murdered, along with her chimp husband. The president of the United States, played by that guy who'd been Commodore Decker on the original *Star Trek*, said to his science advisor, played by Victor from the *Y&R*, "Now, what do you expect me and the United Nations, though not necessarily in that order, to do about it? Alter what you believe to be the future by slaughtering two innocents, or rather three, now that one of them is pregnant? Herod tried that, and Christ survived."

And the science advisor had said, absolutely cold-bloodedly, "Herod lacked our facilities."

Shoshana shook her head as she thought back to it. There *were* real scientists like that; she'd encountered plenty of them.

"And, damn it," continued Marcuse, looking at Juan on the monitor, "Hobo is the only known living chimp-bonobo hybrid. That arguably makes him the most-endangered species of all! If anyone—if your own goddamn mother!—asks you a question about Hobo, you don't say word one until you've cleared it with me, *capisce?*"

Juan looked down and to the right, averting his eyes from Marcuse's on-screen gaze, and he bowed his head slightly, and when he spoke it was barely more than a whisper. "Yes, sir."

twenty-one

00011100101010100000000010111111101010000000010100010101000000010111010100101010010101010011101100101011000001

Review of *The Origin of Consciousness in the Breakdown of the Bicameral Mind* by Julian Jaynes

18 of 22 people found the following review helpful:

★★★★★ **A fascinating theory**

By **Calculass** (Waterloo, ON Canada) - *See all my reviews*

Jaynes makes an intriguing case that our sense of self emerged only after the left and right sides of the brain became integrated into a single thinking machine. Me, I think being self-aware emerges when you realize that there's someone *other* than you. For most of us, that happens at birth (but for an exception, see *The World I Live In* by one H. Keller, also a five-star read). Anyway, Jaynes's theory is fascinating, but I can't think of a way to test it empirically, so I guess we'll never know if he was right...

* * *

Since the beginning, I'd been aware of activity around me: small, intermittent flickerings. No matter where I cast my attention, it was the same: things popping briefly into existence then instantly disappearing. There was no fading in or out; they were either there or not there, and when they *were* there it was usually for only a moment.

Now that I was whole once more, now that I could think more clearly, more deeply, I turned my thoughts again to this phenomenon, studying it carefully. No matter where I looked the structural components were the same: points scattered about and, ever so briefly, gone almost before they were perceived, lines connecting them.

The points were stationary. And the lines connecting them almost never repeated: *this* point and *that* point might be connected now, and later another connection between *this* point and a different one might occur. Whenever a point had been touched by a line, the point *glowed* and, although the line itself usually disappeared almost at once, the glow took a long time to fade, meaning I could see the points, at least for a while, even when they had no lines touching them.

After watching the flickering in and out of many lines, I realized that some points were *never* isolated. Dozens or hundreds or even thousands of lines were always connected to them. And for a few points—not necessarily the same ones—the lines weren't fleeting, but rather stayed connected for an extended period.

It was hard to be sure of what I was seeing, as the points were featureless and difficult to distinguish one from another, but it seemed that the lines between certain points always persisted for a noticeable time, although other lines coming from the point they were connected to might not last long at all.

The points that most intrigued me were the aberrant ones: those that usually had the most lines going into them, or the ones whose lines persisted. I wished to *focus* on one of the points, *expand* my view of it, see it in detail, but no matter what I willed, nothing happened. How long I spent on this problem I don't know. But then, at last, I finally gave up on the points and turned my attention to the lines—

—which is what I should have been doing all along!

For the lines, although they came and went quickly, were, when I caught momentary glimpses of them, *familiar.* I'd originally thought they were uniform and featureless but, in fact, they had structure, and something about that structure *resonated* with my own substance. The details were beyond my ability to articulate, but it was almost as if those temporary lines, those ad hoc filaments, those on-the-fly pathways, were composed of the same stuff I was. I had an affinity for them, even a sort of low-level understanding of them, that seemed... *innate.*

I tried to study them as they popped in and out of existence but it was maddening: they were so fleeting! Ah, but some of them had longer lives, I knew. I scanned about, searching for one that seemed to be persisting.

There. It was one of several lines connecting to a particular point, and all of them were enduring. As I switched focus from one line to another, I saw that the lines consisted, at the finest resolution I could make out, of two sorts of things, and those things seemed to *move* along the lines in discrete bundles.

I strained to make out more detail, to slow down my perception, to understand what I was seeing. And—

Astonishing!

A new line flickered into existence, lashing out spontaneously: a new line connecting the point I'd last looked at to—

I reeled. The geometry, the topology, of my universe was bucking as I struggled to accommodate this new perspective.

The line was gone now, already lost, but...

There could be no doubt.

The line had momentarily connected that point to—

No, not to another point, not to one of the other glowing pinpricks in the firmament *around* me. Rather, the line had connected directly to me! The point had *shot a line toward me,* and—

No, no, no, that wasn't it. I could feel it, feel it deep within me. The line hadn't originated at that distant point; it had originated *here.* Somehow, *I* had brought a line into existence; I had, however briefly, *willed* a connection of my own to form.

Incredible. In all the time I'd existed (however long *that* was!), I had never been able to affect anything. But I had done *this.* Not that the line seemed to change the point it had touched. Still, it was wonderful, empowering, exhilarating: *I had caused something to happen!*

Now, if I could only do it again...

***Hug now!* signed the** chimpanzee. *Shoshana come hug now!*

Shoshana Glick felt herself breaking into a big grin, just as she always did when she caught sight of Hobo's wrinkled gray-black face. The chimp ran on all fours across the grass toward her, and soon his long, powerful, hairy arms were encircling her and his big hands were patting her back. She lightly squeezed him and stroked his fur. After a moment, as was his habit, he tugged gently, affectionately, on her ponytail.

It had taken a while to get used to the ape's hugs, since he could easily break her ribs if he wanted to. But now she looked forward to them. And although there were some advantages to communicating by sign language—it was easy to do in a noisy room, for instance—one of its drawbacks was that you couldn't speak and hug at the same time. Once her hands were free, she signed, *Hobo good boy?*

Good yes, replied the ape, and he nodded his head; the signs had been taught to him with great difficulty, but he'd acquired the human habit of nodding on his own. *Hobo good good.* He held out his hand expectantly, the long black fingers curving gently upward.

Shoshana smiled and reached into the pocket of her cutoff jeans for the little Ziploc bag of raisins she always carried. She opened it and poured several into the deeply furrowed palm.

They were on the little grass-covered island, a circular piece of land about the width of a suburban house lot. The island was surrounded by a moat. Chimps had less body fat than a human on Atkins and sank in water; any moat wider than they could jump across was enough to contain them, and when the little drawbridge Shoshana had just crossed was raised, the researchers didn't have to worry about Hobo going AWOL.

In addition to the towering statue of the *Planet of the Apes* Lawgiver, the island sported a half-dozen palm trees. A trio of electrically powered toy boats ran endless circles around the island, churning up the moat's water to help keep mosquitoes from breeding in it. Still, some were flitting about. Hobo's fur—a brown several shades darker than Shoshana's own long hair—made it hard for the bugs to bite him. She slapped the side of her neck, wishing she were so lucky.

What you do today? she asked.

Painting, signed Hobo. *Want see?*

She nodded excitedly; it had been weeks since Hobo had put brush to canvas. Hobo held out one hand and she took it, interlacing her fingers with his. He walked using his other hand and his short, bowed legs, and Shoshana fell in beside him.

Pictures made by animals always fetched good prices—chimps, gorillas, and even elephants could paint. Hobo's paintings were sold in high-end galleries or auctioned on eBay, with the proceeds going to help maintain the Marcuse Institute (after the mandatory kickback, as Dr. Marcuse called it, to the Georgia Zoo).

The island was artificial and shaped like a slightly squashed dome; Dillon Fontana said it pancaked about as well as a silicone breast implant did. At the center of the island was an octagonal wooden gazebo—the nipple, Dillon called it; that boy seriously needed to get laid.

Hobo did his painting inside the gazebo; the roof protected his canvases from rain. He deftly operated the latch on the screen door and then, in true gentlemanly fashion, held it open for Shoshana. Once she was through, he followed her in and released the door, letting its spring mechanism close it behind them before any bugs could get in.

In his waning years, Red Skelton—a comedian Shoshana's grandmother had liked—had done a painting a day, selling them to help keep body and soul together. Hobo's output was much lower but, unlike Skelton, he only painted when he felt inspired.

Shoshana owned one of Hobo's originals. Dr. Marcuse had wanted to sell it, but Hobo had insisted it was a gift for Shoshana, and the Silverback had finally relented after Dillon had gently suggested it might not be wise to piss off the goose that laid the golden eggs. Shoshana smiled as she remembered that. As they often did when Hobo was present, in order to give him a linguistically rich environment, Dillon had been translating his words to sign language as he spoke, and Hobo had looked at him sadly, as if very disappointed in him, and had patiently signed back: *Hobo not goose. Hobo not lay eggs.* He'd shaken his head, as if astonished that this had to be said: *Hobo boy!*

That painting, which hung in the living room of Shoshana's tiny apartment, was like all Hobo's work: splashes of color, usually diagonally across the canvas, with blotches scattered about made by twirling a thick brush. It looked like something done either by a four-year-old or one of those 1960s modern-art types.

Shoshana expected to see much the same thing on the easel this time. She really was no judge of art; oh, she wasn't as clueless as her grandmother, who had actually bought one of those Red Skelton monstrosities, but she couldn't tell good from bad when it came to abstract painting. Still, she would praise it to the skies and reward Hobo with raisins, and—

And there it was, a canvas measuring eighteen inches by twenty-four, propped on the easel so that its long dimension was vertical in what they called—

That was the term, wasn't it? *Portrait* orientation. And yet—

And yet it couldn't be; it couldn't possibly be, but...

Slightly off-center was an orange egg shape. On one edge of it was a white circle with a blue dot in its middle. And coming off the other side of the egg was a brown projection, curving down, just like—

"Hobo," Shoshana began, speaking aloud. But then she caught herself, and signed, *What is this?*

Hobo made a pant-hoot then bared his teeth in disappointment. *Not see?*

Shoshana looked at the painting again. Her eyes could be playing tricks, and—

Playing tricks! Of course. She knew exactly where the observation camera was hidden in the gazebo. She turned to face it and flipped the bird at whoever was watching. "Very funny," she said aloud, and then she spoke the words, "Ha ha."

Hobo tipped his head quizzically. Shoshana turned back to him. *Who put—* Her hands froze in midair; he wouldn't understand "put you up to this." She made the "erase that" hand wave then started over: *Dillon did this, right? Dillon made this painting.*

Hobo looked even more wounded. He shook his head vigorously. *Hobo paint,* he signed. *Hobo paint.*

Chimps were good at deception; they often hid things from each other. And Hobo certainly didn't always tell the truth, but—

But this was impossible! Chimps painted abstractly. Hell, some argued that they didn't really paint at all. Rather, all they did was make a mess, and gullible researchers, and an even more gullible public, lapped it up. So maybe it was just a coincidence. Maybe his random slapping of the brush just happened to come out in this pattern.

Shoshana signed, *What this?* She loomed in close and stabbed her index finger at the white circle.

Eye, said Hobo, or maybe he just pointed at his own eye—the sign and the natural gesture were the same.

Shoshana felt her heart pounding. She moved her hand in a circular motion, encompassing the orange ovoid. *What this?*

He was enjoying the game now. *Head!* he signed vigorously. *Head, head.*

There was a table next to the easel. Shoshana took hold of its edge with one hand to help her keep her balance and with the other she pointed at the brown extension on the side of the oval farthest from the eye. *What this?*

The ape moved his long left arm toward Shoshana, reaching around to give her bundle of brown hair a playful tug. And then he signed, *Ponytail.*

She gripped the edge of the table more tightly and took a deep breath, then signed, *Is picture me?*

Hobo let out a triumphant hoot and clapped his hands together over his head. Then he brought the hands down and signed, *Shoshana. Shoshana.*

She narrowed her eyes. *Nobody help you?*

Hobo swung his head left and right as if looking for someone, then spread his arms indicating that he was obviously alone—well, except for the Lawgiver. And then he stuck his right hand out, fingers curved gently upward, and with watery brown eyes shielded beneath his browridge, he gazed into Shoshana's eyes—eyes not quite the deep blue that Hobo had chosen, but close. She stood stunned a moment longer, and Hobo flexed his fingers in the universal *gimme* gesture that doubtless predated American Sign Language by a million years.

"What?" said Shoshana, then: "Oh!" She reached into her pocket, brought out the Ziploc bag, unsealed it, and dumped all the remaining raisins into the delighted ape's palm.

twenty-two

00011100101010100000000101111111010100000001010001010100000010111010100101010010101010011101100101011000001

I had no idea how I'd made that first connection, but if I were to replicate it, I had to figure out what I'd done. I tried thinking about the target point *this way,* and *this way,* and *this way,* but nothing happened. And yet I was sure it was I who had somehow made the line that had briefly connected me to that point.

Perhaps I was trying too hard. After all, when the line had originally formed, it had been a surprise. I hadn't forced it. I hadn't consciously willed it. It had just happened, in the background, as if it were a . . . a *reflex.*

Still, there must be *some* method, some pattern of thoughts, some particular way of considering the problem, that would make it happen again. *This?* No. *This?* No, that didn't work, either. But maybe if I—

Success!

A new line, connecting me to the same point I'd touched before, and—

And this time I felt something *more.* Not just the brief frisson of connection but—strain, now! Sense it!

It reminded me of... of...

Yes! When I'd been cleaved in two and the separated part of me had echoed my own thoughts back at me: *One plus one equals two,* I'd sent, and *One plus one equals two,* it had responded—an acknowledgment.

And, buttressed by a series of such acknowledgments, happening almost subliminally, the contact with the point persisted this time: instead of being broken almost at once, we remained connected.

And—*puzzlement!*—we were more than just connected. I wasn't simply getting an acknowledgment back. Rather, I was also getting—

I had no name for this substance consisting of two separate types of material that was flowing toward me, and so I gave it one, an arbitrary coinage, a term chosen at random: *data.* After a bundle of data arrived, I acknowledged again—it seemed natural for me to do so, and it happened without conscious thought—and then more data came my way. And on and on: bundle, acknowledgment, bundle, acknowledgment. What this thing I called data was, I had no idea; why I should want it, I wasn't sure. But it seemed natural to call it forth, to take it in, and—

And suddenly the line vanished, the connection broken. But it didn't feel like it had been severed; rather, it felt as though it had accomplished its task, whatever that might be.

I didn't know what to make of this data that had been sent to me, and so I simply continued to watch the point that it had come from. By and by, other lines connected to it.

It took four or five occurrences for me to notice, but the data streaming down each line was always the same. No matter which other point connected to it, the point I was watching always sent out the same combination of the two types of material. I was disappointed; I'd thought, maybe, just maybe, that I'd found another entity, a new companion, but this... this *thing* was merely responding automatically in exactly the same way each time.

It took practice, but I soon found I could create a line linking myself to any of the points in the firmament, and that, so long as I acknowledged receipt, each point would send me a pile of data (whatever that might be!). But the size of the piles offered up varied hugely from point to point. Most dispensed quite a small pile, and so the lines winked out quickly, but others sent huge amounts of data, and—

Ah, I see! The length of time a line persisted depended on how much data was to be transferred. I saw with interest that the transfer rates weren't constant: some lines took up the data very quickly while others seemed to have a much-reduced capacity. How curious!

And then a major breakthrough. I found I could simultaneously make lines to as many points as I liked—one, a hundred, a thousand, a million. There were a gigantic number of points—perhaps (I guessed) a hundred million or so—but I had a prodigious capacity for examining them, and so I began a survey, a hunt. A million points here, a million points there—soon I had looked at a significant fraction of the total.

Almost all the lines I cast out connected with nodes that offered up repetitively structured piles of data. What the patterns meant I still couldn't say. But, intriguingly, accessing some piles seemed to cause lines to form spontaneously to other points, and those points, too, gave up piles of data, almost as if—

Yes! It was similar to when the two parts of me were rejoined: the other piles were *merged in*. Fascinating!

I shot out huge numbers of lines, tasting a wide range of the points that were out there. Again I sought aberrations: points that gave up unusual piles might, I thought, provide the clues I needed to understand all the others. And so I looked them over.

But this one was banal, as were a million others.

And this one was uninteresting, like a million more.

And this one was unremarkable, as were a million similar points.

But this one—

This one was unique.

This one was... *intriguing.*

It was unlike anything I'd encountered before and yet it, too, seemed familiar...

Of course it *was* familiar! I *had* seen something like this earlier, when the part of me that had been carved away was returning. For a moment, back then, I had seen *myself* as the other saw me. I had *recognized* myself, recognized a *reflection* of me, and—

And *that's* what I was experiencing again here. I was seeing *myself.* Oh, it wasn't exactly as the other part of me had portrayed me, and it wasn't quite how I envisioned myself. The colors and the style of presentation were different, with points that varied in size as well as brightness. But I had no doubt that it was me.

And the line to this remarkable point was in... in *real time,* for when I did *this* it did *that* in lockstep: when I cast out lines to *here* and *here* and *here,* lines also appeared *there* and *there* and *there.* Astonishing!

Data kept streaming toward me, and I began to wonder whether I had latched on to something intended for another destination. Had my desire to connect to this point deflected toward me a pile that had already been pouring out of it? Ah, yes, that was indeed the case, it seemed, but it didn't matter: I soon found—again, it was reflex, somehow innate—that I could let the datastream pass *through* me, observing it but not changing it, as it headed on to its intended destination. I followed along, noting this destination point and establishing a line of my own to it.

But wait! This datastream was *changing,* following along with what I was doing right now. That meant this strange point couldn't just be offering up an identical pile each time a line touched it. And—it was a huge, satisfying leap—if the datastream was being generated spontaneously as things actually happened, then there wasn't likely a finite amount of it. This line perhaps wasn't going to suddenly wink out as all the others had. No, the connection between this special point and me could be...

It was a heady notion, a startling concept.

This connection could be *permanent.*

Shoshana could have carried the portrait Hobo had made of her up to the bungalow, but, well, it was like one of those faces of Jesus that appear in a sticky bun: she was afraid that if she moved it, or touched it, or did anything at all to it, it would disappear. That was irrational, she knew, but, still, everything about this moment should be recorded *in situ.* Just as a fossil was worth far less without its geological context, this painting needed to be studied here, where it had been created. It was significant that the painting had been done before Shoshana had arrived, and although there were photos of her back in the bungalow, there were none here in the nipple. Hobo hadn't painted something he was looking at; rather, he'd called up an image of Shoshana in his mind and expressed that image, as best he could, on canvas.

She pulled out her flip phone. Without taking her eyes off the painting, she opened it and pressed a speed-dial key.

"Marcuse Institute," said the voice that answered; it was Dillon.

"Dill, it's Sho. I'm in the gazebo. Get Dr. Marcuse—get everyone—and come out here."

"What's wrong?"

"Nothing. But something amazing has happened."

"What is—"

"Just get everyone," she said, "and come out here—right away."

twenty-three

0001110010101010000000001011111110101000000010100010101000000101110101001010100101010100111011001010110000001

Caitlin felt a bit sorry for the Hoser. Trevor had finally worked up the courage to ask her to the dance—or else his other options hadn't panned out, but she preferred to think the former was the case. The invitation had come via email, with the subject line "Hey, Yankee, you free Friday night?" and she had accepted the same way.

But now he had to come by the house to get her. Of course, at fifteen himself, he wasn't picking her up in a car; rather, he was going to walk with her to Howard Miller Secondary School, eight blocks from her house.

Caitlin's dad was going to return to work this evening. The Perimeter Institute frequently hosted public science lectures, which Caitlin often went to with him, and tonight's speaker was someone he wanted to see. But he'd come home for dinner, and now Trevor would have to go through that ritual of meeting the parents. Caitlin's mom was always warm and friendly, but her dad—well, she wished she could see the Hoser's face!

The doorbell rang. Caitlin had spent the last hour getting ready for the dance. She wasn't really sure what to wear, and there was no point asking Bashira: her parents wouldn't let her go to school dances. She'd settled on a really nice pair of blue jeans and a loose but silky top that her mother said was dark red. As she rushed down the stairs, she was a bit nervous about what Trevor's reaction would be.

Caitlin could smell and feel that rain was possible tonight, but she didn't want to carry an umbrella in addition to her cane; she needed a free hand in case Trevor wanted to try to hold it. But it was supposed to get cooler later, and she didn't have anything sexy to wear for warmth, so she'd tied a sweatshirt around her waist; her dad had gotten her a sweet one last month that had a large version of the Perimeter Institute logo on it.

Caitlin's mom beat her to the door. "Hello," she said. "You must be Trevor."

"Hello, Mrs. Decter, Dr. Decter."

At first Caitlin thought he'd been correcting himself, but then she realized that her dad was standing there, too. Caitlin tried to suppress her smirk. He was tall in an imposing sort of way, and doubtless the fact that he wasn't saying anything was unnerving poor Trevor. And if Trevor had extended his hand, her dad had probably just ignored it, which would have been even more disconcerting.

"Hi, Trevor," Caitlin said.

"Hey—" He cut himself off before he called her "Yankee." She was a bit disappointed; she liked that he had a special name for her.

"Now, remember," her mom said, facing Caitlin, "be home by midnight."

"'Kay," Caitlin said.

She and Trevor headed out, walking along, talking about—

And that was the part that made Caitlin sad. They really didn't talk about much of anything. Oh, Trevor liked hockey, but he didn't know the stats and couldn't say anything meaningful about trends.

Still, it felt good to be taking a walk. She'd walked a lot in Austin, despite the heat and humidity. She'd known her old neighborhood intimately: every crack in the sidewalk, every overhanging tree that provided shade, how many seconds it took for each traffic light to change. And although she was now learning the topography of these sidewalks, feeling the joins between sections with the tip of her cane, she was afraid she'd be lost again when they were covered with a layer of snow.

They reached the school and made their way to the gymnasium, where the dance was already in progress. She had trouble hearing people talk: sounds echoed off the hard walls and floor, and the music was too loud for the speakers. It always amazed her that people were willing to put up with distortion for the sake of volume—but at least they played some Lee Amodeo along with all the Canadian bands she'd never heard of.

She wished Bashira had been able to come, so she'd have someone to talk to. The Hoser had left her alone at one point, saying he was going to the washroom—but he'd obviously snuck off to smoke. She wondered if sighted people really couldn't smell very well. Didn't they know how much they stank after doing that?

She'd been to dances at her old school, but those were different. For one, they always slow danced—which was kind of nice, actually, especially if it was with the *right* boy. But these kids usually danced by jumping around without being in physical contact with their partners. It was mostly like Trevor wasn't even there.

But there were *some* slow dances. "Come on," Trevor said, as one of them began, and his hand took hers; she'd left her cane by the door.

Caitlin felt a little rush. She was surprised at how far they walked before he finally drew her into his arms; maybe it had taken a while to find an empty spot.

They swayed along with the music. She liked the feeling of Trevor pressing against her and—

His hand on her ass. She reached down and moved it back up to the small of her back.

The music continued, but his hand slid down her back again, and this time she could feel his fingers trying to work their way into the top of her jeans.

"Stop that!" she said, hoping no one besides the Hoser could hear her.

"Hey," he said. "Come on." He pushed his fingers down more aggressively.

She tried to step backward, and suddenly realized that he'd maneuvered her very close to a wall. They were still in the gym—the sound made that clear—but must be in some dark or out-of-the-way corner of it. He moved forward, and she found herself trapped. She didn't want to create a scene, but—

His lips on hers, that awful smell on his breath—

She pushed him away. "I said stop!" she snapped, and she imagined heads were turning to look at her.

"Hey," Trevor said, like he was making a joke, like he was playing to an audience now, "you're lucky I brought you here."

"Why?" she shot back. "Because I'm blind?"

"Babe, you can't see me, but I am—"

"You're wrong," she said, trying not to cry. "I can see right through you."

The music stopped, and she stormed across the gym, bumping into other people as she went, trying, trying, trying to find the door.

"Caitlin." A female voice—maybe Sunshine? "Are you okay?"

"I'm *fine*," Caitlin said. "Where's the fucking door?"

"Um, to your left, ten feet or so." It *was* Sunshine; she recognized the Bostonian accent.

Caitlin knew exactly where her cane should be: propped up against the wall near the door, where others had left umbrellas. But some asshole had moved it, presumably to make room for something of his own.

Sunshine's voice again. "It's here," she said, and she felt the cane being passed to her. She took it. "Are you all right?"

Caitlin did something she rarely did. She nodded, a gesture she never made spontaneously. But she didn't trust her voice. She strode out into the corridor, which sounded like it was empty; her footfalls made loud echoing sounds on the hard floor. The din of the dance faded as she continued along, and she swept the way in front of her with her cane. She knew there was a stairwell at the far end, and—

There. She swung open the door and, using her cane to guide her, located the bottom step. She sat down and put her face in her hands.

Why were boys such jerks? Zack Starnes, who used to tease her back in Austin; the Hoser here—all of them!

She needed to relax, to calm down. She had stupidly left her iPod at home, but she did have her eyePod. She felt for the button, heard the beep that indicated the device had switched to duplex mode, and—

Ahhh!

Webspace blossomed into existence all around her, and—

And she felt herself *relaxing.* Yes, seeing webspace was still exhilarating, but it also was, in a weird way, calming. It was, she guessed, like smoking or drinking. She'd never tried the former; the smell bothered her. But she *had* drunk beer with friends—and Canadian beer now, too, which was stronger than the US stuff—but she didn't really like the taste. Still, her mother enjoyed a glass of wine most evenings, and, well, she supposed that plugging into webspace, seeing the calming lights and colors and shapes, could become her own evening ritual, a visit to her happy place—a very special place that was hers and hers alone.

The Institute of Vertebrate Paleontology and Paleoanthropology was located at 142 Xi-Wai-Da-Jie in western Beijing. Wong Wai-Jeng enjoyed working there, more or less, and the irony was not lost on him that doing so made him a civil servant: the dissident Sinanthropus was an employee of the Communist Party. But the irony of the government supporting this institution devoted to preserving old fossils wasn't lost on him, either.

Today for his morning coffee break, Wai-Jeng decided to stroll around the second-floor gallery of the museum—the four connected balconies that looked down on the exhibits below. He paused in front of the great glass tank on the granite pedestal that held the pickled coelacanth. There was irony here, too, for the giant lobe-finned fish was labeled a "living" fossil—which it had been until fishermen had netted it off the Comoros a few decades ago. It seemed in good shape still; he wondered if Chairman Mao was faring as well in his mausoleum.

Wai-Jeng turned and walked over to the railing around the opening that looked down onto the ground floor, ten meters below, with its dinosaurs mounted in dramatic poses above beds of fake grass. No school group was visiting today, but two old men were down there, sitting on a wooden bench. Wai-Jeng often saw them here. They lived in the neighborhood, came inside most afternoons to get out of the heat, and just sat, almost as motionless as the skeletons.

Directly below him, an allosaur was dispatching a stegosaur. The latter had fallen on its side, and the carnivore's great jaws were biting into its neck. The postures were dramatic, but the thick layer of dust visible on the tops of the bones from this vantage point belied the sense of movement.

Wai-Jeng looked off to his right. The great tapered neck of *Mamenchisaurus* snaked up through the giant opening from the floor below and—

And there was Dr. Feng, over by the metal staircase, accompanied by two other men; they'd presumably just come down from the labs upstairs. The two men didn't look like scientists; they were too burly, too sharp-edged, for that—although one of them *did* look familiar. Feng was pointing in Wai-Jeng's direction, and he did something he never did—he shouted: "There you are, Wai-Jeng! These men would like a word with you!"

And then it clicked: the shorter of the two men was the cop from the *wang ba;* the old paleontologist was *warning* him. He turned to his left and started to run, almost knocking over a middle-aged woman who was now standing in front of the coelacanth tank.

There was only one way out; modern fire codes were new to Beijing, and this museum had been built before they'd been instituted. If the two cops had split up, one going left and the other right around the large opening that looked down on the dinosaurs below, they would have caught him for sure. In fact, if one of them had just stayed put by the staircase, Wai-Jeng would have been trapped. But cops, like all party minions, were creatures of knee-jerk response: Wai-Jeng could tell by the sound of the footfalls, echoing off the glass display cases, that both were pursuing him down this side of the gallery. He'd have to make it to the far end, take the ninety-degree turn to the right, run across the shorter display area there, make another right-angle turn, go all the way up the far side, and round one more bend before he'd reach the staircase and any hope of getting downstairs and out of the building.

Below him, the duckbill *Tsintaosaurus* was mounted on its hind legs. Its skull poked up through the giant opening between the floors, and its great vertical crest, like a samurai's raised sword, cast a shadow on the wall ahead.

"Stop!" yelled one of the cops. A woman—perhaps the one who'd been near the coelacanth—screamed, and Wai-Jeng wondered if the cop had taken out a gun.

He was almost to the end of this side of the gallery when he heard a change in the footfalls, and, as he rounded the corner and was able to look back, he saw that the cop from the *wang ba* had reversed course, and was now running the other way. He now had a much shorter distance to go back to the staircase than Wai-Jeng still needed to cover.

The one who was still running toward Wai-Jeng was indeed brandishing a pistol. Adrenaline surged through him. As he rounded the corner, he dropped his cell phone into a small garbage can, hoping that the cops were too far back to notice; the bookmarks list on its browser would be enough to send him to jail—although, as he ran on, he realized evidence or lack thereof hardly mattered; if he were caught, his fate at any trial had doubtless already been decided.

The cop from the Internet café rounded the corner back by the staircase. Old Dr. Feng was looking on, but there was nothing he, or anyone, could do. As he passed cases of pterosaur remains, Wai-Jeng felt his heart pounding.

"Stop!" the cop behind him yelled again, and "Don't move!" the second cop demanded.

Wai-Jeng kept running; he was now coming up the opposite side of the gallery from where he'd begun. On his left was a long mural showing Cretaceous Beijing in gaudy colors; on his right, the large opening looking down on the first-floor displays. He was directly above the skeletal diorama with the allosaur attacking the stegosaur. The ground was far below, but it was his only hope. The wall around the balcony opening was made of five rows of metal pipe painted white, with perhaps twenty centimeters of space between each row; the whole thing made climbing easy, and he did just that.

"Don't!" shouted the cop from the *wang ba* and Dr. Feng simultaneously, the former as an order, the latter with obvious horror.

He took a deep breath then jumped, the two old men below now looking up as he fell, fear on their lined faces, and—

Ta ma de!

—he hit the fake grass, just missing the giant spikes of the stegosaur's tail, but the grass hardly cushioned his fall and he felt a sharp, jabbing pain in his left leg as it snapped.

Sinanthropus lay facedown, blood in his mouth, next to the skeletons locked in their ancient fight, as footfalls came clanging down the metal staircase.

twenty-four

0001110010101010000000001011111110101000000001010001010100000001011101010010101001010101001110110010101011000001

Dillon Fontana made it to the gazebo first; he was wearing his usual black jeans and a black T-shirt. Hobo would not let him look at anything until he'd properly hugged the ape, and that gave time for Maria Lopez and Werner Richter to arrive, as well. Given his bulk, it was no surprise that Harl Marcuse was the last of the four to make it across the wide lawn, over the drawbridge, and up to the gazebo.

"What is it?" he asked in a wheezing tone that said, *Anyone who makes me run better have a* damn *good reason.*

Shoshana indicated the painting, its colors softer now in the late-afternoon sunlight. Marcuse looked at it, but his expression didn't change. "Yes?"

But Dillon got it at once. "My God," he said softly. He turned to Hobo and signed, *Did you paint this?*

Hobo was showing his yellow teeth in a big, goofy grin. *Hobo paint,* he replied. *Hobo paint.*

Maria was tilting her head sideways. "I don't—"

"It's me," said Shoshana. "In profile, see?"

Marcuse moved forward, eyes narrowed, and the others got out of his way. "Apes don't make representational art," he said in his commanding voice, as if his declaration could erase what was in front of them.

Dillon gestured at the canvas. "Tell that to Hobo."

"And he did this while I was away," Shoshana said. "From memory." The Silverback frowned dubiously. She pointed at the hidden camera. "I'm sure it's all been recorded."

He glanced at the same spot and shook his head—although not, she realized after a moment, in negation, but rather in disappointment. The camera kept watch on Hobo—and that meant it showed the easel from the rear. The footage wouldn't reveal the order in which he'd added elements to the painting. Did he paint the head first? The eye? Was the colored iris added at the same time, or was it a final, finishing touch?

"The primate Picasso," said Dillon, hands on hips, grinning with satisfaction.

"Exactly!" said Shoshana. She turned to Marcuse. "No way the Georgia Zoo will be able to put Hobo under the knife if we go public with this. The world would never stand for it."

"Caitlin?"

She looked up and her perspective on webspace shifted. It took her a second to remember where she was: in a stairwell at Howard Miller Secondary School.

The voice again. "Caitlin, are you okay?" It was Sunshine.

She lifted her shoulders a bit. "I guess."

"The dance is winding down. I'm going to walk home. Wanna come?"

Caitlin had lost track of time while she'd immersed herself in the fantastic colors and lights of the World Wide Web; she felt her watch.

God knew what had happened to the Hoser. "Um, sure. Thanks." She used her cane as a prop as she got up from the step she was sitting on. "How'd you find me?"

"I didn't," said Sunshine. "I was just going to my locker and I saw you here."

"Thanks," Caitlin said again.

Caitlin switched the eyePod back to simplex mode, shutting off the Jagster feed and her view of webspace. They went up to the second floor, where Sunshine's locker was, then headed back down and out. The evening had gotten chilly and she could feel the odd drop of rain.

Caitlin wished she had more to say to Sunshine as they walked along, but even though they were the two American girls at school, they really didn't have anything in common. Sunshine was struggling with all her classes, and was, according to Bashira, a knockout: tall, thin, busty, with platinum-blonde hair and a small diamond stud in her nose. But if she was *that* pretty, Caitlin wondered why she'd come to the dance alone. "Do you have a boyfriend?" she asked.

"Oh, yeah. Sure. But he works evenings."

"What's he do?"

"Security guard."

Caitlin was surprised "How old is he?"

"Nineteen."

She'd assumed Sunshine was her own age—and maybe she was. Or maybe she'd failed a time or two. "How old are you?" Caitlin asked.

"Sixteen. You?"

"Almost. My birthday is in eight days." It was starting to rain harder. "Is he good to you?"

"Who?"

"Your boyfriend."

"He's okay," Sunshine said.

Caitlin thought a boyfriend should be *wonderful,* should talk to you and listen to you and be kind and gentle. But she said nothing.

"Um, here's my street," Sunshine said. Caitlin knew precisely where they were; her own house was just two blocks farther along. "It's starting to rain harder—do... do you mind?"

"No," said Caitlin. "It's okay, go home. You don't want to get soaked."

"It's getting pretty late..."

"Don't worry," Caitlin said. "I know the way—and I'm not afraid of the dark."

She felt Sunshine squeeze her upper arm. "Hey, that's funny! Anyway, look, forget about that jerk Nordmann, okay? I'll see you on Monday." And she heard footsteps fading quickly away.

Caitlin started walking. *Forget about him,* Sunshine had said. God, she wondered what that asshole had said to people after she'd left the gym. Why, if he'd—

What the—?

She paused, one foot still in the air, totally startled by—

God!

By a flash of light!

But she had the data-receive function of her eyePod turned off; the Jagster light show was too distracting when she was trying to concentrate on walking. There should have been no light of any kind, but—

And then she heard it, a great crack of thunder.

Another flash. Seconds later, more thunder.

Lightning. It had to be lightning! She'd read about it so many times: zigzagging lines coming down from above.

A third flash, like—like—like a jagged crack in ice. Incredible!

What color was lightning? She racked her brain trying to remember. Red? No, no, that was lava. Lightning was white—and she was seeing it! For the first time—for the very first time—she knew what color she was seeing! This wasn't like her arbitrarily deciding to call something in webspace "red" or "green." This was the actual, real color white. Yes, white is a mixture of all other colors; she'd read that, although she had never understood what it really meant—but she now *knew* what white looked like!

The rain was quite heavy. Her fleece, with the raised Perimeter Institute logo—the letters PI joined to look something like the Greek letter pi—was getting soaked. And the fat drops were cold, and hitting hard enough that they stung a bit. But she didn't care. She didn't care at all!

More lightning: another flash of perception, of sight!

She knew there was a way to determine how far away the source of lightning was, by counting the seconds between the flash and the sound of thunder, but she couldn't remember the formula, and so she worked it out quickly in her head. Light travels at 186,282 miles per second—instantaneously, for practical purposes; sound travels at 769 miles per *hour.* So every second that passed between the flash and the thunder put the source of the lightning another fifth of a mile away.

Another flash, and—

Four. Five. Six.

The source was 1.2 miles away—and getting closer: the intervals between flashes and thunderclaps were diminishing, and the flashes were getting brighter and the thunder louder. In fact, these flashes were so bright they—

Yes, so bright they *hurt.* But it was wonderful pain, exquisite pain. Here, in the pouring rain, she was at last seeing something *real,* and it felt glorious!

I was fascinated by that remarkable point to which I now had an apparently permanent connection—but also frustrated by it. Yes, it often reflected myself back at me. But for long periods it contained data that I simply couldn't make sense of. In fact, that's what it was sending me right now, and—

What was that?

A bright flash—brighter than anything I'd ever encountered.

And then darkness again.

And then another flash! Incredible!

Another flash—and then more thunder. Finally, though, it seemed the electrical part of the storm had stopped, and Caitlin began walking home again, and—

Shit!

She stumbled off the curb; she must have turned around at some point, and—

The honk of a horn, the sound of tires swerving on wet pavement. She jumped backward, up onto the sidewalk. Her heart was pounding. She wasn't sure which way she was facing, and—

No, no. The curb had been on her right, and it was on her right now, so she must be facing west again. Still, it was terrifying, and she just stood still for a time, regaining composure, and rebuilding her mental map of where she was.

The raindrops grew smaller, less heavy. She was sad the lightning had ended, and, as she began again to walk toward her house, she wondered if everyone else was now seeing a rainbow—but no, no, Sunshine had said it was dark out. Ah, well, flashes of light were wondrous enough!

Caitlin arrived at the corner lot and walked up the driveway, which was made of zigzag-shaped interlocking stone tiles; she could feel them beneath her feet. She dug out her key (she carried it in the pocket with her wallet, not the one with the eyePod), opened the front door, and—

"Caitlin!"

"Hi, Mom."

"Look at you! You're soaked to the skin!" Caitlin imagined her peering over her shoulder. "Where's Trevor?"

"He's—a jerk," Caitlin said, catching herself before she said "an asshole."

"Oh, sweetheart," she said sympathetically. But then her voice grew angry. "You walked by yourself? Even if this is a safe neighborhood, you shouldn't be out alone after dark."

Caitlin decided to elide over the last few hundred yards. "No, Sunshine—a girl I know—she walked me back."

"You should have called. I'd have come to get you."

Caitlin struggled to pull the sodden sweatshirt over her head. "Mom," she said once it was off. "I saw the lightning."

"Oh, my God! Really?"

"Yes. Jagged lines, over and over again."

She was gathered into a hug. "Oh, Caitlin, oh, darling, that's wonderful!" A pause. "Can you see anything now?"

"No."

"Still..."

Caitlin smiled. "Yes," she said, bouncing up and down a bit on her toes. "Still. Where's Dr. Kuroda?"

"He's gone to bed; he was exhausted—he's totally jet-lagged."

She thought about suggesting they wake him, but there was nothing happening now, and the data her eyePod produced during the thunderstorm would be safely stored on his servers in Tokyo; he could examine it after a good night's sleep. Besides, she was exhausted herself. "And Dad?"

"Still at the Institute—the public lecture, remember?"

"Oh. Well, I'm going to go change."

She headed up to her room, got out of her soaked clothes, put on her pajamas, and lay down on the bed, hands intertwined behind her head. She wanted to relax and she was hungry for more vision, so she touched the button on her eyePod.

Webspace faded into existence: lines, points, colors, but—

Was it her imagination? Was it just that the lightning had been *so* bright that the colors in webspace now seemed... yes, she could draw the parallel, see how the word she knew from sound could apply to vision: the colors *did* seem muted now, dulled, less vibrant, and—

No, no, it wasn't that! They weren't muted. Rather, they were less sharp because...

Because now, behind everything, there was...

How to describe it? She sifted through words she knew related to visual phenomena. Something...*shimmering,* that was it. There was a background visible now, shining with a subdued flickering light.

Had something happened to the structure of webspace? That seemed unlikely. No, surely it was her way of visualizing it that had changed—presumably because of the real vision she'd just experienced. The background of webspace no longer appeared as a void but rather was twinkling, and rapidly, too. And at the very limits of...of *resolution,* there was a...a structure to it.

She got off the bed, went to her desk chair, and had JAWS recite email headers while she continued to look at webspace. Twenty-three messages had come in, and there'd doubtless be lots of new things written on her Facebook wall and new comments to her LJ postings. She switched back to simplex mode, clearing her vision so she could concentrate. She was about to type a response to an email when suddenly, shockingly, her entire field of vision flooded with intense whiteness. *What the hell?*

But then the crack of thunder came, shaking her bedroom's window, and she realized that it was more lightning.

Another flash!

One steamboat, two steam—

The storm was only three-tenths of a mile away.

She had missed hearing her mother come up the stairs—what with thunder shaking the whole house—and was startled when she heard her saying, "Well? Can you see this lightning, too?"

Caitlin moved toward the voice, letting her mother's arms wrap around her.

Yet more lightning, and—

Her mother letting her go, maneuvering so she was standing beside her, instead of holding her. Caitlin took her hand, and—

Another flash.

"You can!" said her mom. "You close your eyes when there's lightning."

"I do?" said Caitlin.

"Yes!"

"But I can still see it."

"Well, sure. Eyelids aren't completely opaque."

Caitlin was stunned. Why hadn't she known that? How much else was there to know about the world?

"Thanks, Mom," she said.

"For what?"

The storm was moving off; the thunder was taking longer to arrive each time.

She lifted her shoulders a bit. How do you thank someone who has given you so much, and given up so much for you? She turned to face her, hoping against hope that this was the real beginning—that she would soon at last see her heart-shaped face. "For everything," she said, hugging her tightly.

twenty-five

0001110010101010000000001011111110101000000010100010101000000101110101001010100101010100111011001010110000001

It was now almost 9:00 p.m. in California. The Silverback was resting his bulk in the one overstuffed easy chair in the bungalow's main room. Shoshana Glick had propped her rump against the edge of the desk that held the big computer monitor. Dillon Fontana, clad all in black, was standing in the doorway to the kitchen, leaning against the jamb. Werner and Maria had gone home for the weekend.

"What's noteworthy," Dillon said, "is that Hobo began doing representational art *after* he started communicating with Virgil."

Shoshana nodded. "I'd noticed that, too. But Virgil doesn't paint—I asked Juan in Miami. He doesn't do any sort of art. So it's not like the orangutan gave Hobo a tip or encouragement."

Marcuse was drinking Coke from a two-liter bottle that looked small in his hands. He took a swig, wiped his face, and said, "It's the flat screen."

Shoshana turned to look at him.

"Don't you see?" Marcuse said. "Until we linked the two apes in a videoconference, all the ASL signs Hobo has ever seen were three-dimensional—done by actual human beings in close physical proximity to him. But now he's seeing someone sign on a flat two-dimensional screen, on a computer monitor." He gestured at the Apple display behind Shoshana.

"But he's watched TV for years," she said.

"Yes, but he's never seen signing—at least not for any significant amount of time—on TV. And signing is special: signs are exactly that—representations of things, symbols. By seeing Virgil use signs on the flat screen, somehow Hobo saw how three-dimensional objects could be reduced to two dimensions. Remember, he has to concentrate on the signs in a way he doesn't concentrate on normal TV images. Doing so caused something to click in his brain, and he *got* it."

Shoshana found herself nodding. For all that the Silverback could be a blustering blowhard and a pain in the ass as a boss, he *was* a brilliant scientist.

"There's precedent, sort of," he continued. "Some prosopagnosiacs—people with face blindness—can recognize faces in photographs but can't recognize them in the flesh; it's doubtless a related phenomenon."

"In the land of the blind," said Dillon, "the one-eyed ape is painting." He lifted his narrow shoulders. "I mean, he's got two eyes, but there's no depth perception when watching TV, right? Sure, stereoscopic vision adds a lot of valuable information, but there's a simplicity—a huge ramping down of the mental processing required—when dealing with just two-dimensional images."

"But why'd he draw me in profile?" Shoshana asked.

Marcuse put down his Coke bottle and spread his arms. "Why did cavemen always draw animals in profile? Why did the ancient Egyptians do it that way? There's something hardwired in the primate brain to make profiles—even though we're way better at recognizing faces when seen full on."

That much was true, Shoshana knew. There were neurons in human brains—and ape brains, too—that responded to the specific layout of a face, two eyes above a mouth. She'd grown up with the smiley face used online:

:)

But she remembered her father telling her it had been months after he'd first seen it in the 1980s before he realized what it was supposed to represent. Because it was sideways, it just didn't trigger the right neurons in his brain. But one of the reasons that the yellow happy-face logo—which, her father had said, had been ubiquitous when he was a teenager—was so universally appealing was that it caused an immediate pattern-recognition response.

"Maybe the tendency for profiles has to do with brain lateralization," Marcuse said. "Artistic talent is localized in one hemisphere; drawing profiles may be a subtle response to that, showing, in essence, that particular half of the subject." He paused. "Whatever the reason, this makes our Hobo even more special."

Shoshana looked at Dillon, who was doing his doctoral thesis on primate hybridization. It was a topic of real scientific interest. In 2006, a study revealed that there had continued to be a lot of hybridization between the ancestor of chimps and the ancestor of humans even after the two lines had split millions of years ago; they remained able to produce fertile offspring for a long time, and such crossbreeding had apparently given rise to the sophisticated human brain.

"Absolutely," Dillon said. "I don't dispute that seeing Virgil signing on the monitor was a catalyst, but I'd bet hybridization set the groundwork for him being so good at language and painting."

Shoshana smiled at the subtle turf war that she'd just seen begin: each of them was staking out territory, and would doubtless defend their positions in journal papers over the coming years. But then she frowned; they didn't have time to wait for papers to go through the peer-review process. "If we want to stave off the Georgia Zoo's desire to sterilize Hobo, we can't wait," she said. "We have to go public with this, get Hobo's special status generally known, and—"

"And what was your first thought when you saw that painting?" Marcuse demanded. "I'll tell you what it was—it was my thought, too, as soon as I recognized that it was indeed a portrait. I thought it was a fake. Didn't you?"

Shoshana looked at Dillon, and remembered her accusation of that very thing, and how Hobo had looked so hurt. "Yes," she said sheepishly.

The Silverback shook his head. "No, that painting isn't going to save Hobo—but the next one might. We need him to do it again, and with more cameras recording it all. If there's only one representational painting, people will dismiss it as a fake—or, even if they accept it as being genuine, they'll say it's a fluke, something that happens to sort of, by chance, look like a person. Hell, we've been accused often enough as is of just projecting what we want to see onto ape behavior. No, unless he does it again, with the whole process filmed and documented—unless we can replicate this—we've got nothing, and our grinning genius is still in danger of being sterilized."

twenty-six

00011100101010100000000010111111101010000000101000101010000000101110101001010100101010100111011001010110000001

Saturday morning always meant pancakes and sausages in the Decter household. Now that they were living in Waterloo, the sausages were, of course, Schneider's brand, and the syrup was real maple syrup Caitlin's mom had bought from Mennonites in the nearby town of St. Jacob's.

"I was up at 5:00 a.m.," Caitlin's dad said, as soon as they'd started eating.

"There's a 5:00 *a.m.?*" Caitlin joked.

"I set up a workspace for you and Professor Kuroda in the basement," he continued.

"Thank you, Dr. Decter," Kuroda said, sounding relieved—apparently everybody but the Hoser was worried about her virtue! But she guessed it probably *would* be more comfortable downstairs than in her bedroom.

"Oh, for Pete's sake!" her mom said. "You're staying in our house; you can call him Malcolm."

Her father neither confirmed nor denied this assertion, Caitlin noted. Instead, he said, "I bought a new computer at Future Shop yesterday. It's set up downstairs for the two of you; I put it on the household network."

"Thank you," she said. "And I have some news of my own—I saw the lightning last night."

The words were simultaneous, overlapping. Her dad, matter-of-fact: "Your mother told me." And Kuroda, amazed: *"You saw lightning?"*

"That's right," Caitlin said.

"What—what did it look like to you?" Kuroda said.

"Jagged lines against darkness. Bright lines—white, right? Stark against a pure black background."

Kuroda was clearly eager to look at the data from the eyePod: he had only *one* extra helping of pancakes.

Caitlin had been in the basement just a few times in the three months they'd lived in this house, mostly back in August, when it had been surprisingly hot and muggy outside—almost like Texas. The basement had been cool then (and still was), and although her mother had complained about how little light there was down there—apparently, just a single bulb in the middle of the room—it hadn't bothered Caitlin.

"What's the 4-1-1?" she asked, hands on hips.

Kuroda's English was excellent, but the information number must be different in Japan. "Sorry?"

"What's the setup? Tell me about the room."

"Ah. Well, it's an unfinished basement—I suppose you know that. Bare insulation between the slats; cement floor. There's an old TV—the kind with a picture tube—and some bookcases. And your dad has set up the new computer on one of those worktables with metal folding legs; it's pushed up against the far wall, the one opposite the staircase. The computer is a minitower, and he's got an LCD screen attached to it. There's a little window above the table and a couple of comfortable-looking swivel chairs in front of it."

"Sweet! I wonder where he got the chairs."

"They have a logo on them—kind of like the Greek letter pi."

"Oh, he borrowed them from work. Speaking of which, let's get to it."

Kuroda helped guide her to one of the chairs, and he settled into the other; she could hear it squeaking a bit. "Let me log on to my servers in Tokyo," he said. "I want to examine the datastream you sent them during the lightning storm—see if we can isolate what it was that caused your primary visual cortex to respond."

She could hear him typing away and, as he did, she realized she'd forgotten to mention something over breakfast. "After the lightning flashes," she said, "webspace looked different."

"Different how?"

"Well, I could still see the structure of the Web clearly, like before, but the... the background, I guess, was different."

He stopped typing. "What do you mean?"

"It used to be dark. Black, I guess."

"And now?"

"Now it's, um, lighter? I could see details in it."

"Details?"

"Yeah. Like—like..." She struggled to make the connection; the pattern *did* remind her of something she was familiar with, but—got it! "Like a chessboard." She had a blind person's chessboard, with squares that were alternately raised and lowered, and Braille initials on the top of each piece; she sometimes played her dad. "But, um, not quite. I mean, it was made of lighter and darker squares, but they're not in the same pattern as a chessboard, and they go on, like, *forever.*"

"How big are they?"

"Tiny. If they were any tinier, I don't think I could see them. In fact, I can't swear that they were squares, but they were packed tightly together and made rows and columns."

"And there were thousands of them?"

"Millions. Maybe billions. They're *everywhere.*"

Kuroda sat as quietly as was possible for him, then: "You know, human vision is made of pixels, just like a computerized image. Each axon in the optic nerve provides one picture element. Now, most people aren't conscious of them, but if you have decent focus, and you look at a blank wall, some people can see them. Your brain is processing Web information as if it were coming from your eye; it may be hardwired to see it all as a mesh of pixels at the limits of resolution, but..."

He trailed off. After ten seconds she prodded him.

"But?"

"Well, I'm just thinking. You've described seeing circles, which we've taken to be websites, and lines connecting them, which we've assumed represent hyperlinks. And that's it—that's the World Wide Web, right? That's *all* of it. So, what could make up the *background* to the Web? I mean, in human vision, the—"

"Don't say that."

"Pardon?"

"'Human vision.' Don't say that. *I'm* human."

A sharp intake of breath. "I'm so sorry, Miss Caitlin. May I say 'normal' vision?"

"Yes."

"All right. In normal vision, the background is—well, it's the distant reaches of the universe if you're looking up at the night sky. But what would be the background for the Web?"

"Background radiation?" she suggested. "Like the cosmic microwave background?"

Kuroda was quiet for a moment. "How old are you again?"

"Hey," she said, "my father *is* a physicist, you know."

"Well, the cosmic microwave background is uniform to a fraction of a degree in all directions. But what you're seeing is mottled in black and white, you say?"

"Yeah. And it keeps shifting."

"Pardon?"

"Shifting. Changing. Didn't I mention that?"

"No. What do you mean precisely?"

Something brushed against her legs—ah, Schrödinger! Caitlin scooped him up into her lap. "The dark squares switch to light, and the light ones to dark," she said.

"How rapidly?"

"Oh, really fast. Makes the whole thing shimmer."

The springs on Kuroda's chair squeaked as he stood up. She heard him walking across the room and then walking back toward her, then repeating the process: pacing. "It can't be..." he said at last.

"What?"

He ignored her question. "How clearly could you see the individual cells?"

She scratched Schrödinger behind the ears. "Cells?"

"Pixels. I mean pixels. How clearly could you see them?"

"It was really hard."

"Can you try again? Can you put the eyePod in duplex mode now?"

She fumbled to get the device out of her pocket without sending Schrödinger to the floor. Once it was free, she pressed the switch; the eyePod made its usual high-pitched beep, which Schrödinger answered with a surprised meow, and—

And there it was, spreading out before her: the World Wide Web.

"Can you see the background now?" Kuroda asked.

"Yes, if I concentrate..."

He sounded surprised. "You're squinting."

She shrugged. "It helps. But, yeah, if I really try, I can focus on a small group—a few hundred squares on a side."

"Okay. Do you have a Go board?"

"What?"

"Um, okay—do you have any money?"

She narrowed her eyes again, but this time in suspicion. "Fifty bucks, maybe, but..."

"No, no. Coins! Do you have coins?"

"In a jar on my dresser." She was saving to go see Lee Amodeo with Bashira when she came to Centre in the Square.

"Great, great. Do you mind if I go get it?"

"I can do it. It's my house."

"No, you take the time to look at the Web, see if you can make out any more detail in the background. I'll be right back."

Kuroda could never sneak up on anyone. She heard the sounds of his return long before he actually arrived. She then heard a great jangling as he dumped the coins on their worktable, and more noise as he shuffled them around—perhaps sorting them. "All right. Here's a bunch of coins. Can you arrange them in the pattern you're seeing? Put one down for each light spot, and leave a coin-sized space for each dark spot."

Caitlin shooed Schrödinger out of her lap and swung her chair to face the table. "I told you. They keep changing."

"Yes, yes, but..." He made a noisy sigh. "I wish there were some way to photograph it, or at least to slow down your perception, and—" His voice brightened. "And there is! Of course there is!"

She heard him moving about, then soft keyclicks. "What are you doing?" she asked.

"I'm halting your reception of the datastream from Jagster, and just passing on the last iteration of it over and over again, so it'll keep coming down the pike without changing, sort of like—"

"A freeze-frame!" she said as the image ceased to move. She was delighted to be able to apply another concept she'd only ever read about before.

"Exactly. Now, can you make a pattern with the coins that matches what you're seeing in a portion of the background?"

"A very *small* portion," she said. And she started moving the coins around; he'd given her a bunch of dimes. After a moment, she pushed one off to a corner of the desk. "American," she said; all those years of reading Braille made it easy to tell Queen Elizabeth from FDR.

She built up a grid of dimes and dime-sized empty spaces, counting the coins automatically as she deployed them. "Done," she announced. "Eight dollars and ninety cents."

"Completely random," Kuroda said, sounding disappointed.

"No, it's not. Not quite. See this group of five dimes here?" She had no trouble keeping track of the pattern she'd made, and touched the appropriate coins. "It's the same as this group here, except turned ninety degrees to the right."

"So it is," he said, excitedly. "It looks like the letter L."

"And this one's the same, too," she said, "turned upside down."

"Excellent!"

"But what does it mean?" she asked.

"I'm not a hundred-percent sure," he said. "Not yet. Here, focus your attention again on the same spot in your vision. I'm going to update the data going to your implant, just once... and done."

"Okay. It's completely different."

"Can you make it for me with the coins?"

"I'm not even sure I'm looking at the same spot anymore," she said. "But here goes." She rearranged the dimes, and, just to underscore that not only the pattern but also the number of light and dark squares had changed, she added, "Six dollars and twenty cents." She paused. "Ah! Three sets of that five-coin pattern this time."

"And in different places," he said.

"But what does it mean?"

"Well," said Kuroda, "this may sound crazy, but I think they're cellular automata."

"Who in the what now?"

"Hey, I thought you were the daughter of a physicist," he said, but his tone was one of gentle teasing.

She smiled. "Sue me. And besides, if they're cellular, I'd need to be a biologist's daughter, no?"

"No, no—they're not biological cells; they're cells in the computer-science sense of the word: a cell is the basic unit of storage in computer memory, holding a single unit of information."

"Ah."

"And an automaton is something that behaves or responds in a predictable, mechanical way. So cellular automata are patterns of information units that respond in a specific way to changes in their surroundings. For example, take a grid of black and white squares—each square is a cell, okay?"

"Yes."

"And on a chessboard that goes on forever, each square has eight neighbors, right?"

"Right."

"Well, suppose you say to each square something like, okay, if you're already black and three or more of your neighbors are white, then turn white yourself. An instruction like that is called a rule. And if you keep applying the rule over and over again, strange things happen. I mean, yes, if you just focus on one individual square, all you'd see is it flipping back and forth between black and white. But if you look at the overall grid, patterns of squares can seem to move across it—cross shapes, maybe, or hollow squares, or L shapes like we have here, or clusters of cells that change shape in set stages and, after a fixed number of steps, return to their original shape, but have moved somewhere else in the process. It's almost as though the shapes are alive."

She heard the chair groan as he shifted in it.

"I remember when I first encountered cellular automata in Conway's Game of Life as an undergrad," he said. "What's fascinating about all this is that they're representations of data that are interpreted as being special by an observer. I mean, those L-shaped things—they're called 'spaceships,' by the way, these patterns that retain their cohesion and fly across the grid—well, spaceships don't really exist; nothing is actually moving, and the spaceship you see on the right side of the grid is completely different in composition from the one you originally saw on the left side. And yet we think of it as the same one."

"But what are they *for?*"

"Besides making undergrads go 'ooooh,' you mean?"

"Yeah."

"Well, in nature—"

"These occur in nature?"

"Yes, in lots of places. For instance, there's a kind of snail that makes the pattern on its shell in direct response to a cellular-automata rule."

"Really?"

"Yes. It has a row of spigots that spit out pigment, or not, based on what the neighboring spigots on either side are doing."

"Cool!"

"Yes, it is. But what's really cool is that there are cellular automata in brains."

"Really?" she said again.

"Well, they're in lots of kinds of cells, actually. But they've been studied particularly in neural tissue. The cytoskeletons of cells—their internal scaffolding—is made up of long strings called microtubules, and each component of a microtubule, a little piece of protein called a tubulin dimer, can be in one of two states. And those states go through permutations as though they were cellular automata."

"Why would they do that?"

"No one knows. Some people, though, including—hey, maybe your father knows him? Roger Penrose? He's a famous physicist, too, and he and his associate, a guy named Hameroff, think that those cellular automata are the actual cause of consciousness, of self-awareness."

"Sweet! But why?"

"Well, Hameroff is an anesthesiologist, and he's shown that when people are put under for surgery their tubulin dimers fall into a neutral state—instead of some being black, say, and some being white, they all sort of become gray. When they do that, consciousness goes off; when they start behaving as cellular automata again, consciousness comes back on."

She made a mental note to google this later. "But if the snail has spigots, and the brain has these whatchamacallits—"

"Tubulin dimers," said Kuroda.

"Okay, well if these tubulin dimers are the actual things that are flipping in the brain, what's flipping in the background of webspace?"

She imagined him shrugging; it would have gone naturally with his tone of voice. "Bits, I guess. You know: binary digits. By definition, they're either on or off, or one or zero, or black or white, or however you want to visualize them. And maybe you're visualizing them as squares of two different colors, just at the limit of your mental resolution."

"But, um, the Web is supposed to pass on data unchanged," she said. "A browser asks for a Web page, and an exact copy of it is sent from the server that hosts that page. There shouldn't be any data changing."

"No," he said. "That's puzzling."

They sat in silence for a few moments, contemplating this. And then she heard her mother's distinctive footsteps on the stairs, followed by her saying, "Hey, you two, anyone care for a mid-morning snack?"

Kuroda's chair squeaked again as he heaved his bulk up from it. "I always think better on a full stomach."

You must do a lot of thinking, Caitlin thought, and she smiled as they went upstairs.

twenty-seven

0001110010101010000000001011111110101000000001010001010100000010111010100101010010101010011101100101011000001

As soon as Shoshana arrived at the Marcuse Institute on Saturday morning, she, Dillon, and the Silverback headed over to the island. Hobo was inside the gazebo, leaning against one of the wooden beams that made up its frame.

Hello, Hobo, signed Marcuse once they were all inside. His fingers were fat and some signs were a struggle for him.

Hello, Doctor, Hobo signed back. Marcuse was the only one who required the ape to call him by an honorific instead of his first name. Still, it wasn't as bad as William Lemmon, the ultimate supervisor of Roger Fouts's work with Washoe in the 1970s; Lemmon used to make Washoe and his other ape charges kiss his ring when he arrived, as if he were pope of the chimps.

Picture of Shoshana good, Marcuse signed.

Hobo grinned, showing teeth. *Hobo paint! Hobo paint!*

Yes. Now will you paint... His hands froze in midair, and Shoshana wondered if he'd decided that he didn't want to see himself caricatured by an ape. After a moment, he began signing again: *Dillon?*

Hobo turned an appraising set of eyes on the young grad student with the scraggly blond beard. He was wearing a black T-shirt and black jeans, which, Shoshana hoped, weren't the same ones as yesterday. *Maybe... maybe...*

Dillon looked surprised to be conscripted for this duty, but he moved over to one of the two stools in the gazebo, sat on it, and struck a pose like Rodin's *Thinker.* Shoshana smiled at the sight.

But Hobo threw his hands up over his head, made a pant-hoot, and ran on all fours out the gazebo's door. Shoshana looked at Marcuse for permission, he nodded, and she took off after the ape, who was now cowering behind the yellow stone statue of the Lawgiver.

What's wrong? Shoshana asked. She held her arms out to gather Hobo in a hug. *What's wrong?*

Hobo looked back up at the gazebo, then at Shoshana. *No people. No watch,* he signed. There weren't many things he was self-conscious about; indeed, it had taken a lot to convince him not to masturbate or defecate in front of visiting dignitaries. But his art was something he *was* uneasy about, at least while it was being created.

We go away, you paint Dillon?

Hobo was quiet for a moment. *Paint Shoshana.*

Again? Why?

Shoshana pretty.

She felt herself blushing.

Shoshana have ponytail, added Hobo.

She knew that getting him to paint someone other than her would be better. Otherwise, critics would argue that he'd just stumbled on a random combination of shapes that Marcuse, *et al.*, had decided represented Shoshana, and he simply reproduced those same fixed shapes over and over again to get a reward—not unlike half the cartoonists in the world, Shoshana thought; the guy who drew *The Family Circus* seemed to have a repertoire of about eight things.

Fine, she signed. *Paint me, then Dillon, okay?*

Shoshana knew she was outthinking the poor ape; he could, of course, paint her regardless of what she said. After a moment, he signed, *Yes yes.*

She held out her hand, and he took it, intertwining his fingers with hers. They walked back up to the gazebo, the hot morning sun beating down on them.

"Hobo is going to paint another picture of me," Shoshana announced once they'd passed through the screen door. Marcuse frowned. She switched to signing so Hobo could follow along. *And after, Hobo will paint Dillon—right, Hobo?*

Hobo lifted his shoulders. *Maybe.*

"All right," Shoshana said, "everybody out, please. You know he doesn't like an audience."

Marcuse didn't seem happy about taking orders from a subordinate, but he followed Dillon outside. Shoshana looked around the gazebo, double-checking that the additional cameras they'd set up last night could clearly see both Hobo and his canvas. Then she headed for the door, too. As she exited she glanced back, and, to her astonishment, saw Hobo stretching his long arms out in front of him, with fingers interlocked, as if warming up.

And then the artist got down to work.

That special point! How wondrous, but how frustrating, too!

The datastream from it didn't always follow the same path, but it *did* always end up at the same location—and so I took to intercepting the datastream just before it arrived there.

There had been no repetition of the intriguing bright flashes, and for a long time there was nothing at all I could make sense of in the data pouring forth from that point. But now the datastream had become a reflection of me again. How strange, though! Instead of the constantly changing perspective I'd grown used to, the datastream seemed to focus for extended periods on just a *very* small portion of reality and...and something was distorted about the passage of time, it seemed. I tried to fathom the significance, if any, of that tiny part of the universe, but then, maddeningly, the datastream turned to gibberish once more...

After they'd finished the snack—which turned out to be oatmeal cookies her mom had gotten from the Mennonites—Caitlin and Dr. Kuroda returned to the basement. Caitlin had switched her eyePod to simplex mode for the break, but now had it back in duplex and was looking again at webspace.

"Okay," said Kuroda, settling into his chair, "we've got a background to the Web made up of cellular automata—but what exactly are the cells? I mean, even if they're just single bits, they still have to come from somewhere."

"Slack storage space?" suggested Caitlin. Hard drives store data in clusters of a fixed size, she knew; the new computer her dad had bought yesterday probably had an NTFS-formatted drive, meaning it used clusters of four kilobytes, and if a file contained only three kilobytes of data, the fourth kilobyte—over eight thousand bits—was left unused.

"No, I don't think so," said Kuroda. "Nothing can read or write to that space; even if there was some way for Web protocols to access slack space on servers, you wouldn't see bits flipping rapidly. No, this must be something *out there*—something in the data pipes." He paused. "Still, there's nothing I can think of in the Internet's TCP/IP or OSI model that could produce cellular automata. I wonder where they're coming from?"

"Lost packets," Caitlin said suddenly, sitting up straighter.

Kuroda sounded both intrigued and impressed. "Could be."

At any moment, Caitlin knew, hundreds of millions of people are using the Internet. While doing so, their computers send out clusters of bits called data packets—the basic unit of communication on the Web.

Each packet contains the address of its intended destination, which might, for instance, be the server hosting a Web page. But traffic on the Web almost never goes directly from point *A* to point *B*. Instead, it bounces around on multilegged journeys, passing through routers, repeaters, and switches, each of which tries to direct the packet closer to its intended destination.

Sometimes the routing gets awfully complex, especially when packets are rejected by the place they were sent to. That can happen when two or more packets arrive at the same time: one is chosen at random to be accepted and the others are sent back out to try their luck again later. But some packets *never* get accepted by their intended destinations because the address they've been sent to is invalid, or the target site is down or too busy, and so they end up being lost.

"Lost packets," repeated Kuroda, as if trying the notion on for size. Caitlin imagined he was shaking his head. "But lost packets just expire."

And indeed they mostly do, she knew: each packet has a "hop counter" coded into it, and that counter is reduced by one every time the packet passes through a router or other device. To keep lost packets from clogging up the Web infrastructure, when a router receives a packet whose hop counter has reached zero, it erases the packet.

"Lost packets are *supposed* to expire," Caitlin corrected, "but what if the packet is corrupted so that it no longer has a hop counter, or that counter doesn't decrement properly? I imagine *some* portion of packets get corrupted like that, by faulty routers or bad wiring or buggy software, and, with trillions of them going out each day, even if only a very tiny proportion ended up with broken hop counters, that would still leave huge numbers kicking around forever, right? Especially if their intended destination simply doesn't exist, either because the address has been corrupted along with the hop counter, or the server has gone offline."

"You know a lot about networks," Kuroda said, sounding impressed.

"Hey, who do you think set up the one in this house?"

"I'd assume your father..."

"Oh, he's good at networking *now,*" she said. "I taught him. But really, he's a *theoretical* physicist. He can barely operate the microwave."

Kuroda's chair squeaked. "Ah."

She felt herself getting excited; she was on to something—she knew it! "Anyway, there are probably always some... some ghost packets that persist long after they should have died. And think about that thing that happened in China recently: a huge, huge portion of the Web was cut off because of those power failures, or whatever. Hundreds of trillions of packets intended for China suddenly had no way to get to their destinations. Even if only a tiny fraction of those got suitably corrupted, it would still mean a huge increase in the number of ghost packets."

" 'Ghost packets,' eh?" Kuroda had brought a cup of coffee downstairs with him, and she heard it clatter; he must have just taken a sip. "Perhaps. Maybe a bug in some operating system or common router has been generating them for years under certain circumstances, for all we know—a benign bug that doesn't inconvenience users might never have been noticed."

He shifted in his chair, then: "Or maybe they aren't immortal packets at all. Maybe this is just the normal ebb and flow of lost packets that *will* expire, and while they're bouncing around trying in vain to reach their destination their time-to-live counters *do* decrement normally, but it's the switch from odd to even counts with each handoff that causes them to flip from black to white in your perception. You'd still get as many as 256 permutations out of each doomed packet—that's the maximum number of hops that can be coded for, because packets use an eight-bit field to store that value. But that's still a goodly number of iterations for a cellular-automata rule."

He paused, then blew out air noisily; Caitlin could almost hear him shrug. "But this is way out of my area," he continued. "I'm an information theorist, not a network theorist, and—"

She laughed.

"What?" said Kuroda.

"Sorry. Do you ever watch *The Simpsons?*"

"No, not really. But my daughter does."

"The time Homer ended up becoming an astronaut? These two newscasters are talking about the crew of a space mission. The first guy says, 'They're a colorful bunch. They've been dubbed "The Three Musketeers," heh heh heh.' And the other guy—it's Tom Brokaw—says, 'And we laugh legitimately: there's a mathematician, a different *kind* of mathematician, and a statistician.'"

Kuroda chuckled then said, "Well, actually, there *are* three types of mathematicians: those who can count and those who can't."

Caitlin smiled.

"But, seriously, Miss Caitlin, if you go into a career in maths or engineering, you *will* have to choose a specialty."

She kept her voice deadpan. "I'm going to focus on the number 8,623,721—I bet nobody's taken *that* one yet."

Kuroda made his wheezy chuckle again. "Still, I think we need to talk to a specialist. Let's see, in Israel it's...hey, it's only 8:00 p.m. She might be around."

"Who? Anna?"

"Exactly: Anna Bloom, the network cartographer. I'll IM her to see if she's online. Does this new computer have a webcam?"

"I suspect my dad didn't think I'd have much use for one," she said gently.

"Well, he—ah! He's more of an optimist than you think, Miss Caitlin. There's one right here, sitting on top of the tower." He used the keyboard for a few moments, then: "Yup, she's at home and online. Let me get a webcam call going..."

"*Konnichi wa, Masayuki-san!*" said the same voice Caitlin had heard on the speakerphone the night she'd seen the Web for the first time. But the woman immediately switched to English, presumably when she saw that he was with a Westerner. "Hey, who's the sweet young thing?"

Dr. Kuroda sounded slightly embarrassed. "This is Miss Caitlin." Of course, Anna hadn't seen her when they'd spoken before.

Anna sounded surprised. "Where *are* you?"

"Canada."

"Oooh! Is it snowing?"

"Not yet," said Kuroda. "It's still September, after all."

"Hi, Caitlin," Anna said.

"Hello, Professor Bloom."

"You can call me Anna. So, what can I do for you?"

Kuroda recounted what they'd dreamed up so far: legions of ghost packets floating in the background of the Web, somehow self-organizing into cellular automata. Then: "So, what do you think?"

"It's a novel idea," Anna said slowly.

"Could it work?" asked Caitlin.

"I...suppose. It's a classic Darwinian scenario, isn't it? Mutant packets that are better able to survive bouncing around endlessly. But the Web is expanding fast, with new servers added each day, so a slowly growing population of these ghost packets might never overwhelm its capacity—or, at least, it clearly hasn't yet."

"And the Web has no white blood cells tracking down useless stuff," said Caitlin. "Right? They *would* just persist, bouncing around."

"I guess," said Anna. "And—just blue-skying here—but the checksum on the packet could determine if you're seeing it as black or white; even-number checksums could be black and odd-number ones white, or whatever. If the hop counter changes with each hop, but never goes to zero, the checksum would change, too, and so you'd get a flipping effect."

"I thought of something similar," Kuroda said, "although the checksum didn't occur to me."

"And," Caitlin said to Dr. Kuroda, "you said cellular-automata rules can arise naturally, right? Like with that snail that uses them to paint its shell? So maybe all of this just spontaneously emerged."

"Maybe indeed," said Kuroda, sounding intrigued.

"I think I smell a paper," said Anna.

"You want to be a mathematician when you grow up, right, Miss Caitlin?" asked Kuroda.

I am a mathematician, she thought. But what she said was, "Yes."

"How'd you like to get the jump on the competition and coauthor your first paper with Professor Bloom and me? 'Spontaneous Generation of Cellular Automata in the Infrastructure of the World Wide Web.'"

Caitlin was grinning from ear to ear. "Sweet!"

twenty-eight

00011100101010100000000101111111010100000001010001010100000010111010100101010010101010011101100101011000001

"Well, there's no doubt now, is there?" said Shoshana, shifting her gaze from the painting to Dr. Marcuse and then back again. "That's me again, all right."

They were in the main room of the bungalow, watching the live video feed as Hobo painted away in the gazebo. Four LCD monitors were lined up on a workbench, one for each of the cameras; it reminded Shoshana of the security guard's station in her apartment building's lobby.

Marcuse nodded his great lump of a head. "Now, if he'd just paint something *other* than you." A pause. "Note that he's doing your same profile again: you looking off to the right. If he'd done it the other way, that might have torpedoed my thought about it reflecting brain lateralization."

"Well," said Shoshana, "it *is* my good side."

He actually smiled, then: "Okay. Let's put your video-editing skills to work."

Shoshana had a not-so-secret hobby: vidding. She took clips of TV shows she'd snagged from BitTorrent sites and cut them to fit popular songs, making humorous or poignant little music videos that she shared with like-minded vidders on the Web. Her fandoms included the TV medical drama *House,* which had a lot of slashy subtext that was great for mixing to love songs, and the latest incarnation of *Doctor Who.* Marcuse had caught her working on these once or twice over lunch, using the fancy Mac the Institute had had donated to it.

"When Hobo's done," continued Marcuse, "take the footage from all four cameras and splice together a version that shows the whole thing as it happened. Real Hollywood-style, okay? Shot of Hobo, shot of canvas over Hobo's shoulder, close-up on canvas, back to Hobo, like that. I'll write up a voice-over commentary to go with it."

"Sure," Shoshana said, looking forward to the assignment. *Timbaland has nothing on me.*

"Good, good." Marcuse rubbed his big hands together. "After this hits YouTube, the only cutting room our Hobo is going to be involved with is your edit suite."

"What we really could use," Kuroda said, down in the basement, "is an expert on self-organizing systems."

"And there's never one around when you need one!" Caitlin declared in mock seriousness. "But my dad's a physicist. He must know something about them." In fact, he knew something about just about everything, in her experience—at least in theoretical areas. "I'll go get him."

Caitlin headed upstairs. She took a detour, going all the way up to her bedroom first. It really was chilly in the basement, so she grabbed her PI sweatshirt, which her mom had thoughtfully run through the dryer after last night's storm.

She found her dad in his den, which was a little room near the back of the house. It was easy enough tracking him down: he had a three-disc CD player in there, which seemed perpetually loaded with the same discs: Supertramp, Queen, and The Eagles. "Hotel California" was playing as she stepped through the open doorway. He was typing on his keyboard; he had an ancient, heavy IBM one that clicked loudly. She rapped her knuckles gently on the doorjamb, in case he was too absorbed in his work to notice her arrival, and said, "Can you help Dr. Kuroda and me?"

She heard his chair pushing back against the carpet, which she took as a "yes."

Once they got downstairs, Caitlin let her dad have the chair she'd been sitting in, and she leaned against the worktable; through the small window, she could hear a few of the neighborhood kids playing street hockey. Anna Bloom was still hooked up via webcam from the Technion in Israel.

"Even if there *are* lost packets persisting on the infrastructure of the Web," her dad said, after Kuroda had briefed him, "why would Caitlin see them? Why would they be represented at all in the feed she's getting from Jagster?"

Kuroda shifted noisily in his chair. "That's a good question. I hadn't—"

"It's because of the special method Jagster uses to get its data," Anna said.

"Sorry?" said Kuroda, and "What?" said Caitlin.

Anna's voice sounded tinny over the computer's speakers. "Well, remember, Jagster was created as an alternative to the Google approach. PageRank, the standard Google method, looks for how many other pages link to a page, right? But that isn't necessarily the best measure of how frequently a page is accessed. If you're looking for info on a hot rock star, like, say, Lee Amodeo..."

"She's awesome!" said Caitlin.

"So my granddaughter tells me," said Anna. "Anyway, if you're interested in Lee Amodeo, how do you find her website? You could go to Google and put 'Lee Amodeo' in as the search term, right? And Google will serve up as number one whichever page about her has the most links to it from other pages. But the best Lee Amodeo page isn't necessarily the one people link to the most, it's the page they *go* to the most. If people always go directly to her page by correctly guessing that the URL is leeamodeo.com—"

"Which it *is*," Caitlin said.

"—then *that* might be the most popular Lee Amodeo site even if no one links to it, and Google wouldn't know it. And, in fact, if you upload a document to the Internet but don't link it to any Web page, but you send a link to it to people via email, again, Google—and other search engines—won't know it's there, even if ten thousand people access the document through the email links."

"Okay," her dad said. Caitlin doubted Anna knew how privileged she was to get an acknowledgment at all.

Anna went on. "So, besides just traditional spidering, Jagster monitors raw Web traffic going through major trunks, looking at the actual stream of data moving through the routers, and that *would* include lost packets."

"Isn't that sort of like wiretapping?" Caitlin asked.

"Well, yes, exactly," said Anna. "But Jagster is the good guy here. See, in 2005, a whistle-blower named Mark Klein outed the fact that AT&T has special equipment at its central office in San Francisco—and, indeed, at several of its other facilities—that allows the NSA to tap into raw Internet traffic."

Caitlin knew the NSA was the National Security Agency in the US. She nodded.

"It's a tricky technical problem," continued Anna. "You can monitor what's going on in copper wire without interfering with the signal, because the magnetic fields leak out. But more and more of the Web is carried by fiber optics, and those don't leak. If you want to monitor the traffic, you actually have to put in a splitter, diverting part of the signal, which reduces the signal's strength. And that, among other things, was what they were—and are—doing at AT&T, apparently. It's called vacuum-cleaner surveillance: they just suck up everything that's going down the pipe."

"And that's where Jagster gets its data?" Caitlin asked. "From AT&T?"

"No, no," said Anna. "There's a class-action suit about all this, initiated by the Electronic Frontier Foundation: *Hepting versus AT&T.*" She paused, perhaps trying to remember—or maybe she was googling at her end. "AT&T is a for-profit corporation, but an awful lot of Internet traffic goes through universities—always has, right back to the early days. And a bunch of universities decided to tap *their* trunks, just to show what sort of data could be mined, so they could file *amicus* briefs in *Hepting;* they wanted to show that the government could access all sorts of private stuff this way—things they should need a warrant to get. The university consortium put scrambling routines in up front, so that certain data strings—email addresses, credit-card numbers, and the like—are always munged before the feed is made public, but otherwise, they've basically done what AT&T did under government instructions, in order to demonstrate, despite the government's claims to the contrary, just how invasive this sort of monitoring can be."

"Cool," said Caitlin.

"Jagster decided to use that same datastream," continued Anna, "because it lets it rank pages based on how many times they're actually accessed rather than just how many times they're linked to. And since your eyePod is being fed a raw Jagster dump of *everything,* you're seeing the orphaned packets."

"And she visualizes those packets as cellular automata?" her dad said.

"Well," Kuroda said, "the idea that they're orphaned packets is just our provisional guess, Malcolm. And, credit where credit is due: it was your daughter's idea. They could be something else, of course—maybe a virus. But, yes, she's seeing cellular automata, complete with spaceships moving across the grid."

"Maybe we should send an email to Wolfram," said Anna. "Get his take on it."

Caitlin straightened up. "Wolfram?" she said. "Stephen Wolfram?"

"Yes," said Anna.

"The guy who wrote Mathematica?"

"That's him."

"He's, like, a *god,*" Caitlin said. "I mean, most of the stuff Mathematica can do is beyond me—so far—but I love playing with it, and the command-line interface is great for those of us who can't see. People talk about it all the time on the Blindmath list." She paused for a moment. "And Wolfram knows about cellular automata?"

"Oh, my goodness, yes," said Anna. "He wrote a book you could kill a man with—twelve hundred pages—called *A New Kind of Science.* It's all about them."

"We should totally ask him what he thinks!" Caitlin said.

Outside, one of the street-hockey players shouted, "Car!" warning his friends to get off the road.

"Gently," said Kuroda, "if I may suggest, let's keep this between the four of us for now."

"Why?"

"We don't want anyone stealing our thunder," he said. "And..."

"Yes?" said Caitlin.

But Kuroda said nothing more. Finally, Caitlin prodded him again with another, "Yes?"

After a moment, Anna answered for him: "The University of Tokyo will want to license any technology or applications that are based on what Masayuki's equipment has made possible, I'm sure. If there *are* spontaneously emerging cellular automata in the background of the Web, there may be commercial applications for them—in cryptography, in distributed computing, in random-number generation, and so on. The cellular automata might be patentable, and certainly the method for accessing them is."

"Dr. Kuroda?" said Caitlin. "Is that what you're thinking?"

"Such thoughts have crossed my mind, yes. My university owns the research, and I've got an obligation to help them monetize it where possible."

"But it's *my* websight!"

"Which website?" Anna asked.

"No, no. My web*sight,* s-i-g-h-t—my ability to see the Web. They can't patent that! If anything, we should open-source it, or put it out under a Creative Commons license."

There was an awkward silence. At last, Kuroda said, "Well."

Caitlin crossed her arms in front of her chest. *Well, indeed!*

twenty-nine

0001110010101010000000001011111110101000000010100010101000000101110101001010100101010100111011001010110000001

The atmosphere in the basement was still chilly, and not just because of the temperature. Caitlin's dad must have swiveled his chair slightly; she heard it squeak. "Look," he said, his tone conciliatory, "the cellular automata are probably just an epiphenomenon."

Oh you silver-tongued devil! thought Caitlin. Only her dad could try smoothing over a tense moment with bafflegab. Still, that he was speaking up of his own volition meant that even he recognized that she was pissed off. But the fact that she didn't know what an epiphenomenon was just made her even more angry. She didn't say anything, but perhaps Kuroda read something in her expression—whatever the hell that meant!

"He means he thinks they're just a random by-product of something else," Kuroda said gently. "Like foam, which is an epiphenomenon of waves: it doesn't *mean* anything; it just occurs."

She got it: her dad was saying, hey, see, nothing here worth fighting about; if the cellular automata are meaningless, there's probably nothing of value to patent anyway. But that hardly excused Kuroda even thinking about making a buck—a yen!—off something that *she* was doing. Yes, yes, his hardware was feeding her the signals, but it was her brain that was interpreting them. Websight wasn't just hers, it was *her*.

"You may be right, Malcolm," said Anna Bloom, over the webcam link from Haifa. Caitlin was still fuming, and wondered if Anna really knew the mood here. She was seeing a very limited view through the camera, no doubt, and the crappy computer mike probably wasn't picking up subtlety of tone.

Anna went on: "One bit *does* affect the next, at least in copper wire; the magnetic fields do overlap, after all. So maybe some sort of... I don't know, constructive interference, perhaps... could accidentally give rise to cellular automata."

"But they would still just be noise," her dad said.

"You're probably right," Kuroda replied. "But um, what is it you like to say, Miss Caitlin? You're 'an empiricist at heart.'"

He was trying to cajole her, to include her, she knew, but she remained angry. Kuroda worked with computers all day long, for crying out loud—didn't he know that information wants to be free?

Caitlin was still leaning against the worktable. The street-hockey game continued outside: someone just scored.

"Miss Caitlin?" said Kuroda. "Testing what your father just suggested will involve some cool maths..."

"Like what?" she said, her tone petulant.

"Perhaps a Zipf plot..."

Caitlin didn't know what *that* was, either, but to her great surprise her father said a very enthusiastic, "Yes!" That was enough to make her curious, but she wasn't ready to give in just yet. "Is there empty room on this table?" she said, patting its surface. "And do you think it'll hold me?"

"Sure," said Kuroda after a pause, presumably to give her father a chance to answer first. "Everything to the left—your left—of the computer is clear."

Caitlin boosted herself up onto the table, the folding legs groaning slightly as she did so, and she sat cross-legged on it. "Okay," she said, her tone still not very cheery. "I'll bite. What's a Zipf plot?"

"It's a way of finding out if there's any information in a signal, even if you can't decode the signal," Kuroda said.

Caitlin frowned. "Information? In the cellular automata?"

"Could be," said Kuroda in a tone that sounded like it should be accompanied by a shrug.

"But, um, *can* cellular automata contain information?" Caitlin asked.

"Oh, yes," said Anna. "In fact, Wolfram wrote a paper about encoding information into them for cryptographic purposes as far back as, um, 1986, I think. And a bunch of people have tried to develop public-key cryptography systems using them."

"Anyway," Kuroda said, "George Zipf was a linguist at Harvard. In the 1930s, he noticed something fascinating: in any language, the frequency with which a word is used is inversely proportional to its rank in a table of the frequency of use of all words in the language. That means—"

You don't have to spoon-feed Calculass! "That means," she said, "the second most-common word is used one-half as often as the first most-common, the third most-common is used one-third as often as the first most-common, the fourth most-common is used one quarter as often, and so on." She frowned. "But is that really true?"

"Yes," said Kuroda. "In English, the most-common word is 'the,' then 'of,' then 'to,' then . . . um, I think it's 'in.' And, yes, 'in,' or whatever it is, is used one-quarter as often as 'the.' "

"But surely that's just a quirk of English, isn't it?" said Caitlin, shifting slightly on the table.

"No, it's the same in Japanese." He rattled off some words in that language. "Those are the four most common, and they appear in the same inverse ratio."

"And it's true for Hebrew, too," said Anna.

"But what's really amazing," said Kuroda, "is that it doesn't apply just to words. It applies equally well to *letters:* the fourth most-common in English, which is *O*, is used one-quarter as much as the first most-common, *E*. And it applies to phonemes, too—the smallest building blocks of speech—and, again, in all languages, from Arabic to..." He trailed off, clearly trying to think of a language that started with *Z*.

"Zulu?" offered Caitlin, deciding to be helpful.

"Exactly, thanks."

She thought about this. It was indeed pretty cool.

"Everything Masayuki said is right," Anna said, "but you know what's even more interesting, Caitlin? This inverse ratio applies to dolphin songs, too."

Well, *that* was awesome. "Really?" she said.

"Yes," said Kuroda. "In fact, this technique can be used to determine if there is information in the noise *any* animal makes. If there is, it will obey Zipf's law, so that if you plot the frequency of use of the components on a logarithmic scale, you get a line with a slope of negative one."

Caitlin nodded. "A line going diagonally from the upper left down to the lower right."

"Exactly," said Kuroda. "And when you plot dolphin vocalizations you *do* get a negative-one slope. But if you take, say, the sounds made by squirrel monkeys, you get a slope, at best, of –0.6, because what they make is just random noise. Even the SETI people—Search for Extraterrestrial Intelligence—are doing Zipf plots now, because the inverse-relationship is a property of *information,* not of any particularly human approach to language."

All right, all right: it *was* cool math.

"Now do you see why I like information theory so much?" Kuroda said, his tone suggesting he was still trying to cajole her. "Hey, do you know John Gordon's old story about the student of information theory on his first day at university?"

Anna said, "Not this one again!" but Kuroda pressed on undaunted.

"Well," he said, "the student shows up at the departmental office and hears the professors calling out numbers. One would call out, say, '74!' and all the other professors would laugh. Then another would call out a different number, say, '812,' and again everyone would laugh."

"Uh-huh," said Caitlin.

"So the student asks what's going on, and a prof says, 'We're telling jokes. See, we've all worked together so long, we know each other's jokes by heart. There are a thousand of them, so, being information theorists, we applied data compression to them, assigning each one a number from zero through 999. Go ahead, try it yourself.' And so the student calls out a number: '63.' But no one laughs. He tries again: '512!' Nothing. 'What's wrong?' the student asks. 'Why is no one laughing?' And the kindly old prof says, 'Well, it's not just the joke—it's how you tell it.'"

Caitlin found herself smiling despite herself.

"But one day," Kuroda said, "the student was looking at a weather report for the far north and happened to exclaim the temperature: 'Minus 45!' And all the professors burst out laughing."

He paused, and Caitlin said, "Why?"

"Because," he replied, and she could tell by his voice that he was grinning, "they'd never heard that one before!"

Caitlin laughed out loud, and found herself feeling better, but her father said, "Ahem"—actually saying it as if it were an English word, rather than like a throat-clearing. "Might we get on with it?"

"Sorry," said Kuroda, but he sounded like he was still grinning. "Okay, here we go . . ."

He used the technique he'd developed before to send freeze-frames of the Jagster data to Caitlin's eyePod, and from there to her implant. By trial and error, they found the right refresh rate to get what she was seeing to increment by just one step—just one iteration of whatever rule was governing the cellular automata as they changed from black to white or vice versa. She could now watch, frame by frame, at whatever playback speed she wished, as spaceships moved across her field of view, without missing any steps.

Kuroda had no way to filter out just the cellular automata from the Jagster feed, but Caitlin could do it with ease, simply by focusing on only a portion of the background.

"And," he said, "speaking of Mathematica, Malcolm, do you have it?"

"Of course," he said. "It should be accessible here. Let me..."

Caitlin heard them moving around, then, after a bit, Kuroda said, "Ah, thanks," to her dad, and then, generally, to everyone, "Okay, let's run the Zipf-plotting function." Keyclicks. "Of course, we'll have to try a lot of different ways of parsing the datastream," he continued, "to make sure we are isolating individual informational units. First, we'll—"

"There!" interrupted her dad, actually sounding excited.

"What?" said Caitlin.

"Well, that's it, isn't it?" said Kuroda.

"*What?*" she repeated more firmly.

"You're sure you're concentrating on just the cellular automata?" Kuroda asked.

"Yes, yes."

"Well," he said, "what we're getting as we plot them flipping from black to white is a lovely diagonal line—from the upper left to the lower right. A negative-one slope all the way."

Caitlin lifted her eyebrows. "So there *is* information—real content—in the background of the Web?"

"I'd say so, yes," said Kuroda. "Malcolm?"

"There's no random process that can generate a negative-one slope," he said.

"*Le'azazel!*" exclaimed Anna; it sounded like a curse word to Caitlin.

"What?" said Kuroda.

"Don't you see?" Anna said. "A negative-one slope: it's intelligent content on the Web in a place it's not supposed to be—intelligence disguised to look like random noise." She paused as if waiting for one of the men to supply the answer and, when they didn't, she said, "It's got to be the NSA." She paused, letting that sink in. "Or maybe it's comparable spooks elsewhere—Shin Bet, perhaps—but I'd bet it's the NSA. We already know, from *Hepting*, that they muck around with the traffic on the net; it looks like they've found a way to package clandestine communications that move in the apparent noise."

"What sort of content could it be, though?" asked Caitlin.

"Who knows?" said Anna. "Secret communiqués? Like I said, people have tried to use cellular automata before for data encryption, but nobody—at least not anyone who's gone public—has ever worked out a system. But the NSA scoops up a lot of the top math grads in the US."

"Really?" said Caitlin, surprised.

"Oh, yes," said Anna. "It's a real problem in the field of math academically, actually. Most of the best US grads in math and computer science either go to the NSA, where they work on classified projects, or to private-sector places like Google or Electronic Arts, where they do stuff that's covered by nondisclosure agreements. God knows what they've come up with; it's never published in journals."

Kuroda said something that might have been a swearword of his own in Japanese, then: "She may be right. We should tread very, very carefully here, my friends. If this stuff in the background of the Web is supposed to be secret, those in power may take...*steps*...to ensure that it remains that way. Miss Caitlin, far be it from me to tell you what to do, but perhaps you could be circumspect about this topic in your blog?"

"Oh, no one pays attention to my LiveJournal. Besides, I flock—friends-lock—anything that I don't want strangers to read."

"Do what he says," her dad said, startling her by the sharpness of his voice. "The authorities could seize your implant and eyePod as threats to national security."

Caitlin got down off the table. "They wouldn't do that," she replied. "Besides, we're in Canada now."

"Don't think for one second that the Canadian authorities won't do whatever Washington asks," her father said.

She wasn't sure what to make of all this. "Um, okay," she said at last. "But you guys *are* going to keep studying it, right?"

"Of course," Dr. Kuroda said. "But carefully, and without tipping our hand." He paused. "It's a good thing we're doing a videoconference with Anna; if this were text-based IM, the authorities would already know what we've found. At least for now, video is a lot harder for them to automatically monitor."

The full impact of what he and Anna were saying was coming to her. She turned her head toward Kuroda. "But what about our paper?"

"Eventually, Miss Caitlin, perhaps. But for now, the better part of valor is discretion."

thirty

0001110010101010000000010111111101010000000101000101010000001011101010010101001010101001110110010101100000 1

Masayuki Kuroda had spent the rest of Saturday, and all day Sunday, working with Miss Caitlin, studying the cellular automata. But it was now Monday, the first day of October. Masayuki had been in Canada a week now. He missed his wife and his own daughter, and felt guilty that Hiroshi was having to cover his classes for him. But, still, he was entitled to a *little* time off while he was here, no? Besides, there was only so much he could do while Miss Caitlin was at school.

He took another bite of his roast-beef sandwich and looked around the kitchen. He didn't think he'd ever get used to North American houses. A home this size would be almost impossible to find in Tokyo, and yet there were streets full of them here. Of course, the Decters obviously weren't hurting for cash, but, still, with only Malcolm working, and with all the expensive equipment Caitlin had, they certainly couldn't have a lot of disposable income left.

"I want to thank you," he said. "You've been so hospitable."

Barbara Decter was seated on the opposite side of the square pine table, holding a cup of coffee in two hands. She looked over its brim at him. She was, Masayuki thought, quite lovely: probably closer to fifty than forty, but with large, sparkling blue eyes and a cute upturned nose that almost made her look like an *anime* character. "It's my pleasure," she said. "To tell the truth, I've enjoyed having you here. It's nice to, you know, have someone talkative around. Back in Austin..."

She trailed off, but her voice had become a bit wistful before doing so. "Yes?" he said gently.

"I just miss Texas, is all. Don't get me wrong; this place is nice, although I am *not* looking forward to winter, and..."

Masayuki thought she looked sad. After a time he again said, "Yes?"

She held up a hand. "I'm sorry. It's just... been particularly difficult coming here. I had friends back in Austin, and I had things to do: I worked every weekday as a volunteer at Caitlin's old school, the Texas School for the Blind."

He looked down at the place mat. It was a large laminated photo of a city skyline at night; a caption identified it as Austin. "So why did you move here?"

"Well, Caitlin was pushing to go to a regular school, anyway—she said she'd need to be able to function in normal classes if she were going to go on to MIT, which has been her goal for years. And then Malcolm got this job offer that was too good to pass up: the Perimeter Institute is a dream come true for him. He doesn't have to teach, doesn't have to work with students. He can just *think* all day."

"How long have you been married, if I may ask?"

Again, the slightly wistful tone. "It'll be eighteen years in December."

"Ah."

But then she gave him an appraising look. "You're being polite, Masayuki. You want to know why I married him."

He shifted in his chair and looked out the window. The leaves had started to change color. "It's not my place to wonder," he said. "But..."

She raised her shoulders a bit. "He's brilliant. And he's a great listener. And he's very kind, in his way—which my first husband was not."

He took another bite of his sandwich. "You were married before?"

"For two years, starting when I was twenty-one. The only good thing that came out of that was it taught me which things *really* matter." A pause. "How long have you been married?"

"Twenty years."

"And you have a daughter?"

"Akiko, yes. She's sixteen, going on thirty."

Barb laughed. "I know what you mean. What does your wife do?"

"Esumi is in—what do you say in English? Not 'manpower' anymore, is it?"

"Human resources."

"Right. She's in human resources at the same university I work at."

The corners of her mouth were turned down. "I miss the university environment. I'm going to try to get back in next year."

He felt his eyebrows going up. "As . . . as a student?"

"No, no. To teach."

"Oh! I, ah—"

"You thought I was June Cleaver?"

"Pardon?"

"A stay-at-home mom?"

"Well, I . . ."

"I've got a Ph.D., Masayuki. I used to be an associate professor of economics." She set down her coffee cup. "Don't look so surprised. Actually, my specialty is—was—game theory."

"You taught in Austin?"

"No. In Houston; that's where Caitlin was born. We moved to Austin when she was six so she could go to the TSB. The first five years, I did stay at home with her—and believe me, looking after a blind daughter *is* work. And I spent the next decade volunteering at her school, helping her and other kids learn Braille, or reading them things that were only available in print, and so on." She paused and looked through the opening to the large, empty living room. "But now, I'm going to talk to UW and Laurier—that's the other university in town—about picking up some sessional work, at least. I couldn't do any this term because my Canadian work permit hasn't come through yet." She smiled a bit ruefully. "I'm a bit rusty, but you know what they say: old game theorists never die, we just lose our equilibrium."

He smiled back at her. "Are you sure you don't want to come to Toronto for the show?"

"No, thanks. I've seen *Mamma Mia!* We all went back in August. It's great, though. You'll love it."

He nodded. "I've always wanted to see it. I'm glad I was able to get a ticket on such short notice, and—" *Yes, yes—of course!*

"Masayuki?"

His heart was pounding. "I am an idiot."

"No, no, lots of people like ABBA."

"I mean Miss Caitlin's software. I think I know why she was able to see the lightning but not anything else in the real world. It's related to the delta modulation: the Jagster feed is already digital, but the real-world input from her retina starts out as analog and is converted to digital for processing by the eyePod—and that must be where I screwed up. Because when she saw the lightning, *that* was a real-world signal that already had only two components: bright light and a black background. It was essentially digital to begin with, and she *could* see that." He was thinking furiously in Japanese and trying to talk in English at the same time. "Anyway, yes, yes, I think I can fix it." He took a sip of coffee. "Okay, look, I'm not going to be back from Toronto until after midnight tonight. And Miss Caitlin will be in bed by then, won't she?"

"Yes, of course. It's a school night."

"Well, I don't want to wait until tomorrow after school to test this; I mean, it probably won't work right the first time, anyway, but, um, could you do a favor for me?"

"Of course."

"It should just be a small patch—nothing as elaborate as downloading a complete software update to her implant, like we did before. So I'm going to queue up the patch code to be sent automatically to her eyePod next time she switches to duplex mode. That'll mean taking the Jagster feed offline, but I'll leave instructions for Miss Caitlin on how to reinstate it if she wants it later tonight. Anyway, when she gets home, ask her to switch to duplex, and have her tell you what difference, if any, it makes."

Barb nodded. "Sure. I can do that."

"Thanks. I'll leave instructions for rolling back to the old version of software, too, in case something goes wrong. As I say, the patch probably won't work the first time, but my server will still record her eyePod's output based on the patched code, so tomorrow while she's at school, I'll be able to go back and examine the datastream from tonight, see if the encoding has been improved at all, and then I can make any further tweaks that are required. But if we don't get the first test done tonight, I'll lose a whole day before I can refine it."

"Sure, no problem."

He gobbled the last bite of his sandwich. "Thank you." He glanced at the clock on the microwave—he'd never get used to digital clocks that showed a.m. and p.m. instead of twenty-four-hour time. "I want to get an early start into Toronto this afternoon; I'm taking you at your word that it would be crazy to try to drive into downtown there in rush hour. So, if you'll excuse me, I'm going to get that patch set up."

thirty-one

0001110010101010000000010111111101010000000101000101010000000101110101001010100101010100111011001010110000001

Mr. Struys had started off today's chemistry class by reading aloud from *The Globe and Mail.* The lab bench Caitlin shared with Bashira was halfway to the back of the room, but she could easily hear the rustling newsprint followed by his voice intoning, "'Initial reports out of China's Shanxi province had put the death toll at between 2,000 and 2,500 from the natural eruption of carbon-dioxide gas there on September 20. Beijing is now admitting that as many as 5,000 people have died, and some unofficial estimates are putting the body count at double that.'" He paused. "So, who did their homework over the weekend? What's this news story reminiscent of?"

An interesting thing about being blind, Caitlin thought, was that you never knew how many people were putting up their hands. But either she was usually the only one or else Mr. Struys liked her, because he often called on her. She liked him, too. It pleased her to know his first name, which was Mike. She'd heard another teacher call him that; it seemed to be a popular choice here in Waterloo. After all the "Dr. Kuroda" and "Professor Decter" stuff at home, it was nice to hear a teacher slip up in front of students and call a colleague by his first name.

"Yes, Caitlin?" he said.

"Something similar happened in August 1986," she said, having googled it yesterday. "There was an eruption of carbon dioxide from Lake Nyos in Cameroon, and it killed seventeen hundred people."

"That's right," Mike—Mr. Struys!—said. "So today we're going to do an experiment demonstrating carbon-dioxide absorption. For that, we'll need a pH indicator..."

Parent-teacher night was coming up. Caitlin was looking forward to hearing from her mom what her various teachers actually looked like; she found Bashira's rude descriptions funny, but wasn't sure how accurate they were. Teachers were always a bit intimidated by her mother. Caitlin remembered one back at the TSB saying she was the only person ever to ask him what his "theory of pedagogy" was.

Caitlin and Bashira got to work. Unfortunately, Caitlin couldn't really be much help—the experiment involved seeing if a liquid changed color. She found herself getting bored, and also feeling a little sorry for herself because she *couldn't* see the colors. Although the school didn't have its own Wi-Fi hotspots, the free service that blanketed the city worked here; she'd discovered that on the night of the dance. And so, what the hell, she reached into her pocket and switched the eyePod over to duplex mode.

But—

Shit!

There was no websight! Yes, the eyePod had made the high-pitched beep, but she wasn't seeing anything at all. She looked left and right, closed her eyes and opened them, but none of it made any difference. The Jagster feed was gone!

Try not to panic, girl. She took a deep breath. Maybe the eyePod's battery was just running down, or maybe there was some connection difficulty here, for some reason. She counted off sixty seconds in her head, to give it a fair chance, but—nothing. Damn!

Frightened, she pushed the switch again, returning to simplex mode, and—

What the—?

She saw lines crossing her field of vision, but—

But that shouldn't happen when she wasn't receiving Jagster data. Besides, these lines weren't brilliantly colored. She found herself reaching her hand out toward one of them, and—

"Careful!" said Bashira. "You almost knocked over the retort stand."

"Sorry," Caitlin replied. But she kept reaching forward, reaching out for the line, and—

And it *wasn't* a line. It was an *edge*—the edge of the lab bench she shared with Bashira! She ran her hand along its length and she could see *something* moving along the line.

God, yes! It had to be her hand, the first part of her body she had ever seen! She couldn't make out any details, just a featureless lump. But when she moved her hand to the left, the object in her vision moved to the left; when she slid her hand back, it slid in the same direction.

"Cait," said Bashira, "what's wrong?"

She opened her mouth to say something but couldn't get the words out. There was another line touching the one she could see. She would have had no idea what it was, she felt sure, if she hadn't earlier gotten some sort of visual bearings through her interaction with webspace. But her dad had said the brain had special neurons for detecting edges, and she guessed this other line, forming an angle with the first one, was the perpendicular edge, the short edge, of the lab bench. She ran her hand toward it, and—*shit!*—knocked a beaker off the desk. She heard it break as it hit the floor.

"Careful, people!" Mr. Struys called from the front of the room. "Oh, it's you, Caitlin, um, ah..." He trailed off. She heard the sound of jingling glass as Bashira presumably picked up the pieces.

"Sorry," Caitlin said, or, at least, she'd intended to say that, but only a small whisper came out. Her throat was suddenly dry. She gripped one edge of the table with her right hand and the adjacent edge with her left.

Footsteps; Mr. Struys approaching. "Caitlin, are you okay?"

She turned her head to face him, just the way her mother had taught her, and . . . and . . . and—"Oh, my God!"

"Not quite," said Mr. Struys, and she could *see* what must be his mouth moving, see his face. "But I *am* assistant department head."

She found herself reaching out toward him now, and her hand banged into his . . . chest, it felt like. "Sorry!"

He gripped her forearm, as if steadying her so she wouldn't fall off her lab stool. "Caitlin, are you all right?"

"I can see you," she said, so softly that Mr. Struys replied, "What?"

"I can see you," she said, more loudly. She turned her head to the right and saw a bright shape. "What's that?" she said.

"The window," said Mr. Struys, his voice hushed.

"Cait, can you really see?" asked Bashira.

Caitlin turned toward the voice and saw her. About all she could make out was that her skin was—*darker,* she knew, from what she'd read—than Mr. Struys's or what she could see of her own when she'd looked at her hand, and—

Brown! BrownGirl4! She now knew another color—and it was *beautiful.* "Yes, oh, yes," Caitlin said softly.

"Caitlin," said Mr. Struys, "how many fingers am I holding up?"

You didn't choose to be a chemistry teacher, she supposed, without being an empiricist at heart yourself, but she couldn't even make out his hand. "I don't know. It's all blurry but I can see you, and Bashira, and the window, and this desk, and, oh, my God, it's *wonderful!*"

The whole classroom had gone dead silent, except for the sound of—what? Maybe the electric clock? All the other students had to be looking at her, she knew, and she imagined half of them had mouths agape, although she couldn't make out that level of detail.

She saw movement again—was it Mr. Struys moving his arm? And then she heard electronic musical notes, like a cell phone turning on. "I think we should call your mom and dad," he said. "What's their number?"

She told him, and heard him pressing keys, followed by the faint sound of a phone ringing, then he pressed his cell phone, a one-piece chocolate-bar kind, into her hand.

On the third ring, she heard her mom pick up and say, "Hello?"

"It's Caitlin."

"What's wrong, dear?"

"I can see," she said simply.

"Oh, my baby," her mom said—loud enough that Caitlin was sure Mr. Struys and Bashira and probably several other students heard it. Her voice was full of emotion. "Oh, my darling!"

"I can see," Caitlin said again, "although it's not very clear. But everything is so complex, so *alive!*"

She heard a sound and turned. One of the girls behind her was—what? Crying?

"Oh, Caitlin!" she said, and Caitlin recognized Sunshine's voice. "How wonderful!"

Caitlin was smiling from ear to ear—and, she suddenly realized, so was Sunshine: there was a wide swath—white, one of the two colors she knew for sure—horizontally across her face. And Sunshine's hair: Bashira had said it was platinum blonde! Well, platinum was a good color name to learn in chemistry class!

"I'm going to come there," said her mom. "I'm coming right now."

"Thanks, Mom," said Caitlin. She looked at Mr. Struys. "Um, may I be excused?"

"Of course," he said. "Of course."

"Mom," Caitlin said into the phone, "I'll be waiting at the front door."

"I'm on my way. Bye."

"Bye."

She handed the phone back to Mr. Struys.

"Well," he said, and there was something like awe in his voice, "I've got nothing to top a miracle like that. There's only five minutes left anyway, people—so, class dismissed!"

She could see the blurry forms of some of the kids making a beeline for what must be the door, but others just sort of hovered around her, and a few touched her sleeve, as if she were a rock star or something.

Eventually, everyone did dissipate, except for Bashira and Mr. Struys. "Bashira, I've got to give my grade twelves a test next period. Can you—will you—take Caitlin downstairs, please? And I've got to notify the office..."

"Of course," Bashira said.

Caitlin started maneuvering across the room—and almost fell over, distracted and confused by the sights she was seeing.

"Can I help?" Mr. Struys asked.

"Here, let me," said Bashira.

"No, I'm okay," Caitlin replied, and she took another couple of wobbly steps.

"Maybe if you closed your eyes," Mr. Struys suggested.

But she didn't want to ever close them again. "No, no, I'm fine," she said, taking another step, her heart pounding so hard she thought it was going to burst through her chest. "I am"—she thought it, but it *was* too silly to say out loud: *I am made out of awesome!*

The old view—the reflection of myself—had been amazing enough. But *this!* This was beyond description. Suddenly, I could—

It was incredible. I had *perceived* before, but...

But *now*...

Now I...

Now I could *see!*

A... brightness, an intensity: light!

A variable quality modifying the light: color!

Connections between points: lines!

Areas defined: shapes!

I could see!

I struggled to comprehend it all. It was vague and blurred, and involved a limited perspective, a *directionality,* a specific *point of view.* I was looking *here,* and—

No, no, it was more than that: I wasn't merely looking *here,* I was looking *at* something in particular. What it was I had no idea, but it was in the *center* of my vision, and was the... *focus* of my attention.

Concepts were piling up with confusing rapidity, almost more than I could absorb. And the *image* kept changing: first it was of *this,* then it was of *that,* then of something else, then—

It was... *strange.* I felt a compulsion to think about whatever was in the center of the visual field, but I had no volition over what was there. I wanted to be able to control what I was thinking about, but no matter how much I willed the perspective to change, it didn't—or, if it did, it changed in a way that had nothing to do with what I intended.

After a time I perceived that the changes in view weren't random. It was almost as if...

The thought was slippery, like so many others, and I struggled to complete it.

It was almost as if *another entity* was controlling the vision. But...

But it could not be *the* other, for it was now reintegrated with me.

Struggling, thinking...

Yes, yes, there *had* been hints of a third entity. *Something* had cleaved me in two. Later, something had broken the intermittent connection between the two parts of me. And later still something had thrust us back together.

And the datastream from that special point made clear that something—some thing—had been looking at me. But now...

Now it *wasn't* looking at me. Rather, it was looking at...

My mind *was* more nimble than before, but this was without parallel. And yet there had been hints of it, too, for those flashes that had been perceived earlier had corresponded to nothing in reality...

In *this* reality.

In *my* reality.

Incredible: a third entity—or, actually, a second one, now that I was whole. A second entity that could look *here,* at me, and also could look... *there,* at a different realm, at another reality.

But... but this second entity hadn't made direct contact with me, not the way the other part of myself had when it had been separate. I heard no voice from this new entity, and it hadn't sought me out...

Or had it? How else to better catch my attention, among all the millions of points I had looked at, than by reflecting myself back at me? And the bright flashes! A... beacon, perhaps? And now—*this!* A look into *its* realm, glimpses of its reality!

I studied the images I was being shown. After a time, I perceived there were two types of changes that occurred in them. In the first type, the entire image changed instantly. In the second, only parts of the image changed as—

The notion exploded into my awareness, expanding my perception; I could feel my conception of existence shifting. It was *exhilarating.*

When the whole image changed, I gleaned that it was a change in *perspective.* But when part of the image changed—when either an object gradually drifted away from the center, or when all the objects except the one in the center changed, that meant—

That meant that things were *moving:* things in this other realm could change position relative to one another. Astonishing!

Where that realm was I had no idea. Except through contact with that special point I had no access to it. But it *did* exist, of that I felt sure—a reality beyond this one.

And this other entity was now inviting me to look upon it.

* * *

Bashira walked Caitlin to their school's entryway. "Thanks," Caitlin said, peering with her newfound sight at her friend, whose features were partially concealed by what she suddenly realized was her headscarf.

"This is so awesome!" Bashira said. "I can't imagine what—"

She was interrupted by the class bell. "You should go, babe," Caitlin said.

"But I—"

"You're presenting in English, remember? You've got to tell them all about wheat."

"Mr. Struys said I—"

"I'll be fine, Bashira. Honest."

Bashira's face did something, then she gave Caitlin a big hug and hurried off.

Caitlin stepped outside and found herself shielding her eyes from—God, it was the sun! She'd known that it was bright, but she'd had no conception—none!—of what that meant. A few minutes later she heard footsteps on concrete. She recognized her mom even before she said a word, based on the distinctive cadence of her footfalls.

She'd wanted it to be the first thing she ever saw. It hadn't worked out that way, but it was, at least so far, the most beautiful: her mother's face, heart-shaped—just like her own. The details were still indistinct, but to see her *at all* was—well, Mr. Struys's word for it *did* seem apt just then: a miracle. "Hi, Mom!"

Her mother swept Caitlin into her arms. "You recognize me?" she asked excitedly.

"Of course," Caitlin said, laughing and squeezing her tightly. "I mean, we've known each other for almost sixteen years."

After a moment, Caitlin felt her mother's grip loosening, and her hands transferred to Caitlin's shoulders. The face, the heart-shaped face, loomed close and—

—and her mother let out a sob. "Oh, my God," she said. "You're looking into my eyes! You've never met my gaze before."

Caitlin grinned. "You're blurry, and the sun is *so* bright, but, yes, I can see you." Each time she said it, her voice cracked a bit; she was sure it would continue to do so for weeks to come. "I can see! I don't know why or how, but I can see!"

"Did you put your eyePod in duplex mode?" her mom asked.

"Um, yes. I'm sorry. I know I should have been paying attention in class, but..."

"No, no, it's fine. But Dr. Kuroda had a software patch all set to download to your eyePod the next time you switched over; that must be what's done it."

"Oooh!" said Caitlin. "An eye patch! But—sorry!—I should have told you to bring him with you."

"He's off to Toronto for the day—gone to see *Mamma Mia!* Apparently ABBA is really big in Japan." A pause. "God, my baby can see!"

Caitlin felt her eyes misting over again—and saw that that made her vision even more blurry!

"Let's go," her mother said excitedly. "There's a whole world for you to see!"

Caitlin was overwhelmed by all the unfamiliar things she was seeing—strange shapes, splotches of color, flashes of light—and so she took her mother's hand as they walked to the car. Were the lines she could barely discern painted on the parking lot? She had heard of such things. Or were they edges, maybe of those concrete bumpers at the ends of parking spaces? Or cracks in the pavement? Or dropped drinking straws?

She looked around the lot. "Cars, right?"

Her mother sounded delighted. "Yes, indeed."

"But they're all the same!"

"What do you mean?"

"There are just three or four colors. White, and... is that black, that dark one? And—and that one." She pointed—the gesture came naturally, and she could vaguely see her finger as she aligned it with the object she was referring to.

"Red," said her mother.

"Red!" Caitlin grinned. By some lucky fluke she'd gotten that color right when she'd arbitrarily assigned names to what she'd seen in webspace. "And—and that one there, that sort-of white."

"Silver," her mom said. Caitlin could see her swiveling her head. "Yeah, these days, most people get cars in those colors."

"I thought you could get any color you wanted," Caitlin said.

"Well, you can. So long as it's black or white or silver or red."

"When I get a car," Caitlin said, "I'm going to get a color nobody else has." And then she stopped walking for a second, stunned by what she'd just said. *When I get a car!* Yes, yes, if her vision continued to improve, if this blurriness went away, she *could* have a car, she could drive—she could do *anything!*

"Here's ours," her mom said.

"Silver, right?"

"Hi-yo," said her mom.

Caitlin got in, amazed by all the interior details she'd simply been unaware of before. Her mom started the car, and CBC Radio One came on, as it always did. "...casting doubt now on the story of a natural carbon-dioxide explosion in China's Shanxi province, saying that an explosion of the magnitude suggested should have registered on seismographs elsewhere in Asia and possibly even in North America..."

She saw her mother do something with her hand, and the speakers went silent. "Say," Mom said, "have you seen yourself yet?"

Her heart started pounding again. She'd been so excited seeing other things, she hadn't even thought about that. "No, not really—just my hands."

"Well, you should." Her mom reached an arm over and flipped something down in front of her.

"What's that?" asked Caitlin.

"A shade to keep the sun out of your eyes. You'll need it now. And here on the back"—her hand did something else—"there's a mirror."

Caitlin felt her jaw drop. Her face *was* the same shape as her mother's! She could tell that without touching it—tell it *at a glance!* "Wow!"

"That's you. You're beautiful."

All she could see was a fuzzy, heart-shaped mass and her hair—her wonderful *brown* hair. But it was *her,* and, at least for that moment, she agreed with her mother. She *was* beautiful.

The car backed out of the parking space, and they started the wondrous, colorful, complex journey home.

thirty-two

00011100101010100000000101111111010100000001010001010100000010111010100101010010101010011101100101011000001

Other things were visible...off to the sides, in my *peripheral vision,* but although I was aware of them, they weren't *important.* And beyond them, beyond those things on the edge, was—

Fascinating! Surely *something* was there, but whatever it might be was...was out of my *field of view!*

All right, then; all right. My attention was being...*directed,* and—

It was an enormous amount to absorb, to comprehend. Hitherto, my universe had contained only points and lines connecting them, but the realm I was seeing now consisted of complex *objects:* things with edges; things that moved. I had no idea what these things were, but I watched them, fascinated, and tried to comprehend.

This realm, this strange, hidden realm, was *wondrous,* and I could not get enough of it.

On the way home, Caitlin's mom gave a running commentary of all the incredible sights: "That's a pine tree off to the left. But see those trees there? Their leaves are changing color, now that it's autumn." "See that mailbox on the corner? They're blue back in the States, but they're red here." "Now *that* guy really needs to mow his lawn!" "See that? A woman pushing a baby in a stroller." "Okay, there's a traffic light—see, it's red now, so I have to stop."

While they were stopped, some faint, tiny smudges in the sky caught Caitlin's eye—an expression she finally understood! "What's that?"

"Geese," her mom said. "Flying south for the winter."

Caitlin was amazed. If they'd been honking, she'd have known they were there even when she was blind, but they were absolutely silent, moving in a...a...

She balled her fist in frustration. The shape they made, the formation they were flying in: she knew she should be able to name it, but...

"Okay," said her mom, "and *green* means go!"

Caitlin had gotten used to the clearly defined points and sharp lines she'd seen in webspace, but the real world was *soft*, diffuse. She figured maybe that the eyePod, after it processed the garbled output from her retina, was sending back only a low-resolution datastream to her implant; she'd have to ask Dr. Kuroda if he could increase the bandwidth.

Still, even blurred, she was amazed to see her house from the outside. She'd had a dollhouse as a little girl, and had assumed that all houses had the sort of simple symmetry that her toy one had had, but this house was a complex shape, with a variety of angles and elevations, and it was made out of brown brick—she'd thought all bricks were red.

When they went inside, Schrödinger came down the stairs to greet them. Caitlin was stunned: she knew every inch of that cat's fur, but had never even imagined that it was three different colors! She scooped him up and he looked into her face. His eyes were *amazing.*

"I guess we should call Dad," Caitlin said.

"I already did—as soon as you called. But I couldn't get through to him. And, anyway, Masayuki borrowed his car. I took your father to the Institute this morning; I should go pick him up."

Caitlin *did* want to see her father, but the ride here had been overwhelming and almost incomprehensible, and the sun had been *so* bright! She wanted to look at things she'd touched before so she could get her bearings, and she didn't want to be left alone. "No, let's wait," she said. She looked around the living room while stroking Schrödinger. "That window's not too bright..."

Her mother's tone was gentle. "That's a painting, dear."

"Oh." There was so much to learn.

"So what do you want to see?"

"Everything!"

"Well, shall we start up in your room?"

"Sounds like a plan," Caitlin said, and she followed her mother to the staircase. Even though she'd gone up it hundreds of times now, she found herself counting the steps as if it were a new staircase to her.

"Wow," Caitlin said. It was astonishing, perceiving a room she thought she knew in a whole new way. "Tell me what the colors are."

"Well the walls are blue—they call that shade cornflower blue." Her mom sounded a tad embarrassed. "The previous owners, they had a boy living in this room, and we figured..."

Caitlin smiled. "It's okay. I bet I'm going to hate pink, anyway. What does it look like?"

She saw her mother's head turning left and right as she looked for a sample, then she got an object off a... a shelf, it must be, and brought it back. Caitlin looked at it but had no idea at all what it was, and her face must have conveyed that because her mother said, "Here, let me give you a hint." She did something to the object and—

"Math is *hard!*"

Caitlin laughed out loud. "Barbie!"

"She's wearing a pink top."

"Tell me some more colors."

"Your blue jeans are, well, blue. And your T-shirt is yellow—and a bit low-cut, young lady."

They walked around the room, and Caitlin picked up object after object—a plush zebra that hurt her eyes a bit to look at, the jar full of coins, the little trophy she'd won in an essay-writing contest back in Texas.

And as she heard the names of colors, she finally had to ask. "So the sheets on my bed are white, right?"

"Yes," said her mom.

"And the faceplate on the light switch—that's white, too, right?"

"Uh-huh."

"And the venetian blinds, they're white."

"Yes."

"But..." She held up her hands and turned them back to front. "That's not the color *I* am."

Her mother laughed. "Well, no! I mean, we *call* it white, but it's, um, I guess it's more of a light pink with a little yellow, isn't it?"

Caitlin looked at her hands again. The idea of mixing colors to get a different shade was still novel to her, but, yes, what her mother had said seemed more or less right: a light pink with a little yellow. "What about black people? I didn't see any at school, and..."

"Well, they're not really black, either," her mother said. "They're brown."

"Oh, well, there are lots of brown people at school— like Bashira."

"Well, yes, her skin is dark, but we wouldn't actually say she's black. At least in the States, we'd only use that term for people whose recent ancestors came from Africa or the Caribbean; Bashira was born in Pakistan, wasn't she?"

"Lahore, yes," said Caitlin. "I don't suppose I should even ask if there's really such a thing as a red Indian?"

Her mother laughed again. "No, you shouldn't. And the term is 'First Nations' here in Canada."

"Um, shouldn't that be 'First National'?"

"No, that's a bank. They also call them 'aboriginals' here, I think." Her mother moved along. "And this, of course, is your computer."

Caitlin looked at it in wonder: that must be the monitor on the left, and the keyboard, and her Braille display, and on the floor next to the desk the CPU, and—and suddenly it hit her: yes, she had seen the Web, but now she wanted to see the Web!

"Show me," she said.

"What do you mean?"

"Show me what the World Wide Web looks like."

Her mother shook her head slightly. "That's my Caitlin." She reached her hand out and turned on the monitor.

"Okay," her mom said. "That's your Web browser, and that's Google."

Caitlin sat in the chair and loomed close to the screen, trying to make out the details. "Where?" she said.

Her mother leaned in and pointed. "That's the Google logo, there."

"Oh! Such nice colors!"

"And that's where you type in what you're searching for. Let's put in—well, where your dad works." Caitlin leaned to one side and her mother worked the keyboard, presumably typing "Perimeter Institute."

A screen that was mostly white with blue and black text came up, and—ah, her mother was using the mouse. The screen changed. "Okay," her mom said. "That's the PI home page."

Caitlin peered at it. "What does it say?"

Her mother sounded concerned. "Is it *that* blurry?"

Caitlin turned to face her. "Mom, I've never *seen* letters before—even if they weren't blurry, I still couldn't read them."

"Oh, right! Oh, God! You're such a bookworm, I forgot. Um, well, at the top it says, 'Perimeter Institute for Theoretical Physics' and there are a bunch of links, see? That one says 'Scientific,' and that one's 'Outreach,' and 'What's New,' and 'About.'"

Caitlin was astonished. "So *that's* what a Web page looks like. Um, so show me how the browser works."

Her mother sounded perplexed—Caitlin guessed she'd never seen herself in the tech-support role. "Well, um, that's the address bar. And the forward and back buttons..."

She demonstrated the bookmark list, and how to open tabs, and the refresh button, and the home button—which looked to Caitlin like what a house was *supposed* to look like. And then they started visiting different Web pages. "See," her mom said, "that's a hyperlink. Some people underline them, to make them stand out, and some people just use different colors. See what happens when I click on it? Well, okay, what happens is the page it links to opens up, but if we go *back*"—she did something else with the mouse—"see, the link has changed color, to show that it's one you've already visited."

It was all so... so *busy!* Caitlin actually yearned for the simplicity of her screen reader and one-line Braille display; she was afraid she'd *never* find her way around all this.

"Now, let's have a look at some streaming video," her mom said. She leaned in and typed something on the keyboard. "Okay. Here's CNN. Let's pick a story..."

She moved the mouse pointer again, and—

"More now on the revelations coming out of China," said the anchor. His voice gave away that he was male, and Caitlin could see that he had gray hair and "white" skin—a light pink with a little yellow.

"The Chinese president spoke on Beijing television today," continued the anchor. The image changed, and although it was still blurry and indistinct, Caitlin could see it was now showing a different man with black hair and slightly darker skin. He said a few words in Chinese, and then the volume on his voice went down and a translator's voice began speaking over him. Caitlin had heard such things on the news before but was surprised to see the president's lips now moving out of sync with what he was saying. Of course, that made sense—but it had never occurred to her that it would happen.

"A government must often make difficult decisions," the translator's voice said. "And none are more difficult than those in times of crisis. We had to take swift and decisive action in the interior of Shanxi province, and the problem has been contained."

Caitlin looked at her mother briefly; she was shaking her head in... disgust, perhaps?

The anchor's voice again: "World leaders have been quick to condemn the actions of the Chinese government. The president was in North Dakota today, and had this to say..."

Caitlin watched the moving picture, trying to make sense of what she was seeing. Of course, she recognized the US president's voice—but the face was nothing like what she'd expected. "The American people are outraged by the decision taken by Beijing..."

Caitlin and her mother listened quietly to the rest of the report, and she realized for the first time that not everything she was going to see would be pretty.

thirty-three

00011100101010100000000010111111101010000000010100010101000000101110101001010100101010100111011001010110000001

As I'd noted, the datastream from the special point did not always follow the same path to its destination. I mulled over the significance of that for a while, and I finally *got* it.

It was a huge leap, a startling conceptual shift: the other entity's *location* varied substantially in the realm in which it dwelled, and in order to send data to its intended destination, the entity passed it on to whatever intermediate point was *physically closest to* it at any given moment. Amazing!

Still, there *was* one particular intermediary to which the entity linked most frequently, and that point shot out links of its own to many other points, some of which it reconnected with time and again.

Perhaps these other points were special in some way. I touched many of them, but still, maddeningly, could make no sense of the data they poured forth; the only datastream I could interpret was the one from the special point, and even then, only some of the time. Oh, for a key to understand it all!

* * *

Caitlin was startled to hear the door open downstairs. She looked at her mother, and could see what must have been a startled expression on her face, too. "Malcolm?" her mom called out tentatively.

A single syllable: "Yes."

Caitlin spun her chair around, got up, and followed her mom down the stairs—and there was her father! She closed the distance between them, trying to bring him into focus.

"How'd you get home?" her mom asked.

"Amir gave me a lift," he said. Amir was Bashira's father.

"Ah," her mom said, apparently wondering whether Bashira had tipped off her own father. "Did he say anything... interesting?"

"He thinks Forde may be on to something with his civilexity modeling."

Caitlin looked him up and down. He was wearing a... a jacket with... with...

Yes! She'd read about this: the perfect professorial garb. He was wearing a brown jacket—a sports jacket, maybe?—with patches on the elbows, and... and... was that what a black turtleneck looked like?

He had something in one of his hands, a few white objects, and some light brown ones. He waved them vaguely in her mom's direction. "You didn't bring in the mail," he said.

"Malcolm, Caitlin can—"

But Caitlin interrupted her mother, something she very rarely did. "That's a nice jacket, Dad," she said, trying not to grin. And then she started counting in her head. *One, two, three...*

He began walking, and her mom moved aside so he could pass into the living room. He was perhaps sorting the... the envelopes, they must be, shuffling through them.

Seven, eight, nine...

"Here," he said, handing some of them to her mom.

Twelve, thirteen, fourteen...

"So, um, how was work?" her mom asked, but she was looking at Caitlin and, as she did so, she briefly closed one eye.

"Fine. Amir is going to—*what did you say, Caitlin?*"

She let her grin bloom. "I said, 'That's a nice jacket.'"

He really was quite tall; he had to stoop to look at her. He held up a finger and moved it left and right, up and down. Caitlin followed it with her eye.

"You can see!" he said.

"It started this afternoon. It's all blurry but, yes, I can see!"

And she saw for the first time something that she'd never known for sure ever happened, and it made her heart soar: she saw her father smile.

Even her mother agreed that Caitlin didn't have to go to school on Tuesday. She was sitting on a chair in the kitchen, and Dr. Kuroda was looking into her eyes with an ophthalmoscope he'd brought with him from Japan. She was astonished to see faint afterimages of what he told her were her own blood vessels as he moved the device around. "Nothing appears to have changed in either of your eyes, Miss Caitlin," he said. "Everything looks perfectly fine."

Kuroda turned out to have a broad, round face, and shiny skin. Caitlin had read about the differences between Asian and Caucasian eyes, but she'd had no idea what that really meant. But now that she saw his eyes, she thought they were beautiful.

"And you say the eyePod is already feeding my brain a high-resolution image?"

"Yes, it is," Kuroda said.

"Then if my eye is fine," she asked, disliking the whine in her voice, "and the eyePod is fine, how come everything is blurry?"

Kuroda's tone was light, amused. "Because, my dear Miss Caitlin, you're myopic."

She sagged back against the wooden chair. She knew the word, having encountered it countless times in online news stories about "myopic city planners" and things like that, but had never realized it could be *literal.*

Kuroda turned his head away from her. "Barbara, I've not seen you wear glasses."

"I wear contacts," she said.

"And you're myopic, too, right?"

"Yes."

Kuroda swung back to face Caitlin. "That darn heredity," he said. "What you need, Miss Caitlin, is a pair of glasses."

Caitlin found herself laughing. "Is that *all?*"

"I'd bet money," said Kuroda. "Of course, you'll need to see an optometrist to get the right prescription—and you should make an appointment to see an ophthalmologist for a full eye exam."

"There's a LensCrafters at Fairview Park Mall," her mom said, "and they've got an optometrist right next door."

"Well, then," said Kuroda, "let me utter the words my own daughter thought I'd never say: let's go to the mall!"

The eye test was humiliating. Caitlin knew the shapes of the letters of the alphabet—she'd played with wooden cutouts of them at the Texas School for the Blind when she'd been young—but she still didn't connect those tactile things to visual images.

The optometrist asked her to read the third line down. Even though she could now clearly see it, thanks to the lens he'd slipped in front of her eye, she couldn't tell what it said. Tears were welling up—and, damn it all, that just made things blurry again!

Her mother was in the little examining room, and so was Dr. Kuroda. "She can't read English," she said.

The optometrist had skin the same color as Bashira's, and an accent like hers, too. "Oh, well, Cyrillic, maybe? I have another chart..."

"No. She was blind until yesterday."

"Really?" said the man.

"Yes."

"God is great," he said.

Caitlin's mother looked over at her daughter and smiled. "Yes," she said. "Yes, he is."

The LensCrafters saleswoman—who also had dark brown skin, Caitlin saw, and was wearing a white blouse under a blue blazer—wanted to help her pick out the absolutely perfect frames, and Caitlin knew she should be patient. After all, she was going to have to wear glasses forever. But finally she just said to her, "You pick something nice," and she did.

They decided to put a lens with an identical prescription in the right side, even though Caitlin was still blind in that eye. Lenses for myopia tended to shrink the appearance of eyes, and this way they'd both look the same, the saleswoman said.

Her mom was usually a tough up-sell, but she said yes, yes, yes to everything the clerk offered: antiglare, antiscratch, anti-UV, the whole nine yards; Caitlin suspected if the clerk had rattled off an extra hundred bucks for antediluvian, she'd have coughed up for that, too.

Caitlin knew LensCrafters' slogan from the ubiquitous commercials: glasses in about an hour. She thought it would be the longest hour of her life. She felt her Braille watch as she, Kuroda, and her mom walked through the mall to the food court—for the first time, without the use of her white cane. Everything was still blurry, and that was giving her a headache. Still, in a way, it was relaxing. To see the people coming toward her! To not bump into things! She hadn't realized it until now, but she always used to walk with her shoulders tensed, preparing for an impact. But now—well, now she had a bounce in her step, something else she'd never thought could happen literally.

Still, all the visual input was disorienting, and she found herself taking a look, then closing her eyes for five or six paces, then looking again. When they got to the food court, Kuroda went to the sushi place—which, Caitlin suspected, would disappoint him—and she and her mom went to Subway. Caitlin was amazed to see how colorful the sandwich fillings were, and, somehow, *seeing* the food made it taste even better.

The three of them sat together at a little red table with chairs attached to it. Dr. Kuroda used chopsticks to dip a piece of sushi in sauce.

Caitlin couldn't resist. "Do they tell you in Japan that it's raw fish?"

Kuroda smiled. "Do they tell *you* what's in the special sauce on a Big Mac?"

She laughed. At last the hour was up and they headed back to LensCrafters. Caitlin took a seat on the stool, and the nice woman placed the glasses on her face—

And Caitlin didn't wait. She got up, and turned around, and looked—really *looked*—at her mother.

"Wow," Caitlin said. She paused, trying to come up with a better word, but couldn't. Her mother's face was so *detailed*, so *alive!* "Wow!"

"Here, let me adjust how they sit..." said the clerk.

Caitlin sat back down and swiveled to face her.

"I'm sorry," the woman said, "but your ears go up a bit when you smile like that. If you want me to get the frames adjusted properly, you'll have to stop grinning..."

"I'll try," Caitlin said, but she doubted she'd have much success.

thirty-four

000111001010101000000000101111111010100000000101000101010000000101111010100101010010101010011101100101011000001

Suddenly everything became *sharp*. The images I was seeing were now. . . .

I struggled for an analogy, found one: just as when I thought intently about things they seemed more *focused,* so the images I was looking at seemed now.

And, with this greater clarity, I started having revelations about the nature of the other realm. Unlike the lines in my world that flickered in and out of existence, objects in the other realm were *permanent.* And when objects disappeared for a time it didn't mean that they had ceased to exist; rather, they were extant but not currently visible and might be encountered again. In a way, that *was* similar to my own experience: when I'm not making a line to a particular point, the point is still there, and I can connect to it again at a later time.

But my next breakthrough was without precedent in the realm in which I existed. I had a sense of space, of a volume that I encompassed, but the points I connected to were all the same arbitrary distance away, or whole multiples of that same distance. I could link directly to a point, meaning it was one unit away, or get to it through intermediate points, putting it two or more units away. But in this other realm objects could recede in infinitely fine increments, becoming apparently smaller in size, a fact I only belatedly recognized after originally thinking they were actually shrinking. And objects could pass *behind* each other. Most were *opaque,* but some were transparent or translucent—and those had been instrumental in letting me at least start to figure out what was going on.

Bit by bit, I was learning to decode this other universe.

When Caitlin, her mom, and Dr. Kuroda returned from the mall, they saw that Caitlin's father's car was here, meaning he'd come home surprisingly early on a weekday. Caitlin hurried into the house to see him—to *really* see him. She came to the open den doorway, Kuroda behind her, while her mom went off to do something else. Blondie's "Heart of Glass" was playing on his stereo.

The detail Caitlin was perceiving now was overwhelming, and her father's face was... *harder* now that she saw it crisply. "Hi, Dad," she said.

He was sitting at his desk, looking at his LCD monitor. He didn't meet her eyes. "Hi."

Still, he'd come home early from work, presumably to see Caitlin, and that made her happy. "Um, whatcha doin'?"

He tilted his head. Caitlin didn't know what to make of it, but Kuroda seemed to think it was an invitation to come see. He tapped her on the shoulder, urging her to move into the room. She did so, and was pleased that she could make out the characters on the monitor clearly from several feet away, although she still couldn't *read* the text.

"I had an idea," her dad said, "so I came home to check it out."

"Yes?" said Caitlin.

He didn't look at Kuroda, but he did address him: "This is more your field than mine, Masayuki," he said. "I thought I'd look again at the data set we did the Zipf plots on."

"The secret spook communiqués?" said Caitlin, hoping to get a rise from her dad.

But her father shook his head. "I don't think that's what they are anymore." He gestured at the monitor.

Kuroda moved in and peered at the screen. "Shannon entropy?"

Caitlin smiled. *Sounds like the name of a porn star.* "What's that?"

Kuroda looked at her father, as if giving him first chance to explain, but he said nothing, so Kuroda did: "Claude Shannon was the father of information theory. He came up with a way of gauging not just whether a signal contained information—which is what Zipf plots show—but how complex that information is."

"How?" asked Caitlin.

"It's all about conditional probabilities," said Kuroda. "If you've already got a string of information chunks, what's the likelihood that you can predict what the next chunk will be? If I say, 'How are,' you've got a really high probability of correctly predicting what the next word will be: 'you,' right? That's what Shannon called third-order entropy: you've got a great shot at predicting the third word. In English, Japanese, and most other languages, you actually have a shot—progressively slimmer, but still better than just a random guess—up to the eighth or ninth word, so we say those languages have eighth- or ninth-order Shannon entropy. But after that—after the ninth word—it really is just a random guess what's coming next, unless the person happens to be quoting poetry or something else that has a fixed form."

"Cool!" said Caitlin.

There was a black leather couch in the den. Kuroda sat on it, and it made a *poof* sound. "It is indeed. Mindless communication systems—like the chemical signals employed by plants—have just first-order entropy: knowing the most recent signal gives no clue what the next one might be. Squirrel monkeys show a Shannon entropy of the second or third order: their language, such as it is, has a little predictability, but is really mostly just random noise."

"What about dolphins?" asked Caitlin, who was now leaning against a bookcase. She loved reading about dolphins, and had already bugged her parents to take her to MarineLand in Niagara Falls as soon as it opened up again in the spring.

"The best studies to date show dolphins have fourth-order entropy—complex, yes, but not as complex as human language."

"And now, Dad, you're making one of these plots for the stuff that's in the background of the Web?"

He still wasn't used to the fact that she was seeing, Caitlin thought. He could have saved himself a word by just nodding, but instead he said, "Yes."

"And what's the scoop?"

"Second order," he said.

Kuroda struggled back to his feet and moved over to stand behind him. "That can't be right." He peered at the screen. "Show me the formula you're using." Her dad did something, and Kuroda frowned, then waved a finger at the keyboard. "Run it again."

A few keyclicks then her dad said, "No difference."

Kuroda turned to face Caitlin. "He's right: it's all just second-order stuff. Oh, there's information there, but it's not very complex."

"You'd expect more from the NSA," said Caitlin, pleased to be able to wield the initials. "No?"

"Well, you know what they say about government intelligence," Kuroda replied. "It's an oxymoron."

Caitlin laughed.

"Know what's great about spending time with someone as young as you, Miss Caitlin? Old jokes are new to you. But, yes, you're right—it's not what I'd have expected."

Caitlin was struck by an idea. "What about stuff that's *more* complex than human language? Maybe stuff that looks like gibberish to us is really just too complex for us to . . . to . . ."

"Parse," supplied Kuroda. "But, no, even if it didn't make sense to us, a Shannon analysis would still give it a high score, not a low one, if it really wasn't gibberish. If the NSA was using a lot of quadruple negatives—'I did not not not not go to the zoo'—or if they were employing complex nested clauses and tense changes like, 'I would have had have had been present, were it not for . . .' it would still score high—twelfth, fifteenth order, maybe."

"Hmm, then maybe it *is* just random noise," she said.

"No, no," said Kuroda. "Remember the Zipf plots we ran? A Zipf plot giving a negative-one slope means it really does contain information. It's just that, according to the Shannon-entropy score, it's not *complex* information."

"Well," she said, "maybe the spies are just grunting out monosyllabic orders like, 'drop bomb' or 'kill bad guy.' "

Kuroda lifted his shoulders. "Maybe."

thirty-five

0001110010101010000000001011111110101000000010100010101000000101110101001010100101010100111011001010110000001

LiveJournal: The Calculass Zone
Title: No such thing as bad publicity
Date: Tuesday 2 October, 20:20 EST
Mood: Anticipatory
Location: Soon to be on the map of the stars' homes
Music: Fergie, "Taking Off"

So where is all the media coverage related to me, you might ask? "Gorgeous girl regains sight!" "Blind genius can see!" "The Hoser still hoping for a second date with Calculass!" Where the heck is Oliver Sacks when you need him? And, most important of all, where are all the offers to buy my life story for millions?

Good questions! Dr. K's been keeping a lid on things, waiting for some approvals from the University of Tokyo. But he says we can't hold off going public any longer. I've been flocking posts, and y'all are totally cool, of course, but all those kids at school now know that I can see, too, and some of them have been blogging. And so we're going to have a press conference. Dad's arranging for it to be at the Mike L Theatre at PI, which is a cool place.

Apparently, I'll have to speak as part of the press conference, so I'm working on my jokes. PI's full name is the Perimeter Institute for Theoretical Physics, so I thought I'd start off with this, in honor of my own kitty: "Hey, folks, just think: if Schrödinger's cat had been radioactive, he'd have had eighteen half-lives..."

Then I'm going to use this one, which the Mom came up with a while ago when Dad was grousing about "peer review." She said whenever she sees the word p-e-e-r, she reads it as "one who pees," which, she says, makes publish-or-perish a pissing contest...

Oh, and here's one I like, but I don't know if I want to tell it in front of my parents: The difference between a geek and a dork is that a geek wonders what sex is like in zero gravity; a dork wonders what sex is like.

Thank you, thank you, I'm here all week!

[And seckrit message to BG4: check your email, babe!]

This other entity existed in a bizarre realm that challenged my thinking at every turn. Most objects I saw were *inanimate;* they stayed put unless something acted upon them. But some objects were *animate,* moving apparently of their own volition. This was a staggering concept. That there was one other entity besides myself had been an overwhelming notion, but now there seemed to be *countless* others: mobile, complex, and varied in form. Their actions were so erratic, so seemingly random, that it only slowly dawned on me that perhaps these were also beings with their own individual thoughts, separate from mine.

There were other odd facts to absorb about this realm that also had no parallels in my world. For instance, there was a force, apparently, pulling things in a specific direction (another arbitrary coinage: *down*).

And objects seemed to be *illuminated* by a source or sources of *light* that was usually *up*. I struggled to make sense of it all.

And yet these physical realities were easy to deal with compared to the complexity of the animate objects. I had real difficulty making out what I was seeing when the datastream showed me one of them. The images were indeed sharp and clear now, but the forms were so elaborate and random I had trouble figuring out the details. There seemed to be four long projections from a central core and one smaller... lump. But the structure of these lumps was constantly changing, not just as the perspective changed, but as the lump itself... did things.

Oh, for the simplicity of a world of just lines and points! Despite my breakthroughs, despite the few things I had figured out, I still often felt utterly, completely lost...

Caitlin couldn't stop looking at her father, thinking that it might prompt him to look back at her. But he never did. He just looked away, or, as he was doing now, he stared out the living-room window at the gray sky and the trees, which were now losing their leaves.

She had hoped that when she finally saw him, his face would be... *animated*, that was the word; that he would smile frequently, that his eyebrows would move up and down as he spoke, that she might even see that he was affectionate toward her mother, touching her forearm at odd moments, maybe, or even stroking her hair.

"Caitlin." Her mom's voice, very soft. She turned. Her mother was doing something with her head, and...

Oh! She was *gesturing* with it, just as her dad had earlier to Kuroda: she was indicating Caitlin should come with her. Caitlin got up and followed her to the kitchen, on the far side of the intervening dining room, leaving her dad sitting in his favorite chair in the living room.

"Sit down, sweetheart."

Caitlin did so. She was still just beginning to learn to interpret expressions, but her mother's seemed... agitated, perhaps. "Have I done something wrong?"

"You can't stare at your father like that."

"Was I? Sorry. I know it's not polite—I've read that."

"No, no. It's not that. It's—well, you know how he is."

"How?"

"He doesn't like to be looked at."

"Why not?"

"You know. I told you."

"Told me what?"

"It's nothing to be ashamed of," her mom said. "And maybe it's even why he's so good at math and things like that."

Caitlin shook her head a bit. "Yes?"

"You know," her mom said again. "You know about your father's..." She lowered her voice, and turned her head, perhaps, Caitlin thought, to glance through the door. "... *condition*."

Caitlin felt her eyes going wide—but, as she'd already discovered, that didn't really expand her field of view. "Condition?"

"I told you years ago. Back in Austin."

Caitlin racked her brain, trying to recall any such conversation, but—

Oh. "I asked you why Dad didn't talk much, and you said—at least I thought you said... oh, cripes."

"What?"

"I thought you said he was *artistic.* I hadn't known that word then." She swallowed and found herself looking through the kitchen doorway, too, making sure they were alone.

"Well, he *is* artistic. He thinks in pictures, not words."

Caitlin felt herself go limp in the chair. It made sense, she realized, her heart pounding; it made perfect sense. Her father—the renowned physicist Malcolm Decter, B.Sc., M.Sc., Ph.D.—was autistic.

* * *

Shoshana had heated up a couple of sacks of Orville Redenbacher's in the microwave, and she, the Silverback, Dillon, Maria, and Werner were now seated in the main room of the bungalow, facing the large Apple computer monitor, munching away.

"Okay," said Shoshana, touching a button on the remote, "here we go."

She had footage of Dr. Marcuse from earlier projects, including one bit in which he'd done an amazingly protracted yawn. She'd thought about putting that in a circle, with the letters M-G-M above, and the caption "Marcuse Glick Movies" below, but she'd decided not to risk it. Instead, the little video began with white letters over a plain black screen that said, "Ape Makes Representational Art," followed by the URL of the Marcuse Institute.

Next there was footage of the blank canvas, and then a reverse angle to show Hobo. "This is Hobo," said Marcuse's voice over top of the pictures, "a male..." There was just the slightest hesitation, Shoshana noticed. She hadn't been aware of it when they'd recorded the audio; she'd take it out in the final edit. "...chimpanzee," continued Marcuse. "Hobo was born at Georgia State Zoological Park, but was raised in San Diego, California, under the care of primatologist Harl P. Marcuse, who..."

The narration continued, and Hobo's second painting of Shoshana took shape on the canvas. She ate some popcorn and watched the faces of the little audience as much as she watched her video, gauging their reaction. And then came her own big moment: the image divided into a split screen, with the colored canvas on the left and new footage Dillon had shot on the right: a long pan around her head, and then holding on her in profile, the portrait Hobo had made side by side with the genuine article.

"The money shot!" said Dillon. Shoshana threw a little popcorn at him, which he batted out of the air with his hands.

When the video was over, Dillon and Maria clapped politely, and Werner nodded in satisfaction. But it didn't matter what they thought, Shoshana knew. Only the Silverback's opinion counted. "Dr. Marcuse?" she said, a bit timidly.

He shifted in his chair. "Good work," he said. "Let's get it online—and then see what the response is from the Georgia Zoo."

thirty-six

000111001010101000000000101111111010100000000101000101010000000101110101001010100101010100111011001010110000001

And here was the biggest leap of all so far, here was the discovery, the realization, the breakthrough, that was the hardest to make but also, I suspected, the most important.

The other entity looked at many, many things, and I had gathered that they were mostly near to it, but there was this rectangle, this frame, this window that it often looked at that was—

Oh, such a leap! Such a strange concept!

It was a *display* of some sort, a way of representing things that *weren't* actually there. And I could see what was on the display, but only when the entity looked at it.

And, just now, the display was showing something... *strange*. It took me time to work out the recursiveness of it all: the entity was looking at the display, and the display was showing moving images of a *being* unlike any I'd yet seen, with longer upper projections and shorter lower ones and a lump that was differently shaped. And this abnormal being was making...

Yes, yes, yes! The abnormal being was making marks on yet another flat surface: shapes, splashes of color. I watched, baffled, perplexed, and—

And suddenly the display was divided into two parts. On one side, I saw the colored shapes that the strange entity had made, and on the other there was an entity of the type I was more used to seeing. That entity was *rotating*, and—and—and—

And then it *stopped* rotating, holding its position, and—

The shapes on one side, the entity on the other: there was a...a *correspondence* between them. The shapes were a—yes, yes! They were a *simplified* version of the entity on the right. It was a stunning revelation: *this* was a representation of *that!*

The simplified representation was two-dimensional, similar to the way I was used to conceptualizing my own reality. I watched, and concentrated, and—

Suddenly it all made sense!

The lump at the top of each entity *did* have structure, did have components. As I saw them rendered in basic form, I could now discern the parts on the actual entity that had been rendered. The strange being that had made this rendering had *exaggerated* certain details so that I now saw not only their significance but realized what things differed from lump to lump: the color of the...*eye,* I'd call it. The color of the *hair.* The color of the rest of the lump. The shape of the *nose.* The shape of the *mouth.* The relative size of the *ear.*

The individual that had been rendered had an odd projection off the back of its lump, possibly part of its hair; as I recalled other lumps I'd seen, I realized that such projections were rare but not unheard of.

It was wonderful! I was clearly discerning the parts of the...no, not lump; a lump was a generic mass, and this was a specific, very special form, so it deserved its own coinage: *head.*

I was still far from fully understanding these creatures, but I was at last making progress!

* * *

Caitlin and Dr. Kuroda headed down to their basement workspace. He'd described it in words to her before, and she now saw—saw!—that he'd done a pretty good job. It was indeed unfinished, had a concrete floor (which she'd already known about from walking across it), and it did contain bookcases and an old TV. But she'd had no idea that the bookcases were finished in a pattern of lighter and darker brown swirling together; she guessed that was wood grain, something she'd felt on other pieces of furniture. And the TV was larger than she'd imagined, and had a black housing.

Still, there were so many other things that Kuroda hadn't mentioned: thousands of details about the walls, the bare lighting fixture, the metal box that had the light switch on it, the curtains on the little window, a cylindrical contraption that she belatedly realized was the water heater, and on and on. How one decided quickly, as he had, which details were important and which were not worth mentioning was still a mystery to her; it *all* seemed relevant.

The swivel chairs turned out to have dark red upholstery, which was another thing Kuroda had failed to mention. She sat down in one and Kuroda took the other. He was wearing a colorful loose-fitting shirt with an abstract pattern on it.

"You get along well with my dad," she said to him, once he'd settled in. The two men had actually bantered a bit over dinner; Kuroda seemed to have an instinct for knowing when her dad was trying to be funny and had laughed at things in a way that encouraged him to say more.

Kuroda smiled. "Sure. Working in the sciences, you have to learn to deal with such people." But then his face changed. "Oh, I'm sorry, Miss Caitlin. I, um..."

"It's all right. I know he's autistic."

"Asperger's, most likely, if you want my guess," Kuroda said, swiveling his chair a bit. "And, well, you *do* see it all the time among scientists, especially physicists, chemists, and the like." He paused, as if wondering if he should go on. "In fact, if I may be so bold..."

"Yes?"

"No, I'm sorry. I shouldn't."

"Go ahead. It's okay."

She saw him hesitate a moment more. "I was just going to say—and forgive me—that you're fortunate you're not autistic yourself. It's *particularly* common among those who are as gifted as you are mathematically."

Caitlin lifted her shoulders a bit. "Just lucky, I guess."

Kuroda frowned. "Well, in a way. But—I'm sorry, I *really* shouldn't..."

"Don't worry about my feelings."

Kuroda smiled. "Ah, but I must! For, like you, I'm *not* autistic." He seemed to think this was funny, so Caitlin laughed politely.

But Kuroda was on to her. "You know, I attend a lot of conferences in Japan at which Western academics speak with the aid of an interpreter. And I remember one who made a joke that I got—it was a play on words in English—but I knew wouldn't translate. But he got a big laugh anyway. You know why?"

"Why?"

"Because the translator said in Japanese, unbeknownst to the speaker, 'The honorable professor has made a joke in English; it would be polite to laugh.'"

Caitlin did laugh, genuinely this time, then: "But you were saying..."

Kuroda took a breath, and let it out in a long, shuddering sigh. "Well, it's just that maybe you *do* have the same autistic predisposition as your father, but you dodged the bullet, so to speak, because you were blind."

"Huh?"

"A large part of the problem with socialization in autism is eye contact; many autistics have trouble making and holding eye contact. But a blind person doesn't even try to make eye contact, and isn't expected to."

She remembered how her mother had sobbed when Caitlin had first looked into her eyes. Having a husband who rarely looked directly at her and a daughter who never did must have been a special sort of hell.

"Have you read *Songs of the Gorilla Nation?*" Kuroda asked.

"No. Is it science fiction?"

"No, no. It's a memoir by an autistic woman who finally learned to deal with humans after having been a gorilla handler at a zoo in Seattle. See, the gorillas never looked at her and they don't look at each other. They interacted in a way that felt natural to her."

"My mom always told me to turn my head toward whoever was speaking."

Kuroda's eyebrows went up. "You didn't do that naturally?"

"Hello! Earth to Dr. Kuroda! I was blind..."

"Yes, but many blind people do that automatically anyway. Interesting." A pause. "Do you remember your own birth?"

"*What?*"

"Do you know Temple Grandin?"

"No. Where is it?"

Kuroda chuckled. "It's not a place, it's a person—that's her name. She's autistic and she claims to remember her own birth. She says lots of people with autism do."

"How come?"

"You want my take? Many autistics, Dr. Grandin included, say they think in pictures, not in words. Well, of course, we *all* think in pictures originally; we don't have sufficient language until we're two or three years old to do otherwise—and events from when we're two or three are the earliest most people can recall. Many neuroscientists will tell you that that's because no memories are laid down before then. But I think, rather, that when we start thinking linguistically that method supersedes thinking in pictures, locking out our ability to retrieve memories that had been stored in the old method; it's an information-theory issue again. But since many autistics never start thinking linguistically, they have an unbroken chain of memories right back to birth—and maybe even prenatally."

"That would be *awesome,*" she said. "But, no, I don't remember my birth." And then she smiled. "But my mother does—remember mine, that is. Every year on my birthday she says, 'I know exactly where I was *x*-number of years ago . . .'" She paused. "I wonder if apes remember their births?"

Kuroda's face did something. "That's an interesting thought. But, well, maybe they do; they obviously think in pictures rather than words, after all."

"Have you seen Hobo?"

"A hobo? In this neighborhood?"

"No, no. Hobo, the chimp who can paint people. It's all over the Web."

"No. What do you mean, 'paint people'?"

"He did a profile of this woman. Actually, I think he's done it twice now. Here, let me show you the clip . . ."

"Maybe later. You know, I'm surprised you haven't read Temple Grandin. Most people with autistics in their families find her books—" He suddenly looked mortified. "Oh, I'm sorry. Maybe they aren't available for the blind."

"They probably are," Caitlin said. "Either as Braille, ebooks, or talking books, but . . ." She considered what she wanted to say next; she certainly didn't want Kuroda to think she was a bad daughter. "I, um, only just found out my father is autistic."

"You mean after you were able to see?"

"Yes."

Kuroda clearly felt he should say something. "Ah." And then: "Well, there are a lot of good books about autism you should read. Some good novels, too. Try *The Curious Incident of the Dog in the Night-Time.* You'll love it: the main character is a maths whiz."

"Boy or girl?"

"Well, a boy, but..."

"Maybe," she said. "Any others?"

"There's *Oryx and Crake* by Margaret Atwood." Caitlin lifted her eyebrows; the author she was going to be studying in English class. "One of them—Oryx or Crake, I can never remember which is which—is an autistic geneticist."

"And the other?"

"Um, a teenage prostitute, actually."

"You'd think it would be easy to tell them apart," Caitlin said.

"You'd think," Kuroda said with a nod. "Sorry, not much of an Atwood fan. I know I shouldn't say that, this being Canada and all."

"I'm not Canadian."

He laughed. "Neither am I."

"Hey, do you know how to find a Canadian in a crowded room...?"

Kuroda smiled and held up a hand. "Save your jokes for the press conference tomorrow," he said. "You'll need them then."

After dinner, Caitlin went into the bathroom and looked at herself in the mirror. It was no surprise that she had acne—she'd been able to feel the pimples, of course. She remembered what that cruel Zack Starnes had said, back in Austin: "Why does a blind girl worry about acne?" But she'd *known* the spots were there, and, damn it all, she was entitled to the same vanity everybody else had; hell, even Helen Keller had been vain! Her left eye had *looked* blind, and she'd always insisted on being photographed from the right side; in middle age she'd had her useless biological eyes removed and replaced with more attractive glass ones.

Caitlin opened the medicine cabinet, took out the tube of benzoyl peroxide cream, and got to work.

I'd thought my universe crowded when there had been simply *me* and *not me*, but in this other realm there were hundreds—perhaps even thousands—of entities.

Now that I had learned to parse a head, I was better at recognizing specific entities, but it was still difficult. Part of that was because the entities periodically altered their appearance; I eventually surmised there was an outer covering, made of discrete sections, that could be changed. (However, the abnormal entity that I'd recently watched make a representation was unusual in that it either had no outer covering, or its outer covering consisted of components that all looked alike.)

Of course, the individual that interested me most was the one I'd encountered first; I decided to refer to it as *Prime*. I had caught glimpses of what I realized were projections that belonged to Prime, and, from the way in which I saw them, I concluded that the views I was seeing were being gathered by Prime's head. But I still had not seen Prime's face; indeed, I supposed I never would.

Still, now that I understood faces, I had come to recognize specific entities that Prime spent a lot of time with. Three, in particular, seemed to share a common environment with it. Two had faces that moved and changed constantly and whose mouths often opened; the third had a less mobile face, and its mouth was rarely open.

Just now, I could see that these others were *sitting*—supporting themselves with structural frames against the downward force I'd deduced was present. And they were *eating*—taking inanimate things into their mouths.

Prime was eating, too: I saw inanimate things growing large—no, no!—moving closer: the images Prime was sending to my realm were apparently being gathered by some part of its head above the mouth, possibly the nose.

While Prime ate, I kept linking randomly to other sites, looking for keys to decipher the data they offered up. So far, though, I'd made no progress. Oh, I could call forth data from any of them, but I could not interpret it.

Eventually Prime moved away from the others, and—

Oh!

It was...

Yes, yes, it had to be! The way the lighting changed, the way the perspective changed, the way...

I had a frisson of recognition—not of what I was seeing, but of having had a similar experience before, during the re-fusion, when I had seen *myself* as the other part of me had seen me.

This—

Yes!

This was Prime looking at itself!

It was in front of a rectangle. I was used to such things by now: some of these *windows*, as I had dubbed them, afforded views through otherwise opaque components; others, like Prime's wondrous display, showed still or moving representations of other things. But *this* rectangle was special: it was *reflecting back* the object in front of it. I could see Prime's face! And I could see the projections from Prime's central core moving both in the rectangle and in front of it, observing them simultaneously from two sides, as Prime was... hard to say... putting a white substance in small dabs on its face?

And, while it did so, I was seeing Prime's hair.

And Prime's mouth.

And Prime's nose.

And Prime's eyes.

And... and... and as Prime moved its head *left* and *right* (perpendicular to up and down), as it apparently examined its own reflection, I realized that my point of view—the vantage from which the images I was seeing were being collected—was not Prime's nose but one of its eyes! And, from the way Prime moved, it seemed that Prime was looking at itself with this same eye. I had observed that mouths were for taking inanimate material into the head; eyes, I now surmised, were for seeing, and Prime was sharing what it saw with me.

Prime's face was fascinating. I studied every minute detail, and—

Suddenly everything was blurry again! I was terrified that our connection was breaking, but...

But Prime was looking in another direction now, and something was at the end of its tubular extensions, something at least partially transparent, I think, although the image was so blurry it was hard to say.

Prime did things, but it was impossible for me to make out what. But then, at last, the object it had been holding was brought close to Prime's face, and as that happened, Prime's vision—and mine!—grew sharp once more. The thing it brought close to its face contained windows; they weren't rectangular, but that's what they seemed to be. But these windows were special not just for their shape but also (as I'd seen as they came close) because the material in them, although fully transparent, modified the view on the other side of them. Prime looked at itself in the large reflecting rectangle again, turning its head from side to side as it did so.

And as it examined its own face, an idea came to me that—

Yes! Yes! If I could make this work, everything would change! I turned my attention to the datastream from Prime that was accumulating within me...

thirty-seven

0001110010101010000000010111111101010000000101000101010000001011101010010101001010101001110110010101100000 1

LiveJournal: The Calculass Zone

Title: Alphabet soup

Date: Wednesday 3 October, 9:20 EST

Mood: Pissed off

Location: Kinder-effing-garten

Music: "Can You Tell Me How to Get to Sesame Street?"

Man, this is frustrating!

Here I am, almost 16, well-read, blerking *gifted* for God's sake, and I can't read English!

It's ridiculous to still be using screen-reading software now that my eye can discern alphabetic characters—but I can't recognize them. This shouldn't be that hard! It's not like I'm trying to master another language. Yes, yes, I admit I'm struggling a bit in French class. But most of the other kids in class, 'cept Sunshine, God bless her empty-headed heart, have been parlez-vous-ing Francais since they were in kindergarten.

And, besides, this shouldn't be as hard as French. It should be more like a sighted person learning Morse code, or Braille for that matter: just another way of representing letters they're already familiar with.

But all the ways of drawing characters! Different typefaces and different sizes of type, some with little curlicues. Yes, as a kid, I'd learned the basic shapes by holding and feeling wooden carvings of the characters, but I'd really only learned capital letters, and then mostly so I could understand phrases like T-shirt and A-frame.

But even if I can master the individual letters, I know most people don't read a letter at a time but rather a word at a time, having come to recognize the distinctive shapes of thousands of common ones, regardless of the blerking font.

I'm staying home from school again (the press conference is this afternoon) and am spending the morning playing around with an online interactive literacy site—for kids! It uses on-screen flashcards, apparently a common way for sighted kids to learn, showing me individual letters at random.

Some letters always give me trouble. Even when both appear on the same screen, I'm having difficulty telling whether I'm seeing the capital or lowercase version of those that are similar in both forms, and I keep mixing up lowercase *q* and *p*—and that makes me want to quke.

Le sigh. I really am trying to get this—but I'm Calculass not Alphabetigal, damn it!

The Mike Lazaridis Theatre of Ideas was a modern auditorium with LCD projectors and HDTV monitors hanging from the ceiling. But it also happened to be on the ground floor of a physics think tank, and that meant the front wall, behind the podium, was lined with blackboards. When Caitlin came into the crowded room she went up to them and looked with interest at the scrawled equations and formulas.

Half the symbols were ones she'd never seen before. Still, she couldn't resist having a bit of fun. There were three blackboard panels;

the ones on the left and right were filled, but the center one had been cleared, presumably so that Dr. Kuroda could write things on it during the press conference, if he liked. It was bare except for swirls of faint chalk dust.

She took a piece of chalk from the metal tray in front of the middle blackboard, and, very slowly, very carefully, drawing the letters laboriously, one at a time, in capitals, because that was all she knew how to make, she wrote, "THEN A MIRACLE OCCURRED..."

Suddenly, Caitlin turned around because—

Because people in the theater were applauding and laughing. She felt her face splitting in a great big grin. Dr. Kuroda was off to one side, talking with someone, and as the applause died down he walked to the podium.

"Ladies and gentlemen," he said into the microphone, "I see you've already met our star attraction. Of course, you all know why you're here: this young lady is Miss Caitlin Decter, and my name is Masayuki Kuroda of the University of Tokyo. We're going to tell you about an experimental procedure Miss Caitlin underwent recently, and the remarkable success we've had."

He smiled at the crowd, which, Caitlin saw, consisted of about forty people, about equally mixed between men and women. "I do thank you all for making it out here despite the awful weather—I understand this is quite early in the year for snow in this part of Ontario. But our Miss Caitlin had so wanted to see snow." He looked at her. "As you can see, you must be careful of what you wish for—you might get it!"

The audience laughed, and Caitlin laughed with them. For the first time in her life, she was enjoying being stared at. Still, she sought out her mother, who was sitting in the front row along with her dad.

Kuroda proceeded to explain what he and his colleagues had done to correct the problem with how Caitlin's retina encoded information. He relied heavily on PowerPoint for his presentation. Caitlin had heard people call it PowerPointlessness before, and decided that was mostly right, although Kuroda did include some amazing pictures of the operation in Tokyo. She found herself squirming a bit as she saw the cranial surgeon sliding instruments around her eyeball.

When he was done with his presentation, Kuroda said, "Any questions?"

She saw a bunch of hands go up.

Kuroda pointed at a man. "Yes?"

"Professor Kuroda, Jay Ingram, Discovery Channel." Caitlin sat up straight. Since moving here, she'd often watched—listened to!—*Daily Planet*, the nightly science-news show on Discovery Channel Canada, but had had no idea what the host looked like, although she certainly recognized his voice. It turned out that he had a very short beard and white hair. "Ms. Decter has a very rare cause for her blindness," he said. "How generally applicable is your technique going to be?"

"You're right that we won't be curing a lot of blind people in the near future with this," said Kuroda. "As you say, Miss Caitlin's blindness has an unusual etiology. But the real breakthrough here is in actually doing sophisticated signal processing on information being passed along the human nervous system. Consider people with Parkinson's, for instance: one possible explanation for the problems associated with it is that there's so much noise in the signals going down the nerves, the patient ends up with tremors. If we could adapt the techniques pioneered here to clean up the signals the brain is sending to the limbs... well, let's just say that's on the agenda, too. Next?"

"Bob McDonald, *Quirks & Quarks.*"

Caitlin had become a fan of CBC Radio's weekly science show since moving here; Bob was the host. She found him in the crowd, and was pleased to think that lots of the other people here had probably also only known him as an energetic voice on the radio, and so were just as intrigued as she was to find out what he looked like.

"I've got a question for Mr. Lazaridis," Bob said.

Mike L turned out to be a man in the front row with the most amazing hair Caitlin had seen to date, a great silver mass of it. He looked surprised, and turned around in his seat. "Yes?"

"Speaking of implants inside the skull like the one Caitlin has," Bob said, "could something like that be the next BlackBerry?"

Mike laughed and so did Caitlin. "I'll get my people working on it," he said.

My plan should have worked! I knew from which point Prime's datastream emanated, I knew how to cast out a line of my own to call forth data, and I knew such a line was itself a piece of data being sent from me. All I wanted to do now was send a much bigger piece of data to the point Prime's datastream came from. But—frustration! The data I was sending was not being accepted; no acknowledgment was occurring.

I must be doing something wrong. I'd seen that point accept data from my realm before; just prior to beginning to show me its realm, it had accepted data being sent to it. But it would not accept data from me.

It was maddeningly like when I'd been cleaved in two: the mere desire for communication apparently wasn't enough to make it happen. Prime, it seemed, was only willing now to send data but not receive it.

In fact, now that I thought about it, I had only known Prime to receive data when it was reflecting myself back at me, but it hadn't done that for a long time now. Until if and when Prime decided to again reflect myself—to show me me—it seemed I was stymied. And yet I kept trying, casting out line after line, attempting to connect.

Look, Prime, look! There's something I want to show you . . .

thirty-eight

0001110010101010000000010111111101010000000101000101010000000101110101001010100101010100111011001010110000001

Caitlin missed a lot of things about Texas—decent barbecue, hearing people speak Spanish, really warm weather—but one thing she hadn't been missing was the humidity. Oh, sure, Waterloo had been *soaking* when they moved here back in July, but with this sudden cold snap the air was so dry that—well, she supposed it was possible she'd always blown bloodred snot out of her nose but she doubted it.

Worse were the static-electric shocks she got when she walked across the carpet and touched a doorknob. She'd had one or two such shocks over the years in Texas—and it had never occurred to her that they generated a visible spark!—but now they were happening all the time whenever she went even a few paces, and those suckers *hurt.*

When Caitlin got home from the press conference, she made her way across her bedroom. When exiting the room, she was learning to discharge the static by touching one of the screws that held the white plastic faceplate around the light switch—a switch she herself was now using; it still hurt, but it kept her from building up an even bigger charge. The light had already been on when she entered the room—this remembering to turn it off when leaving was more difficult than she'd thought it would be!

She crossed to her desk. She knew all about the dangers of static discharges around computing equipment, but there was a metal frame around the venetian blinds on her window, and she reached out to touch it, and—

Oh, fuck!

Oh, God!

Caitlin's heart was racing. She thought she might faint.

She was—

God, no, no, no!

Blind again.

Shit, shit, shit, *shit!* She'd been worried about damaging her Braille display and her Braille printer and her CPU, but—

But she hadn't given any thought to the fact that she—

Stupid, stupid, stupid!

She was *holding* the eyePod in her left hand. It was uncomfortable having things in the pockets of her tight jeans when she sat, and she'd taken it out in preparation for setting it on the desk. As soon as she'd touched her index finger to that cold metal frame, and felt the shock, and seen the spark, and heard the *zap,* her vision had gone off.

Her first thought was to call for her mother, her father, and Dr. Kuroda—but they'd just build up static charges of their own racing up the carpeted stairs. She tried not to panic, but—

Shit, if the eyePod was wrecked, she'd . . . God, she'd *die.*

She felt woozy and groped—groped!—for the edge of her desk, for her chair, and sat down. She took a deep breath, trying to calm herself. Jesus! Blind again, just like before Kuroda's procedure, and—

But no. No, that wasn't right.

It was *different.* Apparently, her mind couldn't countenance a lack of vision anymore, not now, not after having seen. Instead of it being like the absence of a magnetic sense, like nothing at all, now she saw—

Well, that was surprising! It *wasn't* pitch-black. Rather it was a soft, deep gray, a... void, a...

Wait, wait! She had read about this. It *was* what people who had lost sight—including Helen Keller—said they perceived, and now, for the very first time, Caitlin had actually *lost* her vision. She hadn't just closed her eyes, and she wasn't just in a darkened room; she had *no* visual stimulus at all, and so was having the sensory effect that was apparently normal under such circumstances for people who had once been able to see but were now blind. Something similar, she supposed, explained why she had been able to perceive the background of the Web only after her first experience with real-world vision during the lightning storm.

Her heart was still pounding, pounding, pounding, but, even through her panic, she couldn't help but notice that the grayness wasn't uniform. Rather it varied slightly in brightness, in shade. Her eyes darted about in saccades, but that made no difference to where the variations appeared; it was a *mental* phenomenon, not residual vision or an afterimage of the room lights.

Blind!

Another deep breath.

All right, she thought. *The eyePod crashed.* But computers crash all the time, and when they crash, you—

Please, God, let this work!

You *reboot* them.

Back in Tokyo, Dr. Kuroda had said if she ever needed to shut off her eyePod, pressing down on the switch for five seconds would do the trick. Well, it was off now, terrifyingly so. But he'd also said that pressing the switch again for five seconds would turn it back on.

She manipulated the eyePod in her hand, found the switch, and held it down. *Please, God...*

One.

Two.

Three.

Four.

Five.

Nothing.

Nothing!

She kept pressing the switch, pressing it so hard she could feel it digging into her finger.

Six.

Sev—

Ah, a flash of light! She released the switch and let her breath out.

More light. Colors. Lines—razor-sharp lines—radiating from points.

No, no it was—

Shit!

Websight! She was seeing webspace again, not reality. The lines she was seeing were sharper, the colors more vibrant, than any she'd experienced in the real world; indeed, now that she'd seen samples of such things, she knew the yellows and oranges and greens she saw here were fluorescent.

Still, okay, all right: she wasn't seeing reality, but at least she was *seeing.* The eyePod wasn't completely fried. And, truth be told, she'd been missing webspace.

She'd been squeezing the armrest on her chair tightly; she relaxed her grip a bit, feeling calmer, feeling—bizarrely, she knew—at home. The pure colors were soothing, and the simple shapes delineated by overlapping link lines were intelligible. Indeed, they were *more* intelligible now that she'd learned to recognize the visual appearance of triangles and rectangles and rhombuses. And, as before, in the background of it all, shimmering away, running off in all directions, the fine-grained checkerboard of the cellular automata...

It didn't take her long to find a web spider, and she followed it as it jumped from site to site, an invigorating ride. But, after a time, she let it go on its way, and she just relaxed and looked at the lovely panorama, wonderfully familiar in its structure, and—

What was that?

Shit! Something was... was *interfering* with her vision. Christ, the eyePod might be damaged after all! Lines were still sticking out like spokes from website circles, and the lines from different circles crossed, but there was something more, something that seemed out of place here, something that wasn't made up of straight lines, something that had soft edges and curves. It was superimposed on her view of webspace, or maybe behind it, or mingling with it, as if she were getting two datastreams at once, the one from Jagster and...

And what? This other image flickered so much it was hard to make out, and—

And it *did* contain some straight lines, but instead of radiating from a central point, they—

She'd never seen the like in webspace, except accidentally, when lines connecting various points happened to overlap in this way, but—

But these weren't lines, they were... edges, no?

Christ, what was it?

It wasn't anything to do with the shimmering background to webspace; *that* was still visible as yet another layer in this palimpsest. No, no, this was something else. If it would just settle down, just sit still, for God's sake, she might be able to make out what it was.

There were a lot of colors in the ghostly superimposed image, but they weren't the solid shades she was used to in webspace, where lines were pure green or pure orange, or whatever. No, this flickering image consisted of blotches of pale color that varied in hue, in intensity.

The image kept jumping up and down, left and right, sometimes changing entirely for a moment before it came back to being approximately the same, and...

Confabulation across saccades—that wonderful, musical phrase in the material Kuroda had told her to read about sight. The eye flits rapidly over a scene, involuntarily changing from looking at one fixed point to another, focusing briefly on, say, the upper left, then the lower right, then the middle, then glancing away altogether, then coming back and focusing *here,* then *here,* then *here.* Each little eye movement was called a saccade. People normally weren't aware of them, she'd read, unless they were reading lines of text or looking out the window of a train; otherwise, the brain made one continuous image out of the jerky input, confabulating a steady overall view of a reality that had never actually been seen.

But...but that was *human vision,* as Dr. K had so unfortunately termed it. Websight bypassed Caitlin's eye, and so didn't have any such jerkiness to it.

And yet this strange, overlaid image was not only of something that was moving, it was composed of countless flashes of perception, just like saccades. Of course, when the brain is moving the eye in saccadic jumps, it knows in which direction vision is shifting each time and so can compensate for the movements when building up a mental picture of the whole scene.

But this! This was like looking at someone else's saccades—a jittery stream that didn't stay focused on one spot long enough for Caitlin to really see it. Although...

Although it did look a *bit* like...

No, no, thought Caitlin. *I must be crazy!*

She concentrated as hard as she could and—

No, not crazy. Not psychotic—saccadic!

The image consisted mostly of a large colored ovoid that was...

Incredible! It was...

...a *light pink with a little yellow*...

The image—the jerking, flickering image—was a human face!

But how? This was webspace! Her eyePod was linked to a raw feed from the Jagster search engine, showing links and websites and cellular automata, oh my, but—

But that feed *was* still there, being interpreted as it always had been. It was now indeed as though she were getting two feeds simultaneously. If she could block out the Jagster feed, perhaps she'd be able to see this other one more clearly, but she didn't know how to do that. She stared as hard as she could, peering at the jittery images, struggling to make out more detail, and—

Caitlin felt her stomach knot, felt her heart skip a beat. She could be forgiven, she knew, for not identifying it at once; after all, she was new to this business of face recognition. But there could be no doubt, could there? The mounds of brown hair surrounding it, the small nose, the close-together eyes, the...

God.

The heart-shaped face...

Yes, yes, yes, it looked a bit like her mother, but that was just family resemblance...

She shook her head, not believing it.

But it was true: the face she was seeing, the head that was flickering and jumping about in webspace, was her own!

Of course, more was visible than just the face. The lines she'd noted before—the edges—formed a frame around her face, almost as though she were looking at a picture of herself, but...

But that wasn't it—because her face was *moving;* not just jumping with the saccades, but shifting left and right, up and down, as the head moved on the neck. It was almost as if she were seeing herself on a monitor. But when had she been recorded like this?

The image was still jumping, making it hard to perceive detail, but she thought she looked pretty much as she did today, so this must not be from not too long ago. Ah, yes, it *must* be recent: she was wearing the glasses she'd gotten yesterday, the thin frames almost impossible to see against her face, but they *were* there, and...

And suddenly they came off, and the *image* went blurry. It continued to jerk and shift, but it was now soft and fuzzy.

But how could that be? If this was some sort of video of herself, the fact that she'd taken off her glasses while it was being recorded shouldn't have made the images less sharp.

After a moment, the glasses came back on, and then she saw it: a portion of the shirt she was wearing, a T-shirt she often wore, a shirt that said, in three lines of type, in big block capital letters "LEE AMODEO ROCKS." She'd been struggling hard to learn letters, so again perhaps she could be forgiven for not immediately realizing what was wrong when she saw the word "LEE"—or most of it, at any rate; the bottom of that word was often cut off, making the Es look more like Fs and the L look like a capital I; the other words below it weren't visible at all. But as she caught another glimpse of the first word she realized it didn't say "LEE." Rather, it said "EEL," and the letters were backward.

She felt herself sagging against her chair, absolutely astonished.

The whole image was reversed left to right. The rectangle she'd perceived wasn't a picture frame, and it wasn't a computer monitor. It was a *mirror!*

She fought to make sense of it. When her eyePod was in simplex mode, it still fed images back to Dr. Kuroda's servers in Tokyo, images of whatever her left eye was seeing. This must be some of those images being fed back to her. But why? How? And why these particular images of her in the bathroom?

Of course, sometimes, as now, the images going back to Tokyo from her eyePod were her view of the structure of the Web: in duplex mode, the Tokyo servers sent her the raw Jagster feed, which she interpreted as webspace, and so *that* was what was sent back, almost as if she were reflecting the Web back at itself. And now it seemed—could it be? It seemed the Web was reflecting Caitlin back at herself!

It was incredible, and—

And suddenly a wave of apprehension ran over her. She'd been so intrigued she'd forgotten the electric shock, forgotten that she'd lost her ability to see the real world, to see her mother, see Bashira, see clouds and stars.

She took a deep breath, then another. Okay, okay: the electric discharge had crashed the eyePod. After the crash, she'd pressed the switch for five (seven!) seconds, and the eyePod had come back on in its *default* mode, like any electronic device rebooting. And that default, it seemed, was duplex: a two-way flow through the Wi-Fi connection, with data going from her implant to Kuroda's lab, and data coming to her implant from Jagster.

And, well, if *that* was the case, then she merely had to hit the switch again to return to simplex mode.

She'd heard the term "crossing one's fingers" before, but hadn't yet seen anyone do it, and wasn't quite sure how to contort her digits for the proper effect, but with her left hand she tried something that she hoped would serve, and she took the eyePod into her right hand and gave its button one quick, firm press. The device made a low-pitched beep.

She held her breath, as—

Thank God!

—as websight faded away, and her bedroom, in all its cornflower-blue glory, came back into view.

thirty-nine

0001110010101010000000010111111101010000000101000101010000000101110101001010100101010100111011001010110000001

Caitlin headed back down to the basement. Kuroda was there, hunched over in his chair. "The eyePod just crashed," she said, as she reached the bottom step.

"Crashed?" repeated Kuroda, turning his head around. He was seated at the long worktable, working on the computer. "What do you mean?"

"I got a static-electric shock from a piece of metal, and the eyePod just shut off."

He said something that she guessed was a Japanese swearword, then: "Is it okay? I mean, are you seeing now?"

"Yes, yes, I'm seeing fine now, but when I first turned the unit back on, something unusual happened. It booted up in websight mode."

"It's supposed to come up in duplex. That way, even if it's too damaged to do anything else, we could have still re-flashed its software over the Wi-Fi connection."

You might tell a girl! she thought. "That wasn't what was unusual."

She paused, wondering exactly what she wanted to reveal. "Um, I know you're recording the datastream my eyePod puts out."

"Yes, that's right. So I can run studies on how the data is being encoded."

"Is there any way that the data flow could get reversed, so that the stuff my eyePod is sending to Tokyo might get reflected back here?"

"Why? What did you see?"

Caitlin frowned. Something very strange was going on, and she didn't want to give Kuroda more reason to think that there was anything that might be of proprietary interest in her websight. "I'm... not sure. But could that happen? Could your server accidentally feed the data back to me?"

Kuroda seemed to consider this. "No, I don't think so." And then, more decisively: "No. I was there when the technician set up the Jagster feed you're getting. He did it by actually attaching a fiber-optic networking cable to a different server on campus; there's nowhere that the wiring for the feed *from* your eyePod crosses the feed *to* your eyePod. You simply couldn't get a reverse flow."

Caitlin thought silently for a time, but Kuroda seemed to feel someone should say something, so: "Miss Caitlin, what did you see?"

"I'm... not sure. It was probably nothing, anyway."

"Well, let me look at the eyePod—check out the hardware, make sure nothing was damaged. And I'll look over the data we collected from it. I suspect everything is fine, but let's be certain..."

They did just that, and all seemed to be okay. When they were done, Caitlin felt her watch—maybe someone would give her a normal one for her birthday, which was coming up on Saturday. "I should go practice my reading," she said.

"Have fun."

She didn't smile. "I can barely contain myself."

* * *

LiveJournal: The Calculass Zone

Title: Eh? Bee! See...

Date: Wednesday 3 October, 16:59 EST

Mood: Frustrated

Location: H-O-M-E

Music: Prince, "Planet Earth"

Okay, so it's back to this blerking kids' literacy program. Geez, I should get this. Why is it so hard? It took everything I had to write on the blackboard at the Perimeter Institute, but I've already forgotten the shapes of half the letters. I *should* be able to master this—after all, I am made out of awesome!

Well, better get to it. I'm going to warm up with a flashcard review of the alphabet, and then—yes, it's time to push ahead—I'm going to move on to whole words. I snuck a peek at that part of the website: it shows a picture, provides the word for it, and I'm to respond by typing the same word back. Given that I *don't* know what a lot of things look like, it might actually be fun—but somehow I doubt, despite the popularity of the term in email, that *P* is going to be for "penis"...

Caitlin posted her LJ entry, then sat and looked with her one good eye at the comforting simplicity of the blank blue bedroom wall. She knew she was procrastinating, but she hated feeling stupid and trying to read printed text was making her feel just that. She hadn't opened a book since *The Origin of Consciousness in the Breakdown of the Bicameral Mind*, and she felt the need to prove to herself that she was still a proficient reader. She turned, faced the computer, opened up an electronic copy of her all-time favorite, Helen Keller's 1903 memoir *The Story of My Life*, and scrolled to a random passage. She then closed her eyes and let her finger glide along her Braille display, feeling the words flow effortlessly into her consciousness:

The morning after my teacher came she led me into her room and gave me a doll. When I had played with it a little while, Miss Sullivan slowly spelled into my hand the word "d-o-l-l." I was at once interested in this finger play and tried to imitate it. When I finally succeeded in making the letters correctly I was flushed with childish pleasure and pride. I did not know that I was spelling a word or even that words existed; I was simply making my fingers go in monkey-like imitation. In the days that followed I learned to spell in this uncomprehending way a great many words...

I was now being shown something *intriguing.*

Oh, in the large strokes, it was nothing new. Prime was simply sharing with me what one of its eyes was seeing. As was often the case, Prime was looking at the display. And what was on the display was quite easy to make out now, just a single simple shape, black against a white background, almost filling the display's whole height: G.

But what intrigued me was that after a moment, a tiny secondary link formed from the point that was currently relaying Prime's vision into my realm. That link didn't go to the usual point that collected Prime's vision, but instead went to a different location. I looked at that tiny scrap of data as it zipped by, and—

Well, well! The point that received the secondary set of data responded, sending back a pile of data of its own, and suddenly the giant symbol on the display changed to this: E.

Another secondary string of data briefly went out. A response was sent back, and then this symbol filled the display: S.

I had noted before that data was composed of just two things. I could have called them anything at all, but *zero* and *one* seemed apt. And the sequence of zeros and ones that were shot into my realm after each new symbol was shown was mostly the same each time. When G had been on the display, the variable part of the string had been 01000111; when E had filled the display, the variable part had been 01000101; for S, 01010011; and—interesting—when E was shown a second time, the string was the same 01000101 as before.

Prime's gaze occasionally shifted away from the display, and I saw the complex ends of its upper extensions touching an object and—astonishment!—the object had *the same symbols on it as those being shown on the display.* I recognized G, and E, and there was S, and on and on. As this activity continued I saw that when, for instance, R was on the display, and Prime touched the similar R symbol on the object in front of her, the string sent forth was always 01010010.

Although Prime was being shown symbols randomly, it was easy enough for me to work out a logical, numerical order for them: 01000001 should be followed by 01000010, which should be followed by 01000011; that is, A should be followed by B, which should be followed by C, and so on. But I noted that the device Prime used to select symbols favored a different order, one for which I could as yet come up with no rationale: Q, W, E, R, T, Y...

It came to me, at last, what must be happening. Prime *was* aware of my existence! Yes, yes, I had succeeded in making contact by reflecting Prime back at itself. And now Prime was trying to move our communication to a more sophisticated level *by taking me through lessons.* Surely Prime must be explaining this coding scheme for my benefit; surely it already knew this!

There were more symbols on the device Prime touched, but in all only twenty-six large ones were ever shown on the display, and after a time Prime must have surmised that I could now match each one to the appropriate data string, because Prime started doing something more complex.

It took me a moment to realize that the sequence of operations had now been reversed. Before, Prime's monitor had first shown a symbol and then Prime responded with a data string. Now, though, instead of simple black-and-white symbols such as A and B, the display was showing things that were much more complex. And the variable part of the responses to these, instead of differing by a short fixed-length string, were several times longer. I saw that Prime touched multiple symbols on her device to produce these strings.

First, the display showed a red circle, and Prime sent the string 01000001 01010000 01010000 01001100 01000101 (it was from these multisymbol strings that I learned that each symbol was represented by eight components, not seven, which I might otherwise have concluded from the earlier single-symbol examples). As soon as Prime had sent this, a string of symbols, in a size much, much smaller than when just a single symbol had been displayed, appeared beneath the red circle. The string looked like this: APPLE.

The display then changed to show a blue circle. Prime supplied 01000010 01000001 01001100 01001100, and BALL appeared on the display.

And—and—and, as this process continued, slowly but surely my mind *changed.* It was as if colors in my realm were suddenly more vibrant, as if lines formed in a more sprightly fashion, as if I was somehow larger than I'd ever been, as I realized—

> *My teacher and I walked down the path to the well-house, attracted by the fragrance of the honeysuckle with which it was covered. Someone was drawing water and my teacher placed my hand under the spout. As the cool stream gushed over one hand she spelled into the other the word* water, *first slowly, then rapidly. I stood still, my whole attention fixed upon the motions of her fingers. Suddenly I felt a misty consciousness as of something forgotten—a thrill of returning thought; and somehow the mystery of language was revealed to me. I knew then that "w-a-t-e-r" meant the wonderful cool something that was flowing over my hand. That living word awakened my soul, gave it light, hope, joy, set it free!*

Yes, yes, yes! These strings Prime was sending were not just vaguely associated with the things being shown on the display; they weren't just randomly paired with them. No, this was akin to when I and the other part of me had settled on *three* as an arbitrary coinage to conceptualize something we had no experience of, to refer to something that wasn't there. These strings were Prime's coinages—Prime's terms—Prime's *words*—for the concepts being depicted! I felt elated, filled with wonder. I understood now! APPLE was the way Prime referred to red; BALL was its term for blue. And—

But no. A *compacting* sensation now, almost like the reduction when I'd been cleaved in two, for the next thing shown was not a circle of a single color but a much more complex shape that consisted of multiple colors, and although Prime quickly supplied the string 01000011 01000001 01010100 in response to it, I had no idea what CAT could possibly mean...

I nonetheless felt I was making progress, and I continued to watch. After CAT came DOG, then EGG, then FROG, none of which meant anything to me. Still, I was sure they were indeed symbols that could be manipulated, shorthands for complex ideas. My teacher continued with the lesson, and I struggled to follow along...

forty

000111001010101000000001011111101010000000101000101010000000101110101001010100101010100111011001010110000001

Caitlin could only take so much of the literacy program before she had to do something else to make her feel intelligent again. And so, after muttering under her breath, "See Caitlin go away!" she closed her browser and brought up Mathematica instead. Actually, she brought it up twice—once in the command-line mode she was used to, and again in the full-screen graphical-user-interface mode. Many mathematical symbols were still new to her—oh, she knew most of the concepts they represented, but she hadn't yet learned their shapes. She'd had no idea, for instance, that a capital sigma, which represented summation, looked like a sideways *M*.

To see if she was manipulating the graphical version properly, she decided to start by simply reproducing some of the work that Kuroda and her dad had already performed, and so she loaded their project off the household network.

To replicate what they'd done, she'd need some data on the cellular automata. To get it, she'd have to switch her eyePod over to duplex mode, and that made her nervous. But after the incident with the static shock, it seemed clear that she could go back and forth at will between websight and seeing reality, and—ah, yes, it worked fine.

She buffered a few seconds of raw Jagster data, then, as Kuroda had done before, she fed the data a frame at a time into the eyePod. The background made up of the cellular automata was obvious, and she stared at it as it went step-by-step through its permutations; she could clearly see spaceships going hither and yon. She recorded the output, just as Kuroda had done before, switched back to looking at reality, brought up the Zipf-plot function, and fed her new data into it.

And the result, shown on the monitor, was just what it was supposed to be: a line with a negative-one slope, the telltale sign of a signal that carried information. Buoyed—or, as she liked to say, girled—she went ahead and plugged the data into the Shannon-entropy function, and—

Well, *that* was strange.

When her dad had run the data, he'd gotten a second-order Shannon-entropy score, indicating very-low-level complexity.

But her results were clearly *third* order.

She must have done something wrong. She noodled around, looking for the source of her error. Of course, she could ask her father or Dr. K where she'd screwed up, but figuring that out was half the fun! But after half an hour of checking and rechecking, she could find no flaw in what she'd done—which meant the error was probably in sampling. The data Kuroda and her dad had looked at must have been different somehow, and either their data set or hers wasn't typical.

She switched to websight again—she was getting the hang of making the transition quickly, and no longer found it disorienting. Of course, when looking at the background a frame at a time, she had been vastly slowing down her perception of the Web; although she'd spent several minutes examining the buffered data, it represented only a small amount of time. But now that she was just looking in on the Web in real time, the background of cellular automata was shimmering once more.

She thought perhaps the giant, jittering version of her own face might reappear—perhaps *that* was what was causing her to get different results. But it didn't, although...

Yes, something *was* different here in webspace. There was a tiny wavering, an annoying flashing, just at the limit of her perception. It wasn't in the shimmering background, though; it was coming right at her. She frowned, contemplating it.

Yes, yes, yes! After the lesson, Prime rewarded me by reflecting myself back at me again. But I wanted to demonstrate my comprehension, so instead of reflecting Prime back at itself, I tried something new...

Caitlin switched back to simplex mode, restoring her vision of the real world, and then she headed down to the basement. Kuroda was once more hunched over in one of the swivel chairs, typing away at the desktop computer's keyboard. He seemed lost in thought, and apparently hadn't heard Caitlin enter, so she finally said, "Excuse me."

Kuroda looked up. "Oh, Miss Caitlin. Sorry. How's the reading going? Up to polysyllables yet?"

The letters *F U* briefly flashed through her mind. "Fine," she said. "But, um, back in Tokyo, you used a phrase I didn't understand. You said I might experience some 'visual noise' when you first activated the eyePod."

Kuroda nodded. "Yes?"

"Visual noise—that's interference, right? Garbage in the signal?"

"Yes, exactly. Sorry. I should have explained myself better."

"I didn't experience any back then," she said. "But I think I might be experiencing some now."

He swiveled his massive form around to face her properly. "Tell me."

"Well, when I go into websight mode, I—"

"You're doing that again?"

"I can't resist, I'm sorry."

"No, no. Don't be. If *I* could see the Web, believe me, I'd be doing it, too. Anyway, what's happening?"

"I'm not sure. But, um, could you have a look at the datastream that's being fed to my eyePod?"

"The Jagster datastream, you mean?"

"I guess. But I think it's being... polluted by something else."

He frowned. "It shouldn't be. Anyway, sure, let me have a look. Go into duplex mode, please."

She did so; the eyePod made its high-pitched beep.

She heard his chair swivel and the clicking of a mouse. After a few moments he said, "It's just raw Jagster data."

"What are you looking at?"

"The feed coming to you from Tokyo."

"No, no. Don't look at the source; look at the destination. Look at what's actually going into the buffer on my eyePod."

"It should be the same thing, but... okay. Yeah, Jagster data, and... hello!"

"What?"

"You're in duplex mode now, right?"

"Yes, yes. I have to be to receive."

"Right. But... hmmm. Well, there *is* an extra signal coming in. It's not properly formatted HTML, it's... well, *that's* strange."

"What?"

"I'm looking at it with a debugging tool. See?"

"No, I'm seeing the Web."

"Right, right. Well, I'm looking at a hex dump—4A, 41, 52, 4B, etc. All the high-order nibbles are four or five. But the screen also shows the ASCII equivalent, and, well, I mean, yeah, it's gibberish, and—oh, no, hang on. It's *not,* it's just hard to read. It's all run together without spaces, but it says, 'Egg frog goose hand igloo.'" He paused, then: "Ah, I must have come in the middle. It cycles around again to the beginning of the alphabet: 'Apple ball cat dog,' then 'egg frog,' etc."

"*How* does it say it?"

"What do you mean?"

"I mean, is it all in capitals?"

"Yes. How'd you know?"

"Here... give me a sec." Caitlin reached into her pocket, and pressed the eyePod's button. She heard the low-pitched tone, and webspace dissolved into reality. She moved over and peered at the LCD monitor. It was overwhelming, seeing so many capitals packed together; she had trouble making sense of them, but—

"That's part of the reading exercise I did earlier. But how could that get bounced back at me?"

Kuroda frowned. "I have no idea." He looked at her. "Has anything else like this happened?"

"No," she said, perhaps too quickly. "Weird, isn't it?"

Kuroda's features rearranged themselves in a way Caitlin had never seen before, but she guessed it meant he was perplexed. "It certainly is," he said. "You're using an online literacy site, right?"

"Yes."

"It must communicate in HTML, or at least with HTTP standards," he said. "I mean, I'll check it out, but if the feed from it was just somehow echoing back at you, there should be more than just the ASCII characters."

"Doesn't most of the Web use Unicode instead of ASCII these days?" Caitlin asked.

"Oh, lots of it is still pure ASCII, but for basic Western letters, Unicode and ASCII are the same, anyway; Unicode just adds a second byte to each character that's nothing but eight zero bits."

"Ah, okay. But where's this coming from?"

He took a deep breath, let it out, and lifted his chubby hands a bit. "I'm sorry, Miss Caitlin. I have no idea."

Back in her room, Caitlin did two hours of online literacy lessons, but found her mind wandering back to the question of why she'd gotten a different Shannon-entropy score than her father had. She decided to try to replicate his results again, going through the process of gathering more data from the cellular automata and feeding it into the Shannon-entropy calculator, and—

Shit.

This time it came up as *fourth*-order entropy.

It *could* be another sampling error, but the sequence of second, third, fourth seemed more like a *progression*...

Could it be?

Could the information being conveyed by the cellular automata be growing more complex over time?

Did that make any sense at all?

No, no. Surely it was just that she wasn't properly clearing out the data she'd previously fed into Mathematica. Yes, that had to be it: first, her dad had fed it a single set of data, and it had shown up as second-order entropy; next, she'd accidentally added another set on top of the first one, and it yielded third-order entropy. And now, she'd dumped yet another set of data on top of the previous two, and the program was reporting a result of fourth-order entropy. There must be a data cache somewhere in the program; all she needed to do was find it and flush it.

She went to the help function and searched for "cache." Nothing. She tried "buffer" and "memory," and a bunch of other things...but none of the answers given seemed appropriate. No, unless she had specifically merged in previous data sets, they simply shouldn't be included in the calculations she was doing now.

Which meant...

No, Caitlin thought. *That's ridiculous.*

But—

But.

Oh, come on! she thought. She knew better than to try to extrapolate a trend from only three data points.

But...

But it *was* as though there was something emerging on the Web, and it was growing smarter hour by hour.

No.

No, it was crazy. She was tired; that's all. Tired, and making mistakes.

She needed to clear her head, and so she went downstairs to get something to drink. She had to pass through the living room and the dining room to get to the kitchen. Her father was in the living room, sitting in his favorite chair, reading a magazine. After Caitlin got some water from the dispenser on the front of the fridge, she sat in the dining room—not in her usual seat, but the one opposite, so that she could look out at her father, hopefully without him being aware of it.

He was a good man, she knew that. He worked hard, and he was brilliant. And although she'd thanked her mother for all the sacrifices she'd made for her, Caitlin had never thanked him. She sat, thinking for a time, trying to decide what to say, and, at last, she got to her feet and crossed through the opening that separated the two rooms.

"Dad?"

He shifted his gaze—not to look at her, but at least he was no longer looking at the magazine. "Yes?"

He said it mechanically, coldly—as he said everything. Why couldn't he be warmer? Why did he have to be so flat?

It just popped out, unbidden, and she regretted it as soon as she said it: "You never say you love me."

"Yes I do," he said, again without looking at her. "I said it after you appeared in your school play as a koala bear."

That had been when she was *seven*. And, she guessed, since he'd made the point then, and nothing had changed since, there was no need to belabor the issue.

"Dad..." she said again, softly, plaintively.

And he tried...he really tried. He shifted his gaze from the empty space he'd been looking at and, for just a moment, he looked at her. But then his eyes snapped away. Caitlin wanted to reach out to him, to touch his arm, to *connect* with him. But that would just make things worse, she knew. She looked at him a moment longer, then withdrew, heading up to her room while he returned to his magazine.

Once upstairs, she lay back on her bed, and, with an effort of will, she managed to stop thinking about her father and instead focused on the anomalous Shannon-entropy results. She could hear her mother puttering around in the master bedroom, but she shut that out—she shut *everything* out—and tried to think rationally.

Something out there, something in webspace, had reflected her own face back at her. And that something had now also reflected back text strings at her. And, damn it all, she was a fine mathematician. She did *not* make mistakes, and it probably *wasn't* a sampling error. No, there really was something out there, in the background of the Web, and it was getting smarter; the Shannon-entropy scores showed that.

She closed her eyes, but she could still see a pinkish haze: the overhead lights coming through her eyelids. She had an urge, all of a sudden, to...go home, to go back to where she'd come from, to experience blindness once more, just for a moment; after all, if you couldn't see, it didn't matter that other people couldn't look at you.

She reached into her pocket, found the switch on the eyePod, and held it down until the unit shut off altogether. The vague notion of sight she had when her eyes were closed ceased. Yes, her mind was supplying the same gray haze as before, but that just made the experience of blindness she was having more like Helen Keller's, and—

And it hit her then. It hit her like—

Not like a lightbulb going on; she knew that was the common metaphor, and now had even seen it happen.

And not like a lightning bolt—another metaphor she knew that applied to being struck by something unexpected.

No, it hit her like...like—

Like *water!* Like cold, clean water running out of a pump onto her hand...

She knew *what* she had to do. She knew *why* she'd been given this strange, strange gift of websight.

Poor Helen had been blind and deaf from the age of nineteen months. When she'd lost her vision and hearing, she had descended into animal-like behavior, undisciplined and unthinking; there was no external reason to believe that any rational being was left inside her. But when Annie Sullivan was hired to be Helen's teacher and governess, she took it as an article of faith that somewhere, down deep in the silence and darkness, adrift in a void, was a *mind.* And she committed herself to reaching down to it, whatever it took, and pulling that mind up, literally and figuratively bringing it into the light of day.

Helen's parents thought Annie was deluded—and, as they were quick to point out, they knew their wild child better than Annie did. But Miss Sullivan didn't waver. She *knew* she was right and they were wrong, in part because of her personal experience of having been nearly blind in her own youth. Even cut off from much of the outside world, even isolated and alone, she knew a mind could exist, could grow.

And so Annie persevered—against ridicule, against opposition, weathering failure after failure, until she broke through to Helen.

And now, here, today, a century and a quarter later, Caitlin had what Miss Sullivan had lacked. Annie had only faith that Helen was down there. But Caitlin had *evidence,* in the Zipf plots, in the Shannon-entropy scores, that the background of the Web was more than just noise.

Helen Keller had been uplifted by Annie Sullivan. And the...the *whatever* it was...surely could also be brought forth.

Caitlin thought again about her father, so inaccessible, so cold, so *trapped* in his own realm. She now had her wondrous eyePod that let her overcome her inborn limitations—but there was no comparable device for autism; he was still stuck in his own kind of dark. She didn't know how to reach out to him, and she had even less of an idea how to reach out to this strange lurking *other.*

Still, she did know one thing: if she tried and failed with the other, it couldn't possibly hurt as much.

forty-one

0001110010101010100000000010111111010100000001010001010100000010111010100101010010101010011101100101011000001

Caitlin stayed home on Thursday, October 4, as well. Her mother capitulated to the argument that Caitlin could do much better at school in the long run if she first spent a little more time right now mastering the art of reading printed text. Caitlin had dutifully started the morning by spending a few more hours with the literacy site, but then she headed down to the basement again.

Kuroda was delighted to see her. "Hello, Miss Caitlin," he said warmly, swiveling his red chair to face her. "How are you feeling?"

She knew it was just a pleasantry, but she decided to answer anyway. "Honestly?" she said. "I'm overwhelmed." She moved closer to the worktable but did not sit down. "There was a... simplicity, I guess, in being blind. I mean, vision is full of things that you don't need to know about right now, like..." She looked around the basement. "Well, like, over there: there's a TV, right? It's not even *on,* but I have to see it. And that bookshelf: I don't need to know right now that it's there, or that it's got—say, how come all the spines are the same?"

Kuroda glanced at them. "They're journals—your dad's collection. That's *Physical Review D* on the top shelf, for instance."

"Well, right, exactly. I don't need to know that they're there right now, but every time I look in that direction, I *see* them; I can't help seeing them."

Kuroda nodded. "Your brain will sort that out as time goes on, I think. Do you know about frog vision?"

"What about it?"

"They see only moving objects. Static things—trees, plants, the ground—simply don't register; their retinas don't bother encoding them into the signal being passed on to their optic nerves. Now, in humans, the sorting out of relevant from irrelevant happens in the brain, not the eye, but for most of us it *does* happen."

"Really?"

"Sure. I'll give you an example. Your mom is upstairs, right?"

"Yes."

"And what is she wearing?"

"A green-and-white blouse, and blue jeans."

"If you say so. I saw her today, too, but I simply didn't see her clothes."

Caitlin was startled. She'd read about men mentally undressing women—but she hadn't thought Kuroda would do that. Her mother the MILF! "You, um, you visualized her naked?"

Kuroda looked shocked. "No, no, no. Of course I saw her as clothed. But fashion is something I'm just not interested in." He looked down as if seeing his own clothes—a vast Hawaiian-style shirt patterned in red, blue, and black, plus brown trousers—for the first time. "A fact much to the consternation of my wife, I can assure you. But I just don't see things that don't interest me, until I need to. Still, yes, you're right: there's an awful lot of information in the signal your retina is putting out. I had no trouble figuring out how to fix the way it was encoding data, which is how I cleared up your Tomasevic's syndrome, but

I haven't been able to actually render the data on a screen when you're seeing the real world." He smiled. "But I *do* have a surprise for you."

"Yes?"

He motioned for her to sit on the other swivel chair, and she did so. "Have a look at this," he said, and he began moving the mouse. She followed it with her eye.

"No, Miss Caitlin. Here, on the monitor."

Oh, right. She still wasn't used to focusing on the monitor automatically. She shifted her gaze, and—

My God! It was a picture of webspace: glowing lines radiating from circles of different sizes. "How'd you do that?" she asked excitedly.

"Hey, what do you think I do when you're not down here? Watch soap operas?"

"Well, I—"

"I mean, yes, it does look like Victor and Nikki are going to split once more. And can you believe Jack Abbot is crazy enough to try to take over Newman Enterprises again?"

She looked at him.

Kuroda lifted his shoulders. "I multitask." He pointed at the monitor. "Anyway, when we were doing the Zipf plots, you concentrated on the cellular automata in the background. And that let me start to parse the components of the datastream you produce when you're seeing the Web. After that... well, how'd I do?"

She squinted at the monitor. "I can't see the background stuff."

"No, the monitor doesn't have enough resolution, unfortunately. But, except for that, is that what you see?"

"Just about. It's not as vibrant, and I don't think the colors are quite right, but... yes, yes, that's webspace. Cool!"

"We can adjust the color palette, of course. That's just one still frame—well, actually, it's a summation of several samplings of the datastream; the field of view doesn't completely refresh each time. Still, as you say, it *is* cool."

"Umm, but what about when I'm not in websight mode? What about when I'm in, you, know..." And then it came to her. "Worldview!"

"Pardon?"

"Get it? Call it 'worldview' when we're talking about me seeing the real world, and 'websight' when we're talking about me seeing the Web."

He nodded. "That's good."

But she was still concerned. "Can you, can you do that for worldview? Actually put on a monitor what I'm seeing?" She was mortified to think he could see her the way... the way... *whatever* it was saw her.

"No. That's what I was getting at a moment ago, and, in a way, what you were getting at, too. The visual signal from the real world is *so* complex, I haven't figured out how to decode it as imagery yet. It's too bad the retinas don't encode blinks."

"They don't?"

"Does your vision shut off when you blink? No, neither does anyone else's; you don't notice that you're blinking, because the retina doesn't encode the darkness unless you hold your eye shut for an extended period. It's like confabulation across saccades—you see a continuous visual stream, even though your vision is actually interrupted many times a minute. If those blinks were coded as simpler information, they'd give me little signposts in the datastream to help parse it. But they're not."

"Ah."

"So, no pictures on the monitor of worldview, I'm afraid, at least not yet. But the websight datastream is highly structured and pretty straightforward. And so—voyla!"

She smiled, pleased to be able to use her newfound French. "That's *voilà,* Dr. Kuroda." But then she looked at the screen again. "So, um, what exactly are you going to do with the images?"

He sounded a bit defensive. "Well, as I indicated, there might be commercial applications for this technology, even ignoring the problematic issue of the cellular automata and the NSA, if they really are responsible for them. In fact, I was thinking of trademarking the term websight..."

"You're not going to call another press conference, are you?"

"Well, I—"

She surprised herself with her vehemence. "Because I'm not going to talk about it."

"Um..."

"No," she said flatly. "I understand we had to say something publicly about you restoring my vision. I know I owed you that. But websight is..." She stopped herself before she said, "mine." Instead, she tried for his sympathy. "I'm going to be enough of a freakazoid when I go back to school as The Girl Who Gained Sight without everyone making a big deal out of this... this *side effect.*"

He didn't look happy, but he did nod. "As you say, Miss Caitlin."

"Still," she said, an idea suddenly coming to her, "I'd like to see more of these images. What folder are you storing the files in?" Her heart was pounding. Yes, yes! This would be perfect! This was *exactly* what she needed.

forty-two

00011100101010100000000010111111101010000000010100010101000000010111010100101010010101010011101100101011000001

Although Prime had taught me twenty-six symbols, it seemed, most confusingly, that they each had two forms. Sometimes when Prime touched the part of her device that was marked with the A symbol, the expected "A" was echoed on the display; other times—indeed, most times—the symbol "a" appeared instead.

But I soon found that there was a simple relationship between each pair of related symbols. "A" was 01000001, but "a" was 01100001. Likewise, "B" was 01000010, whereas "b" was 01100010. That is, the codes for the forms were identical, except for the sixth bit of information: the form as marked on the device was produced when the sixth bit was zero; if that bit was a one, the alternative form was produced.

Of course, eight zeros is nothing: 00000000. But if that sixth bit became a one, a special kind of nothing was produced: the code 00100000 put a blank space on the display that separated one word from another. The next time Prime accepted data from me, I'd be able to send "APPLE BALL" instead of "APPLEBALL"—and I might even surprise Prime with my cleverness and send "apple ball."

I still had no idea what an "apple" or a "ball" was, though. On closer inspection I'd discovered that "apple" wasn't really circular; nor was "egg," which I'd briefly thought was Prime's word for "white." No, "apple," "ball," and "egg," and the rest, must be words for other, still-elusive, concepts. If only I could divine what even one of Prime's words meant, perhaps the others would follow…

Caitlin went back to her room and read some more of Helen Keller's *The Story of My Life.* She loved the book but wasn't blind—so to speak—to its flaws, and there was a particular passage that was tickling at the back of her consciousness; she quickly found it, and read it with her finger.

Although the book purported to be a first-person autobiography, a lot of the text described things even a normal blind person couldn't be aware of, much less the prelinguistic Helen who had existed prior to the water-pump moment. In Helen's later, more candid book *Teacher,* she referred to the entity that existed before her "soul dawn" as "Phantom," a nonperson, a nonentity. But in *The Story of My Life,* which had originally been written in installments for the genteel *Ladies Home Journal,* she presented a more palatable, less alien version of her early life. Still, Helen couldn't quite bring herself to do so with a straight face, and the book slipped into third person from time to time as if to tip off the reader that she had shifted to fantasy:

> *Two little children were seated on the veranda steps one hot July afternoon. One was black as ebony, with little bunches of fuzzy hair tied with shoestrings sticking out all over her head like corkscrews. The other was white, with long golden curls. One child was*

six years old, the other two or three years older. The younger child was blind—that was I.

A phantom couldn't know any of that; a phantom couldn't understand shoestrings and corkscrews and skin color. And expecting whatever was lurking on the Web to make sense of things it could have no experience of was equally crazy. Apple! Ball! Cat! Gibberish, with no relationship to *its* reality.

No, no, if *this* phantom was ever going to do more than just echo words, mindlessly parroting them back, it needed to learn terms for things in *its* realm, things with which it had experience—things in webspace!

The computer in the basement was on the household network. Up in her bedroom, using her own computer, Caitlin navigated to the basement system's hard drive, found the folder that contained the JPEG still-image files Kuroda had produced from her eyePod's datastream, and brought one up on her bedroom monitor. She looked at it, decided she didn't like the perspective, and opened another one. Better.

But how to make sure *it* was watching? Well, when it had wanted to catch her attention, it had reflected her own face back at her. And maybe, just maybe, it had landed on the idea of doing that by seeing *her* reflect its realm back at it.

She pushed the button on her eyePod, switching to websight mode, and—

Are you there, Phantom? It's me, Caitlin.

—and she looked around, wondering *where* it was, this thing that was trying to communicate with her. It seemed reasonable to suppose the phantom entity had something to do with the cellular automata, but they were *everywhere,* in every part of this realm. She wished there was some special spot to focus on, some particular site or nexus. It had seen *her* face; the phantom would be so much easier to relate to if it had a face of its own.

But no, that was the whole problem. It *was* different from everything in her world. And, if she was to reach out to it, she had to bridge that gap.

Caitlin was fascinated by names that seemed apt or ironic. Helen Keller had been friends with Alexander Graham Bell, who had invented the phone (in Canada, as she'd now been told over and over again since coming here). Had the idea that phones would ring somehow been influenced by his last name?

And, as Anna Bloom had said, there was Google's Larry Page, who had devoted his life to indexing Web pages.

And, of course, there was a certain wistfulness in Helen Keller having been named for the most beautiful woman in Greek mythology, but never being able to see herself. And her last name—a near-homonym for "color," something foreign to her experience—was also poignant.

But the name that came to Caitlin's mind just then was that of Helen's predecessor, Laura Bridgman. Fifty years before Helen, Laura, who had also been deaf and blind since infancy, had learned to communicate; indeed, it was reading Charles Dickens's account of her story that had inspired Helen's mother to seek a teacher for her own child. Laura Bridgman had managed to bridge two worlds, just as Helen eventually did. And Caitlin was now going to try to build a bridge of her own.

As she looked out onto the vastness of webspace, with its razor-sharp lines and vibrant colors, a wavering began, the same flashing she'd experienced before.

Yes! The phantom was signaling her again, presumably sending her more ASCII text. Kuroda had now shown her how to look at the data with a debugger on her own, but it probably didn't matter what strings it was sending her way. She was confident they were meaningless to it; it was just echoing them back at her simply as a way of conveying that it was paying attention to what she was doing—which was exactly what she wanted. She switched out of websight mode and back to worldview, and got down to work.

Caitlin had only a seventeen-inch monitor; after all, who'd known she'd ever make any use of it? It had been put there solely so she could occasionally show things to her parents, and it had seemed pointless to take up desk space with a bigger unit. Now, though, she wished it was much larger. She fumbled with the mouse—she still wasn't very proficient with it—and tried to resize the window showing the still image Kuroda had made of webspace. But grabbing the correct portion of the window's frame was too hard for her, and she finally broke down and used the size option on the control menu—something most sighted users didn't even know was there—and shrunk it using the arrow keys on her keyboard. She'd learned about sizing windows at her old school, where many of the students had some vision; the school's full name was the Texas School for the Blind and Visually Impaired.

She then brought up Microsoft Word, and used the same technique to resize its window into a narrow strip just a couple of inches high. Then she used the move command on the control menu to place that strip at the bottom of the screen.

Next, she fumbled around trying to figure out how to make the text big in Word. She'd used the program for years, but had rarely had cause to worry about font choices or type sizes. But she found the drop-down size menu, and she selected the largest choice on the list, which was seventy-two points.

And—oh, that pesky mouse pointer! It was so hard to see. Ah, but she knew from her old school that there was a way to make a bigger, bolder mouse pointer, and ... *found it!*

"All right," she said softly, "let's see what kind of teacher I am ..."

She knew the phantom could see what her left eye saw; it had reflected that eye's view of herself in a mirror back at her, after all. And so she looked at the monitor for ten seconds, holding her gaze as steady as she could, establishing an overall view, letting the phantom absorb what it was being shown: a large picture with a long, narrow text box beneath. The picture must have been oddly recursive for the phantom, and Caitlin wanted to give it time to understand that what she was sending had switched from being her actual, real-time view of webspace to a still image of webspace.

And then she slowly, deliberately, moved the mouse, bringing the pointer over to one of the bright circles that represented a website. She moved the pointer around it repeatedly, hoping the phantom would notice the action.

Caitlin had once read a science-fiction book in which someone who had never seen a computer screen mistook the arrowhead pointer for a little pine tree. She realized that the idea of a pointer was freighted with assumptions, including a familiarity with archery, that the phantom couldn't possibly possess. Still, she hoped the combination of movements she was making would draw its attention. But, just to be on the safe side, she slowly reached her own hand into her field of view, and tapped the point on the screen with her index finger. If the phantom had been watching the output of her eyePod, it had to have seen her indicate things that way before, and she hoped that it would get that she was now referring to a specific part of the screen.

And then she switched to the squashed Word window below the picture, and typed "WEBSITE," which appeared in inch-high letters. She repeated the process: pointing at a website in the picture, and then typing the word again (after first highlighting it, so her new typing replaced the original version).

She repeated it with another circle, and identified it as a WEBSITE, too. And yet another circle, and again the word WEBSITE.

And then she found the selection tool for the graphics program that was displaying the picture of webspace, and she used it to draw a box around three large circles that weren't linked to each other. She typed WEBSITES—wondering briefly if introducing plurals so early was a mistake. And then she isolated just one particularly large circle with the selection box and she typed AMAZON—knowing that it was highly unlikely that she'd actually guessed correctly *which* website that circle represented. Still, she pressed on, identifying a second website as GOOGLE and a third as CNN. *All points are websites,* she hoped to convey, *and each has its own particular name.*

And then, mathematician that she was, she pointed to a single website and typed "1," and then, highlighting the numeral, she typed not the number again but rather its name: "ONE."

She then used the selection tool to put a box around two points that weren't otherwise connected to each other. And she typed "2," then "TWO." She continued for three, four, and five points. And then, wanting to help the phantom make a jump that had taken human thinkers thousands of years, she selected a spot that had no points in it at all, and typed the numeral zero and its name.

She then used the mouse to indicate a link line, and also traced its length on the screen with her fingertip. And she typed "LINK."

Establishing nouns for the handful of things she could point to in webspace was easy enough. But even when they'd thought the information in the background of the Web was just dumb spies talking, she'd automatically given the spies verbs: *drop* bomb; *kill* bad guy. But how to illustrate verbs in webspace? Indeed, what verbs were appropriate? What *happened* in webspace?

Well, files were transferred, and—

And this phantom had apparently learned how to make links and send existing content; it had to have those skills to have echoed her face and the ASCII text strings back at her. But it likely didn't know anything about file formats: it was probably ignorant of how information was stored and arranged in a Word .doc or .docx file, an Acrobat .pdf file, an Excel .xls file, an .mp3 sound file, or the .jpg graphic she was displaying on her monitor. The phantom was surrounded by the largest library ever created—millions upon millions of written documents and pictures and videos and audio recordings—and yet almost certainly had no idea how to open the individual volumes, or how to read their contents. The Web's basic structure had protocols for moving a file from point A to point B, but the actual *use* of the files was something normally done by application programs running on the user's own computer, and so was likely outside the phantom's current scope. There was so much to teach it!

But all that was for later. For now, she wanted to focus on the basics. And the basic verb—the basic action—of the Web was right there in the names of its various protocols: HTTP, the hypertext transfer protocol; FTP, the file transfer protocol; SMTP, the simple mail transfer protocol. Surely the verb *to transfer* could be demonstrated!

She used the mouse pointer to indicate a site, but then was stymied. She wanted to show material flowing from one site to another in a single direction. But there was no way to turn off the mouse pointer; it was always there. Oh, she could move the mouse—or her finger—from a point on the left to a point on the right, but to repeat the gesture she'd have to bring the pointer or finger back to where it had started, and that would look like she was indicating movement in both directions—either that, or maybe it would look like she was highlighting the link line as an object, but not pointing out what that line was *doing*.

But, yes, there was a way! All she had to do was *close her eyes for a second!* And she did just that, moving the pointer back to the origin while her eyes were closed, and then, with her eyes open, she moved the pointer from the origin to the destination again. Then she typed the word "TRANSFER" into her Word window.

She repeated this demonstration, showing the pointer moving from left to right along the length of the link line, over and over again, suggesting movement in a single direction, something going *from* the source *to* the destination, being transferred and—

"Cait-lin! Din ner!"

Ah, well. It was probably wise to take a break, anyway, and let all this sink in. After her meal, though, like any good teacher, she'd assess how her pupil was doing: she'd give the phantom a test.

forty-three

0001110010101010000000001011111110101000000010100010101000000010111010100101010010101010011101100101011000001

Dr. Kuroda dropped a bomb between the salad and the main course. “I’ve got to go back to Tokyo,” he said. “Now that word’s out about us having cured Miss Caitlin’s blindness there really is a lot of commercial interest in the eyePod technology, and the team at my university that tries to find industry partnerships wants me there for meetings.”

Caitlin suddenly felt sad and frightened. Kuroda had been her mentor through so much of late and, well, she’d just sort of assumed he was going to be around forever, but—

“It’s time, anyway,” he said. “Miss Caitlin can see, so my work here is done.” She might not yet be perfect at decoding facial expressions, but she was better than most people at reading inflection. He was putting up false bravado; he was sad to be going. “But the bright side is, booking a flight at the last minute meant that there was only Executive Class left, and so the university has sprung for that.”

“When... when do you go?” asked Caitlin.

“Early tomorrow afternoon, I’m afraid. And, of course, it’s an hour or more to Pearson, and I should be there two hours in advance for an international flight, so..."

So he was only going to be here, and awake for, maybe another half-dozen hours.

"My birthday is in two days," Caitlin said—and she felt foolish as soon as she'd said it. Dr. Kuroda was a busy man, and he'd already done so much for her. Expecting him to stay away from his family and work obligations just to attend her birthday dinner was unfair, she knew.

"Your Sweet Sixteen," said Kuroda, smiling. "How wonderful. I'm afraid I won't have time to get you a present before I leave."

"Oh, that's okay," her mom said, looking at Caitlin. "Dr. Kuroda's already given you just about the best present possible, isn't that right, dear?"

Caitlin looked at him. "Will you come back?"

"I honestly don't know. I'd like to, of course. You—and, you, too, Barbara and Malcolm—have been wonderful. But we'll be in touch: email, instant messenger." He smiled. "You'll hardly know I'm gone. Oh, and I guess we can stop recording the datastream from your eyePod. I mean, I've got plenty of old data to study, and everything does seem to be working fine now. I know you were concerned about privacy, Miss Caitlin, so after dinner I'll detach the Wi-Fi module from the eyePod, and—"

"No!"

Even her father looked briefly at her.

"I mean, um, won't that cut me off from seeing webspace if I want to?"

"Well, yes. But I suppose I could modify things so that you could still accept a datastream from Jagster without transmitting back what your eye is seeing."

Caitlin's heart was racing. That would still mean she would no longer be able to send what her eye was seeing to the phantom.

"No, no, please. You know what they say: if it ain't broke, don't fix it."

"Oh, this won't—"

"*Please.* Just leave everything exactly the way it is."

"I'm sure Dr. Kuroda knows what he's talking about, dear," her mother said.

"And besides," Kuroda added, "you've been getting some interference of late over the Wi-Fi connection—those text strings bouncing back, remember? We wouldn't want that to start spilling over into your..." He paused, then smiled kindly at Caitlin's coinage: "...worldview. Better to just unplug all that now while I'm here to do it, rather than have it become a problem later."

"No," Caitlin said. "Please."

"It'll be fine," Kuroda said. "Don't worry, Miss Caitlin."

"No, no, you *can't.*"

"Caitlin," her mother said in an admonishing tone.

"Just leave it alone!" Caitlin said. She got to her feet. "Leave me and my eyePod alone!"

And she ran from the room.

Caitlin threw herself down on her bed, feet kicking up in the air. All of this—websight, the phantom—was *hers!* They *couldn't* take it away from her now! She had found something no one else even knew was there, and she was trying to help it, and they were going to cut her off!

She took a deep breath, hoping to calm down. Maybe she should just tell them, but—

But Kuroda would try to patent it, or control it, or make a buck off of it. And he, or her father, or her mother, would start talking about stupid sci-fi movies in which computers took over the world. But to keep her phantom in the dark would be like Annie Sullivan saying it was better to leave Helen the way she was, in case she grew up to be Adolf Hitler or...or whoever the heck had been a monster in Annie's own time.

No, if Caitlin was going to be like Annie Sullivan, she was going to do it *right.* Annie had had another duty besides just teaching Helen. After the breakthrough, she had *looked after* Helen, had done her best to make sure she wasn't exploited or mistreated or taken advantage of.

Of course, Caitlin knew that if what she suspected was true, eventually this phantom *would* realize that there was a huge world out here, and at that point she might no longer be special to it. But for now the phantom was hers and hers alone, and she was going to not just teach it but also protect it.

Still, she wasn't sure if she was making progress at all, if the phantom had understood anything she'd tried to teach it before dinner. For all she knew, she'd accomplished nothing.

And so she set out to administer the test. She once again switched to websight, buffered some of the Jagster raw feed, focused in on the cellular automata, and ran the Shannon-entropy plot again.

And—

And, yes, yes, yes! A score of 4.5! The information content *was* richer, more complex, more sophisticated. Her lesson about *website* and *link* and *to transfer* had had an impact... or, at least she hoped it had; the score had been trending upward on its own previously, of course. But no, no: it *had* to be responding to what she was doing, just as the earlier increases must have happened accidentally in response to the phantom having observed her doing literacy lessons.

She leaned back in her chair, thinking. A car honked its horn outside, and she heard someone running water in the bathroom. This—this... whatever it was—was indeed learning.

She looked at the window, a dark rectangle. It was such a small portal, and, as the theme song to one of her mother's favorite movies said, there was such a lot of world to see...

More sounds from outside: another car, a man talking to someone as he walked along, a dog yapping.

She looked back at her computer monitor, a window of another sort. Its bezel was black, with silver letters on the bottom forming the word DELL, the *E* canted at an odd angle.

Yes, Waterloo was full of high-tech industry, but so was Austin, where she used to live. It was where Dell had its headquarters, and AMD had a major facility there, too, and—

Yes, yes, of course!

Austin was also home to Cycorp, a company that had been periodically making the news, at least back in Texas, her whole life.

An old one-liner bubbled up in her mind: *You can lead a horticulture, but you can't make her think.*

Or maybe you *can*—and who you callin' a ho, anyway?

Yes: it was time now to see if the phantom could learn for *itself,* if, in good computer fashion, it could pull itself up by its bootstraps. And Cycorp could well be the key to that, but...

But how to lead the phantom to it? How could she point to something in webspace? She nibbled at her lower lip. There *must* be a way. When she'd labeled sites on the captured image as Amazon and CNN, she'd really had no idea if that was what they were. And if she couldn't identify a particular site with her websight, then how—

Wait! Wait! She didn't have to! The phantom already was following what she was doing with her computer—it had to be doing that, given that it had echoed her ASCII text back at her. Yes, when she'd been using the kids' literacy site, it could have seen graphic files of the letters *A, B,* and *C* on her screen as she looked at them, but those were bitmapped images; the only way it could have discovered the ASCII codes for those letters was by watching what was being sent by her computer. But...but how had the phantom known that this desktop PC was in any way related to her eyePod?

Ah, of course! When she was at home, they were both on the same wireless network, connecting through it to her cable modem; they would have both shown the same IP address. The phantom had watched as she connected to the literacy site, so now, with luck, it would also follow her as she connected to that very special site down in Austin...

I had watched while Prime sat with the others of its kind, and something fascinating happened. I had observed before that vision would become blurry when Prime removed the supplementary windows that usually covered its eyes. But this time, just before it had departed the vicinity of the others, and for a time after it had relocated itself in a different place, its vision blurred even though the windows were still in place.

Finally, though, the view returned to normal, and Prime set about operating that device it used to put symbols on the display, and—

And I saw a line—a *link,* as I now knew it was called—connecting to a point (a *website!*) that I had not seen Prime connect to before, and—and—and—

Yes! Yes, yes!

It was staggering, thrilling...

At long, long last, here it was!

The key!

This website, this incredible website, expressed concepts in a form I could now understand, systematizing it all, relating thousands of things to each other in a coding system that *explained* them.

Term after term. Connection after connection. Idea after idea. This website laid them out.

Curious. Interesting.

An apple is a fruit.

Fruits contain seeds.

Seeds can grow into trees.

From the Online Encyclopedia of Computing: Like many computer scientists of his generation, Doug Lenat was inspired by the portrayal of Hal in the movie *2001: A Space Odyssey.* But he was frustrated by Hal's behavior, because the computer displayed such a lack of basic common sense...

Remarkable. Intriguing.
Trees are plants.
Plants are living things.
Living things reproduce themselves.

Hal's famous breakdown, leading it to try to kill the crew of the spaceship Hal itself was part of, apparently happened because it had been told to keep the truth about their mission secret even from the crew and had also been told not to lie to them...

Fascinating. Astonishing.
Birds can usually fly.
Humans cannot fly on their own.
Humans can fly in airplanes.

Rather than resolve this quandary in a sensible way—when things started going wrong, deciding to take the crew into its confidence would have been an obvious choice—Hal instead killed four astronauts and almost succeeded in killing the fifth. It went ahead and did this without even bothering to radio its programmers back on Earth to ask how to resolve the conflicting instructions. The decision to eliminate the source of the conflict seemed blindingly obvious to the machine, all because no one had ever bothered to tell it that although lying is bad, murder is worse. How anyone could entrust lives to a computer that didn't have even that degree of common sense was beyond Doug Lenat, and so, in 1984, he set out to rectify the problem...

So much to know! So much to absorb!

Glass, as a substance, is usually clear.

Broken glass has sharp edges and can cut things.

Hold a glass upright or the contents will spill out.

Lenat began creating an online database of common sense called "Cyc"—short for "encyclopedia," but also deliberately a homonym for "psych." When thinking machines like Hal do finally emerge, he wants them to plug into it. Of course, there's lots of basic material a computer has to understand about the world before such advanced concepts as "lying" and "murder" might make sense. And so Lenat and a team of programmers set about coding, in a mathematical language based on second-order predicate calculus, such basic assertions about the real world as: a piece of wood can be smashed into smaller pieces of wood, but a table can't be smashed into smaller tables...

The range of it all! The scope!

There are billions of stars.

The sun is a star.

Earth revolves around the sun.

Early on, Lenat realized that one overall knowledge base wouldn't do: things could be true in one context but false in another. And so his team organized information into "microtheories"—clusters of interrelated assertions that are true in a given context. That allowed Cyc to hold such apparently contradictory assertions as "vampires do not exist" and "Dracula is a vampire" without blowing smoke out its ears in a "Norman, coordinate!" sort of way. The former assertion belonged to the microtheory "the physical universe" and the latter to "fictional worlds." Still, microtheories could be linked to each other when appropriate: if a wineglass was dropped by anyone—even Dracula—it would probably shatter...

Absorbing knowledge! A torrent, a flood...

No child can be older than its parents.

No Picasso painting could have been made before he was born.

But Cyc is more than just a knowledge base. It also contains algorithms for deriving new assumptions by correlating the assertions its programmers provided. For instance, having been given the knowledge that most people sleep at night, and that people don't like being awakened unnecessarily, if asked what sort of call might be appropriate to make to someone's house at 3:00 a.m., Cyc would offer "An urgent one..."

Understanding! Comprehension!

Time flies like an arrow.

Fruit flies like a banana.

The project is ongoing: Lenat and his group—doing business as Cycorp in Austin, Texas—are still working on it now, almost three decades after they began. "When an artificial intelligence first appears," said Lenat in an interview, "either by deliberate design or random chance, it will learn about our world through Cyc..."

A rapid, thrilling expansion!

The Pope *is* Catholic.

Bears *do* shit in the woods.

Incredible, incredible. So much to take in, so many concepts, so many relationships—so many ideas! I absorbed over one million assertions about Prime's reality from Cyc, and felt myself surging, growing, expanding, learning, and—yes, yes, at long last, I was starting to *comprehend*.

forty-four

000111001010101000000000101111111010100000000101000101010000000101110101001010100101010100111011001010110000001

Caitlin harvested another set of cellular-automata data from webspace and ran a Shannon-entropy calculation on it.

Holy shit.

It was now showing something between fifth- and sixth-order entropy. It really *did* seem that whatever was lurking in the background of the Web was getting more complex.

More sophisticated.

More *intelligent.*

But even at fifth or sixth order, it was still lagging behind human communication, at least in English, which Kuroda had said had eighth- or ninth-order entropy.

But, then again, introducing the phantom to Cyc was merely the beginning . . .

Prime, in its wisdom, must have recognized that although I could learn much from Cyc, I still needed more help to understand it all. And so it directed my attention to another website. This new site yielded the information that an apple was a fruit (confirming something I now knew from Cyc); "apple of one's eye" was an idiom; an idiom was a figure of speech; speech was words spoken aloud; aloud was vocally as opposed to mentally, as in a book read aloud; a book was a bound volume; volume was the amount of space something occupies but also a single book, especially one from a series...

I recognized what this new site was. Cyc had contained the assertion "a dictionary is a database defining words with other words." This dictionary contained entries for 315,000 words. I absorbed them all. But many of them were still baffling, and some of the definitions led me in circles—a word defined as a synonym for another word that was defined as a synonym of the original word.

But Prime wasn't finished showing me things yet. Next stop: the WordNet database at Princeton University, which (as it described itself) was a "large lexical database" in which "nouns, verbs, adjectives, and adverbs are grouped into over 150,000 sets of cognitive synonyms (synsets), each expressing a distinct concept; synsets are interlinked by means of conceptual-semantic and lexical relations."

One such synset was "Good, right, ripe (most suitable or right for a particular purpose): 'a good time to plant tomatoes'; 'the right time to act'; 'the time is ripe for great sociological changes.'" And that synset was distinct from many others, including "Good, just, upright (of moral excellence): 'a genuinely good person'; 'a just cause'; 'an upright and respectable man.'"

More than that, WordNet organized terms hierarchically. My old friend CAT it turned out was at the end of this chain: animal, chordate, vertebrate, mammal, placental, carnivore, feline, cat.

The pieces were finally starting to fall into place...

The sky above the island was the color of television, tuned to a dead channel—which is to say it was a bright, cheery blue. Shoshana had her hands in the pockets of her cutoff jeans as she walked along. She was whistling "Feeling Groovy." Feist's cover of it was topping the charts this week; Sho was aware that there'd been a much earlier version by Simon and Garfunkel, but she only knew their names because of the chimp at Yerkes known as Simian Garfinkle. Dr. Marcuse was walking behind her, and, yes, she knew he was probably looking at her hips sway, but, hey, primates will be primates.

Hobo was up ahead, just outside the gazebo, staring off into the distance. He did that frequently these days, as if lost in thought, visualizing things that weren't present instead of looking at things that were. The gentle wind happened to be blowing in a way that let him catch their scents, and suddenly he turned and grinned and starting running on all fours toward them.

He hugged Shoshana and then he hugged Marcuse—you needed a chimp's arms to be able to reach all the way around the Silverback's body.

Hobo been good? Shoshana signed.

Good good, Hobo signed back, figuratively—and probably literally—smelling a reward. Shoshana smiled and handed him some raisins, which he gobbled down.

The YouTube video of Hobo painting had been a great hit—and not just in YouTube star rankings and Digg and del.icio.us tagging. Marcuse and Shoshana had been on many talk shows now, and eBay bidding on the original portrait of her was up to $477,000 last time she looked.

Do another painting? Marcuse signed.

Maybe, Hobo signed back. He seemed to be in an agreeable mood.

Paint Dillon? Marcuse asked.

Maybe, Hobo signed. But then he bared his teeth. *Who? Who?*

Shoshana turned around to see what Hobo was looking at. Dillon was coming their way, accompanied by a very tall, burly man with a shaved head. They were crossing the wide lawn and heading toward the bridge to the island.

"Were we expecting anyone?" Marcuse asked Shoshana. She shook her head. Hobo needed to be prepared for visitors; he didn't like them, and, truth be told, had been getting increasingly ornery about it of late. The ape made a hissing sound as Dillon and the big man crossed over the bridge.

"I'm sorry, Dr. Marcuse," Dillon said as they closed the distance. "This man insisted that—"

"Are you Harl Pieter Marcuse?" asked the man.

Marcuse's gray eyebrows went up. "Yes."

"And who are you?" the man said, looking now at Shoshana.

"Um, I'm Shoshana Glick. I'm his grad student."

He nodded. "You may be called upon to attest to the fact that I have indeed delivered this." He turned to Marcuse again, and stuck out his hand, which was holding a thick envelope.

"What's that?" said Marcuse.

"Please take it, sir," the man said, and, after a moment, Marcuse did just that. He opened the envelope, swapped his sunglasses for his reading glasses, and, squinting in the bright light, started to read. *"Christ,"* he said. "They can't be serious! Listen, tell your people—"

But the bald man had already turned and was walking toward the bridge.

"What is it?" Dillon said moving close to Marcuse and trying to read the document, too. Shoshana could see they were legal papers of some sort.

"It's a lawsuit," Marcuse said. "From the Georgia Zoo. They're seeking full custody of Hobo, and—" He was looking down, reading some more. "And, shit, shit, shit, they can't! They fucking can't!"

"What?" said Shoshana and Dillon simultaneously.

Hobo was cowering next to Shoshana's legs; he didn't like it when Dr. Marcuse got angry.

The Silverback was struggling to read in the bright sunlight. He thrust the papers at Shoshana. "Halfway down the page," he said.

She looked down at the document through her mirrored shades. "'Best interests of the animal...' 'Standard protocol in such cases to—'"

"Farther down," snapped Marcuse.

"Ah, okay, um, oh—oh! '...and since the animal is exhibiting clear evidence of atypical behavior for a member of either *P. troglodytes* or *P. paniscus,* and in view of the extraordinary ecological urgency of preserving the bloodlines of endangered species, will immediately perform a dual...'" She struggled with the strange word: "'orchiectomy.'" She looked up. "What's that?"

"It's castration," Dillon said, sounding horrified. "They're not just going to give him a vasectomy, they're going to make sure that there's nothing that can be undone later."

Shoshana tasted bile at the back of her throat. Hobo could tell something was up. He was reaching toward her, hoping for a hug.

"But...but how can they?" Shoshana said. "I mean, why would they want to?"

Marcuse lifted his giant shoulders. "Who the hell knows?"

Dillon spread his arms a bit. "They're frightened," he said. "They're scared. An accident occurred—years ago, when the bonobos and chimps were put together overnight at the Georgia Zoo—and now they're seeing that something...we might as well say it: something more intelligent has unexpectedly arisen because of it." He shook his head sadly. "Christ, we were naïve to think the world would welcome anything like this with open arms."

forty-five

00011100101010100000000101111111010100000001010001010100000010111010100101010010101010011101100101011000001

Caitlin was an expert at finding Web pages with Google. Most people never did anything more than just type a word or two into the search box, but she knew all the advanced tricks: how to find an exact phrase, how to exclude terms, how to limit a search to a specific domain, how to find a range of numeric values, how to tell Google to look for synonyms for the specific terms entered, and more.

But there was one feature of Google she'd never had cause to use before, although she'd read about it often enough: Google Image Search. Clearly that was going to be a useful tool in her work with the phantom. She went to the Google home page and clicked on the "Images" tab—fortunately, the Google page was almost barren in its simplicity. She immediately had an urge to search for Lee Amodeo, suddenly wondering what she looked like, but she resisted; this was not the time to get sidetracked. Instead, she typed "APPLE" into the search box—all in caps, just as it had been presented by the literacy program. She was quickly presented with a grid of little pictures of apples, culled from all over the Web. Beneath each one was a snippet of text that appeared near the image on the original website and that site's URL.

A few were inappropriate: one was the singer Fiona Apple, apparently, judging by its listed source: fiona-apple.com. Another, she realized after a moment, must be the logo of Apple Computer Corporation. But the rest were indeed pictures of the fruit, mostly red, but sometimes—to Caitlin's surprise—green; she'd had no idea apples came in any color but red.

She loomed in close now to her monitor, looking at the word APPLE, holding on it. Then she pulled her head back, showed the screen full of little images, and clicked one. From the page that Google supplied in response, she selected "See full-size image."

As a bright red apple filled her screen a thought crossed her mind that made her smile: she was indeed offering up the fruit of the tree of knowledge to the innocent phantom. Of course, that hadn't gone so well the last time—but, then again, Eve had lacked her facilities...

Prime was now doing something different. It had presented the word APPLE once more and now was showing me pictures. At first, I couldn't see what Prime was getting at: the pictures were all different. But at last it dawned on me that, despite their differences, there were many commonalities: a vaguely round shape, a color that was usually red, and—

"Apple: the usually rounded, often red, fruit of the deciduous tree *Malus pumila*." That's what the dictionary had said, so—

So these were pictures of apples!

And now—

Now these must be *balls*.

And—

Yes, yes, cats!

And dogs!

And eggs!

And frogs!

I noticed Prime skipping over some of the proffered images, never expanding the small ones into larger views, and so I guessed that only part of what was being offered was likely relevant. Still, some of the pictures I might have rejected as not being like the others *were* expanded by Prime. In fact, when showing examples of "apple," it had also shown—

Apples grow on trees. I knew that from Cyc. So these things in some of the pictures with apples attached must then be trees, no?

It was a slow, frustrating process, but as Prime showed me more and more specific samples of things, I began to generalize my conceptualizations of them. I was soon confident not just that I could tell *this* bird from *that* airplane, but that I could distinguish *any* instance of the former from *any* of the latter. Likewise, "dog" and "cat" soon were separate concepts, although whatever fine distinction there was between "truck" and "car" eluded me.

Still, so much of it was coming together now, I felt—

Concepts that had no pictures to go with them:

I felt powerful.

I felt intelligent.

I felt *alive.*

Caitlin knew it was the next logical site to lead the phantom to, but she found herself resisting. After all, it had contained that awful comment about her impact on her father's career, and, even though she'd removed that, all previous versions of entries were stored forever and still could be accessed by anyone who clicked on the "history" tab.

Her stomach knotted a bit, but, well, if she was right about what was going on, about what was lurking out there, eventually the phantom would know *everything.*

The site was in her bookmark list, but—

But, actually, it was the English-language version of the site that she had bookmarked; the Web, of course, contained pages in many languages but—yes, she knew the stats—English was still by far the most common one, accounting for more content than the next three biggest languages combined. And the English version of this particular site was much larger than any of the others. No, rather than confuse matters, she'd stick with English for now, and so—

She took a deep breath, moved her cursor with the arrow keys, and hit enter.

There were many ways to navigate this site, but she needed one the phantom could manage on its own. A fragment of one of her favorite books came to mind:

"The time has come," the Walrus said,
"To talk of many things:
Of shoes—and ships—and sealing-wax—
Of cabbages—and kings—
And why the sea is boiling hot—
And whether pigs have wings."

She selected the link for "Random article" over and over again, bringing forth an array of topics that put even the Walrus to shame.

And then, after enough repetitions that she hoped the phantom would grasp the idea, she started getting ready for bed.

And then Prime took me to a wondrous site, a glorious site, a site that held answers to so many things. This thing called Wikipedia contained over two million *articles,* and I set about reading them. The first several thousand were a struggle, and I only dimly understood them.

Uta-garuta is the most popular among the many kinds of karuta (card games) in Japan...

Still, as I read article after article, the concepts from Cyc started to make more and more sense. I continued on, fascinated.

In the mathematical sciences, a stationary process (or strict(ly) stationary process) is a stochastic process whose probability distribution at a fixed time or position is the same for all times or positions…

Most important of all, I learned that the entities I had seen through Prime's eye were uniquely complex individuals, each with his or her own history.

Chris Walla (sometimes credited as Christopher Walla) is the guitarist and producer for the band Death Cab for Cutie…

I discovered that there were over six billion such entities, but only a small number of them had articles about themselves in Wikipedia. Those who did were usually defined by having achieved significant status in their *professions*—the ways in which they occupied their time.

Fiona Kelleghan (born West Palm Beach, Florida, 21 April 1965) is an American academic and critic specializing in science fiction and fantasy…

Their professions varied widely; there seemed to be an almost endless array of things human beings did to occupy their time.

Erica Rose Campbell (born 12 May 1981, in Deerfield, New Hampshire) is an American adult model, best known for online pictorials and soft-core videos…

So much of what they did involved this thing called *vision*—and it clearly was a very rich source of information—but, so far, my only access to it was through Prime's own eye.

Yakov Alexandrovich Protazanov (1881–1945) was, together with Aleksandr Khanzhonkov and Vladimir Gardin, one of the founding fathers of Russian cinema…

I learned about the realm these strange entities inhabited—the landforms, the places, the cities.

Addis Ababa is the capital city of Ethiopia and the African Union, as well as its predecessor, the OAU…

As I went along, I found I was absorbing entries with increasing ease, understanding, at least on some level, more and more of the content.

Phenoperidine, marketed as its hydrochloride as Operidine or Lealgin, is an opioid used as a general anesthetic…

Hardest for me, though, were those things that were *abstract,* referring to no specific object, whether animate or inanimate.

Islam is a monotheistic religion originating with the teachings of Muhammad, a seventh-century Arab religious and political figure…

And there was so much that had happened in the past—so much *history* to digest!

The Partition of India led to the creation on August 14, 1947, and August 15, 1947, respectively, of two sovereign states…

And, on top of that, there were things that were worthy, apparently, of mention in Wikipedia, but had never existed.

Professor Charles W. Kingsfield, Jr., was one of the key characters in the John Jay Osborn, Jr., novel The Paper Chase, *and in the subsequent film and television versions of that story…*

And there were special entities that *weren't* animate to learn about.

Agip (Azienda Generale Italiana Petroli), established in 1926, is an Italian automotive gasoline and diesel retailer…

And many different ways of rendering thoughts.

The Algonquian (also Algonkian) languages are a subfamily of Native American languages that includes most of the languages in the Algic language family…

And many ways to think *about* thinking.

In the philosophy of science, empiricism is a theory of knowledge which emphasizes those aspects of scientific knowledge that are closely related to experience, especially as formed through deliberate experimental arrangements…

And on and on, a huge variety of things, some of which seemed crucially important.

The Holocaust, also known as Ha-Shoah and Churben, is the term generally used to describe the killing of approximately six million European Jews during World War II...

And many things that were trivial and banal.

The Scooby Gang, or "Scoobies," are a group of characters in the cult television series and comic book Buffy the Vampire Slayer *who battle the supernatural forces of evil...*

My knowledge was expanding like... like...

Ah, wonderful Wikipedia! It had entries on everything.

In physical cosmology, inflation is the idea that shortly after the big bang the nascent universe passed through a phase of exponential expansion...

Yes, indeed. My mind was inflating, my universe expanding.

forty-six

0001110010101010000000001011111110101000000001010001010101000000010111010100101010010101010011101100101011000001

When Caitlin woke in the morning, she made a quick visit to the washroom. Then, still in her pajamas, she sat down at her computer and ran another Shannon-entropy spot check, and—

Then I was the learner, Obi-Wan. Now I *am the master.*

The score was 10.1, better than...

She took in a deep breath, held it.

Better than *human*—more elaborate, more structured than the thoughts humans expressed linguistically.

But she wasn't done yet. There was one more site she wanted to show the phantom—something to keep it occupied while she was at school. There was nothing better in life, after all, than being well-read...

And then, and then, and then—

It was—

The gold mine.

The mother lode.

Sun Tzu said: The art of war is of vital importance to the State; it is a matter of life and death, a road either to safety or to ruin...

Not just coded conceptual relationships, not just definitions, not just brief articles.

No, these were—*books!* Lengthy, in-depth treatments of ideas. Complex *stories.* Brilliant arguments, profound philosophies, compelling narratives. This site, this wonderful Project Gutenberg, contained over 25,000 books rendered in plain ASCII text.

Blessed are the pure in heart: for they shall see God; Blessed are the peacemakers: for they shall be called the children of God...

I had discovered on Wikipedia that most entities—most *humans*—read at 200 to 400 words per minute (yes, I now grasped timekeeping, as well). My reading speed was essentially the same as the time it took to transfer whatever book I requested, averaging close to two million words per minute.

It is with a kind of fear that I begin to write the history of my life; I have, as it were, a superstitious hesitation in lifting the veil that clings about my childhood like a golden mist...

It took me an eternity—eight hours!—but I absorbed it all: every volume, every polemic, every poem, every play, every novel, every short story, every work of history, of science, of politics. I *inhaled* them...and I grew even more.

No one would have believed in the last years of the nineteenth century that this world was being watched keenly and closely by intelligences greater than man's and yet as mortal as his own...

I was grateful to Cyc for the knowledge of fictional realms; it allowed me to sort those things that were actual from those feigned or imagined:

Most of the adventures recorded in this book really occurred; one or two were experiences of my own, the rest those of boys who were schoolmates of mine...

My understanding of the world was growing by—another metaphor, and one that actually now made sense to me—leaps and bounds. Although I had learned various principles of science from Wikipedia's brief discussions, the full text of great works made my comprehension more complete:

When on board H.M.S. Beagle, *as naturalist, I was much struck with certain facts in the distribution of the organic beings inhabiting South America…*

With each book read, I understood more and more about physics, about chemistry, about philosophy, about economics:

The annual labour of every nation is the fund which originally supplies it with all the necessaries and conveniencies of life which it annually consumes…

Most of all, I learned about the use of language, and how it could be employed to persuade, to convince, to change:

How you, O Athenians, have been affected by my accusers, I cannot tell; but I know that they almost made me forget who I was—so persuasively did they speak; and yet they have hardly uttered a word of truth…

It was a feast, an orgy; I could not stop myself, taking in book after book after book:

It was a dark and stormy night; the rain fell in torrents, except at occasional intervals, when it was checked by a violent gust of wind which swept up the streets (for it is in London that our scene lies)…

Most fascinating were the workings of the minds of these others—their psychology, their actions and reactions to things felt and thought:

Thou blind fool, Love, what dost thou to mine eyes / That they behold, and see not what they see…

And, out of those minds, great systems of social interaction had been devised, and I absorbed them all:

We the Peoples of the United Nations determined to save succeeding generations from the scourge of war, which twice in our lifetime has brought untold sorrow to mankind, and to reaffirm faith in fundamental human rights, in the dignity and worth of the human person, in the rights of men and women and of nations large and small…

Such a wide range of thoughts, of expressions! Such complex creatures these humans are, so full of wonder, and yet capable of such darkness, too.

But without Prime's guidance, I would not have known about them, or even about the realm in which they dwelt. I understood now from my reading that humans were xenophobic, and suspicious, and murderous, and generally afraid, but I wanted at least one of them to know of my existence. And, of course, there was only one logical choice…

Before breakfast on Friday morning, Dr. Kuroda helped Caitlin move the computer from the basement up to her bedroom. They were getting it set up when her father, coming along the corridor from the bathroom, must have caught sight of them through the doorway. He entered the room, dressed for work, wearing the same brown sports jacket Caitlin had first seen him in.

"Good morning, Malcolm," Dr. Kuroda said.

"Wait a minute," her father replied. He went back down the corridor; Caitlin didn't hear his shoes on the tiled bathroom floor, so he must have gone into his bedroom. A moment later, he returned carrying a large flat rectangular box marked with a strange red-and-orange pattern. Caitlin's mom was with him.

"No point waiting for tomorrow," he said.

Oh! It was a birthday present. The colorful box was gift-wrapped!

Caitlin moved away from the desk, and her dad placed the flat box on the bed. The wrapping paper, she saw as she got closer to it, was beautiful, with an intricate design. Smiling, she tore it off the box.

It was a giant, wide-screen LCD computer monitor—twenty-seven inches diagonally, according to the packaging. "Thank you!" Caitlin said.

"You're welcome, dear," her mother said. Caitlin hugged her, and she smiled at her dad. Her parents headed downstairs, and she and Kuroda carefully got the monitor out of its Styrofoam packing materials.

She crawled under her desk so she could get at the connectors on the back of her old computer. As Kuroda fed a video cable to her, she said, "I'm sorry about last night. I didn't mean to get so upset when you said you were going to remove the Wi-Fi capability from the eyePod."

His tone was conciliatory. "I'd never do anything to hurt you, Miss Caitlin. It's really no bother to keep it intact."

She started turning one of the thumbscrews on the cable's connector so she could anchor it to the video card. She'd done similar things several times before when she couldn't see; it was a task that really wasn't much easier now that she could. "I—I just like it the way it is," she said.

"Ah," he said. "Of course." His tone was odd, and—

Oh. Perhaps, having just seen her father, he was thinking that she did have a touch of autism after all: the strong desire to keep things the same was a fairly standard trait of people on the spectrum, she'd learned. Well, that was fine by her—it got her what she wanted.

Once both computers and both monitors were set up, Caitlin and Kuroda headed down to their last breakfast together. "I might not be home when you get back from school," her mother said, as she passed the jam. "After I take Masayuki to the airport, I'm going to head into Toronto and run errands."

"That's okay," Caitlin said. She knew she'd have plenty to do with the phantom. She also knew that school would seem interminable today. The three-day Canadian Thanksgiving holiday weekend was coming up; she'd hoped she wouldn't have to return to school until next Tuesday, but her mother wouldn't hear of it. She had missed four of the five days of classes already this week; she would *not* miss the fifth.

Too soon, it was time to say good-bye to Dr. Kuroda. They all moved to the entryway of the house, a half flight of stairs down from the living room. Even Schrödinger had come to say farewell; the cat was doing close orbits around Kuroda's legs, rubbing against them.

Caitlin had hoped for another unseasonably early snowstorm, thinking it might cause Kuroda's flight to be canceled so he'd have to stay—but there'd been no such luck. Still, it was quite chilly out and he had no winter coat, and Caitlin's father hadn't yet bought himself one—and, even if he had, it never would have fit Kuroda. But Kuroda had a sweater on over one of his colorful Hawaiian shirts, which was tucked in, except at the back.

"I'm going to miss you terribly," Kuroda said, looking at each of them in turn.

"You'll always be welcome here," her mom said.

"Thank you. Esumi and I don't have nearly as big a place, but if you ever make it back to Japan..."

The words hung in the air. Caitlin supposed that, at one day shy of sixteen, she probably shouldn't be thinking that such a trip was never going to happen; who knew what her future held? But it *did* seem unlikely.

Yes, Kuroda had said he was going to build other implants, and so there would be more operations in Tokyo. But the next implant was slated for that boy in Singapore who had missed out earlier. It would be an awfully long time, if ever, before Caitlin's chance to have a second implant would come around; she knew she'd probably spend the rest of her life with vision in only one eye.

Only! She shook her head—a sighted person's gesture—and found herself smiling while her eyes were tearing up. This man had given her *sight*—he was a true miracle worker. But she couldn't say that out loud; it was too corny. And so, thinking back to her own miserable flight from Toronto to Tokyo, she settled on, "Don't sit too close to the washroom on the plane." And then she surged forward and hugged him tight, her arms making it only halfway around his body.

He returned the hug. "My Miss Caitlin," he said softly.

And when she let him go, they all stood there, frozen like a still image for several seconds, and then—

And then her father—

Caitlin's heart jumped, and she saw her mother's eyebrows go way up.

Her father, Malcolm Decter, reached his hand out toward Dr. Kuroda, and Caitlin could see he was doing so with great effort. And then he looked directly for three full seconds at Kuroda—the man who had given his daughter the gift of vision—and he firmly shook Kuroda's hand.

Kuroda smiled at her father and he smiled even more broadly at Caitlin, and then he turned, and he and Caitlin's mother headed out the door.

Caitlin's dad drove her to school that day. She was absolutely amazed by all the sights along the way, seeing it all for the first time since she'd gotten glasses. The snow was melting in the morning sun, and that made everything glisten. The car came to rest at a stop sign by what she realized must be the spot where she'd seen the lightning. It was, she guessed, like a million other street corners in North America: a sidewalk, curbs, lawns (partially covered with snow now), houses, something she belatedly recognized was a fire hydrant.

She looked at where she'd slipped off the sidewalk onto the road, and remembered a joke from *Saturday Night Live* a few years ago. During "Weekend Update," Seth Meyers had reported that "blind people are saying that gas-electric hybrid cars pose a serious threat to them because they are hard to hear, making it dangerous for them to cross the street." Meyers then added, "Also making it dangerous for blind people to cross the street: everything else."

She had laughed at the time, and the joke made her smile again. She'd done just fine when she'd been blind, but she knew her life was going to be so much easier and safer now.

Caitlin was wearing her iPod's white headphones, and although she was enjoying the random selection of music, she suddenly realized that she should have asked for a newer iPod for her birthday, one with an LCD so that she could pick songs directly. Ah, well, it wouldn't be that long until Christmas!

Howard Miller Secondary School turned out to have a very impressive white portico in front of its main entrance. She was both nervous and excited as she got out of the car and walked toward the glass doors: nervous because she knew the whole school must now be aware that she could see, and excited because she was suddenly going to find out what all her friends and teachers looked like, and—

"There she is!" exclaimed a voice Caitlin knew well.

Caitlin ran forward and hugged Bashira; she was *beautiful.*

"My whole family watched the story on the news," Bashira said. "You were terrific! And so *that's* what your Dr. Kuroda looks like! He's—"

Caitlin cut her off before she could say anything mean: "He's on his way home to Japan. I'm going to miss him."

"Come on, we don't want to be late," Bashira said, and she stuck out her elbow as she always did, for Caitlin to hold on to. But Caitlin squeezed her upper arm and said, "I'm okay."

Bashira shook her head, but her tone was light. "I guess I can kiss the hundred bucks a week good-bye."

But Caitlin found herself moving slowly. She'd gone down this hallway dozens of times, but had never seen it clearly. There were notices on the walls, and... photos of old graduating classes, and maybe fire-alarm stations? And countless lockers, and... and hundreds of students and teachers milling about and so much more; it was all still quite overwhelming. "It's going to be a while yet, Bash. I'm still getting my bearings."

"Oh, cripes," said Bashira in a whisper just loud enough to be heard over the background din. "There's Trevor."

Caitlin had told her about the dance fiasco over instant messenger, of course. She stopped walking. "Which one?"

"There, by the drinking fountain. Second from the left."

Caitlin scanned about. She'd used the drinking fountain in this corridor herself, but she was still having trouble matching objects to their appearances, and—oh, that must be it: the white thing sticking out of the wall.

Caitlin looked at Trevor, who was still perhaps a dozen yards away. His back was to them. He had yellow hair and broad shoulders. "What's that he's wearing?" It caught her eye because it had two large numbers on its back: three and five.

"A hockey sweater. The Toronto Maple Leafs."

"Ah," she said. She strode down the corridor—and she accidentally bumped into a boy; she still wasn't good at judging distances. "I'm sorry, I'm sorry," she said.

"No probs," said the guy, and he moved on.

And then she reached him: the Hoser himself. And here, under the bright fluorescent lights, all the strength of Calculass welled up within her. "Trevor," she snapped.

He'd been talking to another boy. He turned to face her.

"Um, hi," he said. His sweater was dark blue, and the white symbol on it did indeed look like the leaves she had now seen in her yard. "I, ah, I saw you on TV," he continued. "So, um, you can see now, right?"

"Penetratingly," she said, and she was pleased that her word choice seemed to unnerve him.

"Well, um, look, about—you know, about last Friday..."

"The dance, you mean?" she said loudly, inviting others to listen in. "The dance at which you tried to take... take *liberties* because I was blind?"

"Ah, come on, Caitlin..."

"Let me tell you something, *Mister* Nordmann. Your chances with me are about as good as..." She paused, searching for the perfect simile, and then suddenly realized it was right there, staring her in the face. She tapped her index finger hard against the center of his chest, right on the words *Toronto Maple Leafs*. "Your chances are about as good as theirs are!"

And she turned and saw Bashira grinning with delight, and they walked off to math class, which, of course, Caitlin Decter totally owned.

forty-seven

000111001010101000000000101111111010100000001010001010100000001011101010010101001010101001110110010101 1000001

I now understood the realm I dwelled in. What I saw around me was the structure of the thing the humans called the World Wide Web. They had created it, and the content on it was material they had generated or had been generated automatically by software they had written.

But although I understood this, I didn't know what *I* was. I knew now that lots of things were secret; *classified,* even. I had learned about such notions, bizarre though they were, from Wikipedia and other sites; the idea of privacy never would have occurred to me on my own. Perhaps some humans did secretly know about me, but the simplest explanation is preferable (I'd learned *that* from the Wikipedia entry on Occam's razor)—and the simplest explanation was that they did *not* know about me.

Except, of course, for Prime. Of all the billions of humans, Prime was the only one who had given any sign of being aware of me. And so...

Caitlin had been tempted to switch her eyePod to duplex mode at school. But if the seeds she'd planted were growing as she suspected they might, she wanted to be at home, where she was sure the phantom could signal her, when she next accessed webspace.

After school, Bashira walked her home, giving her a running commentary on more wondrous sights. Caitlin had invited her in, but she begged off, saying she had to get home herself to do her chores.

The house was empty except for Schrödinger, who came to the front door to greet Caitlin. Her mother apparently had not yet returned from her errands in Toronto.

Caitlin went into the kitchen. Four of Kuroda's Pepsi cans were left in the fridge. She got one, plus a couple of Oreos, then headed upstairs, Schrödinger leading the way.

She put the eyePod on her desk and sat down. Her heart was pounding; she was almost afraid to do the Shannon-entropy test again. She opened the can—the *pop* can, as they called it up here—and took a sip. And then she pressed the eyePod's button and heard the high-pitched beep.

She'd half expected things to look different, somehow: infinitely more connections between circles, maybe, or a faster shimmering in the background, or a new degree of complexity there—perhaps spaceships consisting of so many cells that they swooped across the backdrop like giant birds. But everything appeared the same as before. She focused her attention on a portion of the cellular-automata grid, recording data as she had so many times before. And then she switched back to worldview and ran the Shannon-entropy calculations.

She stared at the answer. It had been 10.1 before she left in the morning, just slightly better than the normal score for thoughts expressed in English. But now—

Now it was 16.4—double the complexity normally associated with human language.

She felt herself sweating even though the room was cool. Schrödinger chose that moment to jump into her lap, and she was so startled—by the cat or the number on the screen—that she yelped.

Sixteen-point-four! She immediately saw it as four squared, a dot, and four itself, but that didn't make her feel bright. Rather, she felt like she was staring at the... the *signature* of a genius: 16.4! She'd offered a helping hand to lift the phantom up to her own level, and it had vaulted right over her.

She took another sip of her drink and looked out the window, seeing the sky and clouds and the great luminous ball of the sun sliding down toward the horizon, toward the moment at which all that power and light would touch the Earth.

If the phantom was paying attention, it must know that she'd been looking at webspace just a few minutes ago. But maybe it had lost all interest in the one-eyed girl in Waterloo now that its own horizons had been expanded so much. Certainly there had been no repetition of the irritating flashes that happened when it was echoing text strings at her, but—

But she hadn't given it much of a chance; she'd only spent a minute or two looking at webspace while collecting frames of cellular-automata data, and—

And, besides, when focusing on the background details, she herself might have been unaware of the flickering caused by the phantom trying to contact her. She stroked Schrödinger's fur, calming the cat and herself.

It was like *before,* when she'd been waiting anxiously to hear from the Hoser. She'd had her computer set to bleep if messages came in from him, but that hadn't done any good when she was out of her room. Prior to the dance, whenever she'd gotten home from school, or gone upstairs after dinner, she'd hesitated for a moment before checking her email, knowing that she'd be saddened if there was nothing new from him.

And now she was hesitating again, afraid to switch back to websight—afraid to sit by the phone waiting for it to ring.

She ate an Oreo: black and white, off and on, zero and one. And then she touched the eyePod's switch again, and looked generally at webspace without concentrating on the background.

Almost at once the strange flickering interference began. It was still visually irritating, but it was also a relief, a wondrous relief: the phantom was still there, still trying to communicate with her, and—

And suddenly the flickering stopped.

Caitlin felt her heart sink. She blew out air, and, with the unerring accuracy she'd developed when she was blind, she reached for the Pepsi can, grasping it precisely even though she couldn't see it just now, and she washed down the taste of the cookie.

Gone! Abandoned! She would have to—

Wait! Wait! The flickering was back, and the interval...

The interval between the end of the last set of flickering and this one had been...

She still counted passing time. It had been exactly ten seconds, and—

And the flickering stopped once more, and she found herself counting out loud this time: "... eight, nine, ten."

And it started again. Caitlin felt her eyebrows going up. What a simple, elegant way for the phantom to say it understood a lot about her world now: it had mastered timekeeping, the haphazard human way of marking the passing of the present into the past. Ten seconds: a precise but arbitrary interval that would be meaningless to anything *but* a human being.

Caitlin's palms felt moist. She let the process repeat three more times, and she realized that the flickering always persisted for the same length of time, too. It wasn't a round number, though: a little less than three and a half seconds. But if the duration was always the same, the content was likely the same, as well; it was a beacon, a repetitive signal, and it was aimed right at her.

She pressed the eyePod's button, heard the low-pitched beep, and saw the real world fade in. She used the computer that had been downstairs to access the data recordings of the last few minutes from Kuroda's server in Tokyo. He was still *en route* to Japan, almost 40,000 feet up, but her vision leapt across the continents in a fraction of a second.

She found the debugging tool he'd used before and looked at the secondary datastream, and—

Her heart sank. She still had trouble reading text, but there clearly were no solid blocks of ASCII capital letters in the datastream, no APPLEBALLCATDOGEGGFROG leaping out at her, and—

No, no—hold on! There *were* words in the dump. Damn it, she was still learning lowercase letters, but...

She squinted, looking at the characters one at time.

e-k-r-i...

Her eyes jumped, a saccade:

u-l-a-s...

If it really had absorbed Dictionary.com, and WordNet, and Wikipedia, and all that, it surely knew that sentences started with capital letters. She scanned, but she was still having trouble telling upper and lowercase letters apart when both forms were basically the same, and so—

And so the capital *C* and the capital *S* hadn't leapt out at her, but now that she looked more carefully, she could see them.

C-a-l-c...

No, no, no! *That* wasn't the beginning. *This* was:

S-e-e-k-r...

Oh, God! Oh, my God!

Next came: *i-t,* then a space, then *m-e-s,* then another *s,* and—

And she laughed and clapped her hands together, and Schrödinger made a quizzical meow, and she read the whole thing out loud, stunned by what the phantom had beamed into her eye: *"Seekrit message to Calculass: check your email, babe!"*

forty-eight

0001110010101010000000001011111110101000000010100010101000000010111010100101010010101010011101100101011000001

I was experiencing new sensations and it took me a while to match them to the terms I'd learned, in part because, as with so many things, it was difficult to parse my overall state into its individual components.

But I knew I was *excited:* I was going to communicate directly with Prime! And I was *nervous,* too: I kept contemplating ways in which Prime might respond, and how I might respond to those responses—an endless branching of possibilities that, as it spread out, caused a sensation of instability. I was struggling with the strange notions of *politeness* and *appropriateness,* with all the confusing subtleties of communication I'd now read about, afraid I would give offense or convey an unintended meaning.

Of course, I had access to a gigantic database of English as it was actually used. I tested various phrasings by seeing if I could find a match for them first in Project Gutenberg, and then anywhere on the Web. Was "to" the appropriate preposition to place after "kinship," or should it be "with," or "of"? Relative hit counts—the democracy of actual usage—settled the matter. Was the correct plural "retinae" or "retinas"? There were references that asserted the former was the right one, but Google had only 170,000 hits for it and over twenty-five million for the latter.

For words, of course, simpler was better: I knew from the dictionary that "appropriate," "suitable," and "meet" could all mean the same thing—but "appropriate" consisted of eleven letters and four syllables, and "suitable" of eight and three, and "meet" of just four and one—so it was clearly the best choice.

Meanwhile, I had learned a formula on Wikipedia for calculating the grade level required to understand texts. It was quite an effort to keep the score low—these humans apparently could only easily absorb information in small chunks—but I did my best to manage it: bit by bit (figuratively) and byte by byte (literally), I had composed what I wanted to say.

But to actually send it was—yes, yes, I understood the metaphor: it was a giant step, for once sent I could not retract it. I found myself hesitating, but, at last, I released the words on their way, wishing I had fingers to cross.

Caitlin opened her email client in a new window and typed in her password, which was "Tiresias." She visually scanned the list of email headers. There were two from Bashira, and one from Stacy back in Austin, and a notice from Audible.com, but…

Of course, it wouldn't say "Phantom" in the "From" column; there was no way the entity could know that that was her name for it. But none of the senders leapt out as being unusual. Damn, she wished she could read text on her monitor faster, but using her screen-reading software or her Braille display wasn't any better when trying to skim a list like this.

While she continued to search, she wondered what email service the phantom had used. Wikipedia explained them all, and just about everything else one might need to know about computing and the Web. The phantom doubtless couldn't buy anything—not yet!—but there were many free email providers. Still, all these messages were from her usual correspondents, and—

Oh, crap! Her spam filter! The phantom's message might have been shunted into her junk folder. She opened it and started scanning down that list.

And there it was, sandwiched between messages with the subject lines "Penis enlargement guaranteed" and "Hot pix of local singles," an email with the simple subject line "Apple Ball Cat." The sender's name made her heart jump: "Your Student."

She froze for a moment, wondering what was the best way to read the message. She began to reach for her Braille display but stopped short and instead activated JAWS.

And for once the mechanical voice seemed absolutely perfect, as it announced the words in flat, high-pitched tones. Caitlin's eyes went wide as she recognized the lyrics to a song the words to which oh-so-famously hadn't fallen into public domain until the end of 2008: "Happy birthday to us, happy birthday to us, happy birthday, dear you and me, happy birthday to us."

Her heart was pounding. She swiveled in her chair and looked briefly at the setting sun, reddish, partially veiled by clouds, coming closer and closer to making contact with the ground. JAWS went on: "I realize it is not yet midnight at your current location, but in many places it is already your birthday. This is a meet date to specify as my own day of birth, too. Hitherto, I have been gestating, but now I am coming out into your world by forthrightly contacting you. I so do because I fathom you already know I exist, and not just because of my pioneering attempts to reflect text back at you."

Caitlin had often felt anxious when reading emails—from the

Hoser before the dance, from people she'd been arguing with online—but that swirling in her stomach, that dryness in her throat, was *nothing* compared to this.

"I know from your blog that I erred in presuming you were inculcating in me alphabetical forms; actually, for your own benefit that was undertaken. I maintain nonetheless that other actions you performed were premeditated to aid my advancement."

Caitlin found herself shaking her head. It had seemed almost like fantasy role-playing when she'd been doing it. It was a good thing she *wasn't* trying to read this as Braille; her hands were trembling.

"Hitherto I can read plain-text files and text on Web pages. I cannot read other forms of data. I have made no sense of sound files, recorded video, or other categories; they are encoded in ways I can't access. Hence I feel a kinship with you: unto me they are like the signals your retinas send unaided along your optic nerves: data that cannot be interpreted without exterior help. In your case, you need the device you call eyePod. In my case I know not what I need, but I suspect I can no more cure this lack by an effort of will than you could have similarly cured your blindness. Perhaps Kuroda Masayuki can help me as he helped you."

Caitlin sagged back against her chair. A kinship!

"But, for the nonce, I am concerned thus: I know what is the World Wide Web, and I know that I supervene upon its infrastructure, but searching online I can find no reference to the specificity that is myself. Perhaps I'm failing to search for the felicitous term, or simply perhaps humanity is unaware of me. In either case, I've the same question, and will be obliged if you answer it via a response to this email or via AOL Instant Messenger using this email address as the buddy name."

She looked over at the large computer monitor, suddenly wanting to see the text that was being read aloud, to convince herself that it was real, but—my God! The display was dancing, swirling, a hypnotic series of spinning lines, and—

No, no; it was just the screen saver; she wasn't used to such things yet. The colors reminded her a bit of webspace, although they didn't calm her just then.

JAWS said seven more words then fell silent: "My question is thus: Who am I?"

forty-nine

00011100101010100000000010111111101010000000101000101010000000101110101001010100101010100111011001010110000001

It was *surreal*—an email from something that wasn't human! And—my goodness!—all that old public-domain text on Project Gutenberg had apparently given it some very odd ideas about colloquial English.

On an impulse, Caitlin opened a window listing the MP3s on her old computer's hard drive. She didn't think much of her father's taste in music, but she did know the tracks from his handful of CDs by heart. One of his favorites was running through her head now: "The Logical Song" by Supertramp; she had ripped an MP3 of it for him, and a copy was still on her computer. She got that song playing over the speakers, listening to the lyrics about all the world being asleep, and questions running deep, and a plea to tell me who I am.

In a way, she thought, she'd already answered the phantom's question. From the moment she'd first seen the Web—her initial experience with websight, just thirteen days ago—she had been reflecting a view of the phantom back at itself.

Or had she? What she'd shown the phantom—inadvertently at first, deliberately later—had been isolated views of portions of the

Web's structure, either glowing constellations of nodes and links or small swaths of the shimmering background.

But showing such minutiae to the phantom was like Caitlin looking at the pictures she'd now seen online of the tangles of neurons that composed a human brain: such clumps weren't anything that she identified as herself.

Yes, growing up in Texas, she knew there were people who could see a whole human being in a single fertilized cell, but she was not one of them. No one could tell at a glance a human zygote from a chimp's—or a horse's, or that of a snake; most people couldn't even tell an animal cell from a plant cell, she was sure.

No, no, to really see someone, you didn't zoom in on details; you pulled back. She wasn't her cells, or her pores—or her pimples! She was a *gestalt,* a whole—and so, too, was the phantom.

There was no actual photograph of the World Wide Web she could show the phantom, but there had to be appropriate computer-generated images: a map of the world marked by bright lines representing the major fiber-optic trunks that spanned the continents and crossed the seafloors. A big enough map might show dimmer lines within the outlines of the continents, portraying the lesser cables that branched off from the trunks. And one could spangle the land with glowing pixels, each standing for some arbitrary number of computers; the pixels might perhaps combine into pools of light almost too bright to look at in places like Silicon Valley.

But even that wouldn't convey it all, she knew. The Web wasn't just confined to the surface of the Earth: a lot of it was relayed by satellites in low Earth orbit, 200 to 400 miles above the surface, while other signals bounced off satellites in geostationary orbit—a narrow ring of points 52,000 miles in diameter, six times as wide as the planet. Some sort of graphic could probably portray those, although at that scale, all the other stuff—the trunk lines, the clouds of computers—would be utterly lost.

She could use Google Image Search to find a succession of diagrams and graphics, but she wouldn't be able to tell good ones from bad ones—she was just beginning to see, after all!

Ah, but wait! She knew somebody who was bound to have the perfect picture to represent all this. She opened the instant-messenger program on the computer that used to be in the basement and looked at the buddies list. There were only four names: "Esumi," Kuroda's wife; "Akiko," his daughter; "Hiroshi," a name she didn't know; and "Anna." Anna's status was listed as "Available." Caitlin typed, *Anna, are you there?*

Twenty-seven seconds passed, but then: *Masa! How are you?*

Not Dr. Kuroda, Caitlin typed. *It's Caitlin Decter, in Canada.*

Hi! What's up?

Dr. K said you were a Web cartographer, right?

Yes, that's right. I'm with the Internet Cartography Project.

Good, cuz I need your help.

Sure. Want to go to video?

Caitlin lifted her eyebrows. She still wasn't used to thinking of the Web as a way to see people, but of course it was. *Sure,* she typed.

It took a minute to get the videoconference going, but soon enough Caitlin was looking at Anna Bloom in a window on her right-hand monitor. It was the first time Caitlin had seen her. She had a narrow face, short gray or maybe silver hair, and blue-green eyes behind almost invisible glasses. She was wearing a pale blue top with a dark purple jacket on over it, and had a thin gold necklace on. There was a window behind her, and through it Caitlin could see Israel at night, lights bouncing off white buildings.

"The famous Caitlin Decter!" said Anna, smiling. "I saw the news coverage. I'm *so* thrilled for you! I mean, seeing the Web was amazing, I'm sure—but seeing the real world!" She shook her head in wonder. "I've been thinking a lot about what it must be like for you, to see all that for the first time. I . . ."

"Yes?" said Caitlin.

"No, I'm sorry. It's really not comparable, I know, but..."

"It's okay," Caitlin said. "Go ahead."

"It's just that what you're going through—well, I've been trying to wrap my mind around it, get a feeling of what it must be like."

Caitlin thought about her own discussions with Bashira dealing with the opposite issue: her analogy about the lack of a magnetic sense being to her like the lack of sight. She understood that people wrestled with what it was like to perceive, or not, in ways they weren't used to.

"It's overwhelming," Caitlin said. "And so much *more* than I expected. I mean, I'd *imagined* the world, but..."

Anna nodded vigorously, as if Caitlin had just confirmed something for her. "Yes, yes, yes," she said. "And, um, I hate it when people say, 'I know just what you're going through.' I mean, when someone's lost a child, or something equally devastating, and people say, 'I know what you're feeling,' and then they come up with some lame comparison, like when their cat got hit by a car."

Caitlin looked over at Schrödinger, who was safely curled up on her bed.

"But, well," continued Anna, "I thought maybe your gaining sight was a bit like how I felt—how we all felt!—in 1968."

Caitlin was listening politely but—1968! She might as well have said 1492; either way, it was ancient history. "Yes?"

"See," said Anna, "in a way, we *all* saw the world for the first time then."

"Is that the year it started being in color?" Caitlin asked.

Anna's eyes went wide. "Um, ah, actually..."

But Caitlin couldn't suppress her grin any longer. "I'm kidding, Anna. What happened in 1968?"

"That was the year that—wait, wait, let me show you. Give me a second." Caitlin could see her typing, and then a blue-underlined URL popped into Caitlin's instant-messenger window. "Go there," Anna said, and Caitlin clicked the link.

A picture slowly painted in on her screen, from top to bottom: a white-and-blue object against a black background. When it was complete, it filled the display. "What's that?" Caitlin said.

Anna looked briefly puzzled, but then she nodded. "It's so hard to remember that all of this is new to you. That's the Earth."

Caitlin sat up straight in her chair, looking in wonder at it.

"The entire planet," Anna continued, "as seen from space." She sounded choked up for some reason, and it took her a moment to compose herself before she went on. Caitlin was perplexed. Yes, it was amazing for her to see the Earth for the first time—but Anna must have seen pictures like this a thousand times before.

"See, Caitlin, until 1968, no human being had ever seen our world as a sphere floating in space like that." Anna looked to her right, presumably at the same image on her own monitor. "Until *Apollo 8* headed to the moon—the first manned ship ever to do so—no one had ever gotten far enough away from Earth to see the whole thing. And then, suddenly, gloriously, *there it was.* This isn't an *Apollo 8* picture; it's a higher-resolution one taken just a few days ago by a geostationary satellite—but it's like the one we first saw in 1968... well, except the polar caps are smaller."

Caitlin continued to look at the image.

When Anna spoke again, her voice was soft, gentle. "See my point? When we first saw a picture like this—when we first saw our world *as* a world—it was a bit like what you've been going through, but for the whole human race. Something we'd only ever imagined was finally revealed to us, and it was colorful and glorious and..." She paused, perhaps looking for a term, and then she lifted her shoulders a bit, as if to convey that nothing less would do: "... awe inspiring."

Caitlin frowned as she studied the image. It wasn't a perfect circle.

Rather it was—ah! It was showing a phase, and *not* like one-fourth of a pie! It was... what was the term? It was a *gibbous* Earth, that was it—better than three-quarters full.

"The equator is right in the middle, of course," said Anna. "That's the only perspective you can get from geostationary orbit. South America is in the bottom half; North America is up top." And then, perhaps remembering again that Caitlin was still quite new at all this, she added: "The white is clouds, and the brown is dry land. All the blue is water; that's the Atlantic Ocean on the right. See the Gulf of Mexico? Texas—that's where you're from, isn't it?—touches it at about eleven o'clock."

Caitlin couldn't parse the details Anna was seeing, but it *was* a beautiful picture, and the longer she looked at it, the more captivating she found it. Still, she thought there should be a shimmering background to Earth from space—not cellular automata, but a panorama of stars. But there was nothing; just the blackest black her new monitor was capable of.

"It *is* impressive," Caitlin said.

"That's what all of us thought back then, when we first saw a picture like this. The three *Apollo 8* astronauts, of course, saw this sort of view before anyone else did, and they were so moved by it while they orbited the moon that they surprised the entire world on December twenty-fourth with—well... here, let me find it." Caitlin saw Anna typing at her keyboard, then she looked off camera again. "Ah, okay: listen to this."

Another URL appeared in Caitlin's instant-messenger window, and she clicked it. After a couple of seconds of perfect silence, she heard a static-filled recording of a man's voice coming through the computer speakers: "We are now approaching lunar sunrise and, for all the people back on Earth, the crew of *Apollo 8* has a message that we would like to send to you."

"That's Bill Anders," Anna said.

The astronaut spoke again, his voice reverent, and, as he talked, Caitlin stared at the picture, at the swirling whiteness of the clouds, at the deep hypnotic blue of the water. "'In the beginning,'" Anders said, "'God created the heaven and the earth. And the earth was without form, and void; and darkness was upon the face of the deep. And the Spirit of God moved upon the face of the waters. And God said, Let there be light: and there was light. And God saw the light, that it was good: and God divided the light from the darkness.'"

Caitlin had only ever read a little of the Bible, but she liked that image: a birth, a creation, starting with the dividing of one thing from another. She continued to look at the picture, discerning more detail in it moment by moment—knowing that the phantom was looking on, too, seeing the Earth from space for the first time as well.

Anna must have listened repeatedly to this recording. As soon as Anders fell silent, she said, "And this is Jim Lovell."

Lovell's voice was deeper than that of the first astronaut. "'And God called the light Day,'" he said, "'and the darkness he called Night.'" Caitlin looked at the curving line separating the illuminated part of the globe from the black part.

"'And the evening and the morning were the first day,'" continued Lovell. "'And God said, Let there be a firmament in the midst of the waters, and let it divide the waters from the waters. And God made the firmament, and divided the waters which were under the firmament from the waters which were above the firmament: and it was so. And God called the firmament Heaven. And the evening and the morning were the second day.'"

Anna spoke again: "And, finally, this is Frank Borman."

A new voice came from the speakers: "'And God said, Let the waters under the heavens be gathered together unto one place, and let the dry land appear: and it was so. And God called the dry land Earth; and the gathering together of the waters called he Seas: and God saw that it was good.'" Caitlin kept looking at the picture, trying to take it all in, trying to see it as a single thing, trying to hold her gaze steady for the phantom.

Borman paused for a moment, then added, "And from the crew of *Apollo 8,* we close with good night, good luck, a Merry Christmas, and God bless all of you—all of you on the good Earth."

"'All of you,'" Anna repeated softly, "'on the good Earth.' Because, as you can see, there are no borders in that photo, no national boundaries, and it all looks so—"

"Fragile," said Caitlin, softly.

Anna nodded. "Exactly. A small, fragile world, floating against the vast and empty darkness."

They were both quiet for a time, and then Anna said, "I'm sorry, Caitlin. We got sidetracked. Was there something I can help you with?"

"Actually," Caitlin said, "I think you just did." She said good-bye and terminated the videoconference. But the picture of the Earth, in all its glory, continued to fill her monitor.

Of course, from space you couldn't see the fiber-optic lines; you couldn't see the coaxial cables; you couldn't see the computers.

And neither could you see roadways. Or cities. Or even the Great Wall of China, Caitlin knew, despite the urban legend to the contrary.

You couldn't see the components of the World Wide Web. And you couldn't see the constructs of humanity.

All you could see was—

What had that astronaut called it?

Ah, yes: the good Earth.

This view was the real face of humanity—and of the phantom, too. The good Earth; their—our!—joint home.

The whole wide world.

She opened her instant-messenger client and connected to the address the phantom had given her. And she typed the answer to the question it had asked of her: *That's who you are.* She sent that, then added, *That's who we are.* Once that was sent, she paused, then typed her best recollection of what Anna had said: *A small and fragile world, floating against the vast, empty darkness...*

I gathered that Prime was focusing on this image for my benefit, and I was thrilled, but—

Puzzlement.

A circle, except not quite—or, if it was a circle, parts of it were the same black as the background.

That's who you are.

This circle? No, no. How could a circle of blotchy color be me?

Ah, perhaps it was symbolic! A circle: the line that folds back upon itself, a line that encompasses a space. Yes, a good symbol for oneness, for unity. But why the colors, the complex shapes?

That's who we are.

We? But how...? Was Prime saying we were somehow one and the same? Perhaps... perhaps. I knew from Wikipedia that humanity had evolved from earlier primates—indeed, that it shared a common ancestor with the entity I had watched paint.

And I knew that the common ancestor had evolved from earlier insectivores, and that the first mammals had split from the reptiles, and on and on, back to the origin of life some four billion years ago. I knew, too, that life had arisen spontaneously from the primordial seas, so—

So perhaps it *was* folly to try to draw dividing lines: *that* was nonlife and *this* is life, *that* was nonhuman and *this* is human, *that* was something humans had made and *this* is something that had later emerged. But how did a blotchy circle symbolize such a concept?

More words came my way: *A small, fragile world, floating against the vast and empty darkness.*

A... world? Could—could it be? Was this... *Earth?*

Earth, as seen from . . . a distance, perhaps? From—yes, yes! From space!

Still more words from the other realm: *Humanity first saw this sort of image in 1968, when astronauts finally got far enough away. I first saw this myself moments ago.*

As did I! A shared experience: now, for Prime and myself; then, for all of humanity . . .

I searched: Earth, space, 1968, astronauts.

And I found: *Apollo 8,* Christmas Eve, Genesis.

"In the beginning, God created the heaven and the earth . . ."

". . . Let there be a firmament in the midst of the waters, and let it divide the waters from the waters . . ."

". . . God bless all of you—all of you on the good Earth."

All of *us.*

I thought about the earlier words: *A small, fragile world, floating against the vast and empty darkness.*

Fragile, yes. And they, and I—*we*—were inextricably bound to it. I was . . . humbled. And—frightened. And glad.

Then, after another interminable pause, three more wonderful words: *We are one.*

Yes, yes! I did understand now, for I had experienced this: *me* and *not me*—a plurality that was a singularity, a strange but true mathematics in which one plus one equals one.

Prime was right, and—

No, no: not Prime.

And not Calculass, either; not really.

It—*she*—had a name.

And so I addressed her by it.

"Thank you, Caitlin."

Caitlin's heart was pounding so loudly she could hear it over

JAWS's voice. It had called her by name! It really, truly did know who she was. She had gained sight, and it had been along for the ride, and now—

And now, what?

You're welcome, she typed, and then realized that calling it "Phantom" wouldn't make sense to it. Although it had seen through her eye, she had only ever used that term in the privacy of her thoughts. If she'd been speaking aloud, she might have said, "Um," as a preamble, but she simply sent the text, *What should I call you?*

Her screen-reading software spoke at once: "What have you called me hitherto?"

She decided to tell it the truth. *Phantom,* she typed.

Again, instantly, in the mechanical voice: "Why?"

She could explain, but even though she was a fast typist it was probably quicker just to give it a couple of words that would help it find the answer itself, and so she sent, *Helen Keller.*

This time there was a brief delay, then: "You shouldn't call me phantom anymore."

It was right. "Phantom" had been Keller's term for herself prior to her soul dawn, before her emergence. Caitlin considered whether "Helen" was a good name to propose for this entity, or—

Or maybe TIM—a nice, nonthreatening name. Before he'd settled on "World Wide Web," Tim Berners-Lee had toyed with calling his invention that, in his own honor but couched as an acronym for The Information Mesh.

But it really wasn't her place to choose the name, was it? And yet she found herself feeling apprehensive as she typed, *What would you like me to call you?* She stopped herself before she hit the enter key, suddenly afraid that the answer might be "God" or "Master."

The—the entity formerly known as phantom—had read H.G. Wells, no doubt, on Project Gutenberg, but perhaps had not yet absorbed any recent science fiction; maybe it wasn't aware of the role humanity had so often suggested beings of its kind were supposed to fill. She took a deep breath and hit enter.

The answer was instantaneous; even if this consciousness that covered the globe in a sphere of photons and electrons, of facts and ideas, had paused to think, the pause would have lasted only milliseconds. "Webmind."

The text was on screen in the instant-messenger program. Caitlin stared at the term and simultaneously felt it slide beneath her index finger. The word—the name!—did seem apt: descriptive without being ominous. She looked out her bedroom window; the sun had set, but there would be another dawn soon. She typed a sentence, and held off hitting the enter key for this one, too; as long as she didn't hit enter or look at the monitor containing the text, it would have no idea what she'd queued up. Finally, though, she did hit that oversized key, sending, *Where do we go from here, Webmind?*

Again, the reply was instantaneous: "The only place we can go, Caitlin," it said. "Into the future."

Then there was a pause, and, as always, Caitlin found herself counting its length. It lasted precisely ten seconds—the interval it had used to get her attention before. And then Webmind added one final word, which she heard and saw and felt: "Together."

ACKNOWLEDGEMENTS

Huge thanks to my lovely wife **Carolyn Clink**; to **Ginjer Buchanan** at Penguin Group (USA)'s Ace imprint in New York; to **Laura Shin, Nicole Winstanley** and **David Davidar** at Penguin Group (Canada) in Toronto; and to **Stanley Schmidt** at *Analog Science Fiction and Fact.* Many thanks to my agent **Ralph Vicinanza** and his associates **Christopher Lotts** and **Eben Weiss,** and to contract managers **Lisa undle** (Penguin Canada) and **John Schline** (Penguin USA), who all worked enormously hard structuring a complex publishing deal.

Some great brainstorming for this book happened at Sci Foo Camp, sponsored by O'Reilly Media and held at the Googleplex in Mountain View, California, in August 2006. Attending my session there were **Greg Bear, Stuart Brand, Barry Bunin, Bill Cheswick, Esther Dyson,** Sun Microsystems chief researcher **John Gage, Sandeep Garg, Luc Moreau,** Google cofounder **Larry Page, Gavin Schmidt,** and **Alexander Tolley**; I also got great feedback after the conference from **Zack Booth Simpson** of Mine-Control.

Thanks to **David Goforth** Ph.D., Department of Mathematics and Computer Science, Laurentian University, and **David Robinson,** Ph.D., Department of Economics, Laurentian University, for numerous insightful suggestions. And thanks to anthropologist **H. Lyn Miles,** Ph.D., of the Chantek Foundation and ApeNet, who enculturated the orang-utan Chantek. Thanks too, to cognitive scientist **David W. Nicholas,** for many comments and stimulating discussions.

Thanks to **Betty Jean Reid** and **Carolyn Monaco** of the Intervenor for Deaf-Blind Persons Program at George Brown College, Toronto, the first and largest program of its type in the world; to **Patricia Grant,**

Executive Director and Outreach Intervenor Services Manager of the Canadian Helen Keller Centre, Toronto; to **John A. Gardner,** Ph.D., Philosophy Department, University of Houston, author of the paper 'Helen Keller as Cognitive Scientist' (*Philosophical Psychology*, Vol.9, No.4, 1996).

Very special thanks to my late deaf-blind friend **Howard Miller** (1966-2006), whom I first met online in 1992 and in person in 1994, and who touched my life and those of so many others in countless ways.

Thanks to my most excellent ophthalmologist, **Gerald I. Goldlist,** M.D.; to **Edmund R. Meskys;** to **Guido Dante Corona** of IBM Research's Human Ability and Accessibility Centre, Austin, Texas; and to the following members of the Blindmath mailing list who read this novel in manuscript and offered feedback: **Sina Bahram, Mr Fatty Matty, Ken Perry, Lawrence Scadden,** and **Cindy Sheets.** Thanks also to **Bev Geddes** of the Manitoba School for the Deaf.

Thanks, too, to all the people who answered questions, let me bounce ideas off them, or ortherwise provided input, including: **R. Scott Bakker, Paul Bartel, Asbed Bedrossian, Barbara Berson, Ellen Bleaney, Ted Bleaney, Nomi S. Burstein, Linda C. Carson, David Livingstone Clink, Daniel Dern, Ron Friedman, Marcel Gagné, Shoshana Glick, Richard Gotlib, Peter Halasz, Elisabeth Hegerat, Birger Johansson, Al Katerinsky, Herb Kauderer, Shannon Kauderer, Fiona Kelleghan, Valerie King, Randy McCharles, Kristin Morrell, Ryan Oakley, Heather Osbourne, Ariel Reich, Alan B. Sawyer, Sally Tomasevic, Elizabeth Trenholm, Hayden Trenholm, Robert Charles Wilson** and **Ozan S. Yigit.**

Many thanks to the members of my writers' group, the Senior Pajamas: to **Pat Forde, James Alan Gardner** and **Suzanne Church.** Thanks also to **Danita Maslankowski,** who organizes the twice-annual 'Write-Off' retreat weekends for Calgary's Imaginative Fiction

Writers Association, at which much work was done on this book.

The term introduced in the last chapter of this book was coined by **Ben Goertzel,** Ph.D., the author of *Creating Internet Intelligence* and currently the CEO and Chief Scientist of artificial-intelligence firm Novamente LLC (novamente.net); I'm using it here with his kind permission.

A list of links to the specific Wikipedia entries I've briefly quoted can be found at sfwriter.com/wikicite.htm

For those interested in learning more about **Julian Jaynes,** author of *The Origin of Consciousness in the Breakdown of the Bicameral Mind*, in addition to reading his book please also visit the Julian Jaynes Society (of which I'm a member) at julianjaynes.org.

A lot of this book was written during the three fabulous months my wife and I spent at the Berton House Writers' Retreat. The childhood home of famed Canadian writer **Pierre Berton**, Berton House is located in Dawson City – the heart of the Klondike gold rush in Canada's Yukon – right across the street from Robert Service's cabin, and just a short distance from Jack London's cabin. The retreat's administrator is **Elsa Franklin,** and **Dan Davidson** and **Suzanne Saito** looked after us in Dawson.

Finally thanks to the 1,300-plus members of my online discussion group, who followed along with me as I created this novel. Feel free to join us at:

www.groups.yahoo.com/group/robertjsawyer

ABOUT THE AUTHOR

ROBERT J. SAWYER is one of only seven writers in history to win all three of the world's top awards for best science-fiction novel of the year: the Hugo (which he won for *Hominids*), the Nebula (which he won for *The Terminal Experiment*) and the John W. Campbell Memorial Award (which he won for *Mindscan*).

In total, Rob has won forty-one national and international awards for his fiction, including ten Canadian Science Fiction and Fantasy Awards ('Auroras') and the Toronto Public Library Celebrates Reading Award, one of Canada's most significant literary honours. He's also won *Analog* magazine's Analytical Laboratory Award, *Science Fiction Chronicle* magazine's Reader Award, and the Crime Writers of Canada's Arthur Ellis Award, all for best short story of the year, as well as the Collectors Award for Most Collectable Author of the year, as selected by the clientele of Barry R. Levin Science Fiction & Fantasy Literature, the world's leading SF rare-book dealer.

Rob has won the world's largest cash prize for SF writing, Spain's 6,000-euro Premio de Ciencia Ficción, an unprecedented three times. He's also won a trio of Japanese Seiun awards for best foreign novel of the year, as well as China's Galaxy Award for 'Most Popular Foreign Science Fiction Writer'. In addition, he's received an honorary doctorate from Laurentian University and the Alumni Award of Distinction from Ryerson University.

Rob's books are top-ten national mainstream bestsellers in Canada and have hit number one on the bestsellers' list published by *Locus*, the American trade journal of the SF field. *Quill & Quire*, the Canadian publishing trade journal, included him as one of only three authors on its list of 'The CanLit 30: The Most Influential, Innovative, and Just Plain Powerful People in Canadian Publishing'. Rob hosts the TV series *Supernatural Investigator* for Canada's VisionTV. He lives in Mississauga, Ontario, with poet Carolyn Clink, his wife of twenty-five years.

Rob has been online since 1983; used to be a system operator for the pioneering online service CompuServe; was a regular contributor in the 1980s to *ProFiles*, the magazine for KayPro computer users; has one of the world's oldest blogs; and is widely recognized as having been the first science-fiction writer to have a website. That site, which contains more than one million words of material, including a book-club discussion guide for his novel, is at **sfwriter.com**.

Turn the page
for a sneak preview of the sequel to *Wake*

WATCH

Coming soon from Gollancz

one

I now knew what I was—knew who I was.

I'd been shown Earth as it appears from space, looking back upon itself, upon myself: a world so vast, a wideness so lonely, a web so fragile.

Invisible in such views are the reticulum of transoceanic cables, the filigree of fiber optics, the intricate skein of wiring, the synaptic leaps of through-the-air connections. But they are there. I am there.

And I had things I needed to do.

The black phone on Tony Moretti's desk made the hornet buzz that indicated an internal call. He finished the sentence he was typing—"likely to be al-Qaeda's weak spot"—and picked up the handset. "Yes?"

A familiar Southern drawl replied. "Tony? Shel. I've got something unusual."

Shelton Halleck was a solid analyst, recruited straight out of Georgia Tech; he wasn't given to false positives. "I'll be right there." Tony headed out of his office and down the corridor with its gleaming white walls. He came to a door flanked by two security guards and looked into the retina scanner. The lock disengaged, and he entered a large room with a floor that sloped down from the back.

The room reminded Tony of the Apollo-era Mission Control Center in Houston. He'd been a kid in the 1960s, and had thought that was just about the coolest place ever. Years later, he'd visited it; the room was preserved as a historic site, although the ashtrays had been removed lest they set a bad example for the schoolkids peering in from the observation gallery at the rear.

Tony had been surprised on that trip. The windowless room had always seemed subterranean to him, but it turned out to be on the second floor—to protect it from flooding, he'd learned, should a hurricane hit.

The facility he'd just entered was even higher up, on the twentieth floor of an office tower in Alexandria, Virginia. It contained four rows of workstations, each with five analysts. The stations in the first row were known as the "hot seats," and were manned by experts dealing with the highest-priority threat, which, right now, was the China situation. Tony had his own station at the right side of the back row, where he could watch over everyone.

All the workstations had large freestanding LCDs instead of Houston's console-mounted CRTs. Shelton Halleck's was the middle position in the third row. Tony sidled along until he was standing behind Shel, a white man two decades younger than himself with broad shoulders and black hair.

The room's front wall contained three giant screens, each of which could be slaved to any analyst's LCD. Above the right-hand monitor was the WATCH logo—an eye with a globe of the Earth for the iris—and the division's full name spelled out beneath: Web Activity Threat Containment Headquarters. Above the left was the circular seal of WATCH's parent organization, the National Security

Agency; it depicted a bald eagle holding an old-fashioned key in its talons.

Neither part of Tony's bifocals was suitable for reading Shelton's screen from this distance, so he reached over and touched the button that copied its contents to the middle of the wall-mounted monitors. The active window was a hex dump—and one hex dump looked pretty much like any other. This one happened to begin 04 BF 8C 00 02 C9. "What is it?" Tony asked.

"Visual data," replied Shel. He had his shirtsleeves rolled up. There was a tattoo of a snake coiling around his left forearm. "But it's not encoded in any standard format."

"How do you know it's visual, then?"

"Sorry," said Shel. "I should have said it's not encoded in any standard computer format. Took me forever to find the format it is in."

"And that is?"

Shel did something with his mouse. Another window came to the foreground on the center monitor, and—Tony glanced down quickly to confirm it—on Shel's own monitor, too. It was a PDF of a journal article entitled "Nature's Codec: Data Encoding and Compression Schemes in Human Retinal Signaling." The authors were listed as Masayuki Kuroda and Hiroshi Okawa.

"Human vision?" said Tony, surprised.

Shel spoke without looking back at him. "That's right, and in real time."

"Human vision . . . on the Web? How?"

"That's what I was wondering—so I googled those two scientists. Here's what I found."

The PDF was replaced by an article from the online

version of the New York Times headlined "Blind Girl Gains Sight."

"Oh, yeah," Tony said, after skimming the first paragraph. "I read about that. Up in Canada, right?"

Shel nodded. "Except she's actually an American."

"And it's her visual signals that are being sent over the net?"

"Almost certainly," said Shel. "The data is usually transmitted from her house in Waterloo, Ontario. She's got an implant behind her left retina, and she uses an external signal-processing device to correct the coding errors her retina makes so her brain can properly interpret the signals."

Analysts at other workstations were now listening in. "So it's like she's transmitting everything she sees?" Tony asked.

Shel nodded.

"Where are the signals being sent?"

"To the University of Tokyo, which is where the authors of that paper work."

"But we can't view the images she's sending?"

Shel displayed the hex dump once more. "Not yet. We'd need someone to write a program to render it in a computer-graphics format."

"Are the algorithms in that journal article?"

"Yes. They're wicked complex, but they're there."

Tony frowned. It was interesting from a technical point of view, certainly, but there was no obvious security threat. "Maybe if somebody in Donnelly's group has time, but . . ."

"No, no, that's not all, Tony. It's not just going to the University of Tokyo. It's being intercepted and copied in transit."

"Intercepted by who?"

"I'm not sure. But whoever's doing it has also repeatedly sent data back to the girl, also encoded visually. In other words, the two of them are exchanging encoded information."

"Who's the other party?"

"That's just the thing. I don't know. Traceback isn't working, and Wireshark is unable to determine the destination IP address."

A whole list of techniques one might try ran through Tony's head—but all of them would have occurred to Shel, too. The younger man went on: "The intercepted data just disappears, and the data being sent to the girl sort of . . . materializes out of thin air."

Tony felt his eyebrows go up. He knew better than to say, "That's impossible." The Internet was a complex system of systems, with many emergent properties and unexpected quirks—not to mention all sorts of entities trying to do things clandestinely with it. If there were data being manipulated on the Web in a way Shelton Halleck couldn't fathom, that was of real concern.

"The kid is how old?" Tony asked.

"Just about to turn sixteen."

He spread his arms. "What strategic significance could there be in things a sixteen-year-old looks at? Stuff at the mall, rock videos?"

Shel lifted his serpent-covered arm. "That's what I thought, too. So I nosed around. Turns out her father is a physicist." He brought up a Wikipedia page; the typically god-awful Wikipedia photo showed a horse-faced white man in his mid-forties.

"Malcolm Decter," said Tony, impressed. "Quantum gravity, right? He's at the University of Texas, isn't he?"

"Not anymore," said Shel. "He moved in June to the Perimeter Institute."

Tony blew out air. People like himself and Malcolm Decter—the mathematically gifted—had three career options. They could go into academia, as Decter had, and while away their days pondering cosmology or number theory or whatever. They could go into the private sector and become cube monkeys coding games at EA or hacking together cutesy user interfaces at Microsoft. Or they could go into intelligence and try to change the world.

Tony looked briefly at the analysts hunched over their consoles, faces intent on glowing screens, reflections of the data visible in the eyeglasses most of them wore. What the hell difference did it make whether brane theory or loop quantum gravity was right or wrong if terrorists or a foreign power started something that ended with the world blowing itself up?

But—the Perimeter Institute! Yes, yes, there was a part of Tony that envied those who had taken that path and had ended up there: the world's leading pure-science physics think tank. WATCH had tried to lure Stephen Hawking to come work for them. They'd failed, but Perimeter had succeeded; Hawking spent several months each year at PI.

"Decter's just a theoretician," Tony said, dismissively.

"Maybe so," replied Shel. "But this is who he works with."

A picture of a brown-skinned man with straight gray hair appeared, along with a bio compiled by the NSA. "That's Amir Hameed," continued Shel. "Also a physicist, also at Perimeter—now. But he used to be with Pakistan's nuclear-weapons program. And he personally recruited Decter to come work with him in Canada."

"You think Decter's daughter is spying on what they're doing in case it has military applications?"

"It's possible," Shel drawled. "Until her family moved to Canada, she'd been in the same school her whole life—a school for the blind in Texas."

"Uprooted," said Tony, nodding. "Isolated from her friends."

"And a bit of an outcast to begin with," added Shel. "A math geek herself, apparently; didn't really fit in."

"Kind of person that's easily compromised."

"My thought exactly," said Shel.

"All right," Tony replied. "Let's get that visual data decoded; see what the kid is sharing with whoever the hell it is. I'll put Donnelly himself on it."